SHATTERED
DREAMS

SHIRLEY WILKINSON

To my children, Joseph and Ivy, for reminding me that it is never too late to follow a dream and being thrilled when I did so. Also, to my best friend, Makayla, for being my sounding board, even when I know it got old. Thank you.

CONTENTS

1. ANNUAL GALA

Avila woke with the sun shining in her eyes. She blinked once and turned over to bury her head under her pillow. She had been up off and on all night, and she wanted nothing more than to go back to sleep.

She could hear her parents in the next room, getting ready for the annual gala. They were speculating on what King Rougir de Althmear might have to say in his public address. Every year he talked to the people about bills, proposals, and other projects he had planned for the coming year. It was more than just his speech, however. Each year brought people from all over the world into the capital to share ideas, crafts, and art.

Avila had been going to these fairs for more than a decade, which was as far back as she could remember. She couldn't remember anything before she was thirteen, including her real parents. Most days, it felt as if she had never had any other life.

She finally broke out of her reverie and decided to roll out of bed when she heard her adoptive mother, Lila, call out to her. She slipped a robe on and walked into the combination living-dining room.

"Oh my goodness, will you look at that? It looks like miracles are possible. I thought you were never going to get out of bed." Lila took the sting out of her words by smiling as she said them.

"Must we go today? I didn't sleep well, and I—well, I don't feel like going." Avila had been looking forward to the extras, but she wasn't sure she would have the energy to keep up this time.

"Of course we have to go. Don't you want to see the king?" Lila passed a sly wink to her husband Thomas and added, "I also heard the prince was back from Avier; he might actually be there this year."

Avila gave a soft sigh, then turned to her mother and said, "Please, you both know we probably won't see him there. He's never showed up at the fairs in the past. Why should he now? Besides, even if he did show up, he won't stay long, and he will be surrounded by so many court followers that most of the common people won't even get to see him."

However, she had seen him once. She was fourteen when she saw a boy running through a side street. He was a few years older than she was and looked like any other boy his age, except for how he was dressed, and she didn't realize he was the prince until four flustered guards and a distraught tutor came and escorted him back to the castle. Later that night, there were rumors that the prince had managed to escape his tutor and climb over the castle walls.

She was startled out of her memories and into the present when Lila said something to her, and Avila had to have her repeat it. "Is your head full of fluff today? Is that why you don't want to go?" Her mother then put the back of her hand on Avila's forehead before she continued, "Well, you don't seem sick. You should be fine for a while, at least. Now, go get ready."

Avila sighed as she turned and grabbed a piece of toast. She already knew there wasn't a valid reason for her to get out of going, so she resigned herself to facing the crowds. Hopefully, she would get caught up in the excitement, and her tiredness would go away.

When she walked back into her room, the sun was still shining in through the blinds. It almost made her feel like she was outside. She looked at all the plants she had scattered around the place and wished she could go to the woods at the edge of town instead of the fair. She loved watching the animals, and while she was out there she didn't feel out of place, as she sometimes did while she was in town.

When she first started school in Arinel, her dark hair, skin, and eyes had stood out among the rest of the children's light hair and fair skin. She was often left to fend for herself during playtimes and mealtimes. Eventually, they all got used to her and no longer looked the other way when she passed by; she had even been able to make a few friends. To this day, though, there were times when she preferred to be alone.

Tired of thinking of what she didn't have, she opened her closet and picked out what she would wear that day: a white sleeveless shirt and a pair of tan pants, both of which contrasted with her dark caramel skin. She put them on, then brushed through her thick, wavy hair and deftly put it into a braid that fell to the small of her back. She checked once more in her mirror to ensure that everything was in place, then walked back into the living room, picked up the basket that had been left on the table, and walked out the door with one last sigh.

Avila shook off her feeling of apathy and helped her parents pack the last of their things into the hovercar and get on the way. They made it to the fairgrounds quickly. Since they lived in the capital, they got there early enough to find a good spot to set things up for the picnic. They spent the rest of the morning visiting with family and friends, and a sense of excitement and revelry filled the air.

Avila was sitting on a blanket in the shade waiting for her closest friend, Lissa, who seemed about to burst with excitement when she arrived. "There is so much energy in the air today," Lissa exclaimed, half out of breath from chasing her baby sister around and trying to get her to sit still for just a few minutes.

As Lissa sat down, she glanced over at Avila and saw the look on her face. She must have mistaken the look for boredom, as she quickly added, "I know there is this much excitement every year, but it always seems new." When she looked again, she shook her head. "All right, what's wrong, and I don't want to hear 'nothing,' because you are usually just as excited as I am about all of this."

Avila could hear the note of concern in her friend's voice, so she tried to answer as best as she could. "Sorry, I didn't sleep well last night, that's all."

Lissa didn't look entirely convinced, but it was only a moment later that she stood and grabbed Avila's wrist. "Well, I think I know just what you need to get your energy back. Let's go." As they walked past both sets of their parents, Lissa called out to them to let them know they were going to the Gallery and would be back later that afternoon.

The Gallery was in the middle of the large park at the center of the capital city, Arinel. The main building was where the king would give his annual state of affairs speech, but it was surrounded by a giant open-air market. That was the best part, as far as the two girls were concerned, as that was where people from all over the world came to show off whatever they might have to show off. Some were selling foodstuffs, while others sold homemade goods—some of which were excellently made and highly sought after, since the annual fair was the only time they were sold.

The two young women passed these vendors by, as they were focused on finding their favorite place: the impromptu stages set up behind the main building. People from all over would come to the Gallery stages during the fair to put on short plays or play music.

As the girls walked past the musicians, Avila started getting caught up in the moment. It wasn't long until she was grinning as widely as her friend. The two young women alternated between the slower dances with some of the handsome young men present and the faster-paced music made to get the heart racing.

When they started to run short of breath, they decided to find a seat before the whole place became packed with people looking for a place to hear the king's speech. They walked back past the stalls of fresh food and had to stop; the smells were too much to pass by this time around. They shared a glass of lemonade and split a handheld pie filled with roast vegetables and rice in a savory sauce. After they finished, they started toward the front of the Gallery again, passing the hawkers without a second glance. Looking might mean stopping, and stopping might mean browsing or buying. Neither one was interested in wasting that much time. They knew they would have more time later for that kind of stuff, and even if they never bought anything, it was fun to look.

When they finally made it inside, they headed for the stairs. The higher they could get, the better their view would be; or at least, it wouldn't be blocked by standing people on the lower floor. When they got to the third floor, they noticed that the stairs up were no longer barred. Over the last few months, at the king's request, the city had worked on switching the upper levels from small galleries for the elite to single, large balconies on each of the upper floors. With the advancements in mass teleportation technology, more people from other cities worldwide had attended in the past few years, so the king had decided everyone who could be there should have the opportunity to hear his plans. The change had created plenty of places for everyone to sit for the upcoming fair.

The two girls decided to go to the top. There were a few people up there already, but plenty of seats were still open, especially those near the front. As the girls got closer, they realized why almost no one was sitting up there: there was a section of the railing about fifteen feet wide still missing. Avila had no fear of heights, and of course, if she could do it, then Lissa would also try.

As the girls drew near to the front row, Avila looked over at the magnified image of the stage along the far wall. At first glance, it looked familiar. The seven flags representing each of the Trading Alliance planets were there, but something else caught her eye. There was a new flag there with the others, one she could not remember seeing before but that somehow looked familiar. Its simple design depicted a black dragon and a white dragon intertwined on an azure background. There was a word in an unfamiliar language underneath the dragons, but it felt as if she had known what it meant all her life.

A sense of longing and peace filled her spirit. All she wanted to do was reach out and touch the lovely flag. It felt as if it were only a few steps away. If she could simply close the distance, she would remember what it was that was tickling the back of her brain, and she might finally know a little tranquility. Everything around her blacked out except for the flag; it was the only thing in her line of sight. She started to move forward, but she could feel something pulling her back. She struggled against the force that was holding her and trying to keep her away from her happiness. She finally freed herself and continued to move forward. Then it felt as if she were floating on air. As if there were nothing around her at all. She couldn't ever remember feeling so content. Suddenly, a sharp pain exploded through her head as she came to an abrupt stop, and then Avila slipped into the comfortable, warm darkness that surrounded her.

The first thing Avila became aware of was a word ringing through her mind. It was unfamiliar to her, but after a few moments, she realized she knew what it meant: harmony. Her voice was barely above a whisper when she finally said it aloud. With the silence broken, she began to remember a little of what had happened, including the unusual flag with the unknown word and its strange pull on her. However, she still couldn't recall where she was or how she got there.

She could hear the voices of her family and Lissa not far off, but they were somewhat muffled. As she tried to open her eyes and lift her head, a sharp pain raced through it, starting at the back before pounding its way to the front. At that point, all she could think about was lying still and praying to the goddess that the pain would subside. Avila then heard the voices receding, but it also sounded like someone was approaching. When she felt someone sit down next to her, she debated whether she should try to open her eyes again. She decided to open them, but she wasn't going to try to move her head. The sight that greeted her was entirely unexpected. She found herself looking into a pair of sea-green eyes that didn't belong to anyone she knew.

"Whoa there. You just took a nasty bump to the head, so don't try to move yet, doctor's orders. By the way, my name is Galdren."

Avila realized she was staring, and since she couldn't turn her head, she simply closed her eyes and tried to reply. "Wh-where am I?" It was a simple question, but it started the pounding in her head again. She felt nausea crawling up her throat, so she clamped her lips together to try and hold it in.

The man must have noticed her wince from the pain, so he got a cold, wet cloth and put it on her head. It helped her focus a little better as he spoke again. "Don't try talking; you need more rest first, and then we'll go over what happened. If it helps you relax, you are in my apartment. It's right down the road from the Gallery. I was the one that caught you, and since my place was closer than any other, we brought you here." When she opened her eyes again, the look on his face was full of questions he obviously wanted to ask her. She hoped he wouldn't. She wasn't sure she was up to answering.

Instead of asking anything, he stood and looked down at her. "Your parents just left. The doctor said you would need rest and quiet, and he didn't think you should be moved any more than necessary. I told them it would be all right if you stayed here for a couple of days. They will be back later to see you." He walked to a nearby table, picked up a cup, and brought it back to her. "Here, the doctor left some medicine for the pain in case you woke up before he got back."

The pain was excruciating when she lifted her head, but she got the medicine down with help. When she lay back, she decided that would be the last time she tried moving for a while. After a few minutes, she noticed she was having a tough time focusing on anything or putting together a coherent thought. As she realized it must have been the medicine that Galdren gave her, she lost consciousness altogether.

The young girl was alone, in the dark, and terrified. She could hear noises all around her, but she couldn't identify them at first. She stuffed her fist in her mouth to stifle a scream when she heard an explosion nearby. That was when she understood what the noises were: gunshots. She was petrified, but she knew she couldn't stay where she was. If she did, she would be killed. The explosion had been close.

She groped around in the dark until her hand brushed up against a latch. The door to the secret compartment she had been hidden in swung part of the way open, but something blocked it from opening all the way. She pushed with all her might and managed to get it open far enough to squeeze through. The sight of what had been blocking the door made her efforts to keep silent a lost cause. Her scream was shrill as she looked down at her older brother.

He had been shot several times, and part of his left leg was missing. That must have been the explosion she heard. She could feel her vision going dark, but she pinched her arm to force herself to focus. If she fainted now, she would be found and killed like her brother. She loved him, but she couldn't let his sacrifice be in vain. She turned away from him and started to run without looking back. If she did and saw the look of agony frozen on his face one more time, she would not be able to keep herself from breaking down.

She ran down corridors that should be familiar to her, but she barely knew which way she was going because of the destruction. It seemed everywhere she turned, there was another body. She didn't bother checking to see who they were. She was afraid it might be someone else she knew, or worse yet, another person she loved.

She ran for what seemed like an eternity. Her legs started to go numb, but she couldn't stop. Her mind had already gone blank from the devastation around her. Everything and everyone she knew was either dead or gone. As she ran, she started to realize her life would never be the same again. She didn't have time to think about that now or mourn for the deceased. That would come later, when she knew she was safe; if she could ever be safe again.

She hadn't heard anything for a while, as she had been running away from the sounds of battle. She stopped for a few minutes to collect her thoughts and catch her breath in a courtyard that was mostly untouched. She had to figure out where she needed to go. Her family had contacts outside of the city that could help her get off the planet. She knew who a few of them were, but no one had thought she would be alone if the time ever came to find them. There was nothing for it, though. There was no way she could stay.

As she got up to leave, she heard a noise behind her. She turned around warily but didn't see anything. She looked for a minute, then, satisfied nothing was there, headed for the archway to leave. Before she could reach it, a soldier came into the courtyard from the way she had just arrived. There was no use in hiding; he had already seen her. Without even thinking, she started to run. If she could make it out of the courtyard, she might find a place to hide until the soldier passed. She had to survive.

With that last thought, she heard a shot ring out in the silence. She felt a searing pain on the right side of her head, and then she couldn't seem to stay on her feet. The world started to fade in and out, and her vision grew fuzzy. Her last thought was that her flight had been for nothing, and she was going to die. She heard a shout that seemed like it was worlds away, then she saw a face lean over her. As her eyes drifted shut, all her thoughts faded into darkness.

2. RECUPERATION

Avila awoke with a short scream, which caused a burst of bright colors behind her eyelids and a searing pain in her head. She opened her eyes to find herself in a strange room. The fear that any moment someone would burst in and try to shoot her seemed overwhelming and confusing. After a few seconds, she realized she had only been dreaming, and she was safe in Galdren's room. As if thinking about him made him appear, Galdren stepped through the door.

"Are you all right? I was downstairs, but I had the com turned on in case you needed anything, and I heard you scream." The breathlessness in his voice and look of concern on his face almost made Avila feel normal again.

"Yes, I'm fine." She noticed her voice was stronger now. Also, talking didn't automatically start the bees buzzing in her head if she lay relatively still and kept her voice low. She decided to brave a few more words. "I had a dream that seemed so real, and I was confused when I woke up in unfamiliar surroundings."

"Well, that must have been some dream, because I probably could have heard you without the com. It sounded as if someone was trying to kill you, or you had decided to go for a leap again." He said the last with a smile, but it completely confused Avila. She thought that maybe the bump on her head was making it hard for her to understand things. She decided to leave it at that and not ask any questions, then closed her eyes as a cue that she was done talking for the moment.

Galdren took the hint and turned to go. "I think you probably still need to rest, but I will be around, so if you need anything, speak up. I'll be able to hear you." With that, he softly closed the door as he left.

Avila knew she had been rude, and from what she could gather, she probably owed Galdren her life. However, at that moment, she was too disoriented to deal with anything other than her immediate surroundings and swirling thoughts. He had been right about one thing: that had been one hell of a dream. She was still having difficulty slowing her heartbeat down. As she started to slip back into sleep, she decided the bump on her head had shaken her up worse than she had initially thought.

Over the next few weeks, Avila slept most of the time, but she could tell she was getting better when awake. By the third week, she could sit up in bed and eat real food without it making her sick. The only bad thing was the dreams. Most of the time, they were not as intense as the first one, but they were always enough to shake her up even if she could never fully remember the details. Afterward, when awake, she felt afraid and disoriented. It would take her several minutes to sort through the bloody images and frightening scenes in her head. Galdren was always there whenever she woke up screaming.

Galdren was a perfect gentleman, and when he wasn't around, he had a woman named Olva there to take care of Avila. She didn't speak much, but she was polite. She would help Avila clean up and rebandage her head, and she was always there to assist her with using the amenities when necessary. She would keep up a minimum conversation, but every time Avila started asking questions about her gracious host, Olva would clam up and find something else she needed to do.

After the fourth week, Avila managed to get out of bed on her own and move around some. Her favorite place to sit was by the window. It didn't offer much of a view since it was in the heart of the city, but she could see the park, and there were always birds flitting around. Occasionally she might catch sight of a couple of squirrels chattering to each other or a rabbit hopping across the walkway. She was beginning to feel cooped up, and she often found herself wishing she could be out there with the squirrels and birds.

It wasn't that she was lonely. Her parents came to visit her every day, but they could never stay long. Every time she asked them about when she would get to go home, they shied away from the question. Their constant response was to tell her they would worry about those things, and all she needed to worry about was getting better.

She even had Lissa coming by occasionally to keep her up to date with all the latest gossip at school, but none of it seemed important anymore. More and more, she was getting the feeling she was being kept in the dark about something, though she couldn't figure out what it could be.

Once Galdren realized she was feeling better, he took to visiting with her more often. Sometimes he would come and talk to her for an hour or more at a time. He would keep her up to date on current events, and at his request, she would tell him about herself. Whenever she asked any questions about his personal life, he would give her generic answers and quickly change the subject. Whenever she asked about leaving, he would joke about her not being satisfied with his hospitality. The humor didn't seem to reach his eyes, and he almost seemed hurt that she didn't want to stay longer.

By Avila's rough estimation, she had been at Galdren's for more than two months. She no longer needed constant attention, and she felt she should be able to leave soon. She planned to ask the doctor about it when he came to check on her.

It was nearly time for the doctor's visit, so Avila got up and started moving around so he wouldn't catch her in bed. As she paced, she wondered why Galdren had not been up to visit her yet. Eventually, Avila looked at the timeglass and saw that the time for her appointment had passed, and the doctor was still not there. She decided he must have been held up and was running late, so she went to her favorite place by the window to wait for him.

After a while, she got lost in the antics of a pair of squirrels across the street. She was so engrossed in what she was watching that she didn't hear the door open and close quietly. After a few moments, someone called her name softly, making her jump. She turned and saw Galdren standing by the door watching her.

"I thought you were the doctor come to check on me again." As soon as she said that, she noticed he had a somber look on his face. Not exactly upset, but a little sad and maybe a little anxious. That was a look she had not seen yet, and it was out of place.

"Well, you are partly right; I was just talking to the doctor." The way he said that made a shiver go down her spine, especially when he added, "Why don't you sit back down? I need to talk to you."

Avila felt she had better comply before her heart jumped out of her chest. "So, what was his diagnosis? Surely it isn't that bad. I feel fine. Like I could get back to my regular life." She was trying to lighten the tension in the room and hide the turmoil going on inside her.

He followed her cue and smiled as well. "Of course, you are fine. He recommended you take it easy for a while, but you are cleared to get back to your studies and such." After that, he paused for a moment, but she couldn't find the breath to say anything, so he continued, "Here is where we get to the reason I really need to talk to you." As he said that, he pulled up a chair and sat down across from her. "There are so many things I need to tell you, and I don't know where would be best to start, so I guess I'll start with the basics.

"I know we have spent a lot of time getting to know one another, but I am also aware that you don't know much about me besides my name. Did you ever wonder why my apartments were so close to the Gallery when I first brought you here?" After he asked her the question, he looked directly into her eyes, and for a moment, the intensity she saw there took her breath away.

When she got her breath back, she looked at him carefully before she answered, "I didn't think about it at first, but after the first couple of weeks, I did wonder why you were so close to the castle complex. When we would talk, I noticed that you didn't want to talk about anything too personal, so I figured it would have been pointless to ask, and that you would tell me when you were ready. Anyway, I think I have it figured out." She paused and checked his face for a reaction. He raised an eyebrow and gestured for her to continue.

"The nice apartments, the location, the polite servants . . . you even have the same name as the prince—that one took me a while to figure out. I think you are a royal cousin or another relative, maybe even from another high-ranking family. Perhaps named after the prince in a show of respect for the royal family? You seem as if you are close to his age. Am I warm?"

At those self-assured statements, he smiled, and this time it reached all the way to his eyes, crinkling the edges, but only for a moment. "Well, you truly are as bright as I thought you were, but you underestimate a little. I am Prince Galdren de Althmear, heir to the throne of Aril. I keep apartments both inside and outside the castle proper to use at my convenience."

At first, Avila was too stunned to say anything. Then, as it finally hit her, she tripped over her own feet as she hurried to stand up and bow. "Your Highness, I really had no idea. I don't know how to thank you for everything you have done for me. This must be a burden on your time. I apologize, but I will pay you back for your hospitality in time; all you need to do is tell me what you desire from me." She ended with a low bow since she was afraid to look up.

Her reaction seemed to take Galdren off guard at first, but he quickly regained his composure. "You have no need to act like that for me just because you now know who I am. That is not why I told you." With a soft but firm hand, he pushed on her shoulder. "Sit down before you fall over. You are not fully well yet."

Her face was still flushed, but she did as she was told. After she was seated again, she slowly raised her eyes and met his gaze. "I meant what I said about repaying you for your kindness. I knew you were someone of importance and were going out of your way for me. I had planned on telling you something along the same lines anyway."

At her words, his face became clouded, and it was hard to tell what he was thinking. "We haven't talked about what happened that day. I think we need to now."

The change of subject threw Avila for a moment. "All right, if that is what you would like, but I can only remember bits and pieces. I was hoping that eventually, you would be able to fill in some of the gaps for me." Still confused, she looked at him as he sat there, but he only looked at her intently for a few moments before he began again.

"First, I think you should start with what you can remember from that morning and work your way up to when you can't. I'll add what I know then, and we will see if we can get this figured out." With that said, Galdren sat back more comfortably, clearly trying to look like he was just having a regular conversation. However, Avila could tell he was still tense. This strange day was far from over.

Avila wasn't sure what he meant by the beginning, so she started with when she had met Lissa at the fair. "After we looked at the stages behind the Gallery, we went upstairs to find a seat and decided to sit up front. When we walked up there, I looked at the screen to see the stage. The new flag caught my attention, and then I blacked out. The next thing I remember is being here at your apartments."

Galdren had a strange look on his face, but he didn't say anything at first. Then he leaned over, took her hands, and looked directly into her eyes. "Are you sure that is all you can remember? There is absolutely nothing else? You can't remember what might have made you black out in the first place?"

The contact had Avila flustered again. For some reason, having her hands inside both of Galdren's was disconcerting, and she wasn't sure why. Still, she tried not to show it. She started to tell him that was everything, but then she remembered the inscription on the flag. "I don't know if this might be important, but it is a little strange. Before I blacked out, I noticed the inscription below the two dragons on the new flag: *comhcheol*. I know what it means; I mean, I know that language.

It translates into 'harmony,' but I don't know how I would know that. I have no memory of seeing it before."

"Most people from this planet wouldn't know." Galdren leaned in toward her a little more. "The flag is from one of the planets I visited on my journeys; Talamh. It is somewhat misleading, since they have been going through a lot of civil unrest for more than a decade. It seems as if they are finally settled enough that they are trying to put the past behind them and find allies for the future. They even put in an application to rejoin the Trading Alliance.

"About twelve years ago, when the unrest started, they became totally withdrawn from galactic society and severed all ties with their allies, including the Alliance. There are still too many unsolved mysteries for them to rejoin right now, I think. The issue of what happened to the royal family is a good example. However, my father decided it was better to show acceptance for now rather than make an enemy of them. Therefore, we are flying their flag with our other allies'."

That was a bit much for Avila, and it clearly showed on her face. "I'm sorry, that was too much about politics when all you want to know is why you know that language." He touched her hand again for a moment. "Well, if it is any help to you at all, I think that maybe your family fled when the revolution started. Your parents told me you were adopted and that you had no memory of your early childhood. This could explain a lot of that. Plus, many of the Talamhites fled here to Aril. Since we are neutral, it was a logical destination. Not the only one, but a great many of them have settled here."

The shock of everything he had said was barely able to sink in; she was too overwhelmed. As soon as she could cope with one thing, like him being the prince, something else came up to throw her off-balance. "I don't really know what to say. I had given up on finding out anything about where I'm from. My parents had told me I was a refugee, but they also discouraged me from looking into it more. They always said knowing would hurt more than not knowing. To tell you the truth, I rarely ever think about it anymore." She glanced out the window for a moment, then turned back to face him. "To think, I've found out more in the last twenty minutes than I've ever known; it's a little much to take in."

"Well, when I first brought you here, you were mumbling something. When I figured out you were quoting the flag's inscription, it took me by surprise too. However, you were too weak at first to talk about it, and then the time didn't seem right. After you had been here for a while, I had already talked to your parents and friends enough to form my own theory, but I wanted to wait to talk to you about it.

"There are some other things that don't have answers either. These are a little more serious and harder to figure out," Galdren said the last with a stern expression. "I will try to pick up your story where you left off."

He sat back and glanced to the side, as if he was trying to recall exactly what happened. "I was up on the balcony already, inspecting things to make sure everything was passable for the speeches. When you walked up, it caught my attention because, well, you stand out. Anyway, I watched you walk to the edge, and I was going to use the excuse of getting a look at the stage to get a better look at you."

At that, Avila turned bright red. She didn't trust herself to say anything, so she let him continue with his story. "By the time I reached you, I noticed there was something wrong. Your friend Lissa was trying to pull you away from the edge, but you kept right on walking. I ran up to help her, but you had already pulled away from her, and you had a content expression on your face. You seemed like you were happy. Happy to walk to your death! You walked right off the edge of the balcony. I barely caught you in time. You hit your head extremely hard on the edge, but that was better than the alternative. You would have fallen several stories to your death. It is fortunate I was up there."

Avila was trying, but she could not remember any of it. "I'm grateful you were there. I cannot for the life of me think of what would make me act like that. Honestly, I don't remember." Tears started to well up in her eyes, and she blinked them back. She was scared and frustrated, but she would not break down here. Galdren had done enough for her already; he did not need to be a shoulder for her to cry on too. Besides, just the thought of him seeing her like that, especially now that she knew who he was, made her cringe. She didn't even want to think about the fact that he had been nursing her for more than two months.

Avila pushed those thoughts aside and waited until she trusted herself to speak without her voice cracking. "I'm truly sorry you have been dragged into my personal drama. I'm quite certain you have much better things to be doing. Now that I am better enough to move, I will be out of your way as soon as I can get my things and have someone to come and get me. I will eternally be in your debt."

As she said those words, the same strange look of hurt and guardedness passed over Galdren's face once more. "Avila, that is the other thing I have come to talk to you about." His words sounded ominous, but she was already numb from all the other revelations. She didn't move as he continued, "Are you familiar with our laws?"

Once again, the change of subject had Avila off-balance and searching for what it was he wanted from her. "I am familiar with some of them, but I am no expert. What laws, exactly, do you want to know about?"

He took a deep breath and looked away from her. "Are you familiar with the Life Debt?"

Those simple words sent an icy chill over her, and she couldn't repress a shiver. "I have heard of it before. When a person's life has been saved, the Life Debt states that they literally owe their life to their savior, to put it simply, but I thought it wasn't used anymore. Too many people disputed whether their lives were actually in danger, and other times the savior didn't want the responsibility of holding another person's life in their hands." It was more of a statement than a question, as she was hoping he would only confirm what she had said.

"You are only partially right. It is not required to be enforced anymore because of the problems you have listed and many more. However, there is a provision that if the threat to life is clearly defined and the savior so chooses, they can invoke the Life Debt." He paused for a moment and looked at her intently. "I have already talked to my father and to your parents. They all agree that if I had not helped, you would have died. My father has allowed me to invoke your Life Debt."

The silence and tension in the room at that moment could have been cut with a knife. The realization of what he was saying hit her like an icy wave. She was his, it was already decided, and there was nothing she could do about it. Everything else she had learned that day shrank in comparison.

After a few moments of her utter silence, he stood up. "I realize this is a lot for you to take in right now, but I don't want you to worry about it. I want you to concentrate on getting better. Your parents will be by in the next couple of days, and you can tell them what you need from your old house." Those words had a kind of finality to them, letting her know her old life was over.

"Professor Fredrick Gilbert was my old tutor. I have learned that you have worked closely with him in the last couple of years, so when I spoke to him he agreed to continue your graduate studies here as soon as you feel well enough. I hope that will be all right with you. Also, I will be continuing our visits; I find them absorbing. If you need anything, let Olva know, and I hope you will come to accept this in time. I know it will turn out for the best."

With that said, he turned around, and before she could say anything, walked out of the door. She sat stock-still for a moment, and then it hit her. She would never play in the forests by herself again or sit and chat with her friends. Her life was no longer her own. No matter how much he tried to make it seem like it would continue to be the same, things were changed forever. All because of some stupid twist of fate. Even the formality with which he'd delivered her sentence to her was in stark contrast to his warmth of a few moments before.

She couldn't take it anymore; it was too much all at once. Even the sight of the park from her window seat was depressing. She lay down on the bed and, finally giving in to the tears she had been fighting, cried herself to sleep.

3. NIGHTMARES

The young girl woke up, and her head was pounding. She was completely unfamiliar with her surroundings. When she tried to move, the whole room started to blur and fade out again, so she decided to stay still. When the blurriness passed, she was able to focus on the pain in her head. It was coming from the right side, above the temple. As long as she didn't move her head, she felt all right. She moved her hand slowly and touched the spot where the pain was coming from. She felt a bandage there, but it was wet with something, and when she brought her fingers around in front of her face, they were red. The sight almost made her fade out again, but she refused to let herself get scared by the prospect of a little blood. She couldn't quite remember, but she had the feeling she had seen enough so that it shouldn't bother her.

She slowly put her hand back down and tried again to see where she was, this time without moving her head too much. She could tell she was in some sort of bunk, and by the looks of it, she was on a space liner. The room had one other cot, a desk, a door marked with the lavatory symbol, and a smaller door that was presumably a closet.

After her quick inspection of the room, she closed her eyes and tried to remember how she had come to be there. For the life of her, she could only remember bits and pieces of bloody images that were too outlandish to be real. The only thing she could think was she had somehow taken a nasty bump to the head and, in the meantime, had some scary dreams. All she could do was wait and hope that someone who knew what was going on would be able to help.

Just as she was about to drift off to sleep again, she heard a sound that brought her fully awake. She couldn't identify it at first, but it soon got closer to her room. When she heard it up close, the gunfire brought back memories of her bloody dreams much more vividly, and she began to wonder if they had been dreams at all. There was a great blast almost right outside the door to her room, and it made her jump, which caused the room to spin again. While the explosion was still echoing down the hallway, the door to her room burst open, and she screamed. The face that appeared was battered but somehow familiar. She felt she should know this face, and it was no threat.

"My lady, you are awake. That is good. I don't mean to frighten you, but we really must be going." This calm, matter-of-fact statement seemed almost absurd coming from this man, but all her instincts told her she should listen to him.

"I will try to move as fast as I can. The slightest movements make me dizzy, so I will need your help. Will that be possible?" As she said this, she got up and tried her best not to fall over, fighting the dizziness with every step and using the wall as a prop.

"I am sorry, but they have found us even here. I trapped them in the far end of the hallway, but it will not take them long to find a way through. I will help you as long as I can, but when they start to come again, I will have to stop to take care of them." She was still totally confused about what was going on, but her instincts had kicked in, and they told her now was not the time to ask questions. It also did not escape her attention that he did not sugarcoat the situation by saying "if" they got through. She appreciated his candor; this way, there were no false promises or inflated hopes. She had no idea where all these thoughts were coming from, but they made sense, so she went with it.

They hurried down the hallway, leaving the sounds of intermittent explosions behind them. Soon the sounds stopped altogether, but that only increased her fear. Something told her this was far from over. They only had to stop twice for her to regain her feet after a fit of dizziness. Each time, the strange man would stand over her looking behind him with a gun that he always kept close at hand, even when he was helping her walk.

In her confused state, it felt like an eternity before he called a halt to their frantic pace. But when they stopped, the urgency in his face only seemed more pronounced, and she thought she could hear what sounded like many footsteps in the direction they had just come from. That might explain his frightening expression. He looked straight at her and tried to school the fear out of his eyes; she was sure for her benefit. "My lady, they are gaining, and I cannot hold them all. Behind us is a single person escape pod. I had hoped to make it to the larger one, but that doesn't seem like it will be possible. I need you to get in this pod, and I will set the controls to take you where you should be safe until the next person can pick you up."

For some reason, the thought of being alone again terrified her more than the statement that the unknown assailants were gaining on them. She tried to voice an objection, even tried to convince him she could move faster. She argued that if they left now, they would be able to make it to the bigger pod, even though she had no idea how far that was. She was doing everything she could think of to not be left alone.

He cut off all her excuses and reassured her she would be safe if she did exactly as he said. "We always have a backup plan, and this is one of them. It was decided if we both couldn't get away, you would leave in this pod after I led them past. I will take the larger one to act as a decoy."

She felt helpless but could think of no more valid arguments. She got into the pod and strapped herself in while he took care of programming the pod's computer with the coordinates of where he was sending her. He checked her straps one last time and gently laid his hand on her cheek. "You are so young, but I promise I am not the only one that wishes for your safety. You won't be alone for long." With those words, he walked out of the pod and looked back to see if he could tell it had been disturbed. Apparently, he found things to his satisfaction because, after a moment, he walked off some ways. He stopped, but it wasn't long before he started running.

Before she could even begin to feel scared, the footsteps were right outside. When she heard the voices that went with them, she froze. "Hey, look here. This looks like the bandage the brat was wearing. Here's part of his cloak too. They must have had to stop because she started bleeding again. There's fresh blood up the hall here too; he must be carrying her now. Maybe we can catch them soon."

With every word they uttered, the blood in her veins seemed to freeze a little more. She could hear at least five different voices, but to her amazement, they were going farther and farther down the hall in the direction her unknown helper had gone. Before they were completely out of earshot, she heard something that made her gasp. It was a voice she had not heard yet, and the coldness in it made everyone stop talking. "I have informed the commander the only way for them to escape is the double pod on the port side near the rear of the ship. He has informed me his fighters are on the way there now. Even if they manage to make it that far before we catch up, the fighters will blow them into the vacuum as soon as they take off."

They were too far from her now for her to hear more, but that was enough. She couldn't let him take off. She had to find some way to get to him and tell him it was a trap. As she fought with the straps holding her in, it dawned on her they were locked in place, and they wouldn't come undone. When she realized this, she looked frantically around her and realized the takeoff sequence had begun. Either it was set on a timer, or the man had set it off when he was sure the assailants were past where she was.

Within a few moments, she was jolted by the sudden movement of the pod as it released itself from the main ship. It didn't have a large jet, so there was no noise until it initiated its thrusters to send it in the right direction. Even then, the disturbance was minimal. There were fighter ships out there, and even though they were on the other side of the ship, she knew that had to mean that either a cruiser was close or they were close to a planet.

The question was answered as the pod turned and the planet beneath her came looming into view. She was so awed by the sight that for a moment, she forgot where she was. Then, as the pod turned again, she had an unobstructed view as the other, larger pod took off. Not far from it were two sleek fighters. She couldn't tell what class or style from this distance. The scene unfolded in sickening slow motion. Just as it seemed the other pod would clear them, the two fighters opened fire simultaneously. In a blast that made her need to cover her face with her hands, the pod was gone in an instant.

Avila woke with a start. She didn't scream, but then, she'd been having the dreams long enough that she no longer did that. She did notice when she reached up to rub her face that there were tears streaked down her cheeks.

The next few days went by in a blur for Avila. Her parents came by to talk to her and reassure her they would still be around for her any time she wanted to see them. They had already been told the prince didn't have a problem with it, so they would try to come over as often as possible. They also brought a few of her personal things from her room they knew she would want or need and told her they would get her anything else she thought she might want if she would give them a list.

The one question burning in Avila's mind was if they had known all along that Galdren was the prince and what his intentions were. She was too afraid to ask. The sense of betrayal, that they might have had a clue and had done nothing to warn her or help her in any way, was too much. She couldn't stand to find out for sure.

Avila tried to fight those feelings. She knew there was nothing they could have done even if they had known. Trying to convince her heart of that was a lot harder than convincing her mind.

When Lissa came to visit her for the first time since things had changed, Avila's mood was switching somewhere between frustrated, angry, and outright depressed. Her friend seemed to sense some of that as soon as she saw her.

"Hey, I thought I might drop by and see how things were going since I haven't got to see you for a while; you know, make sure you're feeling better." Avila didn't even know where to begin, so she sat there until Lissa continued like there was no problem, "I was going to come by last week, but your parents said it probably wasn't a good time. I asked them when you might be coming home, and they said you were going to stay here for a while, but they didn't say much else."

Avila knew Lissa was trying to make polite conversation, and that her questions were aimed at finding out what was wrong. However, they brought every feeling she had gone through in the past week back to the front of her mind. She knew she had to say something to stop the questions before she exploded and said something she didn't mean.

"Lissa, stop beating around the bush." Avila realized that had come out a little harsh, so she tried to soften her words with a smile. "I can tell you want to know what is going on, but I barely know myself. If you'll sit down and listen, I might be able to explain what I can."

She paused for a moment, then continued after Lissa sat in the chair by the window, a place Avila tried to avoid these days. "Okay, where do I start? Well, I am going to stay here . . . as long as . . . as long as Galdren wants me to. I don't know how much you know already, but I will start at the beginning. Besides, I could use a friend to talk to right now anyway." At that last statement, Lissa looked sharply at her and seemed like she was going to speak, but clamped her lips shut when Avila caught her eye.

"Do you remember what happened on the day of my accident? I know we haven't talked about it." Before Lissa could reply, Avila continued, "I don't know exactly what happened, but I was told that if Galdren hadn't been there, I probably would have died." Avila repressed a grimace as she said that last part, but she went on anyway. "You know, it feels a little strange to call him that, even though that is what he had me call him from the day we met."

Lissa was clearly trying to follow Avila's broken thought patterns, but she looked totally lost. "What are you talking about? I thought his name *is* Galdren; why would you call him anything else?" The question bothered Avila as soon as it was out, and she felt like she was either about to start crying or laughing hysterically; it was hard to tell which.

She did neither. Instead, she told herself to pull it together. It wouldn't do her any good to lose it again. "I guess they really didn't tell you anything, did they? One of the bombs they dropped on me was his title. His full name is *Prince* Galdren de Althmear, heir to the throne of Aril."

After she said that, she felt a little bit of gratification, because the look on Lissa's face was as shocked as she had felt when she first found out. Unfortunately, the satisfaction wore off quickly, and the despair started to set back in before Lissa could find the words to reply.

Still, Lissa recovered far more quickly than Avila herself had. "Oh, wow! You mean you have been living with the most eligible bachelor in the whole of the Trading Alliance and didn't even know it, and he wants you to keep staying here, and—what are you so upset about?"

Lissa's excited chatter was barely understandable as it tried to all come out at once. It brought a small chuckle out of Avila until what she was saying sank in. It hit her even harder that her situation was not at all what Lissa was thinking. Once again, the tears started to come, and this time she didn't even bother to try and stop them. Lissa had been her best friend as long as she could remember, and if she couldn't cry on her friend's shoulder, then she didn't have anyone she could turn to.

Lissa was obviously shocked by the sudden outburst from her usually levelheaded and sensible friend, but she pulled Avila into a hug anyway. It was exactly what Avila needed.

After a few minutes, Avila had cried herself out and felt she at least owed Lissa an explanation. "Sorry about that. I know it might look like this is every girl's dream, you know, being rescued by the prince and him falling for her, but this isn't exactly like that." She paused to try to figure out how to tell her best friend that she didn't know how much longer she would be able to spend time with her.

"When Galdren—I mean, the prince, rescued me, he saved my life, and now I owe it to him. I mean that literally. He has invoked the Life Debt, and I am now his to do with as he pleases." Avila watched as the look on Lissa's face changed to one of complete shock. "I know it sounds like an old story, but the law still exists. It's rarely used anymore, but it can be. For reasons I haven't even been able to bring myself to ask about, Galdren was granted my life."

Both girls sat there for some time. Lissa in stunned silence, and Avila still trying to come to terms with the reality of what felt like a horrible dream. Finally, Lissa broke the silence in a soft voice as she grabbed Avila's hand. "What is going to happen to you, then? Has he told you anything about what he wants? Are you going to be able to keep seeing the other people in your life, like your parents and me?"

Somehow, Avila managed a weak grin to make Lissa feel she was helping. "I don't know what he wants yet. As far as what will happen to me, I have no clue, but he has told me, for now, I can continue to see my family and friends. I can even keep up with my studies, but it all must be done from here. He hasn't expressly forbidden me from leaving, but every time he says something, it is always 'they can come here anytime they want' or 'you can vo-im anytime.' As far as my studies are concerned, and this is unreal, Professor Gilbert has agreed to come and tutor me privately." She smiled with the last part of her explanation. The fact that her favorite professor also mentored the prince was one of the small miracles helping her keep her sanity.

"Professor Gilbert, what has he got to do with any of this? I knew he was taking time off from teaching. The assistant dean, Professor Dilant, took over his classes with the explanation that Gilbert needed some personal time. Until further notice, we had to deal with her. If necessary, they said we would have a new teacher next year."

Avila stopped Lissa before she could get any more worked up. She knew how Lissa could get when she was excited. "Okay, calm down. There is a logical explanation for it. Professor Gilbert used to be the private tutor for the prince himself. When the prince was done with his studies, the professor still felt he had a lot to teach people, so he went to work for the public system. He agreed to tutor me privately as a personal favor for the prince. I have only talked to the professor once, as I don't officially start back until next week, but he seemed more than happy to do this for me. He carefully avoided the subject of why he has to, though."

"So, that explains why, but didn't he at least try to talk to you about what is going on?" Lissa, being the loyal friend she was, clearly couldn't understand why the professor didn't say anything to make Avila feel better.

"To be honest, Lissa, I'm glad he didn't. I thought I would burst with the need to talk to someone, but I think since we will be working together, it could have made things awkward. Not to mention, I don't know what is going to happen." With a sigh, she stood and strode over to the other window in the room. "I am, however, ecstatic I have you to talk to!" She made sure to face the window so Lissa would not see the fresh tears on her cheeks. It was one thing to need a shoulder now and then, but quite another to burden her best friend with how overwhelmed she was feeling.

4. ACCEPTING REALITY

After Lissa's visit, things seemed to settle into a regular pattern for Avila. After a week of giving her time to think and come to terms with her situation, Galdren resumed his visits. Although at first, he only visited right before Professor Gilbert was done for the day and talked with both of them. He left when the professor did. In some ways, this made things a little easier for her. She was comfortable around the professor. Having him there made the conversation flow smoothly. A small part of her wished she could be alone with Galdren to ask him why, though she was quite sure she wouldn't be able to.

Her first week of lessons was almost enough to keep her from thinking about anything else. She had been absent long enough and had so many other things on her mind that she had almost completely forgotten about her studies. It was difficult to get back into the habit of focusing on her schoolwork like she didn't have any other cares in the world, but she realized quickly if she didn't, she wouldn't pass.

While her classes didn't seem as important to her as they once did, it didn't take her long to become reabsorbed in Professor Gilbert's teaching and to strive for perfection in her grades. It was as much a matter of personal pride as it was the professor's teaching.

"I hope the last papers you turned in were the last ones of that caliber I am forced to grade." It was the end of the second week, and the professor had returned her grades for the first week. "I know things are rough, but I also know you are quite capable of doing much better." That was the first time the professor had even so much as mentioned the situation, even if it was obliquely.

Avila was caught off guard for a moment; she had been thinking about her schoolwork, and the brief intrusion from the real world had caught her unaware. Feeling a bit off-balance, it took her a moment to respond. "I apologize for the lack of concentration on my part last week. I know you are doing me a great favor. My remaining grades will reflect my respect for you and the level of workmanship you have come to expect from me."

In turn, her formality seemed to throw the professor off, but he recovered much more quickly. "You know, I have always admired the tenacity with which you throw yourself into everything you do. You are always diligent, but you are also human, and with everything, it is to be expected. If you would like to talk, I am here for you, and I want you to know it is a pleasure to tutor you, not just an obligation. I wish all my students would try as hard as you do."

Twice in the last few moments, he had mentioned her situation, and Avila was beyond focusing on her work now. She knew the formality of her answer before had probably stung a little, and that if the professor didn't want to be there, he wouldn't be. However, she was in no mood to talk about the situation or the prince with her professor, so she did her best to steer the conversation elsewhere. "Thank you for all you are doing. I know you wouldn't be here if you didn't want to be. I am trying to let you know I will endeavor to make sure the faith you have in me is well-placed, and your time here is not wasted." She said the last with a smile, both as a way of reassuring him she was all right and to apologize for her earlier curtness.

He placed a hand on her shoulder. "You are an amazing girl." He turned to pick up her work and the rest of his papers. "It is time for me to go today. I will get all this back to you next week." He turned to look over his shoulder at her. "Don't forget, there will be tests at the end of next week, but I will have these graded and back to you before then so you will have time to study them."

With his announcement about the time and his earlier statements, she found herself focusing on Galdren. He had not been up to see her today. "Thank you, Professor, for . . . for everything. I will make sure I study, and I will see you next week." She followed him to the door with a smile and closed it behind him after he said his goodbyes.

She walked to the window seat and sat there, staring blankly out at the park. She had avoided looking outside for the last several weeks; it only reminded her of not being able to go anywhere if she pleased. Her thoughts were in tangles, and she wasn't sure exactly what she was feeling. A little upset maybe, but Professor Gilbert had tried to talk about things for the first time and it had rattled her. Also, perhaps a little relieved. Galdren showing up usually put a tense edge on their conversations, even if it was easier to see him while with the professor.

Deep down, though, no matter how much she didn't want to admit it to herself, she was disappointed. She had gotten used to seeing Galdren every day for the last few months, and he always assured her he would be back. Even though it made her uncomfortable being around him, knowing what she did now, she still enjoyed their time together. It was realizing this more than anything else that had her off-balance. Not being sure of how she felt, and worse yet, recognizing that she might like the man holding her life in his hands, made her want to start crying again. It was much easier to rail about her situation when she knew exactly how she felt about it.

She knew next to nothing about the prince, and it scared her beyond belief that she wanted to get to know him more—not just as her master, but as a person as well. The first weeks they had spent talking before she knew who he was and what her straits were, she had always enjoyed it. He had been charming and funny and always concerned about how she felt and in tune with when it had been too long for her and she needed rest.

She almost cursed the fates that had made the man she enjoyed being around the one that was now in control of her destiny. Even if she was grateful to him for saving her, her conflicted feelings were too much on top of everything else. She could feel the tears on her face but made no attempt to wipe them away. What did it matter anyway? She was alone with the cold comfort of the green grass, aloof and untouchable through the glass.

As she sat there staring at nothing, it eventually grew dark outside. She began to see more of her reflection than she saw of the park below. As she focused on the image, noting the tear trails still on her cheeks, she glanced up a little and noticed another. Galdren was standing behind her, studying her appearance in the window.

She almost fell off her seat backward in her effort to get up quickly. As she turned around, the look on his face was unreadable. Neither of them moved or said a word for what seemed an eternity; then he slowly reached out and brushed at the tearstains.

Avila felt her face flush at the brief contact, so she quickly turned her head. "I didn't think you would be up to visit today." She regretted the words as soon as they left her mouth. They were too close to the reason she had been crying, and she didn't want him to know he had that much power over her.

"I had things I had to attend to that took up most of my day." At those words, her face flushed again. She had been thinking only of herself, but he was the prince; of course he had duties to attend to.

Still far too embarrassed to look him in the face, she moved to the chairs across the room and took a seat. "I apologize for taking up your time. I wasn't thinking. I know you are a busy man and have far greater concerns than seeing me every day." She kept her head down and looked at her hands, wanting nothing more than to erase the telltale signs of her inner conflict off her face. She knew the attempt would only draw more attention to them, so she did nothing.

After a few moments, he still had not moved or said another word, so she chanced a glance up. The look on his face was still mostly unreadable, but she caught a glimpse of anger in the set of his mouth and the look in his eyes.

When their eyes caught, he strode over to where she was sitting but did not join her. He stood towering above her for a moment; he did not say a word, but she could not look away from his blue-green eyes if she had wanted to. He was a head taller than she was already, and seated like she was, she had to look almost straight up with him standing so close.

Finally, with a sigh, Galdren took a couple of steps and sat on the opposite chair. His intense stare and the tenseness in his chiseled jaw relaxed. Much more like his usual charming self, he kept Avila's gaze trapped.

"I had something I wanted to talk to you about tonight, and though I did not plan on being this late, I think it may be better." At those ominous words, despite his apparent goal of casualness, Avila had to restrain a shudder.

She tried to match his effort at being nonchalant, but she knew her posture was still tense, and she could do nothing about it, especially after a statement like that. "I am always here at your convenience." She knew there was a touch of bitterness in her words, but she couldn't help that either.

His jaw flexed, but he released it quickly before he replied, "I understand you are probably frustrated, and from what I have seen of you, I doubt you are practiced at trying to cut with words." At that, she turned her head, even though she was sure he could still see her turning red. She could not look him in the eye as he continued.

"I am trying to make this easy on you, and I need you to accept this. I know you are not the type of person for cruelty or grudges, and I want you to know I will do what I can to make this simpler for you, but this tension cannot continue just because we are alone."

She was sure his reason for wanting the tension to ease was not even close to her own, but she didn't voice that thought and schooled the flush they gave her. "You are right, Your Highness; I do not mean to be snippy or hurtful. I apologize for my earlier statement and ask that you please forgive me, as I am under some strain." She managed the whole sentence without a stutter, a flush, or needing to look away. She had to make sure her thoughts stayed only on the task at hand and tried to look at it as a project. He was in control, but it was still her job to do as asked graciously. She had nothing else she could do about it, and she never did anything except for her best.

Her words brought a smile to his face, a real smile that, for a moment, put a spark in his eyes. As she looked at him, she tried not to think of how attractive he was. He had broad shoulders, and his honeyed hair kissed his collar. When he moved, he had the graceful, sure movements of someone who understood economy of motion. As she started to think about how his hips tapered, she realized he was talking to her, and that she was daydreaming again—about something and someone she absolutely should not be. The ends of her lips had upturned the tiniest bit, which he must have taken as a sign of truce. When she realized she had missed his words, the smile left her face immediately, and she blazed red.

She recovered and tried to respond without letting him know she'd been distracted. "I am glad we can move on, and in all honesty, I will be happy to help in whatever way you need me to." She was rattled, and she knew her response was tepid at best. It probably had nothing to do with what he had been saying, but she was still trying to focus away from him.

He looked confused at her answer, and she didn't blame him. "Well, I am glad you didn't call me 'Your Highness.' I want you to know you can call me Galdren. What I started to say was, I hope we can be friends through all this. I enjoy the time I get to spend talking to you. You are an intelligent young woman, and it is nice not to be fawned over by simpering idiots."

"Simpering idiots? Your High—I mean, Galdren, surely you cannot be talking about the people that surround you every day?"

That time he laughed. "I wasn't sure if I had your complete attention. You seemed distracted there for a bit, but yes, some of them are exactly that. They are much more concerned with my title and how to get the most of it for themselves than they are about me personally. It is a refreshing change to talk to you. Even if you are mad at me, you still speak to me like a person and not a title."

So, he had noticed her being distracted; she prayed to the goddess he wouldn't guess why. "I can only be me. Most people are disturbed by my directness. I apologize for not catching everything you said, but you will have my full attention going forward. I am grateful for all you have done for me and for all your patience. I am just glad that being myself can ease your burden." With that, they both chuckled, and she could feel some of the tension leave her body. She decided then and there that even though she had agreed to do whatever was necessary with all her zeal, she would also not let her situation drag her into reacting instead of doing what she could to make the most of it.

5. OVERDUE INFORMATION

Monday morning came, and true to his word, Professor Gilbert was there with her graded papers and much better reports. "These will be handy for you to use as study guides for the test at the end of the week. I have marked the few incorrect answers for you to go back and find what you did wrong. You can let me know if you have any questions before Friday."

The grades on her papers were indeed much better this time. Although they still were not up to her usual level of competence, Avila was in an excellent mood and did not let it bother her. She didn't even allow the thought of the upcoming test to faze her. After her talk with Galdren on Friday, they had come to a kind of truce. There was still a touch of tension between them, but it wasn't because she was nervous around him or because of any lingering resentment. She still struggled with the possibility she might be starting to care for him, but hoped that if she didn't think about it, it wouldn't become an issue. The fact that he'd come over for short visits with no one else there that went smoothly on both Saturday and Sunday was a boost for her mood. She had enjoyed his company so much that she had almost forgotten to contact her parents both days. At least they had not been upset by the late call when they saw her bright smile.

She tried telling herself it was because she was happy she wouldn't have to put up with the uncomfortableness that had been between them before, and not at all because she thoroughly enjoyed spending time with him.

"Avila, I thought we were past the point of distractedness, and you were on to focusing on your studies?" The professor's words brought a sudden flush to her cheeks, and she jumped a little guiltily. She thanked the goddess that he could not read her mind, then focused on the task at hand. Soon enough, all wayward thoughts became nonexistent.

Professor Gilbert was getting started on the last subject when Galdren came in to join them. He quietly sat off to the side to not be a distraction. Although for Avila, just having Galdren in the room was a distraction. She realized it may begin to be a problem and resolved to focus more on what she was doing whenever he was around. Which would probably help with her other issue, as well.

After the professor was done giving his instructions for the last assignment, he stepped over and quietly chatted with Galdren while Avila finished her work. Several times, she found herself trying to listen to them and not focusing. She chastised herself each time and worked harder to finish so she could be done and go join them. Besides, she knew being distracted would not help her grades, which would not make anyone in the room pleased with her.

By the time she finished, Professor Gilbert had started to pick up his things to get ready to leave. She had just enough time to answer the last question before handing it over to him. "Well, well, that must have been a tough lesson. You never take the whole time for the questions. I guess I will have to grade this without going over any of the answers before I leave. If you really need to discuss them, we can try to fit it in tomorrow. I hope it doesn't put us behind." Avila knew Professor Gilbert was saying this pointedly because somehow, he had figured out she had been pre-occupied instead of concentrating on her work. She only hoped the professor had kept Galdren distracted as well. The last thing she wanted to do was try to explain to the prince why she was unfocused.

She managed to school her blush fairly well by turning and focusing on the window as the professor took her papers. It was a beautiful day outside, which sufficed to distract her from all her worries in the room. Unfortunately, it also reminded her she had not been out in ages. Even though she tried to squash it, a pang of regret and something akin to homesickness washed over her.

After she said her goodbyes to Professor Gilbert, she walked over to the window seat without looking at Galdren. At the moment, between the feeling of being locked up and the feeling of being overwhelmed by his presence, she didn't trust herself to not do or say something stupid. The newfound and fragile truce between them was something she wanted to keep, so instead, she focused on watching the leaves that had started to turn bright orange and red fall to the ground. It was another poignant reminder of how much time had passed while she was stuck inside.

Avila placed her hand on the glass, as if she could reach out and grasp the falling leaves if she tried. She had almost forgotten that Galdren was there in her silent inspection of the autumn splendor just outside her reach. Her hand grew cold from the glass, and for the first time in days, she had to fight back the tears again.

In her distraction, she had once again missed Galdren speaking. Luckily, it was getting easier for her to get her wayward emotions under control, and she quickly turned to face him. He was standing in almost the same spot he had been on Friday. The irony of the situation was not lost on her.

"My apologies, Your Highness, I mean—Galdren." She repressed a sigh. "I really am trying, you know. Anyway, I apologize, but I was distracted by my thoughts, and I did not catch what you said. It really is the leaves' fault, you know; they are quite beautiful right now."

His expression grew thoughtful and his eyes were considering as they searched her own. He stood there like that for several moments before he said anything at all, stretching the silence and searching her face until it started to become awkward. Finally, when Avila began to blush under his scrutiny, she decided she had to say something, if only to try to break the silence. It was at that point that he finally spoke again.

"I was commenting on the fact that you seem to be getting back in the habit of studying well again. The professor is pleased with your progress so far and feels like you should be able to graduate only a little later than you would have." Avila wanted to groan at that. Of course, that had been what they were talking about—her grades. It made her feel like she was back in junior school with Lila and Thomas, only it embarrassed her ten times worse with it being Galdren. For some reason thinking of him in the role of her guardian, as the one wanting to keep her in line or making sure she was doing well, made her want to cringe.

He obviously wasn't done, since he still had that look on his face. It seemed like he was trying to figure out what he wanted to say, and Avila was far too embarrassed to say anything, so she waited for him to figure it out.

"Do you want to leave that badly, or do you simply miss spending time as you please, when you please?" He had never asked her what she wanted directly before, and it took her by surprise. Although he was trying to hide it, she could also tell that he wasn't sure if he wanted to know the answer.

Now it was her turn to examine him before she responded. Why would he ask her that question? Surely, he already knew that she would be happier if her life wasn't at someone else's whim, but she tried not to focus on that and instead considered what would drive him to ask in the first place. He'd obviously noted she wanted to be outside. Maybe he did want to make her comfortable, but she also knew there was no way she could leave, even if she said something. So, she decided to tell him the truth—a bit of it, at least.

"Galdren, I am not unhappy here. You have been more than gracious, and I am grateful, but I am an outdoor creature. I always have been. I used to love spending as much of my free time as possible in the forest outside the city. This time of year is particularly beautiful with all the trees dressed in their finery and just the right amount of crispness in the air. It makes everything look brighter and smell cleaner. It makes me feel alive." She closed her eyes while speaking to capture each of those treasured memories again for a moment behind her eyelids while she conjured them for someone else.

When she opened her eyes, Galdren had taken the step that separated them and was looking down at her face intently. He stood there long enough for her to lose her breath entirely due to his proximity and intensity before he stepped past her and to the window himself. He seemed oblivious to the void he had left behind.

"You know, you could almost be called rapturous as you were describing the autumn. I don't think I have ever heard it portrayed that way before. I know I have never heard you mention it that way." He said all of this with his back to her while he was still looking out the window, and it almost seemed as though the longer he spoke, the angrier he was getting.

"As a matter of fact, I don't believe I have ever heard you mention anything about being outside—ever." With that, he finally turned around, and there was no doubt. He was livid, but she was not about to apologize for wanting to go outside. It wasn't as though she ever got to.

"You want me to treat you like a person, well, all right then. Don't you dare get angry with me because I want to go outside! Just because I kept my feelings to myself because I know how things are and know what I can and can't do doesn't mean I don't still have the desire. It certainly doesn't mean if you ask me a question I will not answer you truthfully, even if you may not like the answer." By the time she finished, the look on his face had transformed into one of pure shock.

He stared at her for a moment, clearly not sure how to process what had just happened. Avila was chagrined as she continued, "Um, is that the first time some-one's talked back to you?" She looked up into his face to see if her question might break the pall that seemed to have fallen on the room. Since she had said her piece, she felt terrible for lashing out. It wasn't usually in her nature to get angry like that, and she hoped to bring a little levity back.

It worked, a little at least. He looked chagrined, but he still managed a half-smile as he answered, "No one except my parents has ever thought to tell me openly exactly what they were thinking, except maybe Professor Gilbert. I am sad to say even he hasn't since I have become an adult."

The stormy look came back into his eyes after that, but it was a tempered storm. "I am, however, still angry with you." He paused and held up one hand as she opened her mouth. "No, don't say a word until I am finished, please. I have spent months talking with you, and I thought we were opening up."

Avila couldn't help a small snort at that, but at a look from him, she motioned to let him know she was still listening. "In all our conversations, not once did you mention the fact that you love being outdoors. From the look on your face as you talk about it, I can tell it is a passion for you, and you have not said a single thing about it to me. You talk about desires and what you can and can't do, and that makes no sense because you have never even asked me. How can you know? I am not angry because you want to go outside. I am angry because you never mentioned it. I told you before I would do all I can to make you comfortable, to make this easy for you. Why do you feel it has to be hard?"

Avila was stunned by his words and the earnestness in them. He really did want to make this easier for her, even down to letting her out sometimes. She wasn't sure if she was elated by that news or insulted. She squashed the part of her thoughts telling her it felt like he was taking care of a prized pet and decided to go with elated. She knew the feeling must have shown on her face because Galdren's smile grew as well, which in turn reignited her own warm and fuzzies. She hoped the slight blush would be written off as excitement.

"I did not try to purposely hide anything from you; it is just that I didn't think that, well, you know . . . with the situation being what it is, that I would be allowed to leave. Every time I mentioned visiting anyone, in the beginning, it was always 'they can visit you.' I assumed that meant I was never going to leave here until you figured out what you wanted to do with me." As soon as those last words left her mouth, her hand flew up to her lips to cover them, and she wished she could call them back. She had never asked before what he had planned for her. She was too scared to, and she hadn't meant to now, even in a roundabout way.

He studied her red face for a moment, then turned away and sat down before motioning her to join him. "Would it surprise you if I told you I am taking this one day at a time too?" His simple question opened up a whole new world of possibilities for her. On the one hand, it meant he didn't have any unknown plan he was saving her for that she had to worry about. Then again, if he didn't know why he was keeping her . . . why was he keeping her? She wasn't sure she wanted the answer to that question.

"Galdren, I am not asking you what you are planning for me. I didn't mean for it to come out that way. I will accept things as they come. I have told you I will do what I can to . . . to do this graciously." She stumbled a little when she thought about the totality of what that might entail. Still, she was encouraged by her life with Galdren so far and chose to take heart from that instead of dwelling on the negative possibilities.

Galdren sighed in frustration. "I would like to believe everything you have said is true. You certainly seem to be improving with me, but if I find you are keeping things from me because you think I don't want to know them or you have already decided it doesn't matter without asking, how can I trust you?"

Avila's mouth popped open into a perfect O. It took a moment for her to recover and another for her to realize it would do no good to lose her temper again. She reined it in before she answered, "I have underestimated you, and I apologize for that. I realize now when you say everything, you mean everything. You can decide if it will be right or wrong, not I." She did not mind sharing with him so much as the fact that increasingly, her life was slipping beyond her control, and it was unsettling. Not to mention the fact that the share everything door was still, mostly, one-way. She knew more about Galdren than she had when she first arrived, but he was reluctant to talk about himself. He often changed the subject back to her whenever he could.

"You know, you have a beautiful mouth when you pout, but overall, it doesn't suit you. You are much better suited to a happier mood." His unexpected compliment erased the pout from her face. It was quickly replaced by a beet-red flush that no amount of ducking was going to hide. The fact that she blushed at his compliment brought a laugh to his lips.

"That is more like it." He chuckled again as she gave him a dirty look. She knew he was teasing her for turning red, but she felt much better. She always felt better when he laughed.

Avila started to relax and even to laugh with him at her own expense, but at his next words, she sobered instantly. "Okay, so, let's talk about what I plan on doing with you now." It threw her off a bit, because he was still grinning like a schoolboy. "Hmm, what to do, what to do?" He started tapping his chin as if he were deliberating several possibilities and shooting glances at her from the corner of his eyes. However, the effect was ruined by the fact that he never lost the grin. She realized he was up to some sort of game, but she wasn't sure how she was supposed to play along. This was new.

She stood up to pace, both for effect and to think. She always thought better when she was walking. She occasionally caught glimpses of him watching as she wandered back and forth, with a small smile still playing across his mouth. Obviously, he was in a much better mood, so she didn't want to say anything to make him mad again, but she had no idea what he wanted. The playfulness was a change and something she didn't want to mess up, so what to do? What had made his mood change? When she told him she would tell him everything? Maybe. He had been furious that she was keeping her feelings from him. If that was it, should she just tell him it was up to him, and she would respect his decision like she said she would? Or should she tell him what she wanted? This was more difficult than she thought it would be. She started to feel like she wanted to go back to bed and let his plans be damned.

By the time she decided to say something one way or the other, she turned to find he was leaning against the back of one of the chairs, watching her pace with a small smile. He reached up and put both of his hands on her shoulders in a reassuring gesture. "Have you been deliberating whether to tell me what to do with you or to tell me to just get it over with?"

Once again, she turned red, but this time, she didn't look away, because she was indeed going to tell him one of those two things, if not in quite the same words. Though his next sentence made her smile.

"Or were you going to tell me to go take a leap and take my demands with me?" He said the last with a horrid attempt to hide the laughter that came out with it.

She couldn't stay upset or tense. His poor effort at humor in and of itself was humorous enough to settle her nerves. "Why Your Highness, your attempts at drollery are truly epic, and I am sure I would not know what I should do if you were to do away with yourself." She smirked in satisfaction as he choked on his laughter, and then she couldn't help but laugh too.

After they both settled down, he grabbed her hand to lead her back to the chairs, which instantly had her heart racing. She tried to ignore that side of what she felt whenever he was around her. She was coming to terms with the fact that she did feel something, but she didn't know what, and she didn't want to know. That path was a dangerous one, and not worth exploring.

As soon as she was seated, and he released her hand, she worked to get her traitorous heart under control. By the time he was comfortably facing her with an easy smile on his face, she had erased all signs of her inner conflict.

"Okay, so no leaping. Well then, how would you like to spend the day with me next weekend at Araleen Royal Park?"

He was actually asking; she could turn him down if she wanted to. She could see the choice in his eyes. The alternative, however, was another weekend stuck inside her padded prison. It was no choice at all, and she wasn't all that upset about it. In fact, she had to school herself just to formulate a coherent response.

"Araleen? The large natural preserve some ways to the north of here, in the Berges Mountains?"

"Yes, they call it a park, but it is a preserve, and normally it is off-limits. That is, without the express permission of the royal family . . ." He raised an eyebrow at her and grinned. The sight of it made her roll her eyes. There was no need to point out the obvious.

She somehow managed to keep the laughter from her voice as she responded, "I have never been that far north before, but I have heard it gets cold sooner. I would love to see it." A brightness started in her eyes and crept into her cheeks as she thought about it.

Avila became lost in thoughts of all she had heard of the preserve—the wildlife, the landscape, and the weather this time of year—and was only interrupted from her reverie by Galdren standing up. He no longer wore the half-smile, but he was not in the foul mood he had been in either. "Avila, please don't let this distract you this week. However, if you can promise me you will do your best in your studies, I will bring you all the information I can on the preserve for you to go over before the weekend."

"Of course, you don't even need to ask that; I would love any information you could get me. Thank you." Her smile was radiant, and they both realized at about the same time that it was the first genuine and unchecked smile she had ever given him. She blushed a little but only lowered the smile a notch or so. She was grateful for the chance to see a beautiful piece of their world, one she had already dreamed of seeing.

"I need to go now, but I will see you again tomorrow." His sudden change of mood and brief dismissal were abrupt, but Avila was still in a good enough mood that it didn't bother her. She took him at his word, both that he would be back the following day, and when he came back, it would be with the information he promised.

"Thank you, Galdren, for everything. Good night." Before he had time to take a step and before she had time to think about what she was doing, Avila went with her gut for once and closed the gap between them to fling her arms around his middle. It was only a moment later that she realized what she had done and where she was. Her face started blazing before she could even think to untangle her arms, but the second before she began to step away, she felt his arms encircle her as well.

"You're welcome." The combination of his embrace and his words right next to her ear was almost more than she could handle. The situation was quickly becoming more than what she had expected, and she needed to leave before she did something even more ridiculous than hugging him in the first place.

She told her knees to stop wobbling, even if she could not stop her face from betraying her, and released him. At first, she could still feel the warmth of his breath next to her ear, and his arms didn't move. It took all her remaining resolve to take a step back and break the contact. It would have been too easy to reach out to touch him. Whether he allowed her to or not, both paths would lead to treacherous territory.

She looked at his face for a moment, totally unguarded and almost gentle, but also confused. She could tell he didn't know what to think of her; he probably did not understand why she'd hugged him in the first place or why she pulled away from him, but she could not let him get any further under her skin. He had too much control of her as it was.

She turned and almost ran to the attached bedroom. At the door, she stopped to look at him. From that somewhat objective distance, she said again, "Good night, Galdren." She was still flushed, and she could not look away from him as he stood there, saying nothing at all and clearly trying to figure out what had just happened. His silence only deepened her embarrassment, and she bowed to him for the first time in weeks before retreating to her bedroom with him still staring at her door.

6. DEADLY DREAMS

Her head hurt horribly, and she was having a tough time concentrating on her surroundings; she could hear voices somewhere but, for some reason, could not muster enough strength to sit up and find out where they were, or who they were. Nothing was making any sense. After several tries, she managed to get up on her elbows without the dizziness knocking her flat again. Once she was there, it only took a few more minutes of slow movement to sit up and get her legs over the side of the cot. It looked like she was inside a small tent. The voices were coming from outside, and there were several people. There was also a small fire flickering through a gap in the door flaps. She could see a couple of shadows between the tent and the fire, but knew she had heard voices coming from the other sides of the tent as well.

After a few minutes of sitting and trying to clear her head of the last of the fuzziness, she thought she might attempt to stand up. She was alone in the tent, and there was little in it besides the cot and a small trunk. No one had poked a head in since she had started moving, so she decided she needed to go outside and see if she could find out anything for herself.

She knew it was a mistake the moment her feet touched the ground and she started to stand. Her knees had no strength, and there was no way she could catch herself. All she could do was try to brace herself as she watched the ground approach. She tried not to cry out, but when she hit, an involuntary grunt came out anyway. Between that and the soft thud of her body hitting the ground, there were, within seconds, no less than three heads poking through the front of the tent. One of them belonged to a woman she was sure she had seen somewhere before, but she could not place the face and couldn't even begin to try to think of a name. The woman stepped into the tent when she saw the girl moving and told the others to go back out.

"Your Highness, are you all right? How are you feeling?" As she asked those questions, she helped the girl back up onto the cot, but she did not make her lay back down. Instead, she sat down beside her and took her hand as if she were trying to comfort her.

"My head, it is excruciating, and I feel dizzy and, well, weak, obviously. Much weaker than I thought I was if I can't even stand up . . . but who are you? And why are we here? What is going on?" The girl could tell her questions disturbed the woman even more than she had been when she found her lying on the floor, but the woman didn't let it show in her voice.

"Princess, you were injured while trying to escape the planet, you have a nasty head wound, and you have been traveling from one checkpoint to the next with groups of us. We are all loyal to you and—and your family. We are here to keep you safe. Do you remember any of this?" As the woman spoke, the flashes of bloody scenes that had been haunting the edges of the girl's thoughts and dreams came to the front of her mind, but were gone again before she could focus on them.

"I . . . I thought those were nightmares, but I can only remember flashes. Is that why you look familiar? I feel like I know you, but I don't know why or how." The girl had to look away from the flash of pain she saw in the woman's eyes, as there was nothing she could do to prevent it.

The woman tucked a strand of hair behind the girl's ear, on the side that wasn't injured, and tilted her head to look her straight in the eye. "Avila, I was there when you were born, and they needed a nursemaid. I have been there for you through countless scraped knees and trees climbed, even when you knew you weren't supposed to. Now, with you on the cusp of adulthood, I will be here for you as you learn to be the queen to lead us all. You may not be blood of my blood, but I raised you, and no one will touch you as long as I am here to protect you."

"You—thank you. I know it isn't enough, and I don't know everything, but I know I can trust you. My heart tells me what my memories do not." The girl was now holding the woman's hand, and they sat that way for a few minutes.

"You need to rest, Princess. I won't give you the medicines that will make you sleep until after you have eaten so you can try to rebuild your strength. You have had a fever on top of your injury, and have been out for several days now. We have been able to give you the barest of sustenance, but if you can handle it, some food should make you feel much better." Without another word, the woman walked out, but was back within moments with a bowl of stew that was mostly broth. It smelled delicious.

"I guess I am still to take it easy?" The girl said this with a little bit of a laugh as she sipped at the hot broth and only occasionally caught a vegetable.

"Tell you what, if you can handle all of that, I might be able to see if we have something a little more solid after. Only if that stays down, and you don't start getting too sleepy or start hurting too much." The byplay between them seemed natural and comfortable. The girl could feel herself relaxing, and she hadn't even realized she had been so apprehensive before.

She finished all the stew and handed off the bowl. However, before it could be taken away, there was a commotion outside, and a dirty man almost fell into the tiny tent. "They have found out we have the princess here. I don't know how, but they are on the way. Now." His announcement was made with no preamble at all, but he stopped and stood up straighter and then dipped into a low bow when he saw that the princess was awake and sitting up next to the woman.

"Your Highness, it is good you are awake. Anything we can do to make it easier and faster to get you out of here will make your chances of survival that much higher." At his words, the girl's tension came back with a vengeance.

"My survival? What exactly is going on?" With a surprisingly steady voice that didn't show any sign of the fear she was feeling, she focused on the given answers.

"My lady, we need to move you quickly, before the Trogand forces reach this camp. We managed to reach the planet and set up at least two dozen camps before they found out you survived. We were hoping to move you before they found out which camp you were in. However, your injury was worse than we expected, and they have found us. I was able to leave the city before their troops, but they will be here within the hour. Everyone in this camp has been identified and compromised. I am sorry, I know you are probably not ready to move, but we must leave immediately. No one else from the camp may come. They can all be identified and would give us away. I can hope to hide you, maybe, but not if anyone else is spotted as well." The man was not looking at the girl as he said most of this; even though he was addressing her, he was staring at the woman beside her. The woman's features had turned resolute.

She turned to the girl and once more picked up her hand. Her grip was almost painful. The girl didn't object. Something told her it didn't matter. "Avila, my princess, you will need to leave now, and you will need to be strong. I will not be able to go with you and protect you like I said I would, but I will always watch over you, no matter where we both are, from in here." She gently touched the girl's chest. "You will go now with Mikael, and he will take care of you. You can trust him like you trust me. We all need you to survive. One day, you will be the hope of an entire people. You may not remember right now, but you were born for that, and raised to carry that torch. You will be more than capable of it; I have faith in you, but you must survive. Go! Now!" She helped the girl stand with those last words, which was much easier since she had eaten something. She then turned her over to Mikael.

She turned one last time to look at the woman. Larissa—that was her name. It came floating back to her from somewhere more pleasant than her most recent flashes. "Goodbye, Larissa, and I promise I will do everything in my power to fulfill all of my duties. That includes surviving. Please do the same; I would like to see you again when I can remember more than just your name. Something tells me I want to."

Her words and her remembrance of Larissa's name brought a smile to the woman's lips where there had been only foreboding before. Now, there was a spark of hope. No more words were needed, and the two slipped out of the camp with no fanfare and no one watching which direction they went. If no one knew where they were, then no one could accidentally give that information away.

The girl had to occasionally lean on the man for support, but he reassured her it was not far to where he had a secure transport. They could use it to get them both to a city where they could get lost for a few days, and then get off the planet. They were only about thirty minutes out of the camp when they started hearing explosions behind them. From where they were located on a slight rise, they had the cover of trees but still had a partial view of the camp behind them, and the girl turned to see significant portions of it completely obliterated. Mikael tried to turn her to rush her on, but she stood rooted to the spot.

"Mikael, do you have a spyglass?" Her words were clipped and authoritative, a change from the uncertainty that had been in her voice when she was relying on others for answers.

"Princess, we must keep moving. We are almost to the transport, and if they are already at the camp, they will eventually pick up our trail, even if no one knows where we went. I am sure they will have trackers."

"Those people down there—every single one of them—are down there because of me, are they not?" She looked at him at last, and he stepped back upon seeing the fire that burned in her young eyes. "I may only have vague memories, but I know this is not the first sacrifice on my behalf. I can't even begin to guess how many lives have been lost, and I will not let their sacrifices come to naught, but I *will* honor them. Now, do you have a spyglass or not?"

Mikael stared at her, almost as if realizing for the first time whom he had been protecting. Not just a figurehead, but an actual royal; young she may be. She had been raised to take command, and was clearly ready to do so when the time came. Hope gleamed in his eyes as he gave a curt nod and said, "Yes, Princess, I have a spyglass, but you must hurry."

He handed her the narrow tube, and she quickly used it to search through the remains of the camp for any signs of life. She was hoping that most of the people had left soon after they had. Unfortunately, they had all stayed. They had set up an ambush for the incoming troops, and there was heavy fighting in the camp. The princess swallowed the bile that threatened to come up. She owed it to these men and women to remember them and their sacrifices for her; she would not look away.

She had only planned to look through the camp to see what had happened before they moved on. However, before she got all the way through the battlefield below, the glass landed on the spot near where her tent used to stand. All that was there now was a small pit, and standing several feet away was a group of men holding Larissa up by her arms. She was bleeding from several cuts on her face and arms and smiling widely at the man facing her. He was bald, but that was all Avila could tell since his back was to her.

He gestured wildly, and she watched as Larissa laughed before the man walked away. Then another man with a gun walked up, and while Larissa grinned at him, he shot her in the head.

Avila woke up screaming for the first time in over a month and choking on the sobs she couldn't hold back. She was still overwhelmed by the disjointed images of the dream, and the loss and burning hatred boiling inside her were so intense she couldn't stop the wracking cries that just kept coming.

Suddenly, there was a warm pair of arms around her and a voice in her ear telling her it was just a dream, that it was going to be all right. A gentle hand was on her hair, soothing the cries into submission. She leaned into the muscular chest and let her breathing return to normal.

As she calmed, so did her thinking, and she became aware of her surroundings. It wasn't light yet, so it must have been early morning. Yet here she was in her bed, crying, with Galdren of all people comforting her. She also realized she must have woken him, since he had no shirt on.

"Are you all right now?" He leaned back so he could look at her face, but he didn't release her. She made no effort to get away.

"I am—I am better now." She wanted to talk about the dream, but she was still unsettled by the whole thing. She knew she should probably move, but she couldn't bring herself to leave the comfort of his arms. Instead, she laid her head back on his chest and tried to stem the tears that were still flowing.

He continued to hold her while she calmed down. "Galdren . . . thank you." Her voice was muffled since she hadn't moved. He lifted one hand and gently pushed her hair off her face, then tucked it behind her ear so she could speak more clearly.

"I wasn't sure of what I heard at first; I was still half asleep, but you sounded so scared. I had to come see what was wrong. You didn't even see me; you had no idea I was here." He touched her face briefly to wipe away a stray tear. "It was a little frightening. I knew you had nightmares, but I haven't seen you like that before."

"I am sorry. Sorry for frightening you, sorry for waking you up, and sorry for acting like a child last night. I am sorry for burdening you with my problems when I know you have your own to deal with." She apologized for her actions the night before without even thinking, but as soon as she said it, she knew it was the right thing to do. She had run away from her confused feelings about Galdren instead of facing them. Still, for worse or better, they would have to be dealt with.

"It's all right, Avila. I am not worried about it, and you shouldn't be either. Tell me, if you want to, what happened?" His question erased all thoughts of uncertainties from her mind and brought back the memories of the dream. A fresh stream of tears started that she couldn't seem to stop. She felt foolish, but her emotions were just too raw.

"It was another bloody nightmare, another dream where I was being chased, but . . . I—I have the impression that I knew some of the people, and—and I watched—I watched them being murdered." She had to stop because her voice had started cracking. She needed a moment to get herself under control before she could continue. He gave her the time she needed without pressure. "The people that were chasing me, chasing us, murdered them because I got away. It was my fault all those people died. Why? Why am I haunted by such nightmares?"

She didn't really expect any answers. She was certain it had something to do with the past that was locked away in her mind, and she wasn't so sure anymore it was a good idea to unlock it. Unless . . . there was a chance it was all true? But she didn't want to mention that; it was a crazy thought, and wasn't as though they did her much good when she could only remember bits and pieces. Still, if it were true, by the goddess herself, not a person responsible would be left standing; they would all pay. The image of the bald man's head flared in her mind's eye.

The righteous fire that suddenly blazed inside her finally worked to dry up her tears as she thought about the fact that she did not have to be helpless. She looked up at Galdren, ready to thank him again and move away, but the words died on her lips.

Her resolve must have come across in her body language, and now the flames that had leapt up into her eyes were reflected in his, smoldering and breathtaking. She became acutely aware of every inch of their bodies that was touching. The hand he had used earlier to brush back her hair he now brought up to trace her cheekbone with the back of his knuckles, then her jawline. She couldn't move a muscle and didn't want to. She was so entranced by his eyes that she almost forgot to breathe.

His hand moved to the side of her neck as he slowly lowered his face to hers without their gaze ever breaking. His lips softly brushed hers with almost no pressure at all, but she melted into him. Her eyes closed, and one hand went around his neck while the other splayed across the sleek muscles of his chest as she leaned into him. As he pulled her tighter to him, she couldn't help the small sound that came from somewhere deep in her throat. Desire pooled somewhere in her middle, low down, and it felt as if all the nerves in her body were extra alert to every sensation she was feeling.

His hand had moved a little to tangle in the hair at the nape of her neck, so she couldn't have moved if she wanted to. However, as his mouth moved over hers, she lost all thoughts of pushing away from him. Her right hand had slipped down to rest on his stomach and the left was winding into the fine hairs at the nape of his neck. She was becoming lost in the wonders of this man who was miraculously here in her arms.

In the next moment, however, he pulled away from her. The absence of his arms left coldness in their wake. Then he was holding her by the shoulders and looking at her intently. It took a moment for her desire-drugged mind to realize all was not well.

"Avila, I am so sorry. There is no excuse for me to ever take advantage of you like this." His words were like a splash of frigid water on her fiery skin, instantly cooling any desire she still felt.

"You did not take advantage of me. You kissed me. That is all." She flushed slightly as she said those words. She couldn't believe any of the last few minutes had happened.

His eyes hardened at her words, and he stood to further distance himself from her. "You are vulnerable, in more ways than one, and I—" He turned away from her and walked toward the door. He paused to glance back over his shoulder before he walked out and said, "Do not worry, it will never happen again." Then, just like that, he was gone.

The reality of the situation came crashing down around her ears. It brought home pointedly every reason she had ever told herself to not even allow a fragment of a fantasy about him to flourish. She may belong to him, but his plans for her, if he did have any, obviously did not involve her in that way.

Perhaps it had been a momentary lapse in judgment on his part. Brought on by what, though? That was the question. A lack of sleep and the proximity of a warm body? The goddess herself only knew how many other offers he had, more tempting to be sure and far more experienced. She didn't need to be told. She already knew he was surrounded by people all the time. It was only a wonder that she had never thought that some, if not most, of them were women wanting a part of him. She had no right to be jealous—no reason, or at least no claim to his affection. He may have said "vulnerable," but his actions told her enough. Her inexperience must be no comparison to the other women available to him.

The spectrum of emotions she had run through over the last half hour left her near shattered. There was no way she was going back to sleep. She wasn't even sure she could face looking at the bed anymore, so she got up to prepare for the day. The dawn was still some ways away, but she was better able to face it in her window seat facing the park. As painful as that was now since she was unsure about any part of her future, it was still easier than facing her bedroom for the remainder of the night.

When the professor arrived, he found her still sitting there staring out at the morning. Her eyes were dull when she turned to face him and ringed by dark circles. However, when he thought of asking if something was troubling her, the questions died unasked when their eyes briefly connected. He saw for a moment the pain there before she could mask it. He knew she was a private person and not prone to share. If she wanted to, she would come to him in time, when she was ready, but not before.

7. TRIP CONFIRMED

A vila threw herself into her studies with what seemed like a renewed vigor. For anyone watching her that didn't know her, it would have looked as if she had found a singular focus and drive. For Professor Gilbert, however, it only worried him. Not that he worried about her work ethic or her ability to get her work done, but this single-minded focus was unlike her in so many ways. Avila had a passion for perfection, but she always followed the paths of her ideas, which sometimes led to entirely new ways of thinking. She was an innovator, and this one-tracked absorption was out of character.

It continued through the day, making conversation outside of the school material nonexistent. Avila showed no signs of wanting to talk about what was bothering her, so the professor never pushed, but he was on alert for any signs of what the issue might be.

Toward the end of the day, she became almost distracted. Every time it seemed as though her mind started to wander, Professor Gilbert could see her face harden. It was as if she were chastising herself for something, and then her single-minded resolve would be back in place.

When it was time for him to leave, he realized that he had been so preoccupied with his worry that he hadn't even noticed Galdren's absence. However, based on the deadened expression that still flitted across Avila's face from time to time, it did not seem like a good idea to bring up any small talk with her. A hunch also told him the prince might be an incredibly sore subject.

It pained him beyond words to see her in such a state, especially if it had anything to do with Galdren. He had known them both for a long time and knew neither would intentionally cause this much pain to the other. However, this was a unique situation, and one he could not do much about.

As he gathered up his things to leave, he put his hand on her shoulder; a simple gesture to let her know he would be there for her if needed. She gave him a small smile, and for the first time that day, a little color came to her cheeks. He left with the hope that the woman he was leaving would be as strong as he knew she could be.

After the professor left, the small smile fled. It had clung to Avila's lips in a desperate bid for a little bit of normal but could not be maintained. She appreciated his patience with her and his understanding that she did not want to speak. Without words, he'd let her know he would be there. The fact that he did that meant a lot to Avila, especially now.

She turned away from the door and, for the first time, prayed that Galdren's not showing up yet meant he was not coming that day. She wasn't sure she could handle facing him. She went again to the window seat and found that for once, the weather matched her mood perfectly. It was already so dark outside she couldn't see across to the park, and the rain was coming down in sheets. She leaned her face against the glass and let the cold seep through into her cheek, chilling the tears that had fallen and making watery streaks on the glass. As she sat there unable to stop crying, she vaguely thought Olva might get upset about the marks and resolved to try to clean those up.

The next thing Avila realized, Olva was standing over her with a pillow and a blanket. "I'm sorry for the streaks; I will clean them up, I promise." The words were a little slurred.

Olva just gave her a strange look. It took a moment to register that Olva was bringing the pillow and blanket for her. She must have fallen asleep against the window, and since Olva couldn't move her, she was trying to make her more comfortable. She usually came to the rooms in the evenings to see if anything needed to be done.

"My apologies Olva, I didn't mean to fall asleep here. I didn't sleep well last night, and it must have caught up to me. Thank you for the thought of the pillow and blanket. I will just go to bed now, I think. Oh, and, um . . . the window . . ." Olva glanced over at the window as she mentioned it, understanding lighting her eyes.

"Mistress Durant, please go to bed. You obviously need the rest, and I can take care of this in no time." Avila fought a small blush. She felt guilty for even thinking about letting someone else clean up a mess she'd made and was perfectly capable of cleaning up on her own. However, she also felt more than a little embarrassed because Olva understood perfectly well what had made those streaks in the first place and was trying to be tactful. Avila had always admired the steady housekeeper, even if she did get frustrated by her occasionally. She gave Olva a small smile and thanked her again before slipping into the next room and closing the door behind her.

Faced with her bed, however, she was not quite sure she would be able to sleep at all. She knew she could not go back out into the other room, and she also knew she couldn't keep running from her own bed. There was nowhere else to run, so she decided she might as well face it. She took her time getting ready, and by the time she was cleaned and brushed and dressed again, she felt tired enough. If only that would do the trick.

She climbed into the made bed and realized it wouldn't be quite as bad as she had anticipated. There was absolutely nothing there to indicate that the events of the morning had ever happened. It didn't seem like it could have only been that morning; it felt like a lifetime ago. Yet, the fact that there was no physical reminder only served to make the memories that much starker. She had no idea how long she lay there trying to focus on the sound of the renewed rain, but eventually exhaustion won out, and she finally fell asleep.

The next morning was still slate grey, and the rain had only slowed to a fine mist. It made it impossible for Avila to know what time it was until she checked the timeglass. Also, she thought she could hear voices in the other room. Something in her gut told her if she didn't hurry and rush her usual morning preparations, she would have someone checking on her soon.

It didn't take long for her to get ready, and surprisingly enough, the need to rush had distracted her sufficiently so that her mood wasn't quite as grey as the weather anymore. That lasted only as long as it took her to walk into her common room, where she found Professor Gilbert in a conversation with Galdren. They were both standing next to the outer door, and Galdren had his hand on the knob.

When Avila walked out, the conversation stopped. For a moment, her eyes met with Galdren's, and it seemed as if he were debating whether to go ahead and walk out the door or to stay. The moment passed, and he dropped his hand. He walked back into the middle of the room, and the professor followed.

"We were discussing whether to go get Olva to check on you. Are you feeling well? You never oversleep." Galdren's words were concerned, but she wanted to scream at him. He didn't look any worse for wear from the last day and a half; he was still his stunning self. Luckily, the dripping of the rain in the background gave her the inspiration she needed for her answer.

"I am fine, Galdren, and my apologies to you too, Professor. The storm kept me up most of the night. By the time I finally fell asleep, it must have been early morning, and I slept right through until now." It was definitely not one of her stellar days, but there was no need for him to know she had been up because of him.

She had tried to keep the venom out of her voice, but he obviously heard it anyway. He looked almost as if he had been struck, and his face paled visibly. However, from his expression, it looked as if he could not understand why she might be upset. Although, for the life of her, she couldn't figure out why he wouldn't expect some sort of negativity. It wasn't as if she was the one who walked out.

The satisfaction she got from his expression was short-lived. Even if he did make her crazy, she couldn't bring herself to cause him discomfort on purpose. After a few moments of stretched silence, she finally shrugged with a self-deprecating smile and walked past Galdren to where she usually had everything set up for studying.

Galdren took it as a cue to follow and continue with why he was there in the first place. "Avila, I want to apologize for not bringing this by yesterday. My father had me occupied." He placed an infochip on the table next to her and walked to the door again without catching her eye. "I also must apologize for running out so quickly. That infochip has everything on it I could find for Araleen Park, so you should be more than ready for this weekend. I am sure the rain will let up before then. However, I will unfortunately not be able to come by this week until maybe Friday to go over any of it. If you have any questions, perhaps Professor Gilbert can help you, or you can save them, and I will be happy to talk to you about it then."

She couldn't shake the feeling he was trying to avoid her, even though he probably had valid reasons and was busy. Yet, his other obligations had never stopped him before. Once again, the need to scream was almost overwhelming, but somehow, she held it in. Instead, she gave him one of her biggest smiles; she only hoped it fooled him better than she was fooling herself. "Thank you very much! I am quite sure it will be all right that you will be busy. If there is half as much as I think there is on this infochip, I will be busy myself. I appreciate you bringing it by, and if I have any questions, I will make sure to let the professor know. Maybe I can even convince him to do a section about it."

Her enthusiasm was a little over the top, but it served to brighten her mood. She really was looking forward to getting out, especially now that he'd confirmed it was still happening. Her cheerfulness seemed to get the point across to Galdren that just because he was avoiding her didn't mean she was going to break. He stood there silently for a moment with his hand on the door, staring at the back of her head since she had turned around to face Professor Gilbert.

Before Galdren slipped out, Avila turned and said, "I hope you have a good week, since I won't be seeing you. And thank you again." With that, she turned back around and continued setting up. She didn't want him to think she was ungrateful. Even if she was mad at him, there was no point in being rude—mostly.

Galdren shook his head. "Until Friday, then." With a final nod to the professor, he slipped out the door and was gone. Avila kept her head down and pretended she was engrossed in her schoolwork.

Professor Gilbert only grew more concerned. It was obvious both of the younger people had an issue, and neither of them wanted to confront it. The enormity of the situation between them had to be weighing heavily on them both. He knew the strain of the responsibility was even harder on the prince these days, since word had finally gotten out about his guest. Even if most of the details had been kept secret, what had leaked was enough to cause everyone headaches. Even he had to watch what he said outside of the castle.

Thankfully, Avila remained blissfully unaware. She was having a hard enough time adjusting as it was. She had an independent spirit, and he knew the whole thing had to be chafing for her. She was taking it in stride, and for the most part was gracious. It was a sign of her remarkable nature that she always did her best to make those around her comfortable even when she needed comfort. He truly did admire her.

After Galdren left, Avila did her best to focus solely on her work and, for the most part, did reasonably well—until her gaze strayed to the infochip on the table beside her. It was a mixed reaction every time she saw it. On the one hand, she really did want to get out, and she had a spike of excitement thinking about it. And not just out, but to a place she had never had the pleasure of going before, to an almost untouched area of nature. The prospect was enough to make it hard for her to sit still at times.

On the other hand, it had Galdren written all over it. From the fact that he had given her the infochip in the first place and set the whole thing up, to the reality that he would have to go as well. Something told her she wouldn't be allowed to go without him.

She wasn't sure how she would handle the weekend. How was she supposed to forget they had kissed? That was what she would have to do to face him with any sense of normalcy, but she had no idea how to pretend it never happened. It must be so much easier for him, but she guessed if it wasn't a big deal in the first place, then remembering it would be more of a chore than forgetting.

Thinking in those circles was getting her nowhere, and her work was still waiting for her, but she did decide on one thing. She really would try to see if Professor Gilbert would do a section on the park. Surely there could be something gained from it—geography, maybe history if you stretched it, or even topography or biology. The possibilities were endless if she applied a little imagination. They might even be able to spend an entire day on it.

Around lunchtime, she decided to ask him. "Professor Gilbert, I know we have a lot to cover, and you are helping me play catch-up, but we both know I am not going to graduate with everyone else. Since my situation is unique—" Bringing it up made her need to swallow several times before she could continue. Still, the point had to be made, or she was not going to get anywhere. "That is, it is—I mean—look, can we please take a day and go over the information Galdren left? I am sure we can find ways to integrate it into my classes if you need to. That way, since I have never been, if I have questions, you can help me answer them. I don't want to seem like a total idiot this weekend. Especially since ecology is my focus and reserve management is something I would like to possibly go into."

Professor Gilbert looked at her curiously, but that quickly gave way to a smile. "Avila, I would be happy to see what I can find out. Why don't you keep that infochip for study just like one of your books, and I will see what I can put together as a lesson plan for later this week? By then, I should be able to come up with a full day's worth of classes and not sacrifice anything you will need for your credits."

She couldn't help but get excited. The part of her that was looking forward to the trip was winning out. If she stayed focused on the thought of the forest out there—virtually pristine, just waiting for her to explore it—she could keep other thoughts at bay, mostly.

She realized that plan was the only way she would be able to get through any of this—not just through the trip, but from here on out. She was going to have to find something to throw her attention into. It had to be unhealthy for her to focus on one person anyway. She would find something to keep her occupied, starting with this trip, and then other things moving forward so that she would not always feel like she was ready to burst with thinking about him.

"Thank you, Professor. I will make sure I go over everything on this chip before Thursday." By that point, a good portion of the morning was gone, and Avila realized she needed to concentrate on the rest of the week ahead of her instead of the weekend after, or nothing was going to get done. She spent the rest of the morning trying to make up for the hour she missed, and the afternoon wasn't much better. The one plus was she didn't have time to consider anything other than what she was working on.

8. HISTORY

When it came time for the professor to leave, Avila had the chip in her hand. For the first time in a couple of days, the night didn't seem as daunting. After he was gone, she sat back down in front of the monitor that had been installed in her outer rooms for her use.

She didn't need the monitor often for her schoolwork since the professor brought most of his own study materials. The only time she ever used it was for contacting her family and the few friends she had. Which, by now, had dwindled down to only Lissa, who she spoke to at least once a week. When she tried to explain that she couldn't come back because of an unplanned extended trip, no one even tried to hide the fact that they didn't believe her. She wasn't close enough to any of them but Lissa to tell them the truth.

It was the worst when she tried to explain it to people. That was when she felt the most like a slave, no matter how well treated she was. The thought of telling anyone other than those she knew loved her, "Oh hey, yeah I just happen to belong to this man now and he can do whatever with me on a whim, but it isn't how it might sound because he totally doesn't want me like that," not only made her cringe inside at the thought of belonging to anyone, but the idea of admitting to anyone that she knew for a fact he had no interest in her made her want to curl up in a fetal ball. There was no way she was going to discuss where she was with acquaintances. That's all there was to it. The fewer people who knew her predicament, the better she felt. At least that was one little piece of something she had not lost complete control over—yet.

She pulled herself out of her reverie and looked again at the infochip that was the source of both her excitement and her pain. She knew Lissa would be hurt if she didn't mention anything before she left, but there would be so many questions Avila didn't want to answer. There was no way she could bring herself to talk about the rejection and shame she was feeling, not even with her best friend. It still hurt too much, even if she was trying to bury it in excitement about the trip. She could put off contacting her until Friday; then she could cut the conversation short, using the excuse that she needed to get ready for the trip. She knew it was terrible that she was already thinking of an excuse, but she knew her friend, and Lissa would be excited. She also knew that excitement might be the undoing of any kind of fragile calm she might have gained by then.

Slowly, she picked up the infochip and inserted it into the monitor. She had to admit, as the initial images loaded onto the screen, there was more excitement starting to bubble up than trepidation. No matter what else was going on, it was the opportunity of a lifetime. She had to admit with a wry smirk to herself that she never would have had this opportunity if she had not been in the circumstances she was in. At least not for an extremely long time. Researchers were sometimes granted limited access to the area, but only after a long and distinguished career. Her seeing the place on her own would have been after decades of research, and then only if she were outstanding and lucky.

It didn't take long for her to become engrossed in the information. It seemed there was an excellent reason the area was limited access only: some of the planet's rarest and most dangerous animals were in that part of the world. She could tell as she browsed through the section on fauna that it was likely a poacher's paradise. The thought brought up a wave of old anger.

She had initially decided to go into ecology partially because of the way she felt so much calmer in the middle of forested areas. The other significant reason was that there were many ways the children she went to school with had tormented her in her first year on Aril. Yet, no torment was worse than when they found out what she did when she went out on her own. When they discovered she liked being in the woods and wasn't afraid of the animals, it was just one more piece of fuel to add to their fire. None of the other people at her school acted that way.

It wasn't long at all until things started happening, small at first. She would find pictures of fur coats and such in her personal spaces. That didn't bother her much, since she knew they were only doing it to get on her nerves, and she wasn't interested in playing their games. However, the morning a small group of boys was huddled near her locker, things changed.

When she first saw them, she was more irritated than scared or angry. However, as she approached and they noticed her, two of them grabbed her and forced her to the center of the small circle up against the bank of lockers. Everyone had already vanished, and moments later, classes started. They were alone in the halls of the school.

She had started to yell at them to leave her alone, but before she could even get the words out, one of them covered her mouth with something that kept her from making any sound, almost covering her nose as well. She began to panic. As she was focused on fighting to get away from the two that held her, another stepped in front of her. Something about his eyes and how he held his hands out in front of himself forced her to focus instead on what he was holding, and finally, on the words he was saying.

"—killed it for a coat I was thinking of making, but my mother says the fur isn't even good enough for that. I say it would look just fine on a reject like you. What do you say, boys?" She had been looking at the tiny rabbit he held in his hands the whole time he spoke. Its poor head had been twisted almost all the way around, and she could tell there was no more life in its limp little body.

That was going too far. She wanted to vomit and almost did, but when he started to reach toward her with the lifeless body like he was going to drape it around her neck, something snapped. She couldn't free her arms to stop him, but her legs were free. She kicked out as hard as she could. She wasn't aiming for anything, but she was more than satisfied when her shin connected solidly with the offending boy's groin.

He dropped like a stone, and the surprise of the boys around her allowed her just enough leeway to free herself from their grasp. She started running and spit out the rag they had jammed in her face, but her freedom didn't last long. A couple of them grabbed her before she had managed more than a few steps, and none were happy. Luckily for her, she had lost the gag and could scream before they started showing her just how unhappy they were.

It didn't take long for an adult to show up after she had screamed to break things up. She had only endured a few slaps and a single punch to the stomach. However, emotionally, she was shaken. She was scared, yes, but she was also livid. There was absolutely no reason for what they had done—not to her, but to the rabbit. She at least could try to defend herself.

The school's administration officials decided that the level of cruelty and spite in the boys' actions was so extreme that they were all suspended for the rest of the school year. For Avila, it wasn't enough. Not that she wanted them to be punished more, but she knew their actions, in part at least, were only a portion of a bigger problem that she felt needed to be addressed.

No one at school bothered her after that. They had all heard what happened. It wasn't like she was made out to be the hero, but she had stood up to them. She had fought back. Not to mention that if anyone did happen to catch her gaze during those days, they saw a fire burning in them that was disturbing even for some adults.

She started crusading, for lack of a better word. She would write letter after letter or start petitions for more humane treatment of animals in captivity across all businesses. Even if few people signed them, she hoped she was starting to raise awareness. At least her actions had garnered enough attention that zoos across the planet were forced to take measures to publicly show their facilities did not harm the animals. Some even went so far as to expand their pens to better mimic natural habitats. It didn't get the animals released, but it was a start.

She knew people wouldn't stop wearing furs or eating meat, and she didn't expect them to. However, there had to be better ways to handle the animals while still alive and cleaner, less painful ways to kill them. There had to be a compromise somewhere.

In addition to petitions, she would organize rallies, both in school and out. She even managed to get a bill before the king asking that some urban areas be used as nature preserves. That last idea was one of her most successful. Even though few people thought about it, it was why there were so many parks in the center of most sizable cities across the globe that now boasted wildlife that could be seen regularly.

Thinking about the parks brought her back to the current moment. She'd always wanted to make a difference. To try and help those that didn't have a voice of their own and had no way of helping themselves. Still, even though she knew she would be the envy of every ecologist, zoologist, and biologist, she had absolutely no idea what to do with the experience, or where her life might go from there. What was the point of her finishing her degree? It wasn't like she had a choice in her career any longer.

The thought made a bitter feeling well up, but it also made her wonder—did Galdren think he needed an ecologist? It didn't seem likely, especially since he hadn't known she was the outdoors type. Then again, she guessed some were all labs and no fieldwork, so it might not be that far-fetched. If he thought she could give him advice on farming, then he would be sorely disappointed. While her studies did cover that, it was not her focus. She was studying to go into something that could help preserve endangered species. Preferably with one of the reserves, but there were several options.

Something told her that he'd meant it when he said that he didn't have some grand scheme for her, so she couldn't figure out why he was bothering with helping her finish her studies. Not that she was complaining, but it did make her wonder.

She realized she was getting tired, so she must have been sitting in front of the monitor for far longer than she thought. She got up to look out the window and noticed that her dinner tray was sitting on her small table, waiting for her. She had been so absorbed in what she was doing that she had not even heard Olva come in or leave.

She went to the tray and found that the food was cold. She ate a little anyway since she knew she needed to, even if she didn't have much of an appetite. The last thing she wanted was to have an upset housekeeper watching her eat every bite because she didn't think she was eating enough. Somehow, she could picture Olva doing just that.

She went to bed after that. She was apprehensive again since she had been having such trouble sleeping. However, she found she was so emotionally drained from the last several days that despite her fear of another sleepless night, it wasn't long until sleep claimed her.

Thursday morning Avila felt surprisingly refreshed and looking forward to the day ahead of her. Not that she didn't still feel the sadness that seemed to have made a home somewhere inside her, but the anticipation of what the day's lessons were going to cover was more than enough to keep her thoughts occupied and her mood somewhat lifted.

She was up and ready and waiting before the professor got there. She even had a smile for him when he came in.

His return smile looked relieved. "Good morning, Avila. I see you are ready to get started this morning."

"I have thoroughly gone through all the information on that infochip, and I'm looking forward to the lessons today." Professor Gilbert raised an eyebrow at her statement. Avila couldn't help but notice, and while she couldn't quite bring herself to laugh at him, she did smile before replying to his unspoken question. "Yes, I was up late each night; later than I expected to be, but it was well worth it. I found out a lot of fascinating things."

"Well then, let's get started. I have managed to put together a bit about the geography for that area and the climate and how the local flora and fauna have adapted to the more extreme changes, especially in the winter. Now I know your focus will be on the wildlife, so I have devoted the entire afternoon to studying several of the more researched species in the territory and briefly touching on a few of the others. How does that sound to you?" Avila had forgotten she could get so excited about anything. The thought of going over all of it with someone who would know not only what pertinent details to point out but how to answer her questions was a special treat for her. It was even better that it would be with someone who could honestly share in the beauty of it all.

She had found that Professor Gilbert was a kindred spirit in many ways. When she'd brought her passions with her from senior school to the university, he was always the first to encourage her never to lose faith and remind her she was doing wonderful things. "Professor, I am so glad I have you here to go over all this. I don't think it would be right any other way."

Her words were clearly unexpected, and the older man cleared his throat before responding, "Avila, it has always been an honor and privilege to teach you." He then looked away as he said, "Now, let's get this started."

The morning's lessons were as absorbing as Avila had thought they would be, and she had been right to think she would need to make sure she had the warmest clothes she could find before Saturday. The preserve was in a mountainous region of the world and, as such, was at a higher altitude than the capital where she had spent most of her life. Not to mention, it was also farther north. While autumn was just setting in nicely here and the winter that followed would be cold but not too biting, winter's beginnings might already be starting in that region. At the very least, fall would be over.

The afternoon's lessons brought her into more familiar territory. Some of the animals the professor talked about were on the endangered species list; some because of hunters of old, and now from the dangers of poachers.

She was already familiar with many of the animals and the threats to them from her work as an activist petitioning and organizing rallies. The people she'd met while working on the bill had taught her of the dangers that came with creating preserves—specifically about the people who don't care about what happens as long as they get what they want. She became familiar with the animals they hunted most and what their usual tricks were. She was never directly involved in any of the specifics with creating the preserves—they were assigned teams who would create and populate the preserves and, most importantly, protect them—but she made sure she always kept an eye on what was done. It was almost as though she were watching a child grow up.

When the lesson ended, although her mood was not wholly bleak, Avila was not looking forward to a night alone. Although, the prospect of looking through the information again was promising. It might at least keep her distracted.

9. RENEWED FRIENDSHIP

Before the professor left, he came and sat down next to Avila at the table. "You are an accomplished young woman, driven and capable of doing so much. Please do not let anything get in the way of that." He meant it as a way of reassuring her that she could still do whatever she wanted. However, the horrified look on her face made him realize she must have been thinking he meant she should leave if she wished, which was not at all the case. "Avila, I'm trying to say I know you will still have plenty of opportunities, and this coming weekend is just the first of many extraordinary opportunities that will be available to you."

Her face changed again when he said that, and he could see the spark in her eyes wink out like a cloud was passing over her face. "Professor, I have been thinking about the preserves in the city. I have not been able to see any reports on them since I came here. Unless you count the antics of the squirrels outside my window." She said the last with a passing attempt at a smile, but it didn't last long. "I am guessing things are still running as smoothly as ever?"

While her question was off topic, he let it slide. Especially since it reminded him of a memory that he thought would be good to share. "Yes, they are going as smooth as ever. You know, that was one of the best ideas anyone in this line of work has come up with. So many people enjoy them, myself included. I really have to thank you." At that, she blushed. He knew she never expected thanks from anyone for what she did; she often said she was just satisfied to know that people were happy and the animals were safe.

He knew his compliment would throw her. It was in her nature not to expect it, so before she could try to stammer out some sort of response, he continued, "I don't know if anyone ever told you or not, but the reason Araleen Royal Park and the few others like it are in existence today is that more than a hundred years ago, the royal family saw the same need. They set that aside for the same reasons and continue to maintain it. It isn't just private hunting grounds, as some believe. It is still exactly what it always has been. Now, that being said, when your proposition was placed in front of the whole royal family, they all fell in love with the idea. They couldn't set aside more land to keep away from people; there are just too many people. Still, they thought if they could give the populace small glimpses of why the large parks are necessary and give the animals safe havens, it would be a win-win."

Again, Avila only stared at him. He could tell she had not been expecting that either, but he wasn't finished. Despite her silence, he knew she was ready to hear the last part of what he had to say. "When they found out the bill was set forth by a girl still in senior school, it made no difference to the king's decision at all. However, I can tell you this: the prince was impressed. He could not believe that a girl even younger than him had the drive and intelligence to put together something like that, so he did a little research. When he found out about your activist history and all the changes your work prompted, he was even more amazed. He wanted to meet you then to find out what kind of person could do what you did and still be in school, but he had to leave soon after. I honestly don't think he has connected yet that you and she are the same person."

"You're right, Fredrick. I had not." That simple statement almost made both of them fall out of the chairs they had been sitting in. Since they had both been positioned with their backs to the door and quite engrossed in the conversation, neither had seen nor heard the prince walk in. Nor had they expected him to, since he had already said he would not be back until the following day.

They both stood, but as Avila took a few steps toward Galdren, she found that her mouth was dry and her heart was beating funnily. She didn't understand it, but it might have had something to do with the way he was staring at her like there was no one else in the room.

Neither Galdren nor Avila caught more than passing movement as the professor grabbed his things. When he had everything gathered up, he said his goodbyes, but they both barely heard him as he slipped out the door.

Several moments later, Galdren and Avila were still standing there, looking at each other. He kept staring as if he wasn't sure exactly who she was, and she had no idea what to say to him. Finally, she had to break the silence. "You said you wouldn't be back until tomorrow." It was the thing that kept popping into her head, so of course, it was the first thing that popped out of her mouth.

It worked to break the tension of his stare. He smiled at her and shook his head. "I had some time, so I thought I would stop by. Please sit down; I have a feeling we need to talk." He walked up to her and motioned to the chairs across the room with one hand. She could tell he was careful not to touch her, though.

She obliged him and walked across the room to sit. He sat across from her. The pattern of those motions was getting to be so familiar to her, but at times, times like these, it felt like there was a skip, and something was off. It was probably because she was anxious, of course. She knew he had to have overheard enough of the conversation to have realized what they were talking about, or else he would not have said what he did or been staring at her that way. Still, she wondered how much he had overheard.

Before she could get too worried about it, he started talking, and she soon had more than enough in the way of answers. "Avila, let me start off by saying Professor Gilbert was right about a lot of things, first being those preserves are one of the best gifts to the people we have been able to give, and I too am happy and thankful to have them." To hear the gratitude coming from Galdren was almost more than she could bear. Her entire face had to be glowing with the blush she felt; she had a hard enough time accepting praise when she heard it from the professor. That is when it struck her—if he'd heard that part of the conversation, then he heard all of it and had stood there and said nothing until the end.

Her flush faded almost as quickly as it had come up, and she narrowed her eyes at him. "Why didn't you say something to let us know you were here if you knew we didn't hear you?"

It was his turn to turn pink. It was so fascinating to see it happen that Avila almost lost her line of thought at the sight of it. "Well, honestly, when I came in, and you didn't hear me, I almost did say something. However, when I heard what he said to you, I was—well, I was at a loss. It was completely unexpected to find out you were the girl I had been looking for all those years ago, and so I listened for a few minutes."

Again, his confession that he had been looking for her was too much. She had to get up and walk around. When she turned to face him again, she could see that he hadn't moved but had been watching her pace. He still had more to say. She could see it in his eyes, so instead of trying to be glib, she sat back down.

"Look, Avila, I don't even know if my father had made the connection when he signed those papers so many months ago, but I do know that what you did, what you put together, was an intricate, amazing piece of work. We all thought so, and when I found out it was only the last in a long line of accomplishments for you, I felt like an underachicver." He laughed at his own expense. She knew it was an effort to make her feel better.

His face grew serious again. "I never got to meet you then, but here you are now, and I am at a complete loss because I feel like I should know you more than this, and yet I don't know you at all. Then there is the sense that it shouldn't matter, because I just found out I have had the pleasure of getting to talk to one of the greatest minds of our generation on a regular basis."

Avila didn't know what to say. She knew there was no way she could have told him everything about herself. She didn't talk about the things she accomplished like trophies anyway, so it wasn't likely to come up unless in a roundabout way. There had been no talk about nature or wildlife until recently, so it never did. She felt like his feelings were unjustified, but she could see why he thought that way. As for the last part, it was more than she thought she deserved. She only ever did what she felt needed doing, nothing more and nothing less.

Galdien watched the emotions play across Avila's face. Still, before she could respond, he held up his hand to let her know he wanted to continue. When she saw his hand go up, her eyes went wide before they narrowed, and she pressed her lips together.

He chuckled under his breath at her visible irritation. The fact that she didn't hide it from him, that she didn't play games and was so open even when she was angry, was so refreshing. His chuckle did not improve her mood, so he quickly added, "I know there is no way you could have told me everything about your life, and I accept that there are things I don't know yet, but this is a huge thing. I get it, I really do. I don't like it, but I understand it. I know you enough just from these last several months to know you would not expect thanks for something like that. If I were to guess what you were thinking, it would be that you were doing your job. You don't have to tell me if I'm right; I can see it on your face."

It looked like she was about to respond, but before she could say anything, again he stopped her. "Please let me finish." This time she let him continue without the irritation.

"Thank you. First off, you deserve thanks even if you don't expect it and even if you don't want it. What you did is a big deal, especially for someone as young as you are. You are singularly driven and amazingly brilliant." She blushed again, but he continued as if he didn't notice, "Secondly, I want to get to know you better. I know this is hard, and I—I know I haven't made things any easier."

With his pointed reminder of a couple of nights ago, Galdren watched the instant transformation to Avila's whole body and saw the paleness grow in her face as if she were feeling ill. If just the memory of what happened made her feel like that—he almost lost hope but continued anyway.

"Avila, I apologize for the whole situation. I hate that it makes you feel the way you do, but I want to put it behind us because I want us to be friends." He wanted to tell her that he just wanted to spend time with her, but the words wouldn't come out.

Galdren was confused but hopeful when Avila stopped clutching her middle. "Galdren, I have to apologize as well. I didn't behave in a dignified manner, and even though I know I have said I would make this easy, I haven't been trying my hardest. I do miss spending time talking to you."

He watched as she swallowed once before she looked away. He wasn't sure if it was her nerves about what had happened or something else, but the sight of her wringing her hands had him moving before he thought of the consequences. His hand covered hers to still the movement, and hopefully to comfort her.

He could see the alarm in her eyes when she looked up, so he released her fingers, but he didn't move right away. It was foolish, he knew, but he enjoyed being close to her. "I just want you to know that you will have nothing to worry about, Avila. I promise you that I will never do anything like that again. I don't want to hurt you." He thought he saw a brief flash of pain in her eyes as he spoke, but it was gone before he was sure, and then her face was calm again.

He stood up and backed away, thinking it was probably as far as he needed to push things for tonight. At least it seemed as if they were back on speaking terms again. However, before he could take more than a step, Avila reached up and grabbed his hand. She looked at their two hands for a moment and then up at him.

"Thank you, Galdren, for everything. I know I said it a long time ago, but I want to make sure you know I mean it, for everything in between now and then too. You have been generous and kind and have become a friend, really. I know you mean what you say, and I appreciate the kindness in which your oath was given. I—I am glad that I have had the honor to get to know you even if the circumstances aren't the best, and, well, I'm happy we're on regular speaking terms again." She smiled when she said the last part and squeezed his fingers before letting them go.

She was always so unexpected. Galdren didn't move for several moments, but he was smiling at her. She could be read so easily most of the time, and he knew her personality well enough by now to know how she would react in most situations. Still, at just the right moment, she always seemed to do the unexpected. She wasn't moving either, for that matter, just kind of looking up at him with a silly half-smile on her face. Goddess, they made a pair, but he knew this was not good, and he needed to get out of there.

"Good night, Avila. I will still be back tomorrow as originally promised, and I hope you will be ready for Saturday." With that, he turned to go. At least until she called out.

"Galdren, coats? Will you have all we need to stay warm, especially one to fit me? It is going to be much colder there than it is here, and I have never had a heavy coat." He hadn't really thought about it before, even though he knew they would need extra warmth. He had assumed the castle would have everything they needed, but now that she brought it up, he realized she couldn't wear one of his or even one of the guards'. He probably needed to get her one before the end of the day tomorrow, as well as any other cold-weather gear the guides thought she might need.

"I will have it with me when I come tomorrow." Her bright smile at his simple statement was enough to remind him again why he needed to leave.

Before he made it to the door, he was stopped again by her voice. "Good night to you too, Galdren. May your sleep be untroubled."

Avila wasn't sure where that particular adage had come from, but it seemed familiar, and it felt right. As Galdren closed the door behind himself, though, she wasn't quite sure how she felt about the rest.

She had nearly gotten sick when he reminded her of the kiss they shared, but it had passed when he entreated her to remain friends. After that, she was left feeling confused. She still felt rejected and hurt; he had kissed her, after all, not the other way around, but he wanted to be friends? Being friends with him was easy. Even before that, when they were talking, the conversation had flowed so smoothly that it was a simple matter for her to forget that she was mad at him. If she would admit it to herself, she missed spending time with and talking to him. If a friend is what he wanted from her, then friendship was what it would be.

The idea filled her with relief. There was no use even trying to deny that. She couldn't stand the thought of it being bad between them indefinitely, so this was one step closer to normal, at least. However, there was still an ache in her chest that she couldn't shake. What was the point of deluding herself? She cared about him. Really, truly did, even if he didn't return the feeling. Her internal acknowledgement could make her dealings with him more challenging, but not impossible. There was absolutely no way she could let it go back to the awkwardness that was there before; that was even worse.

Olva brought in dinner not long after Galdren left, which was a welcome distraction. It didn't take long for her to finish the meal, and it was too late to even think about going over any of the information again as she had planned. Instead, she decided that it might be best to call it an early night instead of trying to keep the circling thoughts at bay. Surprisingly enough, she managed to go to sleep almost as soon as she climbed into bed.

10. GEAR

When Professor Gilbert arrived, he was stunned to see the transformation in Avila. There was color back in her cheeks again and light in her eyes. It didn't take him long to be caught up in her mood, and there was an easy banter between the two of them whenever she wasn't too focused on trying to finish something. Before either of them realized the time, her lessons for the day were almost over, and Galdren had quietly slipped into the room.

When Avila noticed him arrive, she gave him a smile and went back to her work. It froze Galdren where he stood for a moment. When the professor noticed the silent byplay between them, he thought it might be appropriate to talk to the prince while Avila finished her work.

"Prince Galdren, how are you this afternoon?" His voice was pitched just low enough not to carry across the room.

"I am well. I had some things that I needed to bring for Avila, but they weren't ready when I left the castle. Someone should be bringing them shortly." Galdren kept looking in her direction as he spoke. It wasn't hard for the professor to see that he was preoccupied.

"Well, I'm sure she will be happy to see it. She has mentioned the fact that she was supposed to be getting cold weather gear today. For the trip tomorrow, that is. I must say, there is something about her today that is quite remarkable. She has been in the most excellent mood. I would almost go as far as to say she is happy, maybe for the first time in some time." Professor Gilbert knew he couldn't ask what was going on, but he did want the best for both young people. However, he also knew that they might not be the best thing for each other, with the situation being what it was.

"Really?" The prince's face split into one of the biggest grins Fredrick had seen on him since he was a child. It didn't take long for him to school his features again, but there was still a small smile playing at the edge of his lips. "Well, I'm glad. To be honest with you, Fredrick, we had kind of—well, we had not really been fighting, but sort of. We made up last night. We decided that being friends was better than the alternative. I am glad she likes the idea too. I want her time here to be as easy as possible."

"So, what are you smiling about? Do you have a surprise for me that you are hiding somewhere?" Avila had finished her work and walked up to them without either one noticing. Thankfully, she had not caught any of their conversation.

"Well, first off, I am smiling because they are contagious, and I caught yours. As for the present, it will be here shortly. I couldn't bring it myself." Avila laughed at Galdren's poke about catching her smile, but when he told her the gear wasn't in yet, she affected a fake pout.

Professor Gilbert didn't miss the subtle shift in the prince, or the young man's slightly widened eyes. He was old enough and had seen enough to know what was going on, even if it seemed the other two people in the room did not. His heart broke for them both. It would likely not end well no matter their desires; not with the mindset of so many of the nobility. Too many had gone far too long without setting foot off Aril, and it often showed. If Avila and Galdren ever figured out their feelings, it was never going to be an easy path for either of them. Someone was going to get hurt, and most likely, both would be.

He knew there was not much he could do except guide where he could and be there when needed. It pained him to feel so useless. He also knew that any chance he would have had to talk further to the prince was past, and it was time for him to leave. While the two younger people carried on, he gathered his things.

"Are you going to leave before my gear gets here, Professor? I won't get to ask your opinion on its weather worthiness." Galdren rolled his eyes at her, and she smiled at his reaction.

"Avila, you know you will not get anything less than perfect, and I am sure you will have an excellent trip tomorrow and discover many exciting things. I am also positive that you will be warm while you are doing it. I do have to get going for the night, however." Professor Gilbert picked up the last of his things as he was talking, and he bid them both good night as he headed for the door.

After he left, the silence stretched for a few moments. It was broken by a knock. When Galdren opened it, Olva was there with two men Avila had never seen before. They quickly deposited the boxes with her new gear and left.

It was boxes, too—several of them to be exact, much more than she had anticipated. She had thought it would be a new coat and maybe some warm socks and shoes, but this had to be much more.

"Well, are you going to stand there and stare all afternoon, or are you going to open them and see what's in them?" She was still hesitating after he asked, so he walked over and handed her one. "Here, open this one first."

It wasn't too hard to pull the fastening back from the top of the box, and when she did, she pulled out a beautiful dark green winter coat. It was made of a material that trapped body heat, but it was comfortable to wear. She threw it on to gauge the fit, and it was perfect. Snug, but she could still move easily, and it covered her past her hips as well. "It's amazing. I don't know what this is made of, but it is so light, and I'm already burning up in here." She loved the color, too, but was so impressed by everything else she forgot to mention it until it was back in its box, and she was on to the next thing.

Galdren was smiling at her enjoyment, and it was only the first box. He handed her another parcel. This one had boots and socks. That covered all she thought she might need, but there were still two more boxes. She went ahead and tried one of the boots on to check the fit. It was so perfect she wasn't even sure the break-in time tomorrow would be that bad.

As soon as she put the boot back in the box, he handed her the next one. In it was a pair of gloves made of the same wonderfully light material as the coat, an old-fashioned knit cap, and a matching scarf, all in a beautiful rust red. They were almost like brilliant fall foliage. She took each piece out and looked at it in wonder before placing it back in the box with care, as though they were all fragile things. She was beyond words now. There had already been much more than she expected, and there was still more to go. She didn't know if she wanted to cry or go and give the man a hug. For the moment, she accepted the last box with a smile.

Avila opened the last box slowly, unsure of what she might find in there. When she finally got it opened, she pulled out a pair of pants. She could tell just by looking that they were more than likely just her size. They were muted brown and tapered off in the leg, so they could easily be tucked into the boots to both be kept out of the way and to conserve warmth. They were also much sturdier than any she had, though they didn't feel like they would be too heavy to wear.

There was only one thing left in the box. When she reached in, her hands felt what had to be one of the softest things she had ever touched. She pulled out a sweater knit so finely that the stitching could barely be seen. It was of the most amazingly soft material—and it was a light sage green. "Galdren, I—I don't know how to thank you for all this. This is gorgeous. I love it."

"Seeing you smile is thanks enough. Besides, you do need to be warm tomorrow. Now I know you will be." Avila was thrilled with everything, but when she saw him blush, she barely heard what he said next. "I hope I didn't go overboard."

That was too much for her to process. She didn't even pause to think about the consequences before she wrapped him in a crushing hug. Almost as if by reflex, his arms wrapped around her as well. With her head still pressed to his chest, she whispered, "You do so much for me. As much for me as anyone ever has, and you never get anything back from me most of the time except for my sharp tongue. I am so sorry, and I am thankful that you are such a wonderful person."

She began to cry into his shirt, but instead of backing away, his arms tightened around her. She stood there for several moments with her head on his chest while his hand lightly caressed the back of her hair in a soothing gesture.

Avila felt silly for starting to cry, but when he pulled her tighter, she couldn't even try to fight it anymore. She wasn't sure why she was crying. It wasn't as though she was angry or sad anymore. Maybe she was learning to live with her situation and be grateful for what she had instead of pining for what she did not. After her tears dried, she stood there a moment longer, feeling his hand on her hair, knowing it was a guilty pleasure but not able to make herself pull away. Finally, when she had no more excuses to be there, she stepped back, and his arms fell away from her. She almost shuddered with the feeling of loss it left behind.

"I go to thank you for doing so much, and you do it again." She smiled at him in a half-deprecating kind of way. She knew there was no point in running away from things anymore. It only seemed to make them worse. Instead, she thought she would try a different approach and see if they could talk about them instead—to a point, anyway. There was no reason to go overboard and make things awkward again, but she could at least talk to him to try to keep things from going back and forth all the time.

"Look, Galdren, I know I seem really emotional, but please understand that even though you are so wonderful with me, this situation is still overwhelming at times. Plus, there have been things that have added some hardship." She looked away from him when she said that. She hadn't wanted to bring up the kiss or ensuing awkwardness, but she knew that she needed at least to get some things out in the open.

"I have had a difficult time dealing with all of this, and I apologize again, but I am trying, really trying, now. I value your friendship, and I don't want you to think I am ungrateful. I am learning acceptance, and I want to make the most of this. Please know that if I do have a moment here or there, they will get fewer and farther between, I am sure. This outburst isn't because I'm sad. I'm not. I'm only adjusting." She finally managed to look up at his face and noticed that although his jaw was tight, his eyes were considering.

"Avila, you have nothing to apologize for. I know this is hard; it is something new for both of us, and I am learning too. I understand why you would be upset and need time to adjust; honestly, if the situations were reversed, I'm not sure I would have handled it nearly as well. Please forgive me for acting without thinking, and for uprooting your life. I know it can't be easy, but I was not exaggerating when I said I believe it is for the best. Please, let us both take this one day at a time. I want you to be happy here, and if you can do that, then I am sure everything else will work the way it should." He stepped forward and reached for her hand with a smile.

"Let's go sit for a bit, and you can tell me about some of the things we have to look forward to tomorrow." Avila was still overwhelmed by his impassioned speech, but allowed him to lead her to the chairs by the hand he still held. Once they were both seated, the sincerity in his eyes and his bright smile were enough for her to let go of her unease, even if she still wasn't sure what to think about how he viewed her.

They spent the next couple of hours talking comfortably about the things she had learned. He updated her on the weather forecast: cold but clear. It was almost like the conversations they used to have before things got complicated, only better in a way. They both were a little more open. There was more laughter and teasing and less worry about what might slip. Although they both kept a few things to themselves, it wasn't hard.

By the time Olva came with dinner, they were engrossed in the conversation. She carried meals for two; she really was a magnificent housekeeper. They would have missed her if she had not made a point of bringing the tray to them and letting Avila know that she would take care of putting the new things away, so they would be ready for the next day. Avila felt guilty about her picking up everything, but Olva waved away her protests before she could even begin.

It was a leisurely dinner since it was interrupted often by their continued conversation. By the time they were both done, it was later than either of them realized. "I've had a wonderful evening sharing conversation with you once again. It is, however, time for me to leave. We both have an early morning, and it is later than I had expected to stay."

Galdren's words sparked excitement anew in Avila. She wasn't sure she would be able to sleep, but she knew she needed to try because they did plan to get an early start to make the most of the day. It was so much easier to see him leave knowing that things were finally starting to settle into a semblance of normalcy. "Good night, Galdren. I will see you in the morning."

He returned her smile with a quick one of his own, only pausing before he slipped out the door to wish her good night as well. Then he was gone. When he left, Avila found that she still had too much energy to go to sleep even though she knew she should, so she decided to call Lissa and go over what was going on. She knew it might turn into a long conversation, and she wasn't dreading it as much as she had been earlier in the week, but she also knew if she didn't, she would never hear the end of it.

Lissa was thrilled with the news, and more than a little jealous, but didn't try to keep her too late. She did, however, extract a promise from Avila for at least one good sketch. It was an easy promise for Avila to make.

Once she shut off the monitor, she stood with a yawn and went to see where her things had been taken. True to her word, Olva had taken care of all the boxes, and everything was laid out nice and neat in the bedroom, ready for her to slip into the next morning. She ran her hand over the sweater one more time, marveling again at its softness.

11. BEAUTIFUL MORNING

It was Saturday morning, and Avila was up before the timeglass had even let her know she needed to be. Her sleep had been fitful at best, but she didn't feel tired for it. She was too excited. She went ahead and got dressed, almost reverently putting on the sweater. The coat, scarf, cap, and gloves, she grabbed and put by the door so she would have them when she left.

She couldn't sit still, so she was pacing when a knock came at the door. She was expecting Olva or maybe one of the rare others that Olva oversaw to be there with the breakfast tray, but when she opened the door, it was Galdren himself. He had breakfast for both of them.

"I was hoping you would be up, but I didn't expect you to be ready and waiting." He smiled at her as he came in and set the tray on the small table by the chairs.

"I've been up for a little bit. I guess I'm excited." She could barely force herself to sit down long enough to eat the breakfast he had brought up.

While he sat down to join her, he took the opportunity to take a look at her in the clothes he had bought for her. "That color looks great on you. I hope you like them as well now that you've had the opportunity to try them on?"

Avila paused with a bite halfway to her mouth and blushed at his compliment. She put the food back on the tray and took the time to clear her embarrassment, at least to the point where it didn't show on her face anymore. "Thank you, and yes, I do love it. I love all of it. Not only are they some of my favorite colors, but everything fits so well. How is that, by the way? How did you know my exact size in everything?"

He grinned at her for a moment and let her wonder, but when she gave him a look that clearly showed her frustration, he relented. "It isn't that big of a secret if you think about it. I had Olva check for me. She is amazing."

Avila realized that made a lot of sense, and since it was no longer a mystery, it was soon gone from her thoughts. She had too many other things to think about. It wasn't long until they had both finished breakfast. Galdren picked up their trays and nodded to her. "Grab your stuff, and I'll take this to the kitchens on our way out. I'll call for the cars downstairs."

This was it. The first time Avila had been out of these rooms since her accident. She was elated when she passed through the doorway. Even though the trip would not take them more than a couple of hours away, just the thought of finally getting out made it seem like a grand adventure. Though, with where they were going, that wasn't too much of a stretch. Being away from her suite was a strange feeling after so long, but one she hoped to get used to again.

In the hallway, she noted that her set of rooms were closest to the stairs, but farther in, there were several other sets of doors. She wondered how large these "apartments" were, but let the thought pass quickly. It wasn't important. He was the prince after all, so having a lot of space wasn't surprising.

She followed him down the stairs and into the foyer, where he asked her to wait. It was a grand area that extended through both stories with rooms going off all sides and under the stairs, where Galdren had disappeared. She was sure that this was not nearly as impressive as, say, the castle, but it was the grandest, most opulent place she had ever been. The fact that he called the building an apartment blew her mind. Although, with how many suites there were, it made sense if she stretched the logic a bit.

Galdren returned in a few moments without the tray. She assumed that meant the kitchens were somewhere behind the stairs. "I have already called for the cars, so they should be here in just a few minutes."

As he told her this, he gently took her coat, scarf, and cap from her. "Here, let me help you put these on." She did not remember ever having someone else help her get her coat on, so the idea of him doing it seemed somewhat strange. Still, when he wrapped the scarf around her neck and knotted it loosely before gently tugging her hair loose, she instantly forgot any hesitations she might have had. It felt nice to have him help her into the coat and fasten it up for her. When he snugged the cap on and tucked her hair behind her ears, so it would be out of the way, she gave him a radiant smile.

Galdren wasn't sure why he had offered to help with her gear, but seeing her smile like that gave him a clue. It didn't matter that brushing her neck and touching her hair were agonizingly sweet tortures. He would have done it a thousand times more to see her smile like that again. He did have to remind himself that they had something to do other than stand there smiling at each other. The hovercars would be there shortly if they weren't already waiting outside.

He had a small com device in his pocket that was one of a set. Each person on the team he had assembled would be carrying one. He went ahead and turned his on. If they were within range, he should be able to communicate with them and know when they could both leave safely. He always had at least two people with him at all times when he was outside. However, since he was not traveling alone, he'd decided to take a whole team. There would be six other people joining them on their trip.

He had not said anything to Avila about it, but word of her staying in his private apartments had gotten out. Once that happened, they had to change the level of security and a full detail was in or around the building around the clock. It made no difference if potential intruders wished them harm or were just looking for a story. The assigned team took their job of ensuring that the place was always well guarded against intrusion seriously.

Avila didn't know it, but the only other people to live in the area were councilors and their families. The part of the park that she could see was kept private for the use of the landowners in that part of the city to preserve their privacy and protection. The only time it was open to everyone else was during the gala, and security for the event was always a nightmare.

The security of the apartment notwithstanding, he wanted to make sure all was safe on their trip, and that there were no mishaps. The longer she went without having to deal with rumors, the better.

A voice came over the com device he held. "Your Highness, this is transport one. We and transport two are outside and ready." The voice was brisk and to the point.

Galdren took Avila's hand, and they stepped outside. He stood and watched her as she closed her eyes and took in a deep breath of the crisp morning air. It didn't matter that they needed to hurry and get into a vehicle; he couldn't bring himself to rush her. He felt a twinge of guilt again at her obvious pleasure when he thought about how long she had been stuck inside that room, but he pushed it aside. He didn't want anything to mar the day.

Finally, Avila opened her eyes and looked at Galdren sheepishly. She realized they were all waiting to get in the hovercars, and it seemed as if they were all standing there staring at her breathing in the autumn air. "Sorry, it's just—it's a gorgeous day." She smiled at him and waved him forward to let him know she was ready to go.

He pulled her closer to the first hovercar. "Avila, this is Randy and Baxter. These two go with me wherever I go."

There was a double chorus of "ma'am," one from each of them. One of the voices was the voice she had heard on the com; Randy, she thought, but she wasn't sure. Once the introductions were done, Galdren continued, "We will be riding with these two. The other four are a team that Randy picked out to help with anything that might come up while we're at the park, not that there should be anything." He added the last when she gave him a look of concern.

"They will be riding in the other hovercar. We can make introductions to everyone else once we are more secure. Everyone have their coms on and fully functioning?" There was a quick chorus of "yes, sir" before he continued, "Each of these will also function as a locator back to mine if the need arises. All right, let's go; anything else can be discussed on the way."

Galdren still had Avila's hand in his, so as soon as one of the guards opened the door of the first hovercar, he pulled her forward and had her in it. He quickly followed, and the door was shut as soon as he cleared it. One of the guards stood outside the prince's door until the other was in the hovercar behind the wheel, then got into the passenger seat.

"Wow, that was efficient. Do you go through that every day?" Avila said it in a whisper; it was a little scary. She knew who he was, and she did think about what it meant sometimes, but it was easy to forget that there was so much more to his world than what she was aware of.

He smiled at her. "No, actually most of the time, it is a much smaller hovercar since it is just the three of us. I even get to drive sometimes, although I'm not sure I should tell anyone that."

She laughed at his quip, but still felt a little unsettled. He seemed to notice, as he continued, "The only reason security is by the book today is because there is a new element: you. I told you it's all new, remember? We are all learning. It could be that it isn't necessary, but to be on the safe side at least this first time, we do it by the book." She relaxed at his reference to their conversation the night before and gave him a more genuine smile.

The trip would take a little less than an hour, so they settled into a quiet conversation, with the only input from the men up front being when Galdren asked for the names of the other four people. One of the names sounded vaguely familiar to Avila, but she couldn't think of why. The actual introductions would wait until they got to where they were going, so she guessed she would find out then.

The mountain range where the park was located was barely visible from the outskirts of the city. Avila had never thought much of them beyond research, since she had never had the opportunity to travel far. The closer they got to the peaks, the larger they loomed on the horizon. Avila found that no matter how much she had thought she was prepared for this, seeing everything up close was going to be something else entirely.

The conversation in the vehicle all but stopped as they got closer, and Avila was drawn more and more to the sights outside the windows. As they floated closer to their destination, Galdren watched Avila as she watched everything pass. They had passed the entrance several minutes earlier, so they were well into the range, and she was staring in wonder at the peaks rising high all around her.

The hovercars pulled into a small side road that was almost hidden and, after only a couple of minutes, came to a stop in a clearing in front of a small building. Soon, all eight of them were inside the tiny structure, where they found a park ranger and a lot of communication equipment. "Hello Darek, I spoke with you yesterday about bringing a party of eight to the reserve today for some general exploration." Avila had been looking around at everything, but when Galdren started talking, she walked over to where he was standing. The man behind the small desk stood up, bowed, and brought out what looked like a ledger.

"Of course, Your Highness. If you could please have everyone sign into this passbook; it's really just a formality." He handed the ledger over to the prince along with a pen. Galdren quickly signed his own name and handed the pen over to Avila so she could do the same.

However, when she signed her name, the man standing behind the desk must have caught a glimpse of it when she set it down. She watched as his eyes widened when he read it, but thought nothing of it. She was across the room by the time he looked up again. Darek looked like he was still debating saying something, but he kept looking over at the prince and seemed to change his mind.

The last person to sign in was the woman from the group of four that had been in the other vehicle. When she passed Avila, she realized that she did indeed recognize the woman. She was one of the people she had spoken with many years ago to get information about the logistics and probable locations for the small preserves. They had worked together several times back then. The woman, Jessica was her name, had been back and forth between the reserve and the capital in her position as a ranger at the time.

"Jessica, Jessica Lyons, that's your name, right?" Avila had walked up to her before she even finished writing. "I don't know why I didn't recognize your name earlier. I guess I was preoccupied, but I remember you, although you may not remember me. Didn't you used to work as a ranger?"

The woman turned and smiled at her. "I understand you probably had other things on your mind earlier, but I do remember you quite well, as a matter of fact. That and the fact that I am still a ranger and know this place as well as just about anyone are the main reasons Randy picked me for this team." She tilted her head to the back a little to indicate the man behind the desk. "I bet you ten to one that Darek remembers you too."

At that opening, Darek started stammering, and Avila was a little confused since she didn't remember meeting him before. Then again, she did recall working with several people remotely, and his name did sound familiar. She extended her hand to shake his. "Darek Summerton, right? I must apologize for not recognizing your name earlier as well, but I really want to thank you now that I have the chance in person. Your work was invaluable to me, as was Jessica's. Everyone from the park that was gracious enough to provide advice did so much to make sure that bill was everything it needed to be to become a living document."

It was like a cross between someone meeting his favorite idol and an old friend at the same time. Darek took her hand like she had offered him a favor and then went on to tell her how he had followed her work for years, even before she started drafting the bill. When she began looking for resource material, he was happy to help, and he was honored that she remembered his name. Eventually, Jessica stepped in and gently reminded him that they did have other things that needed doing.

The whole time the scene was unfolding, Galdren looked on with amusement. It was interesting to see someone else at the center of attention for once. Out of the rest of the crew, Randy, Baxter, and Jessica were the only ones left inside to witness any of it. The rest had gone outside to wait as soon as they signed in, since there was little room. However, it was interesting to note that as soon as his two bodyguards realized what the commotion was about, the way they looked at the young woman they were helping to guard shifted. He was glad for it. He trusted those two with his life daily, and the higher they valued hers as well, the better he felt.

Darek got back to business after being reminded that he did have a job to do. "Your Highness, please forgive my distraction. There is only one other thing we need to finish before you can get started. I know you have been up here several times before, so you should be familiar with the process of registering a com device. If we get any alerts while you are in the park, they will be relayed to you, so you can be kept current with any problems or emergencies."

Galdren motioned Randy forward. "Take care of this, if you would. You know what to do, and you'll be the one that needs to know first anyway. Avila and I will be outside with the others looking at the maps while you finish."

Avila gave a quick wave goodbye to Darek and followed Galdren outside. The two of them were quickly followed by Jessica and Baxter, leaving only Randy inside to finish the com registration. When they walked out, Galdren took Avila's hand and led her to the left of the doorway, where there was a mid-sized screen she hadn't noticed when they went in. It had an overview of the whole park on it, but when Galdren touched a section, it zoomed into a smaller, more detailed map. There were few trails, but it did list known landmarks, specific well-known or highly populated wildlife habitats, waterways, and various other bits of information.

12. INTO ARALEEN

Galdren was just getting to where he could show Avila where they were on the map and where they were hoping to head when Randy came out of the building. Once they were all together again, Randy introduced the other three formally. "Sir, ma'am, this is Byron, Lee, and Jacob. They are all loyal palace guards, and each has served the king on several missions, both diplomatic and military. You already heard Jessica's story inside." All three men and the one woman gave a quick salute to Galdren, which he acknowledged with a nod.

"All right, we all know where we are heading. Let's go." With that dismissal, everyone headed to the hovercars in which they had arrived. They then turned back to the main road and went a little farther into the park. Soon they came to another small, almost hidden trail on the right. That one also terminated in a clearing, but there was no building there.

If Avila remembered the map correctly, there should be a stream less than three miles from the clearing, but no wildlife areas were marked nearby. Regardless, she was excited to get going. She had not had a chance to exercise in ages, and was ready to give her muscles the workout they were craving. She also had a few small specimen bags in her coat pocket that she had gotten from the professor the day before. She was excited to see if she could find something worth taking back and a little afraid she might not have enough containers.

They gathered in a loose group with Jessica and Randy out front, Lee and Byron to each side, and Baxter and Jacob bringing up the rear, which left Galdren and Avila in the center. The formation was set to be flexible, and it had to be since Avila kept finding things she wanted to look at and changing the direction she was walking in randomly.

There was a long, low incline they had to climb before they could even see the stream that Avila wanted to head for, and by the time they reached the top, she realized two things. First, the meager amount of exercise she had been able to do in the set of rooms she had was not nearly enough, and she was utterly out of shape now. Second, she was pretty sure if there had been any animals about, they were probably long gone. The only other person besides herself that moved quietly through the fallen leaves was Jessica. Not even Galdren, with his effortless grace, seemed to know the trick of not scaring off everything within earshot.

At the top of the rise, she stopped for a few minutes to take in the view of the valley below. On the far side, the decline was a little sharper than it had been coming up, but not so much that it would be a tricky descent. Then the valley floor extended to the stream and beyond to where there was a sharp rise, and one of the peaks seemed to touch the sky from where they were standing.

After Avila caught her breath, they started their descent, and this time she stayed in a straight line. Once they reached the valley floor, she could resume her exploration. She had been thankful for her coat up until then since the air was cold, but with the exertion of the hike, she was almost getting too warm. She loosened the scarf just a little.

Once they got to the bottom, she had to stop again. Everyone had a small pack with some supplies for the day in it, so while she was resting, Avila took out a canteen and sipped some water. Jessica came over to her while she sat. "I thought you might find it interesting to know that the packs we're carrying are ranger day packs. If you look through them, you'll find more than just the water canteen and dry snacks; there's also a small first aid kit, a utility knife, a water filter, and a few other things that might come in handy to a person trying to make it in the wild. Not that I expect any of us to need it, but it's always better to be prepared."

As Jessica described those things, Avila went through the small pack's various pockets until she found each item as they were mentioned and then put them back where she found them. "Thank you, Jessica. That is good to know, and even if I don't use any of it, I feel better knowing it's all there."

By then, she was ready to get started again. She couldn't see the stream anymore now that she wasn't on the rise, which meant it was farther away than it seemed. However, it couldn't be that far, and she was still in the mood for a good hike, so she set off in the direction she knew it had to be.

After another thirty minutes and several more stops, she found many things that she considered collecting, but only kept one of them. She felt a little silly about it, but she couldn't pass up the opportunity. While crouched and creating a quick sketch of a rare late-blooming flower, she had found one whole, unbroken giant oak leaf.

Some of the trees in the forest grew quite large, and the leaf looked to have come from the humongous tree a little off to the left. It was the most beautiful shade of vibrant orange and hadn't yet started to dry up and crumble. She couldn't leave it behind. It was too perfect. She carefully placed it in one of the specimen bags and then put the bag in her sketchbook to make sure the leaf did not get bent. Then the whole thing went back into her pack.

She picked up her pack and headed off again. They had almost made it to the creek when Randy's com unit went off. He had it to his ear within moments, and less than a minute later, he was by Galdren's side. He whispered into Galdren's ear, Avila presumed so as not to upset her, but she still caught part of the conversation. Not that she was trying to, but his words seemed amplified by the lack of any other sound. Poachers had been spotted, not too near them, thank goodness, but if they moved and found the vehicles—or worse, found out who had come in them—there could be trouble.

Galdren turned a concerned look to Avila, then cleared his face and took her hand. "Don't worry about it. I don't think it will cause any problems, and we are not going back, but we will be careful. Randy is briefing the others right now." As Galdren spoke to Avila, Randy gathered the others together in a group to let them know what was going on. Within moments, they had all gathered close to Galdren to see how he wanted to proceed.

"All right, I don't see this as a major threat, and I don't want it to ruin our day, but we do need to take some precautions. First, I want Lee and Jacob to go back and get the vehicles. They are designed for off-road travel as well. I don't know if you can get them down the incline on this side, but I want you to get them as close to us as possible. Once you have completed that, let me know where you are, so we will know where to rendezvous with you. Then I want you to stay with the vehicles and make sure no one else gets near them."

Lee and Jacob both saluted, and with a "Yes sir, as quickly as we can, sir," they were both on their way.

"Now for the rest of us. I want us to stick together in a tighter group. The stream isn't much farther, and that was the turning point for the day. Once we get there, we should still have plenty of time for a little exploring." When he was finished, the group walked in a similar formation as before but much tighter and with no more stops until they reached the stream.

They had barely made it to the stream when Baxter pointed out a series of flashes on the side of the peak opposite them. None of them could quite make out what they were, but it was clear that they weren't from any animal. It was still quite a span away, but Galdren decided that he would take Baxter and Randy and cross the stream to see if they could get a better view with the spyglass he had in his pack. He said he didn't plan to go far, but if it was the poachers, he would at least be able to relay a location back to the rangers.

Avila was a little uneasy, and it made looking for anything new difficult, so she sat instead and tried to soak up the calm of the forest around her. That was something that had helped her cope many times before. Jessica and Byron patrolled the area around her while she tried to meditate. Galdren had been out of sight for some time, and the longer he was gone, the more Avila's uneasiness grew. She had to keep telling herself that some form of communication would have occurred if there was any trouble.

Jessica came and sat beside her for a moment. "Avila, I know you're worried, but you don't need to be. This is no big deal, and besides, we are all out here, so you can do a little exploring. It seems to me like it would be hard to enjoy this place if you're sitting there with your eyes closed."

Avila had to smile. She knew the woman was trying to help, and she knew she really shouldn't pass up this opportunity. Still, it was hard not to think about what might be happening.

Once Avila smiled, Jessica stood. "Look, I need to go for just a few minutes and check something out. I did hear something, but it was distant. It may be nothing, and I don't want you to worry, okay? I'll be right back. When I return, we may need to move, so while I'm gone, I want you to make the most of the time you have left here."

Avila almost panicked, but she had to remind herself that they were well-equipped and used to handling difficult situations. She wasn't worried too much about herself; she had been spending time alone in the woods for years. Granted, it wasn't woods like these where the animals that might find you were a lot more dangerous, but that didn't mean she didn't know how to handle herself. She needed to relax and trust that these people knew what they were doing. "All right, Jessica, I'll be here when you get back, and I'll see what I can find while you're gone." She even managed a smile before the woman took off upstream in the same direction Galdren had gone but without crossing the water.

It didn't take long for Jessica to vanish into the trees, even as thin as they grew.

After she was gone from sight, Avila decided she might as well try to do what she had said she would. Maybe that would occupy her mind since nothing else seemed to be working. She walked around for a little bit and decided to pull out her sketchbook to capture what she was seeing. She looked up at the peaks opposite where she was standing. The thought of Galdren being out there made her stomach clench again, but she forced herself to focus on the sight instead. She managed to get a quick likeness of the mountains and a few of the trees around her before she gave up and put her sketchbook back in her bag.

She took the opportunity to walk around again but was too distracted to focus on anything. Finally, she decided to look into the stream. At least she wouldn't be looking at the mountains. She went down to the edge of the water and knelt next to it. It was only a few feet deep there, and the bottom was rocky, not full of mud. It was the kind of place where the water ran fast enough that it was clear in most spots. She had done this kind of search for life before in the streams near the city when she was younger. She knew that even though it might look calm, there should be life all along the banks, hiding under rocks and in the shadowy places.

Before she even had a chance to start exploring the stream, an arm wrapped around her waist and she was pulled back against someone's chest. She was too startled to scream, but she did struggle until she was able to get away and turn around. Byron was facing her. "Why did you do that?"

He looked at her, grinned, and gave her a half-shrug. "You looked like you were about to fall in. I didn't figure you wanted to get soaked or anything, so I helped you out." He was getting close to her again, and before she could step away, he grabbed her.

"What do you think you are doing?" Her anger was rising more than her fear. She knew there were other people out there, and someone was bound to be back soon, but she did not like having his hands on her.

"Ah, look, honey, I'm not gonna hurt you. Just relax. I gotta say, the prince sure did find a sweet one in you, didn't he? He must have paid a pretty penny. I bet your momma must be loving life now. She probably doesn't even have to work anymore since he up and bought you." Avila had been struggling to get away from him until his words hit her. Then she just stopped. His words made no sense at all.

"What are you talking about? My mother? Bought me? What?" He must have taken her lack of struggle as acceptance and was starting to move in closer.

"Oh, don't play coy; I've been to Nerada many times with the king. I've seen the refugees that flooded that spaceport and the surrounding city. There are plenty of them there trying to make ends meet. So many of them look like you. Well, not quite like you, I gotta say. You are an exceptionally pretty one, but a whore is a whore. I don't think the prince will mind too much if I play with his favorite toy, as long as I don't break you." Byron was no longer playful, and Avila had heard enough. She wasn't going to wait for someone to show up; she might not have time. It looked like he was going to try to attack her right then and there.

She thought back to all the self-defense classes her parents had her go through after the disaster at school. Although Byron had her pinned, he was only using one hand to hold both of hers, so he could use the other to grope at her. Since he was holding her so close, she took that opportunity to stomp on his instep and then bring her knee up as hard as she could into his groin while he was off-balance. He had some protection in his clothing, so it wasn't as effective as she had hoped it would be, but it did make him let go of her hands. Instead of running, since she knew he would just overtake her almost immediately, she grabbed him by both of his ears while he was recovering and brought his face down as hard as she could while bringing her knee up to connect with his nose. She felt it break before she shoved him down.

She didn't know if she had knocked him out or not, but the move bought her enough time to get away. She didn't have her pack on, and it was too far away to grab, so she just started running. She had no idea where Galdren had gone or how far he was. She didn't have one of the communicators that could track him, but there was no way she would go back and try to get the one from Byron. However, she did know that she was heading in the direction Jessica had gone. She hadn't been gone that long either, and most importantly, Jessica could track Galdren.

Avila lost track of how long she had been running. It was long enough that it felt as if her sides were on fire, and she finally had to stop. When she did, there were no other sounds around her. She allowed herself just a moment to catch her breath and then pushed forward at a slower pace. It occurred to her that she had gone far enough that she should have run into Jessica already. The other woman had not been running. Since she couldn't hear any sounds of pursuit, she stopped and thought about it for a minute. Jessica said she would be right back; she might have crossed over to go back along the other side of the stream. A few thick patches of woods could have blocked the view if they had passed each other going opposite directions.

Avila wasn't sure if she should try to cross and go back or try to find Lee and

Jacob. She wasn't sure if she wanted to, though. Now that she had a few minutes to sit and think about the whole thing without the immediate threat, she had to wonder why it happened at all. It was evident that the man knew she belonged to Galdren, and he had made assumptions about the hows and whys. Surely, if Galdren's personal bodyguards had briefed the rest of the team, they would have given them accurate information. It seemed as if either they didn't share anything, or no one knew exactly what was going on in relation to her presence in Galdren's life. Whichever it was, there still seemed to be information out there about the fact that she belonged to Galdren.

Avila doubted that Galdren would allow the two that he always had with him to spread any kind of false information, but she could be wrong, or he might not know. After Byron's near attack, she was unwilling to trust any of the other guards yet. Unfortunately, it also made her wonder how many people from the castle knew she belonged to Galdren, if any, in addition to what rumors there might be.

She wasn't sure if she wanted to laugh or cry. The way things looked, everyone probably thought she was Galdren's little trollop, and ironically enough, he didn't even want to touch her. Eventually, tears won out.

She sat there for a while, even after the tears dried up, debating whether she should just go back and gamble on someone other than Byron being there or not. Finally, she realized she didn't have a choice. One way or another, she had to go back. She wouldn't find Jessica by going forward. At least she knew how to be silent in the woods, so if she had to, maybe she could wait and watch until someone she trusted did show up.

As she stood up to return, she heard a small splash from the stream's direction and turned back to see a giant snow lion just on the other side. A small stone had dislodged near it and fallen into the water; that is what she had heard. If not for that, she would never have realized the giant killer was there before it was on top of her. It was still some distance away, but not nearly far enough. She couldn't outrun it and she couldn't outclimb it. She knew she was looking at her impending death, and for some reason, all she could think was that it had to be one of the most beautiful things she had ever seen.

It had a snow-white coat and a small, white mane that was shorter and thicker than its savannah cousins', which extended farther down its back. The whole cat was bigger than any animal she had ever seen—it had paws the size of platters—but the most remarkable thing was its blue eyes.

She only had a moment to admire the great cat before it leapt over the stream in a single bound. Avila did scream then. Fear finally settled into the pit of her stomach, and she knew she was as good as dead. Before the cat could get close to her, a single shot rang out, and the great cat collapsed about ten feet away from where she stood.

Her primal fear was almost instantly turned into rage. She didn't want to die, but that animal was one of only a few of its kind left. To kill it was beyond an outrage. She didn't even care if it was the poachers she had to face. Whoever it was, they were going to know precisely what they did before she was done. When she turned, however, it was Galdren and Jessica that she saw, and neither of them looked happy. As a matter of fact, Galdren seemed so angry as he passed the gun to Jessica that Avila almost didn't say anything. Still, as she looked back at the motionless white mass behind her, the anger flared anew.

"Thank you for saving me. Please don't think I'm not grateful, but do you have any idea what effects your action might have? That animal, that beautiful, rare animal, was one of only a few of its kind remaining. He was one of the reasons this preserve is here in the first place. How could you kill him like that?"

Jessica had a look of shock on her face. Seeing it, Avila, knowing the prince wasn't spoken to like that often, if ever, wondered if she would walk away from the conversation whole—and from the look on the prince's face, she wasn't entirely sure she would.

13. MISUNDERSTANDING

Galdren was taken aback at Avila's attitude. He was so angry at that moment he wasn't even sure he could answer her. Instead, he walked up to her, grabbed her by the arm, and started dragging her back the way they had just come with Jessica following. After a few minutes of stunned silence on Avila's part, Galdren finally responded to her question. "The cat isn't dead; it was a tranquilizer. Jessica was carrying them in case we ran into anything." He couldn't bring himself to say more.

Galdren couldn't look at her; he wasn't sure what he would do if he did. He was angry at her, yes, angrier than he had ever been. However, more than that, he was still trying to deal with the adrenaline rushing through his body from the terror he had just faced. She had almost been killed—if he had been even a minute later, there would have been no way to save her. He didn't know how to cope with what he was feeling in the wake of that. He didn't even know how to explain what he was feeling. Mostly it was coming out in his outrage.

He had come back to camp to find Jessica patching up Byron's nose and Avila nowhere to be found. When he asked for a report, Byron told him that Avila started acting suspiciously after Jessica left to check out a noise. When he tried to find out what she was up to, she attacked him and ran off. Galdren couldn't understand why Avila would run away or how she could have bested a palace guard, but there was no doubt she had definitely at least temporarily disabled the man. From looking at Byron's broken nose and the bruising surrounding it, he wouldn't have been surprised if the man was unconscious for some time.

By that point, they didn't have any time to lose. If Avila was running, then they needed to catch her, and Jessica was the best tracker. He left Byron in the care of the others, and then he and Jessica took off down the way Avila had gone. The trail was easy to find since she had been running and didn't bother to go slow and hide her tracks. While trying to locate her, Galdren had time to try and figure out why she had run in the first place. He didn't like any of the answers he had come up with.

The last week kept playing back through his mind. How she had been so angry with him. Which he didn't blame her for, but he had thought they were past that. If she really was so sick of everything that she had just waited for the first opportunity to come along and then ran, how was he supposed to handle that? He had wanted to make this easy, but if she was going to fight him, he wasn't sure it would be simple for either of them.

When Galdren had first been approached by his father about Avila's Life Debt, he was unsure of how to answer. He could admit that there were many mysteries surrounding the young woman that he did want to figure out, but he was hesitant to take away her life—her freedom. It was only after his father had mentioned that it might be for the best that he even truly considered it. The reasoning had been vague, but his father's eyes had been concerned. It added to her mystery, and he also trusted his father's judgement. His curiosity would not have been enough to push him into invoking her Life Debt, but after speaking to her for a few weeks, and at his father's urging, he decided that it might be a good idea.

When his father explained that he would not only have Avila's life as his, but he would be responsible for protecting it as well, he felt justified in finally agreeing. That was not something that was spelled out in the wording of the Life Debt document. Though Galdren knew there was more to his father's order—and he had no doubt it was an order, even if it was implied and not direct—that fact only served to deepen the mystery around the girl and strengthen Galdren's resolve, so he had taken up the obligation and all it entailed.

However, walking back through the woods with her, he had no idea how he should proceed. The image of her just standing there while the great cat was stalking her from across the water came back to his mind's eye again, and his hand clenched on her arm without thought. He relaxed it when he heard her stifle a cry. The way she turned on him, her anger at the idea of the cat being dead; it was almost like she had some sort of death wish. It made him consider the idea that she had run without a plan, just to get away, and had not cared what happened. The thought did not make him any happier.

They had not even made it back to the rendezvous point at the stream when they were intercepted by their two vehicles. Lee and Jacob had managed to make it down the incline, and once they were to the valley floor, it was easy going to get to the stream.

It was the one good thing that had happened that day. Jessica left to join the three men in the second hovercar, and without letting go of Avila's arm, Galdren opened the door of the first. That was the first time he had even looked at her since they had left the spot where he found her. The tear tracks on her face startled him. The look she gave him was full of anger, yes, but more of hurt. He wasn't prepared for it. He wanted to know why she would run away in the first place when things had seemed to be working out, but if he couldn't trust her words or actions, he didn't even want to talk to her at the moment. No matter how much that look pained him, he was still too angry at her betrayal.

"Get in the transport." He managed to force the words out, but when she looked like she might say something instead of getting in, he just pointed to the doorway. The look on her face was even angrier now, and there were fresh tears, but he couldn't take any conversation.

The first half of the ride back was spent in complete and uncomfortable silence. It was finally broken by Galdren. "Randy, we will not be going back to the apartment straightaway. I want to go to the palace instead. I also need you to contact them and let them know that I need an audience with my father." He glanced at Avila when he said that and then back to the front again. "I need it as private as possible." When he got the confirmation from Randy, he put up the privacy screen but still would not look at or talk to Avila.

Avila felt like she may as well have been invisible, except for the odd glare she caught occasionally. She felt as if she were finally the prisoner she had feared she was going to be all along. That thought was the one that kept circling in her head and coming back to her when she didn't want it to. That thought was the one that kept the tears fresh on her face.

She had been shocked by his reaction at first; maybe she had pushed a little too far when she got angry about the cat, especially since it wasn't dead. But when she thought about it, he had been furious when he first found her, before she even said anything, so that made no sense. She had thought about saying something, maybe asking why he was angry during the march back, but then he had squeezed her arm, and she saw the look on his face. She had barely been able to stop the cry that came out. Not so much from the pain it caused, but he had such a black look on his face that she couldn't begin to fathom why he was so angry at her.

Again, she wanted to ask at the hovercar, but by then, it was evident that whatever reason he had was so bad in his mind that he didn't want to talk to her. She was caught between hurt and fuming. Mad because she had done nothing for him to be angry about; or at least, definitely not that angry, and hurt because she was still jangled from her ordeal. She needed to talk to him about what was going on, but nothing would get solved if he didn't speak to her. The only thing she had plenty of was silence and tears, and she was getting sick of both, but there didn't seem to be an end to either one in sight.

When they got to the castle complex, they stopped the vehicle near an entrance that looked like it was for the royal family's use, out of the way of the main entrance. The second transport kept going. Presumably, to park in the palace's underground garage. When the other car passed into the tunnel, Galdren took down the privacy screen. "Make sure they all meet us in the audience chamber. I want everyone there."

Avila was starting to feel uneasy. If she was being hauled in front of the king, which is what this was beginning to feel like, what exactly did he think she had done? If it were something serious enough to warrant this, she could understand the anger, but she needed to figure it out and set things straight fast if that was the case. "Galdren, I know you're angry, but we need to talk before this gets out of hand."

The look he gave her was pure ice. "Avila, you can talk to me when I am sure—when I know—you know what, you can wait until we are inside." Avila was taken aback by his tone, and wrapped her arms around herself when his jaw clenched. Still, she kept her silence. There was no point in arguing if he was going to be unreasonable. She was sure the truth would come out soon enough.

Randy and Baxter both got out of the vehicle and came around to open the door. Avila got out first, followed by Galdren. Once they were both out, another servant came and took the hovercar away. With the guards on either side of them, Galdren must have felt she wouldn't try to run since he didn't grab her by the arm again. In fact, he made sure to keep enough distance between them to make sure they didn't touch at all, but he made it clear with body language that he expected her to keep up.

Before they passed through the outer doors, Randy reported to Galdren. "The others will meet us in Room Two, Your Highness. Your father is waiting there for you." It didn't take them long to reach Room Two, which was apparently one of the king's offices that he also used as a small audience chamber. It was spacious and contained an ornate desk with more carvings on the edges and legs than Avila thought was possible on one piece of furniture.

When Galdren and his group arrived, the other four that had been with them were not there yet. Still, there were several other guards already in the room with the king. The four of them stepped up to the desk, and then the two guards with Galdren took their places on either side of the room. Before Galdren could even start talking, the other four showed up and silently took their places as well, two along either wall next to Randy or Baxter.

Galdren glanced around the room and then back to his father before he began. "Father, I only need a short amount of your time, but there is a matter that has come up, and I need your unclouded opinion of events and your guidance, if you would share them, please. This matter involves my charge. I know you said to protect her, and I want to make sure that I do just that, but I need to get to the truth here and am having trouble finding it."

With Galdren's speech, Avila looked at both royals sharply, but neither one even spared a glance in her direction. Galdren continued, "I am not asking you to sit in judgment or to assign any punishment; I will need to manage those on my own. I am simply asking for an unbiased look at what has happened today."

"Galdren, I will guide you as I can." At that point, Galdren turned to face Avila fully for the first time since he had seen her in the forest. She could still see the tightness in his jaw that showed his anger. Between that and the king's dispassionate gaze, which was now turned in her direction, it was more than she could handle. She lowered her eyes to the floor, trying and failing to keep the tears that were forming from falling.

"Avila, you know you are in my charge, correct?" Galdren's question surprised her, but she didn't want to look at him with the tears falling freely. Instead, she watched them form spots on the floor and answered him in the strongest voice she could muster.

"Yes, Galdren, I am aware that I am under your *charge.*" She tried not to put too much spite into the last word, but with the way he had been treating her for the last couple of hours, all the hurt was breaking through.

His jaw clenched tighter at her answer, but there was no direct response to the tone. "If you are fully aware of your circumstances, then I will note the allegations." With that, Avila's head did come up. She was being charged with something? This was fast becoming too bizarre for even a dream. "Avila, you are being accused of trying to escape and doing bodily harm to one of the people designated to guard you. How do you plea?"

Her jaw dropped open, and she just stood there for a moment, unable to find the words to respond. He thought she was trying to run away? That could explain why he was acting the way he had been, but it was no excuse for him not to just ask. "I did not try to run away! I was trying to find Jessica!" Her voice came out as a shout when she finally answered him, surprising everyone in the room.

The king stood up, and Avila calmed enough to know she shouldn't have shouted. The king turned to Jessica and motioned her forward. "Your name is Jessica, I presume?"

Jessica nodded. "Yes, Your Majesty."

"Can you please enlighten us as to what she might be talking about?"

"Well, Your Majesty, I had been assigned with one other guard, Byron there, to watch over Avila and keep her safe while the others were away for various reasons. I thought I heard something nearby that might have been a threat, so I went to investigate. When I came back, she was gone, and Byron was injured. Prince Galdren arrived at about the same time I came back, and he took me to search for her. I can say that although where we found her was farther than I had traveled, most of her path followed mine almost exactly."

"Thank you. That is enough." With the king's nod, Jessica turned and glanced at Byron. After a moment's hesitation, instead of going back to her position by Baxter, she went and stood next to the door. She got a raised eyebrow from some of the others, but with her shrug, it was passed off quickly.

Once Jessica finished her brief statement, all eyes were back on Avila. The king was simply looking at her with a mild expression, as if her outburst had not happened at all. Galdren, on the other hand, still looked stormy. "Why would you be following Jessica? Did she not ask you to stay at the rendezvous point? Were you that anxious to get lost in the woods?" This time Galdren's voice had started to rise in his anger, not to a shout, but enough that the surprise was evident in everyone's faces.

Avila almost choked on her own emotion as she tried to get the answer out. She couldn't tell if she was angry or hurt, but either way, her throat was constricting, and she couldn't make a sound at first. When she finally could answer, it started out as a choking stutter, and her tears streamed down, unchecked and unnoticed. "I went to find Jessica because I knew she could find you! I had no idea where you were, and I had been left alone with that man!" She pointed wildly but unerringly to Byron. "I don't know what you are telling your people these days, but since this is on the record: I am not your whore! And as for the man that thought to rape me—breaking his nose wasn't enough, but it was enough for me to get away. Unless there is some punishment for defending myself now, too?"

Her voice, which had risen nearly to a screech, fell to an almost defeated whisper as she finished. She felt as if she should have no more tears to cry, but they still slid down. The silence in the room was absolute.

The quiet was broken by a sudden rustling by the door: Byron. He'd tried to slip away once he saw how things were going. However, with Jessica by the door, it only took a few moments for him to be secured. He was soon held between two of the other guards. While that took place, Galdren turned to face his father. He thought he caught a troubled look on his father's face, but it passed quickly, and then he was facing his father's usual practical self.

"Father, it seems I have wasted your time here today. The only thing clouded here has been my judgment, and I must apologize, both to you and to Avila. There are still issues to address, though, and since Byron is one of your guards, I must ask how you would like me to proceed?" Galdren couldn't bring himself to look at Avila yet. He could only imagine how she must be feeling, and would not be shocked if she hated him. However, he did note that after Byron was secured, Jessica had walked over to talk to her quietly.

"Galdren, I have given you a great responsibility, one I think you are capable of handling. Part of any growth is admitting mistakes and learning. Move forward. Take accountability for all that has happened and deal with it as you think is best. I will stand behind your judgments. I have faith in your abilities." When the king stopped talking, he stepped out from behind the desk and walked toward the exit, followed by the guards that had been in the room with him. Galdren gave him a nod as he passed. Everyone else bowed as he exited the room.

14. RESOLUTION

Once the king was gone, silence reigned for a short time. Galdren knew he would have to face Avila, along with what he had allowed to happen and his own actions after. Everything was a jumbled mess in his thoughts where she was concerned, and he knew it was not an appropriate mindset to be making decisions in. He knew he couldn't ignore her or ignore what happened, but he needed to sort some things out first.

Dealing with Byron was another matter entirely. When Galdren turned to face the man, he had to fight not to let the rage that suddenly reddened his vision show on his face. There had been rumors regarding Avila's presence for some time now, but from what she had said only moments ago, Galdren could guess what Byron had taken those rumors to mean. He knew he would need to find a suitable punishment even if his first impulse was something more direct and violent. First, he needed Avila taken care of, at least until he could see to her himself.

"Jessica, can you please take Avila back to my apartments and stay there with her until you hear otherwise? If you had other duties later today, I will see to it that arrangements can be made. Baxter, I would like you to accompany them and stay there as well. On the way, would one of you please make arrangements to have Dr. Ortiz meet you there?" He didn't look at Avila as he gave his orders to have her taken care of. He was afraid he might do something foolish if he saw the look of anguish she had in her eyes again.

She glanced back once before she left, but he made sure their eyes did not meet. Given the circumstances, he wasn't sure how he felt about the other two guards left in the room besides Randy, but when he faced them, each gave him a salute with faces set in stone. Galdren could see from their expressions that he was not the only one upset by the way things had unfolded. They had all been there to protect both people, not just one.

Satisfied that there would be no trouble from the two men holding Byron, he finally faced the offending man directly. His first thought was one of satisfaction that Avila had managed to do some damage before she escaped, quickly followed by a sudden urge to smash him in the face again anyway. He stifled the thought. No matter how fleetingly gratifying it might be, he needed the whole story before he could figure out what needed to be done, and the man needed to be able to talk.

"Byron, I need you to tell me exactly what happened, and please keep in mind that I will be checking with someone else as well, so mind that you get the details correct, please." Galdren's words were formal but ice-cold. He didn't even bother trying to hide the disdain he was feeling.

The fear was evident in Byron now. Whatever he had been thinking would be the outcome of his actions that day, he evidently had not been expecting this. He had to swallow twice before he could talk. "Your Highness, I have to say up front that I never meant any harm. I swear it looked like she was flirting with me, and with all the talk about her, well, you know, I thought she was asking for it. She didn't even fight me at first. She didn't do anything until I mentioned that she was a kept woman, and then she got all offended and did this to my face. I'm the one that was assaulted here." When Byron finally took a breath and looked at Galdren, the storm brewing on the prince's face stopped his rant before it truly got started.

"That 'kept woman,' as you called her, is a highly educated, well-respected member of our society who has done more for animal rights and the people of this planet than most people many times her age. I wasn't asking you what you thought about her or what you thought she wanted. I told you I wanted the *details* of what happened, so if you please, let's try that again. This time I only want the facts." Despite his best efforts, Galdren's voice almost slipped from his control, and at the rise in volume, Byron paled considerably. In a calmer voice, he added, "From when Jessica left will be fine."

Byron looked as if he wanted to be sick right there, but it didn't take long for him to start talking again. "I'm—I'm sorry, Your Highness. Just the facts—right. When Jessica left, Avila walked around a bit and then went over to the water. After a few minutes, she bent over, and I thought, well, I guess it don't matter what I thought, but I went and grabbed her. She was surprised, but she didn't scream or nothing. We just talked for a few minutes. She didn't fight at first, just kinda pushed me away. I thought she was playing coy. She was asking me questions too. I told her about how I knew about her already and her kind, you know, the ones at Nerada. Anyway, that was about the time she started freaking out. She was fine one minute and then, bam, kicking me and busting my nose the next. She knocked me dizzy, and by the time I cleared my head, she was gone, and I had no idea where she went. I went to try and clean my face up, and then I was gonna go see if I could find her trail, but Jessica showed back up by then, and well, you know the rest."

Although Byron was looking down and the fear was still plain in the way he spoke, by his own words, he did not seem to think he had done anything wrong. Galdren had to turn away from the man so he could think clearly. He was afraid if he stood there watching the lack of remorse for much longer, he might knock the man flat. It would be immensely satisfying in the moment, but not the justice the man deserved.

The four men stood and watched the prince in silence for several minutes as he deliberated. Finally, he turned back to face them. "The fact that you did not commit an even more grievous crime was due only to Avila fighting back. Had she not been so lucky in her strike against you, how much farther would you have gone before you realized just how wrong you were? You say she wasn't *really* fighting, but that means she was fighting some. That tells me you are trying to justify what you were doing by playing her as the courtesan in your head, but she is an innocent. Any hesitation could only have been shock, not coyness as you thought. So now, do I judge the intent as if it were the deed, as it could have been had you not been stopped?" Galdren paused and glared at the man. "Unfortunately, it is not in our laws to judge intent, so I must judge your actions alone. However, you did assault her, and I do have something in mind."

Galdren walked until he was right in front of Byron. He made sure the man was looking him straight in the eye as he delivered the sentence. "Are you aware that when someone who is under the Life Debt runs away from their debtor, they are subject to flogging?" There was a collective gasp from three of the four men in the room as sudden understanding came to them. The situation became much clearer to everyone, and Byron's eyes grew round.

Galdren continued as if he hadn't heard a thing, "The severity of the flogging depends on the circumstances. Your actions today almost caused an innocent girl to face just this consequence. Given your lack of judgment, your actions, and your apparent lack of remorse, I think it would be fitting that you take her place at the pole. I also do not think a guard is a suitable position for someone who cannot take the people they are set to protect with any amount of seriousness. Once the first part of your sentence has been carried out, you can collect your things, and you will leave the castle. Your services will no longer be required here." Galdren held the man's gaze for a few seconds longer to make sure that everything sank in. He thought he saw a spark of something close to anger, but it was soon swallowed by despair.

"You can't dismiss me; I work for the king." Byron's words were somewhere between a plea and a threat, but either way, they were completely ignored.

"Lee, Jacob, please escort Byron to the holding cells until arrangements can be made." After Galdren handed down the sentence, he turned away from the man as if he no longer existed. All his pleas fell on deaf ears, and he soon disappeared out the door with the other two guards.

Now that it was over, Galdren could feel the anxiety for Avila coming back worse than ever, especially now that he had a better idea of what happened. He wondered exactly what Byron had said about the spaceport. He had a bad feeling that this was only the beginning of a rough time. He needed to find out how she was, even if she was still mad at him. "Randy, we need to get back to the apartment, quickly."

Dr. Ortiz had just left, and Avila felt exhausted. She was completely drained after everything that had happened earlier in the day. Jessica had been accommodating and, for most of the evening, had never left her side, not even when the doctor was there. Still, Avila finally convinced her that she wanted to sleep. At the moment, Jessica and Baxter were both in her sitting room. She could just barely make out the murmur of their voices. It didn't matter, though. As strung out as her nerves were, she was still ready to pass out. Not even the fear of nightmares was able to keep her awake. It did not take long until everything faded, and she drifted off.

When they first arrived in the city, the crowds had made her nervous. Around every corner, she expected to see another soldier calling out an alert for her or just aiming a gun at her. Although she did see plenty of soldiers, none of them seemed to notice her from the press of the people around her. They seemed to have their hands full just keeping riots from breaking out in the streets.

To her dismay, her head wound made her blend in more than it made her stick out. The number of wounded people in the streets seemed to increase every day as the toll of the civil war continued to grow. The graceful coup the Trogand had hoped for with the death of the royal family was disintegrating. The people did not accept the merchant group as viable leaders, and fighting was prevalent everywhere.

While she still did not remember much, she could piece together enough to understand what Mikael was teaching her every day. She understood her place, and had come to accept her responsibilities. It was odd to know herself from the outside like that. She felt as though she was a stranger to herself most days, but there was never any time to ponder the feeling. She had too many other worries; just staying alive was at the top of the list.

The anonymity the city provided was unexpected but welcome after her experience in the woods, and it gave her a chance to heal. She was getting stronger every day, even if she wasn't getting her memory back. It helped with her focus. She no longer passed out regularly, so she could walk in the streets with Mikael while they searched for the contacts they needed.

He had hoped to be in the city for only a week, maybe a few days more, but the fighting was only getting worse, and the number of refugees flooding the city grew every day. It was getting harder to navigate the crowded streets even on foot, and getting anywhere on foot fast was impossible in a metropolis the size of Chruinne. It wasn't as large as the capital city of Ithir, but it was still one of the largest on the planet. It was a good thing Mikael had so many contacts and knew how to carry provisions through a crowd of people that were only looking out for themselves.

They were into their fourth week in the city, and Avila knew that if it hadn't been for Mikael, there was no way she would have made it. Her complete lack of knowledge regarding how to live life in the shadows of the streets was an even more significant danger to her than the occasional dizzy spell she still experienced from the wound in her head.

Mikael had gone out earlier to meet another contact to try yet again to schedule them a flight off-planet. Things in the city had been worse than expected when they arrived. With the constant influx of refugees, the Trogand forces were constantly on the lookout for royal sympathizers. It didn't take much at all for them to make an example of anyone who thought to speak out. Everyone coming to the city as a place of refuge from the fighting outside quickly found that it wasn't much safer there.

Avila's only safety was that, although the Trogand forces did look for her in the crowds, they didn't honestly believe her to be there. If they did start a full-scale hunt for her in the city, they would leave no shadow unsearched, but she hoped to be long gone by then. She only prayed to the goddess that her people would not suffer too much for her absence.

She had ventured outside earlier that day to take a short walk around, sticking to the shadows as much as possible. Although she did not like being alone outside, the need to stretch her muscles and get out, to see her people and feel like she could breathe a little again, was more than sufficient motivation to get her out on her own. It was an excellent way to keep from going mad while Mikael secured their escape.

The crowds in the streets were even larger than they were the last time she had been out; something she had expected but still did not like to see. However, they seemed a little less fiery, and if any eyes were not downturned, they were either filled with fear or utterly empty. The pain of seeing her people in such a state weighed heavily on her, but she knew there was nothing she could do about it yet. The task of staying alive against an entire army bent on killing her was almost more than enough to make her want to give up at times.

Shouts and a shrill scream pulled her out of her wayward thoughts. "There she is! I've spotted the princess, right over there, with the bandage on her head!" Those words froze Avila on the spot; she wanted to run, but she couldn't make her feet move.

A spot in the middle of the street, about a hundred feet away from her, suddenly cleared. A small group of soldiers had a girl by the arm. There was a middle-aged woman with them sobbing so hard her words were almost incoherent. "My daughter, please, please—my daughter."

The woman was desperately trying to reach the girl the soldiers now had pinned between them. One of them brutally knocked the woman down, and her sobs ceased immediately. It did not take long for Avila to understand what was going on. Despite both the woman's desperate pleas and the girl's sincere denials, the soldiers were convinced the girl was the missing princess.

The young girl looked similar to Avila, and she was close in age. Avila found that her feet were moving toward the commotion, not away from it, but she had not even taken more than a few steps through the dense crowd before the guards held the girl up for everyone to see. The patrol lead spoke loud enough for everyone within visual distance to hear; no one else talked or moved on what should have been a busy street. "We have orders to shoot any known rebel on sight. If we find the leader of the rebels, we are to bring her body to our president as proof, so we can end this useless rebellion. We are going to show you here and now that we are dedicated to just that!"

Avila realized that in this quiet, stationary crowd, her frantic forward motion was starting to draw attention, but she didn't care. She had to do something. Then a single shot rang out. Several women screamed, and a few even fainted. Crying erupted all over, from women and men alike.

Avila quit her struggling; it was useless. She didn't need to see the girl's lifeless body to know that one more life was given instead of her own that day. This time it was an innocent, one that didn't have a choice. The fires of righteous retribution that had been slowly drowning in despair over the last four weeks suddenly flared anew. She knew now that no matter what, she would make it through every ordeal. It was her responsibility to make sure the Trogand paid for every life they took and every wrong they committed against her people.

With a renewed vow, she made her way back to the shadows to find Mikael. They needed to get off the planet to rebuild before returning and doing what needed to be done.

15. DISTRACTION

Avila woke up feeling better than she had when she went to sleep. She could feel the tears on her face from her dream, but in addition to the profound sadness, she also felt hope. She wasn't sure why, but something about her dream spoke to her of resolution and the ability to face the future, no matter how grim. At that moment, it was exactly what she needed. She couldn't figure out her dreams, especially since they were rarely ever clear and she'd only started having them after her accident. Still, no matter what they were, she was getting used to them.

She was fully awake, but it was still dark outside, so it had to be early. However, Avila didn't feel like going back to sleep. Even though she wasn't as rattled as she had been, the events from the previous day and Galdren's reactions to everything were starting to creep back over her feelings of hope. The thing that bothered her most was that he had never even looked at her, even after discovering the truth. He believed her and had taken care of it from what she had been told, but she couldn't help but feel abandoned. His reaction had hurt more than she liked to admit. She might not have any right to feel the way she did, but even if all they shared was a friendship, she thought he would trust her not to run away.

Not to mention, it did not escape her memory precisely what the punishment was for someone like her running away. Did Galdren plan on enforcing that? Could he have really taken a whip to her? Just thinking about it again made her feel a little sick.

In an effort to not sink any further into the negativity she could feel threatening to consume her, she decided to try and find something to occupy her mind instead. She was sure she had something she could read at least. Even if it was still dark, there was no point in moping until morning, since sleep obviously wasn't an option. A welcome distraction from her present state of mind was exactly what she needed.

She checked the timeglass and was not surprised to see that it was only a little after three in the morning. Since any company was sure to be a long time in checking on her, she didn't even bother changing.

Avila went into her common room and headed straight for her bookshelf. Although she liked to read, between her love of being outdoors and her normal activities, she rarely had time to read anything other than research materials. These last few months had opened up new opportunities for her since she had extra time on her hands, and she had accumulated a small library of things she would like to read or had read recently.

It gave her a small pang when she looked at the bookshelf and realized that she owed the whole collection to Galdren, like almost everything she owned now. Or perhaps she shouldn't say she really owned anything. After the incident earlier, she was starting to rethink her situation. How easy had it been for him to pass judgment on her without even asking; before he even knew the circumstances? She shook her head to try to rid herself of the thoughts that kept circling.

It only took her a moment to find a book she had started a couple of weeks ago but abandoned when all the recent turmoil had started. Looking back over the last week, she could hardly believe so much had happened in such a short time. She wished once again for the comfort of solitude in a quiet glade. At least there she knew what to expect.

That time, she couldn't stop the tears that came. It was too much. Between the back and forth and up and down that kept going on between her and Galdren, the events of yesterday, and her feelings of being utterly betrayed, she was at the end of her emotional rope. No matter how much she tried to hold on, she was slipping fast.

She refused to sink down right there on the floor and cry, no matter how much she might feel like it, so she turned to at least go sit down in a seat and cry it out. When she turned to find one, her sobs turned to a strangled scream that she quickly stifled. Galdren was asleep on the settee. She didn't move for more than a minute to make sure that the noise she had made didn't wake him. He seemed to be sleeping soundly, despite what looked to be an uncomfortable pose. While she stood there watching him, she noticed that he already had a pillow and blanket. Olva must have made sure of it.

Once she was sure he wasn't moving, she quietly walked over to kneel by his side. Her tears were effectively dried up by the distraction of him asleep in her sitting room, even if seeing him did not help her tumultuous thoughts. While he was sleeping, his features were so relaxed. There was no storm brewing in his eyes and no tightening in his jaw. Granted, she couldn't see his eyes light up either, but his mouth was relaxed in a way that was not quite a smile. It made her stomach tighten when she remembered how it had felt when those lips kissed her. That memory did not help either. She was still so confused about everything that had happened, but seeing him there like that made her want to forget her anger. She doubted he would be in her rooms waiting if he didn't care at all.

Although she knew it was a dangerous path, she couldn't resist touching him just once. He was so beautiful; her heart was breaking at the thought that she might never get to see him like this again. She reached out and lightly brushed the hair from his forehead. When he didn't move, she reached out again. She hesitated; she knew she shouldn't. She had no right to touch him in any way, and although he had said they could be friends, things were so complicated now. She started to turn away and leave him alone, but she turned back at the last moment. She placed a light kiss on his forehead and whispered, "May your sleep continue untroubled, my prince."

Before she could turn to go back to her own bed again and give him peace, his arm came up to trap her. She looked over to stare with shock into his sea-green eyes. Without letting her go and without saying a word, he sat up and pulled her into his lap.

The unexpected turn of events had her so flustered she didn't even protest. Although when she realized she was sitting in his lap in nothing but her nightdress, she did turn a bright shade of red, something she tried to hide by ducking her head.

Galdren's hand then cupped her chin and, with gentle pressure, moved her face until they were once again looking eye to eye. With so little space between them, she didn't think her face would ever stop blushing, or her heart stop racing for that matter. She was sure he could feel it speeding. He could probably even hear it; it was pounding so loudly.

"Avila, I wanted to make sure you were all right. I—I know, well, I don't know how you are feeling, but I do know that this has been an ordeal for you, and I apologize for not being there for you like I should have been. I made unfair assumptions without even asking." Avila could only stare at him. His words did nothing to settle her conflicting emotions. Yes, he had apologized, and she could tell he was sincere, but that didn't change anything that had happened or the possible consequences.

When the silence stretched thin, he finally let go of her chin, and she ducked her head again to avoid his gaze. He shocked her when he gently wiped at the still damp tear trails on her cheeks with the pad of a thumb. "I know I am probably the reason for these. You made a promise, and I should never have doubted you. Please believe me when I say I regret that, and it is a mistake that I will not make again."

Avila finally raised her head to look at him. "Galdren, I will not lie to you and tell you I do not feel betrayed. I do. I spent so much time last night not just going over what happened, but going over how you reacted. How could you not trust me after all we had just been through? Then add the fact that I was worried about—about the—the whipping." Her last words were no more than a whisper, but they seemed to have a profound impact on Galdren as his arm tightened around her before he pulled her against his chest again.

She did her best to keep from shaking, but it was a lost cause. Especially when Galdren said, "Avila, you will not be punished for a crime you did not commit."

His words caused relief to flow through her, even if she still wasn't sure what to think. He held her gently for a few more minutes until the tremors passed. Thankfully, he didn't make any moves to try and get her to look at him again.

He spoke to the top of her head as he held her gently. "Would it surprise you to know that most of the reason I was so unreasonably angry with you was because I was so scared for you?" She pulled away from his embrace so she could look up at him again. She felt something somewhere between confusion and consternation.

At least the confusion must have shown through because he continued, "I'm serious; when I came back, and no one knew where you were, I almost panicked. Then, when I saw the lion leap toward you, I acted on instinct. Almost losing you scared me to death. I couldn't keep that image out of my head. I know I should have said something to you, should have asked you why, but I wasn't thinking straight." Avila could see the earnestness in his face, but she couldn't believe what she was hearing. Although she wanted to believe it was true, it just didn't make sense.

"Why would you care so much?" She said the first thing that came to her mind, and she could tell by the hurt in his eyes that her words had wounded him. Her raw feelings were talking instead of her good sense.

"Avila, please, I know we keep coming back to this, but I—" This time, it was Galdren's turn to avert his eyes. For the first time she could ever remember, he was at a loss for words, and something was obviously troubling him. Something inside her was moved in a way she couldn't explain.

She reached up to touch his face like she had wanted to do when he was asleep. This time, while he was awake, she knew it was the right thing to do. She made sure he was looking straight into her eyes. "Galdren, I think, maybe, we might both be a little foolish. I know I am. Even if you told me tomorrow that there was a way for this situation to be changed, I would always cherish your friendship. Since I know that and can admit that, not only to myself now but also to you, I know that no matter what, I don't have to feel like this is a prison or that I will be a hostage to my time here. We can move forward together."

It was the closest she would ever get to admitting to him how she truly felt, but since she did cherish him, at least he should know that much. She had already decided once that fighting with him was too tiresome. There was no point in going backward now, especially not when he was acting like this. His vulnerability touched her in a way she couldn't explain, even to herself.

Without saying a word, he gently put his forehead against hers with his eyes shut and wrapped his arms loosely around her. She wasn't sure how long they sat there like that, but when he finally moved, the sadness was gone from his eyes. She could see a hint of something in the depths that spoke of something lost, but it was hidden before she could figure it out. His smile was soon distraction enough to make her question whether she might have been seeing things.

Galdren had been too overwhelmed by her acceptance to do more than hold her, at least until he got himself under control. When he pulled back, he managed to give her a bright smile. "You're amazing; that is what you are. And I am indeed a fool." He was aiming for a teasing tone to try to break the mood that had taken over.

When she'd touched his face, it was almost more than he could bear. Just sitting with her now was a lesson in willpower, but he only had himself to blame for keeping her so close. He had to talk to her about a few things still, but they were difficult topics, and there had been enough of that already. What he needed to do was get her back in bed before he lost himself again.

"I do need to talk to you about everything, in all seriousness, but not tonight—this morning. I am going to take you back to bed, and I expect you to sleep in. I will check on you later, and we can discuss all the details. There are a few other things I have to check before I come back as well, so it will likely be later in the afternoon." He raised a single eyebrow at her. "If you happen to still be sleeping when I get here . . ." He trailed off and gave her a look from the corner of his eyes with a mischievous smile.

She swung a fist in the general direction of his shoulder, which he easily caught. He chuckled low in his throat at the sight of her narrowed eyes and the smile she was trying to hide. "Like I was saying, if you are still sleeping, it would be understandable, with your ordeal and your present lack of sleep. I will understand, but when you wake, we can go over everything."

He could tell he surprised her when he put one arm under her legs and pulled her closer. Her confused expression lasted only a moment before he stood up with her in his arms. That was when she pushed against him. "Galdren, I am capable of walking; please put me down!"

He only chuckled more. His earlier mood was gone, replaced by a playfulness that he hoped would ease the tension, but he still wouldn't let her walk. "I said I was going to put you to bed, and I fully plan on keeping my word."

Her face was fluctuating between multiple shades of pink, which he found adorable. That made it even more difficult when he continued to ignore her pleas. "Galdren, please, just—just take me to my room. I swear, I will go to bed." The look he gave her was somewhere between exasperation and amusement, but it was a moot point already. They had reached her bed, and he was laying her down. Since her covers were still down from when she got up earlier, he was able to pull them up and tuck them around her.

Once Galdren had Avila in bed, he turned to leave, then stopped and came back. He bent and kissed her forehead. "Good night, Avila, sleep well, and dreamless." His actions took her entirely by surprise. It was bad enough having him put her to bed and tuck her in. Having his lips on her once again was close to torture.

"Galdren . . . thank you. I will see you later." It was the only thing she could think to say that would help her focus on the moment instead of where her thoughts wanted to go. His answering smile was gentle as he turned and finally walked out the door.

Once he was gone, she lay there and tried to comprehend the last few moments. She could not believe he had felt the need to take her to bed like a child. Although, something in her gut was telling her she had objected more than she really felt. The thought that she was looking forward to him being anywhere near her bed again still gave her flutters.

She had believed sleep would not come to her again, but the longer she lay there going over everything, the more she relaxed. It did not take a leap in logic for her to realize that the more she got along with Galdren, the happier she was all around. Not that it helped to clarify her feelings, but for the moment, she was glad things were back to being as normal as they could be. She eventually found that she was too tired to think about it anymore, and her last thought before she drifted off was that she hoped she didn't oversleep by too much.

16. BOMBSHELL

Avila awoke the next day feeling surprisingly refreshed. She wasn't sure if it was the fact that she had been exhausted or if it had something to do with Galdren's wish before he left, but she had finished her night with no more bad dreams. It was nice to have a dreamless night.

She looked at the timeglass and was relieved to see that, while Galdren was right in that she had slept in, it wasn't that bad. It wasn't even noon yet. If he was going to be busy at the castle until later in the day, then hopefully she at least had time to get cleaned up and dressed before he arrived. She got up to do just that.

It didn't take her long to get cleaned up and dressed. She even made sure she didn't leave any mess in the bathing room for Olva to take care of later. Upon looking again at the timeglass, Avila was happy to note that it was still barely after noon. Surely, she was up and ready long before expected. It gave her a small twinge of pride. She hoped she could surprise Galdren when he came in.

When she walked into her sitting room, however, she was the one that was surprised. Galdren was already there, and by the looks of it, Olva had just brought him lunch. Her stomach reminded her loudly as she caught the smells that she was famished.

Galdren looked up when she came in and smiled his bright-eyed smile that she loved. "I can hear your stomach from over here. Why don't you come and join me, and I'll have Olva bring more?" It was not an offer she would turn down.

It took her seconds to cross the room and seat herself across from him. It felt so familiar. The whole scene—sitting with him, eating with him—somehow, along the way, she had become accustomed to it. She wanted to sit across from him and talk to him and eat with him every day. The fact that she was one of a select few people that ever had this privilege never even crossed her mind. It was her every day now, and she was beginning to realize, like it or not, she was falling in love with it.

She had already started eating before she got lost in her musings, so when she came back to herself, she found her piece of toast sitting listlessly in her hand. The fact that Galdren was speaking had also slipped her attention. She had not had such a bad lapse in a while. Luckily for her, he knew her well enough by then not to be offended.

He'd stopped talking and gave her time to collect herself. Part of her was grateful for his kindness, but the look on his face was so full of questions that she knew he wanted to know what had her so distracted. There was no way she could ever confess that, and she was a terrible liar. She only hoped he wouldn't ask her outright.

"Avila—" Before Galdren could get out more than her name, she jumped in excitedly.

"Galdren, look, I know you were talking, and I was off in my own little world again. I apologize. I haven't done that in a while, and I am trying to keep it to a minimum. It's just, I was thinking about the last several months and how much I've changed. How I've decided that being here isn't such a bad thing after all—that didn't—you know, that didn't come out right. I'm sorry." She was trying to do the whole "best defense is a good offense" thing, but she was so nervous it was going horribly wrong.

To her utter surprise, Galdren just laughed. "Don't worry about it." He reached over and firmly handed her another piece of toast and some fruit to go with it. "Eat. I need to talk to you, but you need to eat first. We can worry about flustered daydreams later." He laughed again, but that time she was feeling distinctly less embarrassed and much more angry. She had a feeling that might have been his goal, so she let it go.

While she finished her toast, he started talking again. "First, I want to go over everything that happened yesterday with you. I know it will be hard, but I want to be here for you."

Even though he had told her to finish eating, she was suddenly not as hungry as she had been a few moments ago. The thought of everything that had transpired created a lump in the pit of her stomach that seemed to take up most of the space there. Galdren must have noticed something was amiss and gave her another moment before he continued.

"Avila, please go through what happened yesterday as best you can. From everything I have heard so far, I know you will have as many questions for me as you have answers, so take as much time as you need, and I will do my best to answer them."

It helped Avila loosen the pit in her stomach to see the bright light in Galdren's eyes as he spoke. She could tell he was trying to convey his feelings along with his words, something that she was finally starting to pick up on after being around him for so long. She idly wondered for a moment if he could read the emotion in her eyes as well, but she jerked herself back from those dangerous thoughts before she had time to ruminate on the consequences of that idea.

"Where do you want me to start?" It was a simple question, but she still had to force each word out. It wasn't that she didn't want to talk to Galdren, and she definitely wanted answers, but each word felt like lead being pushed past her lips. The images of what happened, what could have happened, were all crowding back in her mind, and her just-eaten breakfast was acting as if it wanted to come back up again. When she looked back over at Galdren, his expression was alarmed. Surprisingly, that more than anything served to at least ground her enough to focus so her meal would stay put.

Galdren started to stand up like he would somehow come to her aid, but she quickly raised her hand to keep him from doing so. As good as his intentions might be, the last thing she needed was him any closer to her and confusing the matter. "My apologies Galdren, I guess this is going to be harder than I thought. I do have questions, though, and I know you do too, so I will do my best. I can start from the point when he grabbed me."

Galdren had sat back down as soon as she had raised her hand, but the look of concern was not erased, and it didn't keep him from asking, "Do you want me to call Dr. Ortiz?"

As hard as the retelling might be, Avila didn't think it was the hardest thing she had ever faced. She set the rest of her fruit and toast down and squared her shoulders to face Galdren. "No thank you. I can do this." And despite a difficult start, that was what she did over the next several minutes. She didn't leave out any details, though she also did try not to linger on her concern about him being gone so long. The last thing she needed was more issues due to oversharing.

She did not look up the entire time she spoke. Yet, once she was finished, no matter how hard she tried to stop them, the tears of frustration and anger still came. To her surprise, Galdren was right there before the last word was even out of her mouth. His arms were warm around her as he pulled her head to his shoulder.

After a short time, her shudders started to slow, and she fought to get control over her emotions. "Avila, you are an amazing, intelligent, respected young woman that has done more for this planet than most people have ever thought to. The idea of you being anything less is ludicrous. I don't ever want you to think about that again, because there is no way I will ever see you as anything less than what you are. As for the rest of what that man had to say, I know it probably brought up a lot of questions for you, and I will try to answer them when you are ready."

Avila couldn't believe that she had allowed herself the luxury of crying herself out on Galdren's shoulder yet again. As his words sank in, her feelings were mixed. On one side, she was touched that he held her in such high regard, but he'd also made it clear once again that his interest was only academic. Although it was a slight gut punch with her feelings being so raw at the moment, it was a familiar pain, and one that served to help her ground herself again. She found it easier to dry her tears and push away from him.

"Thank you, Galdren. I do believe you, and I do have questions, several in fact. I apologize for breaking down like that." She was already trying to give herself some space and find a napkin to clean up with.

Galdren understood her need for space, so he sat back down and watched her for a moment. The look on her face was so lost and vulnerable. He wasn't even sure if she was aware in that moment of just how open she was. It tore at him that she had to go through this ordeal because she was associated with him. He hoped that the plan he had would help prevent anything like it from ever happening again, but he also knew it would not be an easy thing for her to go through in itself. Either way, they had to get through the moment, and she needed strength. He only hoped she would accept his.

"Avila, please look at me." She did look up at his request, but her eyes were still empty. He almost wished he could go back and punch Byron like he had wanted to yesterday. He quickly squashed the urge; it wouldn't serve any purpose, and there were more significant issues to solve here, like why Byron thought it was all right to act that way in the first place.

"I wish this had never happened, and I tried to keep you safe and protected here, but as I am sure you have figured out, there have been rumors of your presence that have escaped." Her eyes narrowed, and he could tell there was anger mixing in with her hurt. He only hoped she would not shut him out.

"Avila, please, think better of me than to believe that I would ever allow anyone to say anything remotely like that." She stopped narrowing her eyes at him, but he could still see the fire in them. She was also sitting stiffly. He understood she was hurt and angry, and she had every right to be. He needed to make his next words count. "I kept your existence here hidden for a long time, but somehow it got out that someone was staying here. By the time I heard about it, it was general knowledge that the someone was female. However, since then, people—especially the kind of people who like to surround themselves in court intrigue—have come up with a myriad of reasons why I would have a female living in my private apartments separate from the castle. None of them are near the truth, I'm afraid."

He barely heard the derisive noise she made before she said, "Galdren, I know it is not your fault this happened and that it is your aim to keep me protected. I don't know how you can, not like this, not from every little thing. I feel violated, and more from the fact that I feel naked to every person who thinks they can take from me whatever they want because I am a possession than from what happened yesterday. What am I to do the next time, or the next time?"

He could see that her anger was dying, and despair was winning again. "You are right; I can't protect you from everything. I've tried and failed. I can, however, ensure that it is well understood that you are *not* property and that you are *not* a whore, to use your own words." He could tell that she was skeptical, but he kept on. "I do have a plan I would like to discuss with you, but first, I would like to talk to you about Nerada. If you can handle talking about that today, that is."

Despite her continued frown, Galdren could see the curious shift in her eyes and hoped it meant things were looking up as she said, "I understand the fact that Nerada is a spaceport, so it makes sense that there are refugees there. I have figured that much out on my own. My questions are, why only there, and what did he mean about my mother? Could I have come from a family there?"

It was Galdren's turn to hold up his hand. "That is a lot of questions at once. First, the refugees are not all in Nerada. There are small Talamh communities in several cities surrounding the spaceport. Still, they didn't spread far, and they seem to like to stick together."

He could have sworn she nearly laughed at him when he said the planet's name, but since he couldn't be sure, he continued, "We did provide some aide to all the refugees to help them get set up when they first arrived, and most of them have settled into a decent life, although you are the only one I have seen farther than a hundred miles from Nerada. There are a few that are still in the heart of the space-port. It is a true melting pot, and while there are illegal activities that we cannot seem to entirely stamp out, you will find that slave trafficking finds little purchase and great punishment there. We cannot afford to go lightly on that."

Galdren could see the confusion blooming on her face and nodded. "I know what you are thinking; why would Byron think that about you if the laws are so severe? The only conclusion I can come to is that he must have thought I was above the laws since my family writes them. Obviously, from his own actions, he does not hold the law in high regard."

At that, Avila did snort with contempt, but she waved her hand for Galdren to continue. He could tell whatever humor he thought he had sensed in her did not mean she was not still angry. "I can only assume that he has had some dealings with women of a certain . . . type around the spaceport. He has been there often enough with my father."

As much as he understood that she must know at least some of what he was trying to say, it surprised him how much it embarrassed him to speak of such things to her. He realized that thinking of her in relation to those images was such a drastic juxtaposition that he had a hard time putting them together, even if it was for the purposes of explaining.

"There is no need to explain that 'type,' Galdren. I understand perfectly well what you are saying." The acid in her voice was crystal clear. "I have already figured out that he 'had dealings with' women in Nerada on my own, but you don't need to get tongue-tied because of them. You have no idea what circumstances they might be in to drive them to that."

Galdren could see the fire burning in Avila's eyes, and it only took him a moment to realize his mistake. She had misconstrued his embarrassment for condemnation of the lifestyle these unnamed women had to live. He knew he needed to speak up quickly and try to explain the truth. "Avila, look, I am not condemning any of them. We really do try our best to help, but our system isn't perfect, no matter how we try. I don't always understand choices made, and sometimes I pity them, but I do not condemn them. You are right in that I can't know what drove them to those choices in the first place."

He could tell she wasn't entirely mollified, but the explanation seemed good enough. She no longer looked like she was about to blow up on him. "All I can tell you is that I am almost positive that no girls are being sold into slavery for any reason, even to the rich and powerful, but I am having additional inquiries made in the area just to make sure nothing has slipped past us. I honestly believe Byron was trying to justify his actions to himself more than anything."

Avila couldn't sit still. She stood and paced a few feet away to try to think clearly. She wasn't sure if his explanation made her feel better or not, but at least now she knew she wasn't alone on this planet. She wasn't the complete outcast she had felt her entire life. Now that she had found out there were more of her people on Aril, it was a relief to find they were living normal lives, not the awful ones she had feared.

An idea came to her then. It might be a bad time to ask with all the things that had just happened, but now that it had come to her, she couldn't rest until she did. "Galdren, thank you. I don't understand Byron's line of thinking, but I am glad you explained everything. I also have something I would like to ask of you."

Before his face had the chance to turn from mildly interested to confusedly quizzical, she ducked her head and continued, "Now that I know there is a very real possibility that I am a refugee from Talamh specifically, and that there are several Talamh communities in the world, I would love to have the opportunity to visit one."

She had more to say, but that was the hard part. She counted to ten and finally looked up. When she did, she wasn't sure if she was surprised or relieved. His face was considering, and she could tell that he had been waiting for her to look up at him before he answered. At least he wasn't angry.

Galdren stood to join her and put a gentle hand on her arm before he reassured her, "I have told you before that if you want something to ask for it. Don't be afraid to start now just because things have gotten rough. I mean it now more than ever." Galdren wasn't thrilled about the idea of exposing her to the dangers of a city so soon after what had happened, but if she felt she was ready, he wasn't going to stop her. He would, however, make sure to vet every single guard they brought along personally. Not that he didn't trust Randy or Baxter, but Avila's safety was something he had to take care of.

"I can't promise that it will be next weekend, but it will be soon. There are a few things we must take care of first. I promise I will make it happen, though." He could tell that his proclamation eased her mind and put her in a better mood. Hopefully, he could keep things on an even keel.

"Now that we have the details out of the way, there are a couple more things I wanted to go over with you. First, I want to let you know that Byron is being justly punished for the crime he committed." Galdren could see the questions burning in Avila's eyes, but he shook his head slightly to let her know he wasn't going to answer them. "I do not want to discuss that matter any further. It isn't worth your time or mine. I would much rather put it behind us as best we can. I know it won't be easy for you, but I can only promise to trust you in the future and that I will do what I can to protect you—always."

Avila was clearly not satisfied with his answer, but she also seemed to understand it was the only one she would get. "You said you had a couple of things you wanted to talk to me about? What is the other one?"

Galdren took a deep breath. This would be the tipping point. If she wasn't sold on the idea, then he didn't know what his next move would be. "To put it plainly, I think it is time for you to move out of these apartments and into the castle."

17. SAYING GOODBYE

Galdren knew Avila would be shocked, and he could tell she was. It had to be unexpected. Before she could form an answer, he rushed to explain why. He didn't want her to deny him right off. "It might not make sense to you now, but please think about it. If people are going to go on about you, they need to know the real you. There are other benefits, as well. You will have access to nearly the whole castle, the library, the gardens, all of it. I don't *want* to keep you cooped up."

Now that he had said his piece, all he could do was sit back and wait. After a moment of staring at him with an expression he couldn't quite read, she started pacing again. He realized it was a habit of hers to walk while she thought.

While she was walking, Avila's thoughts were in turmoil. She had done her best to keep everything in after the initial shock passed, but she couldn't get her thoughts quite straight. On the one hand, it was true that she did not want to stay in this apartment any longer if she didn't have to, but a move to the castle—that was intimidating, to say the least. How could she possibly fit in? The fact that she would have access to the grounds and the library was nice, but there were other people there. How would she interact with any of them? All told, she preferred solitude unless it was one of a select few close friends. As much as she didn't want to admit it, the thought of going to the castle terrified her, especially now that people already had preconceived notions about who and what she was. It didn't matter that they weren't true.

Thought on top of thought kept crowding in. Would she be expected to stay around Galdren all the time, or would she have more freedom? Oh goddess, if she had to be around Galdren more, did that mean she would have to spend time around the king and queen? She had no idea how she should or would act in those situations. She had become so familiar with Galdren, but somehow, she didn't feel like that would be permitted in front of other people. The move would be hard, to say the least.

She finally stopped pacing and looked at him. Not that she had any kind of clarity, but she was getting nowhere without asking questions. She was somewhat surprised by the look of concern on Galdren's face. She couldn't quite tell if he was worried about her or about her reaction, but either way, it helped calm her a little. She knew he was trying to help, even if it didn't feel like it.

"Galdren, I know that you mean well, but you have to understand that a move like that would be daunting for me. I do not fit into your society; goddess only knows that I can't even have a proper conversation with the crown prince." He coughed to cover up a quick laugh. It helped to relieve some of her tension as well.

"Seriously, though, I don't know how I'll fit in. It would be nice to have access to the castle grounds and a bit of freedom, but really, you don't own a cabin in the woods?"

Two jokes in a row, and there was no keeping his laughter in that time. Although she wasn't trying to be glib, sometimes it happened. His laughter was contagious, and it didn't take long for the last of her anxiety to fade and for her to join him in laughing at her own expense.

"Avila, I promise you will fit in. In fact, once people learn your name, it is highly likely that you will have a longer line of people wanting to see you than me. It isn't every day that one gets to talk to a genius." He could tell his compliment flustered her, but he was not going to let her fade back into that horrible anxiety. She deserved better.

"I know, I know, not a genius, no thanks needed—I have heard it before, but you are what you are, and you can be nothing less. Something a wise woman once told me." He could see her turning red again at the reference to her own words, but she no longer looked as if she was going to protest.

"Good, so, the answer to your earlier question is no, I do not have a cabin in the woods." He winked at her as he said it and was gratified to see her turn a deeper shade of red. Though somehow she still managed to look upset at him. He knew he had made it at that point. "Also, I promise I will do what I can to make the transition easy. Please remember that I want this to work. I am not trying to make your life harder."

When she spoke next, Avila's temper seemed to have faded. "I knew staying here wasn't much of a choice anyway. I just had to wrap my head around it. I am glad you are going to be there with me, and I promise you I will do what I can to not make a fool of either of us."

Galdren looked past Avila to the window and was surprised to find it was dark already. Even though the days were getting shorter, he hadn't realized they were talking for so long. He turned back to her to see she had also looked at the window and was just as shocked to find the blackness beyond the panes.

"Tomorrow will be a long day for both of us. I will talk to Olva before I leave and have her come up tonight to help you start gathering your things before you retire. We will move everything tomorrow. Please make sure you don't stay up too late tonight. It will be rough on you if you do." He could see her anxiety returning a little.

He knew it was a gamble, but he couldn't stand to see her vulnerable. He got up in one swift motion and knelt by her side before taking her hands in his, and was relieved when she didn't pull away. He sat there holding her hands for a few moments, all the while staring into her eyes and willing her to see the comforting thoughts in his. It didn't take long before he realized it was a mistake for him to get so close to her, and that staring into her eyes was a sweet type of torture.

Before he realized what he was doing, he had raised his hand and brushed her hair behind her ear. The sizzling contact of her skin beneath his fingers jolted him back to his senses. He was at a precipice. It took all his strength to cup her head to bend it, so he could kiss her forehead chastely instead of kissing her the way he wanted to.

As soon as his lips left her skin, he was up and away from her before he did something genuinely terrible again. He knew he would need to guard his actions once they were in the castle. And she was worried about her behavior—ha, she was a saint next to him.

He could tell she was confused by his actions, and maybe a little hurt. He damned himself for that last since he was trying to help alleviate her pain, and he knew he had to get out of the room quickly. "I will send Olva up, and I will be back in the morning so we can get everything moved. I will also talk to Professor Gilbert about the venue change. I doubt it will be a problem for him."

He stepped to the door but turned before his hand touched the handle. "Good night, Avila. Sleep well, and I will see you tomorrow." He didn't dare wait for a response.

The endearing sweetness of his kiss to her forehead had shocked Avila, but his more-than-abrupt departure directly afterward left her reeling. She couldn't make sense of any of his actions. She was still sitting there puzzled when Olva showed up a short while later.

The efficient housekeeper had her up and moving in no time, but she packed in a daze. Her books and clothes all went into the boxes that Olva had brought up and made ready, and any conversation Olva made seemed to pass right over Avila. It wasn't that she didn't respond, but her mind was still whirling with all the possibilities, and she had a hard time focusing. Luckily for her, Olva had never been big on idle conversation.

It did strike her before the woman left that she would miss the capable house-keeper being around every day and wondered if she would ever see her again. Somehow, she knew that Olva's post was here and not at the castle. As they were laying out the clothes she would wear the next day, she suddenly turned to Olva and pulled her into a quick hug.

"Thank you for everything you have done for me while I was here. I don't know if I have said it near enough times as you deserve it." Avila could tell Olva was embarrassed, and she understood, but she wasn't about to let her walk out without letting her know how she felt. Still, she didn't force the moment to linger. Once Olva was gone, she took one last look around to make sure nothing was missed and found that she had mixed feelings about leaving.

If she was willing to admit it to herself, the last several months with Galdren had become like a little piece of time outside the rest of the world. Now the rest of the world was getting ready to intrude again. She wasn't sure she was prepared for that, even with all the ups and downs she had been through.

It was amazing how much her life had changed, and herself along with it. She was still trying to figure out if it was for the better or not, but since there was no going back, she just kept trying to go forward, looking for the positive.

Not finding anything left to do and knowing tomorrow would indeed be a long day in more ways than one, Avila turned to her sleeping chambers. She paused as she remembered that she needed to call and let her parents know about the move. Lissa as well. If she didn't, they would all be upset, and she knew the following day was likely to be long.

The next morning, Avila was up before her timeglass had even warned her it was time to awaken. She took her time with her morning preparations. Not that there was a lot to do, but she felt like she needed to savor the moments. Though this was the location of a turning point in her life, she had to admit that it wasn't all bad. She also knew that this place would forever remain in her heart as where she fell in love.

The thought had struck her as she was getting ready. Things were funny that way, she guessed. She hadn't wanted to admit it, not even to herself, but she was in love with Galdren. Not that it mattered any more now than it had the night before. At that thought, she had to stop what she was doing until she could get herself under control. The last thing she needed that morning was for Olva—or worse, Galdren—to walk in and find her crying.

Even if she could admit her feelings to herself, there was no way under the sun she was ever going to burden Galdren with the knowledge. She could be content with sharing his time as a friend and be happy to be around him, at least. She didn't want to imagine the awkwardness any kind of confession might cause.

As she finished packing the last of her things, she heard movement in her sitting room. She hoped it was Olva with breakfast, but knew it could just as easily be Galdren with the movers. Either way, there was only one way to find out.

She headed out and left her packed box behind. She knew they would get it when they came in to get the rest. It was Olva with breakfast, but Galdren was just coming in the door as well.

"Good, you are up already." His smile was warm and crinkled his eyes just a little. With her recent self-examinations, that smile made it hard for her to remember that she was all right with just being friends. She shoved those thoughts into a dark corner of her mind and returned his smile.

"I've been up for a little while. Everything is ready to go as soon as we finish break-fast and the movers get here." She had to laugh a little at his raised eyebrows. "Oh, my apologies Your Highness, did you actually want to do some packing yourself?"

"Your Highness?"

Avila did not miss the flash that marred Galdren's face. Although she had made the remark in jest, it had obviously bothered him in some way. "In all seriousness Galdren, although I have become accustomed to not using your title, I will have to adjust to using it when we are around other people. Somehow, I doubt a flippant attitude toward the crown prince will be allowed. Honestly, I am surprised I wasn't punished because of my outburst in front of your father, even if it was justified."

Galdren took a deep breath, nodded, then answered, "You're right, Avila; I had not thought about that. I like that you don't call me by my title, and having that change will be unfortunate for me too. The fact is there will be a lot of changes, but we can go over the bulk of that once we get you moved. I want to get this part over with early today. We are both still learning; there will be new things all the time."

By that time, Olva had already brought up a second tray, so they both sat down, now in relative silence. Although the mood wasn't dark, they were both contemplative. After they both finished, Olva came back up and cleared away the trays. While they had been eating, men had been taking what few boxes Avila had down to the vehicles. All that was left now was for Avila and Galdren to leave.

Avila had made sure to set her coat out. Although it wasn't as cold in the capital as it had been up in the mountains, it was still starting to get chilly. Once she had her coat on, they walked out the door for the last time. She looked behind her to her window seat, knowing she would probably never sit there again, and gave one last sigh.

As they walked down the hall and toward the steps, it was strange to think that only two days ago, she was walking the same path with such glee for the first time and thinking about all the times to come. Now she was walking it for the last time. She still wasn't sure how she felt about the whole thing, but it didn't feel entirely right, and she had to reprimand herself mentally for starting to lose control.

Once they reached the bottom, Galdren put his hand on her shoulder. "Wait here a moment. I want to make sure they have everything secure before we go outside."

Surprisingly, he didn't use his com unit. He walked out the door, leaving her alone for a moment. She took the opportunity to look around one last time and say goodbye to the life she had come to know and love. When she felt the tears fall, she quickly wiped them away lest Galdren come back and see them. Hopefully, he wouldn't notice anything amiss.

He returned a few minutes later and gave her a quizzical look, but didn't ask any questions. "Everything is ready now. Let's go." He held out his hand to her and waited until she crossed the room. When she put her hand in his, he opened the door again, and they both walked out.

The feeling of déjà vu was even stronger out here. There were two hovercars with Randy and Baxter standing next to the first one. "We'll be riding in the first transport with Randy and Baxter again. There are a few things in that one, but the majority of your things are in the second hovercar with the gentlemen that moved the boxes."

She shook off the eerie feeling and looked at Galdren. Since his instructions were almost identical to the ones from two days ago, she was ready. It was also what she had expected. "Lead the way."

Randy already had the door open, and Galdren helped her in. He followed her quickly, and the door was shut directly behind him. She was beginning to wonder if her life going forward would always consist of such tight security measures if she had to be near him all the time. The thought made her panic just a little. She wasn't sure she could live with all that pomp. Then again, she guessed she didn't have much choice now that she was going to live in the castle.

She closed her eyes and took a few deep breaths to calm herself. When she opened them, she found Galdren watching her. "It will be all right, you know. Different for you, I'm sure, but you are meant to be part of something bigger, and this will only help you." He was so earnest that she didn't have the heart to tell him she'd never wanted to be part of something bigger.

18. INTO THE CASTLE

Since they were so close to the castle, it was an extremely short trip. As they stopped at the entrance they had used before, the same valet came out, but Randy stopped him before he could take the transport. "There are some things of Lady Durant's in this vehicle. Please take it to the dock for unloading and make sure her boxes make it to her suite." The valet nodded his understanding and quickly took the hovercar in the same direction as the other one.

Everyone except for Avila had already started for the entrance. It only took them a few steps before they noticed that she was not with them. As one, they all turned in her direction. "Lady Durant? Did I suddenly develop a title with the move, or is this something you forgot to tell me about?"

Galdren looked embarrassed. "Will you please walk with me while I explain? I didn't mean to keep it secret; I just planned on telling you later, that's all."

While only barely mollified, Avila agreed to move. Once they were in the confines of the long hall, she turned her gaze to Galdren once more. "So, if you didn't plan on keeping secrets, what is going on?"

Galdren blushed slightly. "Well, while I was taking care of things for the move yesterday, I also took care of something else. Something that I feel is far past due. You see, now that I know who you are, I mean, you know, with the Park Bill and all, well, I thought you should be recognized. I went to my father and explained. He agreed."

By that point, Avila had already figured out the gist of the situation, or she thought she had at least, and she was mortified. "You had your father give me a title for doing that? Why? I've told you before, I don't want anything for what I do, I don't do it for reward, and I don't want it." She could feel herself growing red in the face.

Behind them, Randy made a loud noise. Avila heard and turned to look at him. When she caught his eye and he raised a brow, she realized they were still in the middle of the castle hall, and she had just been yelling at the heir. Her hand came up to her mouth, and she turned an even deeper shade of red. She nodded once to Randy and then turned around silently.

Galdren, clearly confused, glanced between her and Randy, then shrugged and continued moving. They went through several turns and saw a few people, but most looked like servants. It seemed to Avila that they might be taking a longer route to avoid castle traffic. When they finally reached her rooms, she saw two men standing outside. She immediately recognized them. "Lee, Jacob, what are you two doing here?"

"Um, ma'am, we're here to guard you and your room." Lee was replying to her question, but he kept looking at Galdren. He and Jacob both bowed when they saw them approach. It seemed they wanted to make sure they didn't mess up.

Avila had to try hard not to roll her eyes, both at the idea of needing a guard and at their evident desire to impress. Instead, she tried her best to be appreciative. "That is very kind. Can we go in now?" At her innocuous question, they both jumped to open the door. Once it was, Randy and Baxter did a quick once over to make sure nothing was amiss in the rooms and then headed back out, presumably to stand guard with Lee and Jacob. Avila and Galdren entered once the room was cleared.

Now that they were alone again, Galdren gave Avila a curious look as she stood there for a few moments, then took a deep breath before she said anything. "I apologize for acting like a harridan. I told you just earlier today I should watch my actions here in the castle, and the first thing I do when we get here is start yelling at you. I have no sense."

Suddenly, a light bulb came on for Galdren. That was why she went silent after Randy caught her attention. It wasn't that she had given up; she realized where she was and didn't want to cause any embarrassment or issues. By the goddess, at least she had brains—more than him, apparently. "Avila, you had enough sense to stop. I must also apologize for not saying anything. I wanted to tell you once we got to your suite, and we had time to discuss it."

By then, Avila's anger had apparently cooled. She sighed and shook her head as she responded, "Okay, we are here now, and I promise I won't blow up again, so please explain to me what happened."

Galdren was shocked that she was so calm now compared to earlier, but he took the opportunity he was offered. "Well, I told you that I went to my father. I explained to him who you are, and all you had accomplished. He is still quite fond of the bill, by the way. When I laid it all out in front of him, I told him that I thought you should be recognized for everything you have done for the planet and the people. He agreed. He granted you the title of lady. There are no lands that go with it since you are my ward, but there is supposed to be a ceremony this coming weekend to mark it. It was official the moment he signed the papers, though. Of course, Randy and Baxter were there to see, so they knew already, and all the guards assigned to you have been briefed."

Avila started pacing immediately. Galdren watched her in silence as she worked through how she would answer. He only hoped she saw the good that would come of the transition, and not just the difficulties.

When she stopped pacing, she finally looked around for the first time. She then turned to him with raised brows. "This room is huge—and opulent. What am I going to do with this?"

Galdren laughed. The tension that he'd been feeling rushed out of him. At least now, he knew the worst of it was over. "The bedroom is almost as big, and you should see the bath. It's handy being able to pull strings. You are in the family's wing of the castle. My room is right next door, and there is an adjoining room between our rooms that can be accessed from either your room or mine. These suites were made this way for siblings, but since I never had any, this room has always remained empty."

He watched her shift uncomfortably, but it passed quickly and he didn't have an opportunity to ask what was wrong as she said, "So, what all is in the family wing besides bedroom suites?"

Galdren could tell something was bothering her, but she had been so mercurial that day that he didn't want to push his luck. He could understand somewhat; the move couldn't be easy on her, and in general, this whole situation had to be hard. "There are a couple of things you might be interested in, but before I get into them, there are a few ground rules we need to go over. Come sit down with me."

Galdren waved her over to a set of chairs circling a large fireplace. Off to the right of the whole thing was a large bay window with a window seat, and on the far right wall was a set of bare bookshelves. Several boxes were set in front of them.

Before they made it to the chairs, there was a knock, and Lee led a group of men carrying boxes in. The movers had brought the last of Avila's things. Galdren waited until they were gone again before he motioned to the chairs once more.

Avila moved to take a seat. "So, you said something about ground rules? I feel like a teenager again." She said the last with a chuckle.

"Well, I hadn't exactly thought about a curfew, but it would be best if you were back in your room before it got too late. The ground rules I am going to lay out are for your safety, so please don't take them lightly." He waited to make sure she was listening and understood the gravity of what he was saying. She gave him a small nod and waved her hand for him to continue.

"First and foremost, I want you to understand that there will be two guards outside this door when you are in this room at all times. If you decide you want to leave, one of them will go with you as protection. The other one will stay here for two reasons. First, to guard the room against intrusion, and secondly so that there will be constant contact regarding your whereabouts back to this location. Each guard will be equipped with a com unit." Avila looked like she was about to object, but Galdren didn't pause.

"Also, I do not want you to go anywhere outside of the family wing without me. This wing is quite large, and you should be able to keep yourself occupied, but beyond that, there are too many variables. I would feel better if I were with you." He finally paused long enough for her to give input if she wanted to.

She couldn't entirely hide the sigh she tried to stifle, but didn't complain. Instead she answered, "I will follow the rules. That's really not a lot to ask. Is there anything else I need to know about?"

Galdren was glad that she wasn't going to make a fuss. It really was for her own good, especially after the past weekend. He didn't know who he could trust yet, but he felt better having her close to him. It would also help alleviate unwanted rumors if people got to know her, or so he hoped. "The only other thing you need to know is that sometime in the next week, they will be coming in to install com units in your rooms, as well as mine. In the meantime, there are standard ones that we can turn on when we go to bed. Please don't forget."

She didn't answer right away, but eventually turned her face down and whispered, "Thank you for everything, Galdren. I will remember it all and heed your advice."

He could hear the slight tremble in her voice but couldn't for the life of him understand why she was upset. He thought all of his requests were reasonable. He was just trying to take care of her, so why did this have to be hard? He took a breath and counted to ten. He didn't want to start an argument if there wasn't one, and she had said she would heed his advice. Maybe it was just the day taking its toll. He did not need to jump to conclusions. "Avila, I promise it will all turn out all right if you let me take care of things."

Despite his reassurances, Avila started to cry in earnest. Galdren sighed in frustration, but he was still at her side in a moment. He knelt in front of her and took both of her hands in his. "Please explain what is going on. I can't fix what I don't know is broken."

Unfortunately, his words only made her cry harder. Though, she did try speaking through her sobs. "I'm—I'm not angry—it's—it's—just that I'm over—overwhelmed."

That was all she got out before she gave up, but it was enough for Galdren to understand. His features softened immediately, and it took him only a moment to pick Avila up and sit back down in the seat she had been occupying with her in his lap. He cradled her head on his shoulder and held her there until he could feel her tears subside.

After a while, Avila sighed almost imperceptibly, and she pushed herself back away from him. She was just glad he was understanding and not upset over her outburst. She knew she was already sick of all her wayward emotions and the tears they caused. There was no way Galdren couldn't be as well.

She eyed his now-ruined shirt and then looked back up at him. "You know, I'm going to have to quit doing this. Not only will it give the rumor hounds something to talk about, but you won't have enough of a wardrobe left to speak of."

He smiled at her attempt at humor. "Let me take care of the rumor hounds, and as for my wardrobe, well, rest assured that I can cover it." He winked at her, and she had to laugh.

Now that she had cried herself out, she felt better, and although she knew she should move, she was having a hard time finding the motivation. Especially since it was so easy to sit there and joke with him. She sighed, then looked at him one last time—and when she did, she thought she caught an echo of the fire she had seen in his eyes once before. She froze. Her breathing became rapid, and she couldn't see anything now but his smile. Eventually, she realized it looked a little strained. She may have been imagining things, but if his smile was strained, that meant she was pushing it and needed to move.

"Thank you for understanding, Galdren." She stood and turned to face him again. "I know I am emotional, but it is only because you do so much for me, not because I think you are restricting me. I feel special because of you."

She almost bit her tongue after that last admission, but with her recent outburst and her addled thoughts, it wasn't a surprise. At least she hadn't confessed to loving him; that would have been a disaster.

He smiled and stood to join her. "You are already special. It's about time you started seeing it."

He grabbed her hand and brought her to stand in front of the bookcase. From there, she could see out the bay window into the gardens, and it was beautiful. She shifted her attention as he pointed to the boxes. "I will need to leave soon, so you will have the rest of the afternoon to unpack and put everything where you want it. I will be sending Etta over to help as soon as I leave. She works in my suites, and since yours are adjoining, she will now work with yours as well."

Avila was having difficulty ignoring the fact that he had not yet released her hand, but she wasn't going to pull away. It was almost a disappointment when his eyes flitted down after his explanation, and he dropped it quickly as he said, "I didn't get the chance earlier to tell you about the other places you can visit in this wing. The first one obviously is the gardens. You can see them from the window here, but you have to go around to one of the hallway entrances to access the area; there isn't an entrance directly from your room, even if it is on the ground level."

He walked to stand in front of the window and pointed out. From there, she could see a layout of large flower beds with winter-blooming plants on display. It seemed that with the shift in season, the gardeners had already been hard at work to update the garden greenery.

She could see what looked like a hedge maze in the distance and what was most likely a hothouse. She had to admit that she was looking forward to exploring the gardens. It wasn't the woods, but it looked beautiful nonetheless.

19. SETTLED IN

vila's attention was drawn from the gardens when Galdren spoke again. "We also have a library in this wing. It isn't as big as the Great Library in the common wing, but it is still well stocked. You are welcome to go there at any time. If you happen to want to visit the Great Library, you can, just let me know when you would like to go and I will make arrangements to take you."

The library wasn't as exciting as the gardens since she had never been as much into reading as she had been into the outdoors. However, it still appealed to her, especially now that she had a newfound love of reading just for the fun of it. "So, the gardens and the library. Is there anywhere else on your recommendations list?"

He smiled at her quip. "Well, those are the two main rooms in this wing. The rest are bedroom suites like yours and mine. There was a time when the royal family was quite large. Now, most of those are empty and kept closed off. Those are all at the far end of the hall. We are at the end of the hall nearest the commons, and my parents are just down and across from here. The library is directly across the hall from your room. You will also find an entrance to the gardens not far from your door here. Just remember to never go anywhere alone, please."

She had to restrain herself from rolling her eyes at his repeated admonition. The only reason she didn't was that she knew he just wanted what was best for her. That, and she still had a clear image of crying on his shoulder just a short while ago. His actions and concern meant too much to her to disrespect him over something so trivial. "I know you want to keep me safe, and I will do my part. I will make sure to always have one guard with me if I am out of this room."

He laughed at her ill-concealed irritation, which made her all the more annoyed. However, before she could do more than glower at him, he gently placed his hand on her shoulder, effectively stopping any retort. "Avila, I know this is another big change for you, but I also know that you will be able to take it all in stride. There have been many big changes for both of us in a short time, but I think you are adapting wonderfully, and I know this move will not be any different. Besides, this will give you more opportunities."

She wasn't sure she wanted anything to do with the opportunities that being at the castle might provide, but she had two choices: either accept it with grace or fight against the inevitable. With a deep sigh, she let her irritation run out of her. She didn't have anything to be mad at Galdren for anyway. He was just trying to do what he thought was best.

With his hand on her shoulder like it was, she was tempted to take a step forward and embrace him, but decided it would be best not to push her luck. Instead, she looked up at him and smiled. "I know there will be changes, but as long as the important stuff stays the same, I can be happy anywhere."

She wasn't sure what moved her to make that confession so suddenly; maybe it was his hand still on her shoulder, but she knew she had to get some distance between them quickly. She took a step back, and his hand fell away. Without him touching her, she felt a little easier, but still embarrassed. She walked across the room to the table under the guise of inspecting it to put a little distance between them.

She glanced up and saw that Galdren looked confused, but he gave her a moment before following her. "I have other duties I need to attend to today, but I think you can take care of unpacking on your own. I will make sure to send Etta in to help. Also, if you need anything, for now, let one of the guards know. Once the com system is set up, you will be able to call whomever you need."

As much as Avila enjoyed his company, she was glad to see him go. She needed to get her emotions under control before she said something she couldn't take back. "Thank you, I would appreciate the help. I hope to see you again later."

"I'll be back around dinnertime. It will be served in the adjoining room. Feel free to take a little time to look around if you want to." He walked to the door. "Until this evening, then."

Just like that, he was gone again. Avila knew she had made a mess of things, but she hoped he could understand the last few days had been a few of her worst. Reeling from an emotional roller coaster was reasonable as far as she was concerned.

There was no use worrying about it, and she had plenty to keep her busy. She decided to start with unpacking her personal things, which would also give her the opportunity to inspect her sleeping quarters and the bathing room.

Once she walked into the sleeping room, she had to stop and stare for a moment.

Although the room was smaller than her sitting room, it was far more opulent. The bed was a large four-post that dominated one wall. On each side of it were tall windows with dark blue curtains drawn back to let in the light. There was also a large armoire and chest of drawers made of a dark, intricately carved wood along the far wall.

This was far too much for just her. She was almost too afraid to look into the bathing room, but she would have to go in there eventually. She decided to take a quick peek and was not surprised to find that it was just as expansive and elegant as the rest of the suite. There was a deep, carved stone tub inlaid into the middle of the floor with a couple of steps on one side and several knobs on the far side. It looked like it was set up to produce water jets once it was full. The rest of the standard amenities were there as well, but in a stylish and tasteful array.

It was too much. She needed a moment to adjust to the enormity of what was all around her and the fact that she would be living like this for the rest of her life unless Galdren changed his mind and decided he wanted to ship her off somewhere.

The lack of control over her own life, the extent of all the changes, and everything she had been through in the last few days finally overwhelmed her, and she broke down again. Before she had much time to cry herself out, she heard a knock on her bedroom door. She tried her best to clear her tears, but she knew it was a futile effort. When she went to answer the door, she had to look twice before she realized she wasn't looking at Olva. The woman standing before her looked similar, but she was obviously younger. "My apologies, I was—I was distracted. You must be Etta. Are you related to a woman named Olva?"

The woman smiled slightly at the question, even though Avila regretted being so nosey as soon as she asked. However, Etta took it in stride. "I had been warned that you were incurably curious. I am Etta ma'am, and Olva is my older sister. Now, I am here to help you unpack if you still need assistance. Is there anything in particular you would like my help with?"

Avila almost felt like weeping in relief. Etta had the same no-nonsense attitude as her sister, and it felt so familiar. It was nice to have a little bit of something familiar with so many things different. "Thank you, Etta. I was trying to start in here with my personal things, so if you could start with the things in front of the bookshelf, this shouldn't take us long."

After that, they both got to work, and true enough, it didn't take long at all to get Avila's few possessions unpacked and put into their places. Every so often, Etta asked where Avila wanted something to go, but other than that, they both worked in silence until the job was done.

Once they were done, Avila dismissed Etta with her thanks. She was surprised to find that it was still more than an hour until dinner. She did not feel like doing any exploring, and instead decided to get a little sleep, which should help with the sheer mental exhaustion.

She lay down and set the timeglass to wake her in forty-five minutes. That should give her enough time to freshen up before dinner. She fell asleep almost instantly.

It hadn't felt like she had slept at all when she felt a hand brushing her hair off her face. Groggily, she looked up and was surprised to see Galdren looking down at her. His face was so tender it made her heart ache. She blinked once, and the look passed. It made her wonder if she had still been half asleep a moment ago.

Avila sat up and looked at the timeglass before she turned back to him. "I had an alarm set, so I guess it's all right that you woke me a few minutes early."

He glanced over at her timeglass and turned it off before it could trill its alarm. "My apologies. I did not mean to wake you, but I did want to check on you. I knew you had a long day, and there was no response to my knock. I didn't think about the fact that you might be asleep. If you want to freshen up a little bit, you can meet me in the adjoining room."

With a nod, he left her to get ready for dinner. Unfortunately, Avila was still groggy. The nap had done her more harm than good, and she felt more tired now than she had before she had lain down. She hoped dinner would be short; she felt like she needed sleep more than food.

She went into the bathing room and splashed a little cold water on her face, which helped some. After she cleaned up and felt more awake, she decided she was ready to face Galdren across a dinner table.

When she went into the adjoining room, she was surprised to see that it was smaller than her sitting room. It was as long, but narrower. It did have a large window at one end that was dark now, although she was sure it would have another spectacular view of the gardens. The third of the room nearest the window was taken up with a dinner table and a sideboard along one wall. The rest of the room was mostly empty except for a few scattered chairs.

Dinner was already laid out, and Galdren was sitting at the head of the table waiting for her. Instead of sitting at the other end of the table, she took the seat to his left. She hadn't noticed Etta standing next to the sideboard when she first came into the room, but as soon as she sat down, the woman started plating the first serving. It looked like it would be a much more formal meal than any she had had before. She only hoped she could make it through.

Galdren seemed to sense her apprehension about the meal. "Avila, this is only a three-course meal, so it will be relatively short. You said yourself that you needed to get used to life here. I thought tonight would be as good a time as any to start. As of next week, we will have our meals with the rest of the household."

Avila reeled a little at that news but tried not to let it drag her down. She was already too close to the edge as it was. After her waterworks earlier, the last thing she needed was another breakdown in front of Galdren. He had probably seen enough of that from her over the last week to last him a lifetime. Not that she didn't have a cause, but she was getting tired of it herself, so she could only imagine how he felt.

She finally looked up at Galdren and realized he had been watching her while she was in her own inner world again. His face was concerned. There was no telling what her face had shown him, and she couldn't muster the willpower to care overmuch. She did want to let him know she was all right, though.

"Galdren, that news is a little bit shocking to me, and after everything else, it is something I will have to let sink in, but not tonight. I am just too tired. I don't want you to worry about me, please. It has just been a long day, as I am sure you can understand." She could tell her speech did not do much to ease his worry.

She suppressed a sigh and looked down at her plate. The food looked good, at least. She picked up her fork in an attempt to try to eat something even though she really wasn't hungry.

"Avila, I will be here to help you and guide you as I can through this. I don't want you to worry about what is going to happen to you."

She looked up at him and smiled before looking back down. He was so serious, and she knew he wanted her to feel safe, but she just wanted to go back to bed. "I know I can trust you, always." She wasn't sure what made her say that, but it felt right, and at the moment, she just didn't care. She had never been drunk before, but she had been a little tipsy. This almost felt like that.

Galdren didn't say anything for so long that it finally caught Avila's attention and she looked up. When she did, he was smiling. "I'm glad to hear it." That was the last thing said, and Avila was glad for it. Even more so when he didn't mention the fact that she hardly touched her food.

As the meal was being cleared away, Galdren finally broke the silence. "Etta, would you please take care of this and then send someone to Avila's room to assist her in getting ready for sleep? I need to make sure the com units are working, so I will escort her to her room." Etta gave a brief curtsy and turned to continue clearing off the remains of the dinner.

Galdren then turned to Avila and offered his hand. Her brain was still foggy, and it took her a moment to realize that he was trying to help her up. She had completely missed his conversation with Etta. He must have realized that she hadn't caught his cue, so he reached down for her hand and helped her to her feet before he gently turned her around. Then with one hand on her shoulder for support and the other on the opposite arm, he gently guided her from the room.

When they reached the sleeping room, he turned her around and had her sit on the edge of the bed. Once she was seated, he pulled two com units out of an inside pocket of the vest he was wearing. "These two com units are supposed to only be dialed into each other. Once they are turned on, they will only pick up signals from their partner. Since this is only a temporary solution, I felt this was the easiest way. The new com units should be installed within the week."

He turned them both on and put one on the bedside table. He then took the other into the bathing room. He came back a second later. "I need to test to see if I can hear you. Once I walk in the other room, please say something." With that, he turned and walked back to the other room again.

Avila felt a little silly, but she knew she wouldn't get any rest until this was over. As soon as the bathing room door was closed, she leaned closer to the com unit and, in a loud whisper, said, "Hello." She couldn't help the giggles that escaped afterward.

Moments later, Galdren walked back out of the bathing room again. He was fighting to keep from laughing himself. Apparently, the com unit worked, and her giggles had been heard. "Well, these seem to work fine. Just make sure you turn it on each night, and we should have no worries."

Even though the sleeping room door was open, there was still a knock. They both looked over to see a young woman standing in the doorway. "Your Highness, I'm here to help the Lady Durant for the night."

"Yes, of course." Galdren put the second com unit back in his pocket and turned to Avila. "Don't forget that Professor Gilbert will be here in the morning. I will see you again for dinner tomorrow evening, but please feel free to explore if you want to. Good night." Then, with a brief nod of his head, he was gone.

The young woman came into the room and gave Avila a curtsy before she asked where her things were, so she could help her prepare for the night. As tired as Avila was, it took a moment for that to sink in. "I'm sorry, but you don't have to help me get ready for bed. I am perfectly capable of doing that myself." As tired as she was, she wasn't sick anymore, so there was no reason why anyone should need to look after her.

Stricken, the girl obviously didn't know what to do. The answer, however, was taken from both of their hands when Avila tried to stand up. Being so drained and then not eating much had taken its toll on her body. When she stood, the world seemed to tilt a little crazily for a moment and go black. By the time she was back to herself, the young woman had her seated again.

This time, she wouldn't take no for an answer. It didn't take her long at all to help Avila change into her nightclothes, and she was securely tucked into her bed soon enough. It took the last of her remaining willpower to remember to set the timeglass to wake her so she wouldn't be late for her first lessons in the castle. She was asleep before her helper had even left the room, and she had never even gotten her name.

20. NEW NORMAL

Avila had managed to find a door in the alley that was unlocked. She shut it as quietly as she could and tried to find a lock. She nearly screamed in frustration when she found the clasp broken. Still, she put it on the door and hoped it would be enough. She didn't dare try to go farther into the building, as, depending on who the place belonged to, that might cause just as many problems as the guards who had been chasing her.

Mikael had gone to gather a few supplies, so she had been walking alone and was spotted in the main street. Thankfully the guards had called out to each other and inadvertently gave her a head start. It also helped that at least a handful of people had been willing to block her from view as she ran, once they realized what was going on. She only hoped the men had been too busy chasing her to understand it had been intentional. She already owed her people so much; the hope they had shown when their eyes caught hers was enough to drive her forward.

There were no sounds coming from the alley, but she doubted that meant she had lost them. Instead, she looked around to see if there was some place she could hide until they passed. That way, even if they looked in, the room would seem empty. She was lucky enough to find a broom closet, which she shoved herself into. The space was cramped, but it was enough. She then focused on quieting her breathing.

Several minutes later, she heard many heavy sets of footsteps racing by. She nearly jumped when she heard the outer door bang open, but she sagged in relief when she heard one of the men call to the others, "This one opened, but it's empty."

Even though they had passed her location, Avila did not move for several minutes. She was in no position to take chances. Mikael had given her a tiny laser pistol and shown her how to use it, but it was for emergencies only. It would do little good against a whole contingent of guards.

She was almost ready to go ahead and see if she could find Mikael when the door to the closet was flung open. Avila screamed as the guard leered down at her, and he just laughed when her pistol came up. "What are you gonna do with that, Princess? You can't even hold it steady. Look at the way you're shaking."

He was right, too. Part of it was that she was scared to death, but not all. When her finger had tightened on the trigger, it struck her that she was about to kill a man. Even if it was in defense of her own life, she couldn't force her finger to move.

The chance was taken from her when the guard grabbed her roughly by the arm and yanked her out of the closet. Her tiny pistol clattered to the ground and she watched it with wide eyes. She was so terrified that she barely heard the guard say, "You might want to speak to your goddess, Princess. As soon as I get you to the others, the commander has a bullet with your name on it."

Avila was still watching her pistol as the man dragged her out into the alleyway. However, her attention was pulled back to the man holding her when she heard a shot ring out. She screamed as the man's head jerked to the side and he nearly fell on top of her. She didn't need to see the blood that oozed from his temple to know that he was dead.

She looked up to see Mikael, but he was frowning at her, not the man he pulled her out from under. He didn't say anything as he looked around before ducking into the room she had been pulled from. He was back in an instant, and his frown deepened as he grabbed her hand and placed the grip of the gun in her palm.

His voice was low when he said, "Princess, no matter what happens, you must live. I will not always be there to save you. You must learn to save yourself. Taking a life is not easy, but you need to think of how many lives will be lost if you give up. It is a choice that you could not make today, but prepare yourself. It will happen again. When it does, do not hesitate. Hesitation will get you killed."

Avila was still shaken by the whole ordeal, but she managed to swallow her tears and gave Mikael a nod. She knew he was right, but that didn't make it easier.

After her nod, he grabbed her hand and raced back the way she had come. The guards were still out, and they needed to get to safety, even if that meant they would have to finally break down and head back to Ithir. At least the capital was the last place the Trogand would expect her to retreat to.

Despite her continued terror, Avila's hand tightened around the grip of her gun as she raced after Mikael. She only prayed that the next time, she would be ready to face her fear.

Avila sat up with a gasp. All it took was the sight of the posts around her bed for her to remember where she was. Thankfully, the comfort of knowing that she was safe was enough to ease her breathing, though she jumped when she heard a shrill ringing. Her alarm was buzzing, and it took her a moment to find it and shut it off.

At the last moment, she thought about the com unit as well, and shut it off with a cringe. She only hoped Galdren had already been up and out before her timeglass went off so insistently. Her only consolation was that he usually seemed to be up and fully groomed well before her most days.

Due to her disorienting start to the day, she had to rush her morning preparation, and wished she had taken a bath the night before. Unfortunately, there was no time, so she settled for a shower. Thankfully, she managed to finish with just enough time to get settled into the sitting room before there was a knock at the door.

With a "yes" from her, the door was opened, and Professor Gilbert was ushered in by Lee. She could see Jacob just past them, still standing outside the doorway. The sight gave her a bit of a start, even though it shouldn't have. She knew they were supposed to be there, but she had forgotten about them already.

With a sigh, she turned to the professor and put on a smile. There was no use worrying about it. "Good morning, Professor Gilbert. I hope this move hasn't put me too far behind, since it was only a day."

"Well, that will be entirely up to you now. Why don't we get started and see what we can make up today?"

Despite his words, his tone put her at ease. It was surprisingly easy to slip back into her typical routine, even if it was a new location. It only took a few moments to set things up.

The only snag came about an hour after they started, when her stomach rumbled loudly and she realized she hadn't had anything for breakfast. No one had brought anything for her, and she hadn't thought to ask. It was remedied quickly enough; she simply stuck her head out the door and asked how she should go about asking for food to be brought to her rooms, or if she had to go somewhere to eat every morning.

She had to repress a sigh of relief when Lee said that for now, if she required anything, to let them know, and they would have it sent to her room.

It didn't take long before another knock sounded at her door. After Avila opened it, Lee led an unfamiliar young man into the room. He put the tray down, bowed, then left. Avila wasn't sure how she felt about that. It was odd having all these strangers in her personal space and not even having names for any of them, but she wasn't given the chance to dwell on it. As soon as the room was cleared again, Professor Gilbert had her back to her work while she ate, and all other thoughts were soon erased from her mind.

The morning passed quickly after that as she fell back into the familiar pattern of study. It was actually a balm to her frazzled nerves. The familiarity was a soothing anchor in the tumult of the last few days.

It seemed as if little time had passed when a new knock came, but when Avila checked the timeglass, she was surprised to find it was time for lunch already. Lee escorted the same young man that had come in earlier in the day to a table in front of the fireplace.

The lad had already placed the trays, bowed, and was getting ready to leave again, but Avila decided to stop him before he reached the door. "Excuse me, um—thank you."

The boy stopped when Avila spoke, but he didn't look up at her. When she thanked him, he turned a slight shade of pink. She could tell he didn't know how to respond, but now that she had stopped him, he seemed at a loss for how to proceed until he was dismissed. "Also . . . I just wanted to know what your name is, if you are going to be working around here often. If you don't mind, that is."

For some reason, her request made his flush go a little brighter, but he still bowed slightly. "My lady, my name is Michael; thank you for asking."

Avila was a little taken aback when he addressed her by title. She had forgotten already that she had acquired one, but things made more sense now. She also realized she would have to let Michael know he was free to go before he would leave.

"Thank you, Michael. I appreciate your time. I apologize if I have taken up too much of it." She smiled at him and hoped it would make him feel a little more comfortable, but for some reason, his eyes just got wider, and he all but fled from the room.

Avila was at a complete loss as she went to join the professor for their midday meal. It took her a moment to realize he was laughing at her. She had known him for too long to get upset with him, but he obviously had some insight into what had happened, and he found it amusing. "So, tell me, since you think that was so funny, what was that about?"

"Well, that young man now has quite a bit on his mind, and I am sure he is completely awestruck." Avila snorted in disbelief at the thought that anyone could be awestruck with her.

Professor Gilbert shook his head. "Think about it, Avila. When you first found out who Galdren was, how did you feel? How would you feel meeting the queen or king?"

Since she had not yet forced herself to contemplate that question, she did so at his request. He gave her a moment before he continued, "All right, so if you can imagine how you might feel in those situations, then think about this; that young man has a job to do, and to do it, he usually stays out of the way. He may see people, but he never speaks to them. They don't speak to him either. Like all the other servants in the castle, they are just part of the castle. There are, of course, some few exceptions, but they are usually personal maids and bodyguards. Knowing that, you should understand that you took him out of his element, and it completely flustered him. From the looks of it, he was a little starstruck as well."

Avila glowered at him. She could understand what he was saying, but it made no sense to her. "I can understand the concept of being awkward around someone like the king, or anyone else of importance for that matter, but I am a nobody. I don't even have any say over my own life; how can I possibly intimidate others?""

After her heated denial, the professor sat and watched her. It didn't take Avila long to realize why. That was the first time she had ever directly spoken to him about what was going on, and she had done so in a forthright way. There was no taking it back.

After watching her face turn from heated to pale to flushed again, the professor spoke. "Avila, no matter what else has happened, you are not now, nor have you ever been, a nobody. The fact of the matter is that you are somebody to be reckoned with, now more than ever. You have a brilliant mind, and now you will have even more opportunities to make things happen. Like it or not, you have been given a title. You will have to get used to the responsibilities of that, along with everything else."

Avila sighed. She knew Professor Gilbert was right. She wasn't thinking about the responsibilities of a title, only the difficulties. She still didn't believe that what she had done was worthy of one, and could see how it might cause conflict with others both in and out of her field. Still, her mentor managed to make her see both sides to the argument, even when she didn't want to. At least he had done so without getting into her outburst. She sent up thanks to the goddess for that small favor.

"You're right, of course. I still can't see myself as the Lady Durant, but I can see what you are talking about and how it could help with my work in the future. I don't have to like it, though. I don't want all the people around me to be strangers. Does it always have to be that way?"

He laughed at her again, earning another glare. "Easy, I don't mean to earn your ire. Take your time, be polite, say thank you, and they will come around. Just don't jump on them like you did that poor young man today. Once they get used to you and see what kind of person you are, they will not be strangers to you, but it will take time."

His answer helped her relax a little. "This is going to take so much getting used to, and I don't have the time to adjust." She almost felt a little hopeless again at the prospect, but she kept her chin up. She didn't want him to see her inner conflict. They ended up passing the rest of the meal in relative silence.

When the young man came back to clear things away, Avila could tell he was nervous, and he kept his eyes averted from her. She did her best to stay out of his way. However, when he was done, she could not stop herself from thanking him before he walked out the door. She didn't make such a big deal of it with the hope of making it less awkward, but the young man still turned bright red as he managed a bow before he left the rooms.

The ordeal left Avila completely frustrated and made it hard for her to concentrate on her work after lunch. How was she going to get used to life in the castle if she not only had to try to avoid embarrassing herself by being foolish around Galdren, but also had to worry about trying to act the way servants think a lady should act? The whole thing was infuriating.

Her work suffered from her distraction, and the professor made a point of saying something about it before he left. "Avila, I know you are going to need some time to adjust, but you are already behind. We can only afford to allow so much time to pass before it becomes a problem."

That was the closest thing to a reprimand she had ever received from him, and it embarrassed her that it was necessary more than it hurt her feelings. She knew he would not have said anything if he wasn't trying to look out for her. It seemed as if everyone was doing that as of late.

"I understand, Professor. I will do my best to focus during the time you are here. You deserve my undivided attention, at the very least, for taking the time to help me." She wasn't able to look at him while she spoke.

He put his hand on her shoulder in a fatherly gesture. She finally looked up at him, and he smiled. "I understand the stress you are under. I know that this is taking a toll on you, and I don't expect you to not be affected, but you can't wallow in it either. Numerous opportunities are waiting just outside this door for you to walk out and discover them. All you have to do is find the courage and the willpower to do so."

She still wasn't convinced that she wanted anything to do with any of those opportunities, but she knew she also wasn't ready to give up either. She gave him a real smile as reassurance that she understood. "Thank you. I promise that I won't give up."

With a small squeeze of her shoulder, he let her go and turned to gather his things. "I will see you at the regular time tomorrow morning."

After his departure, Avila sat in silence for several minutes, trying to wrap her head around the last few days. Her already tumultuous life had taken on so many changes; it was hard to take it all in stride.

After sitting there for several moments, she came to a sudden decision. It was a couple of hours until dinner, and there was no point in sitting there stewing over things. If she was going to get used to her life in the castle, then there was no time like the present to get started.

Timidly, she opened her door, and two heads turned in her direction. Both faces were unfamiliar to her. The shift must have changed, and Lee and Jacob must be gone for the day. "Hello, um, I was wondering if it would be all right if I could go for a walk in the gardens? I know Galdren said—well—would one of you please come with me?" That was a lot more awkward than she had planned, but she was committed now. There was no way she was going back into self-imposed isolation.

The man on the right spoke up first. "Yes, ma'am, I can walk with you anywhere you choose to go in this wing. My name is Angelo, ma'am." He bowed with his introduction. She couldn't help but smile at him. Finally, someone that volunteered their name! She supposed it made sense since they would be working closely with her, and she couldn't just call them "hey you" all the time. It still made her happy.

She looked to the man on the left, and he bowed slightly as well. "Ma'am, I am David. It is an honor." It made her pink up a little bit at his compliment, but she was thrilled that these two didn't seem to be like the servant earlier. Maybe this wouldn't be as bad as she thought.

"Thank you, Angelo and David. I appreciate your help." She smiled at both of them, and she could feel herself relaxing just a little.

"Angelo, I have a couple of hours, or near so, until dinner, and I would like to take a look around the gardens. It looks like a beautiful day to do so. Would it be okay if we just go walk around for a bit?" At her request, he stepped away from the door and turned to look at her expectantly.

Before she could take another step, David stopped her. "Ma'am, if you are going to be walking around in the gardens, you might want to take a coat. It is chilly outside." She chided herself for being so thoughtless and quickly ran to get her jacket.

She was back in just a moment, and then she and Angelo were on their way. She had only gone a short distance when Angelo stopped her and pointed to a small door to her left; the exit to the gardens. She had missed it, since it was set back in a hallway.

She could hardly contain her excitement as she walked outside into the brisk air. Since it was late afternoon, the sun was low in the sky, but there was still plenty of sunlight to explore by. It wouldn't get dark until it was time for dinner. She started to wind her way through the manicured shrubs and flowers, taking her time and thoroughly enjoying the fresh air.

21. MEETING THE QUEEN

Avila got caught up in the beauty of the garden, and noted that whoever took care of the place seemed to be making sure that flowers bloomed year-round. The ones that were currently in bloom would usually not be on Aril, so it had to be a conscious effort.

Still, she knew she didn't have a lot of time and wanted to check the hothouse, so she shook off her marvel and headed that direction. On the way, she noticed there were also small animals around, which made her positively giddy.

When she reached the hothouse and opened the door, she was immediately struck by the strong perfume of hundreds of flowers. Inside wasn't just an array of blooms, but a variety of some of the most exotic flowers Avila had ever seen. She could identify most of them, at least from textbooks, but there were several varieties there that she had never seen before.

After walking around for only a few moments, she was struck by the need to be alone. "Angelo, would it be possible for me to look around here alone for a short time, please?"

She had stopped abruptly, and her question clearly took him off guard, as he didn't answer right away. "Look, I know you are supposed to stay with me at all times, and I don't want to undermine those orders, but this is an enclosed space. If it makes you feel better, you can sweep the room before you leave. I would just like a little bit of privacy to look around before we have to go back, please."

She could tell that her argument had swayed him. There was no good reason for her not to be able to have a little alone time in here, and they both knew it, but he took the precaution of sweeping the room anyway. Once he was done and back by her side, he gave a quick bow. "I'll be right outside when you are ready to leave, ma'am."

"Thank you, Angelo." Once he was gone, she turned to immerse herself in the flowers around her. She went to the back of the room where she found a group of large purple blooms that she had never seen before. They were striking and she wished she had her sketchbook. The next time she came out, she would have to bring it with her.

The perfume they gave off was intoxicating, something close to jasmine but muskier. She liked it. She wanted to touch them, but she wasn't sure how they would react. She was all too familiar with plants that had violent reactions to contact. Until she knew more about that particular specimen, she didn't want to take any chances.

As she knelt to admire the group of flowers, something in the dirt caught her eye. Tiny weeds were growing in the flower bed. Just a few; someone probably hadn't been to see to these in a few days. It could be the pests were meant to be there, but she doubted it. They were common weeds, a fast-growing and problematic plant in most gardens. With their size, they had probably only been growing for a matter of days, but left unattended, they could choke out other plants in no time at all.

She made a spur of the moment decision and bent down to pull them up. She was careful not to touch the unnamed flowers, but she dug into the dirt and made sure she got the weeds out from the root up. She was so engrossed in what she was doing that she didn't hear the slight rustling behind her, and it wasn't until someone called out that she realized she wasn't alone.

She managed to stifle a scream, but she jumped up, barely missing the flowers on the way and dropping her handful of weeds. To her complete embarrassment, it was the most attractively dressed woman she had ever seen. She was immaculate in a business suit and heels, and her long, honey hair was the same shade as Galdren's, although some of it was going grey. She was beautiful. As Avila stared, it finally struck her that this woman was probably the queen, and she was doubly mortified as she stood there with her muddied hands.

Before Avila could make a move or say anything, the queen smiled at her, which took her completely by surprise. "You must be Avila. I am Queen Lorne. Your guard told me I could find you in here somewhere, but I wasn't expecting to find you digging in my garden. Are my gardeners not doing their job well enough?"

She was still smiling, so Avila didn't think she was too upset, but this was the queen, after all. She finally found the sense to move again and bowed low. "Your Majesty, my apologies if I have offended you. I was caught up in the moment and saw these small weeds growing. I only thought to pluck them before they got any larger."

The queen's tinkling laughter took Avila entirely by surprise. "Please, relax. I am not concerned that you pulled up a few weeds. I am only surprised to find you bold enough to do so. Although, to be honest, from everything I have heard, I suppose I should not have been. Though, I am happy to see the care with which you treated the other flowers while you did so."

Avila was even more shocked now than she was before. Still, she supposed it wasn't surprising that the most powerful woman in the world had heard about her and her doings; she was Galdren's mother, after all. "Please, there is a wastebasket over here where you can dispose of those, and a bench where we can sit and speak."

Avila picked up the weeds she had dropped and followed the queen around the corner. She was pleased to see a small fountain with benches on three sides she had missed earlier. She tossed the weeds in the indicated wastebasket and sat stiffly beside the queen.

"Now, would it surprise you to learn this is all my doing—the gardens, the hothouse, all of it?" The queen waved her hand around as she spoke to indicate everything around them, and Avila was awestruck. The flowers in the hothouse were extraordinary. It struck her then that the queen may also have planned for the animals to be in the gardens outside.

"Ma'am, if I may, this place is beautiful, and there are things in here that I have never even heard of and—well, I know that may not mean anything to you, but I study these kinds of things, and—this is really something." She knew her compliment was a little tepid, but she was sincere, and she hoped that it came through over her awkwardness. She would eventually get over that, she hoped.

The queen laughed again, but it was muted this time. "I can see why my son admires you. You are sincere and straightforward. Those traits are not always easy to find, and it's refreshing." Avila blushed at the mention of Galdren. She blushed even brighter when it struck her that the queen was saying that Galdren had told her he admired Avila.

The queen continued smiling while she gave Avila a moment to collect herself. While Avila struggled with her swirling thoughts of what Galdren had been saying to his mother about her, she was also trying to figure out what to say to this impressive woman. That was when she remembered her encounter earlier in the day and how the servant had reacted to her; she knew she couldn't keep stumbling over herself. She recognized the queen's polite smile; she had been trying to use the same one earlier herself.

Recognizing that gave Avila a slight boost of confidence. Although she still felt intimidated, she could tell the queen really was interested in speaking to her. "Well, Your Majesty, I hadn't always believed I would be appreciated for being so outspoken, but thank you for the compliment." Avila was finally able to return the queen's smile, and she could feel something loosening up inside herself.

This time the queen's smile broadened, and Avila could tell it was with sincere pleasure. "Please, Avila, there is no need to continue to call me Majesty, ma'am will be fine."

Something told Avila that level of comfort with the queen was not a regular thing. Still, given her history with Galdren and her own personal proclivities, she wasn't going to complain. If the queen was all right with things being a little less formal, it was okay with Avila.

"Thank you, ma'am. I will try to remember that." Now that Avila was able to calm down, she was overcome again by the fact that these gardens were all there by the queen's will.

"Ma'am, can you tell me more about the flowers in this hothouse? There are so many that I don't recognize, and some even look like they might not be from Aril."

The queen's smile became even brighter than it had been. "It is wonderful that you were able to figure that out with just a brief examination! There are several here that come from a variety of planets. The one you were examining comes from Maru. It has a great deal of tropical and subtropical climate areas. That particular specimen grows to be much larger in the right climate, but it is somewhat stunted here."

Avila could tell the plants were a passion for the queen, and she couldn't help but get excited. She had never had many people to talk to that were as interested as her in the variety of plant life. If she had not been called into ecology to further her goals, she would have gone into botany.

Before she could get on a roll and start asking questions, they were interrupted by a quiet noise behind them. They both turned at the same time to see Angelo and another guard standing a short distance away. "Your Majesty, my apologies for interrupting, but I just received a call from Prince Galdren. He asked that I remind the Lady Durant that dinner will be served in thirty minutes and to ask her to please not be late," Angelo said with a bow, then waited for a response.

Avila noticed the queen suppress a quick sigh. "Thank you for the notification. If you could wait outside for a moment, I will make sure she will be out shortly."

She then turned back to Avila, but her smile was not as warm as it had been.

"I had hoped that we would have more of an opportunity to talk. I will be looking forward to continuing our conversation at some point soon." With that, the queen stood up, and Avila quickly followed.

"If you have no problem with it, I would like to visit with you. I can send a message ahead to make sure you are available." Avila was surprised—both at the fact that the queen was asking her instead of commanding an audience, and, most surprisingly, that the queen seemed to be looking forward to it.

"Thank you, ma'am. That would be wonderful. Any afternoon would work fine—or any time you are available, of course," Avila finished with a blush.

"I would not disturb you while you are in class, so an afternoon will be fine, or perhaps this weekend, before the party. By the way, speaking about the party, do you have anything to wear?" The question took Avila by surprise. She had not thought about what to wear, much less having to get anything.

"I'm not sure, ma'am. What would be appropriate?"

The queen smiled knowingly at her response. "Well, since it is going to be a formal affair, a formal dress would be most appropriate. We can make sure you have something, of course. I will come by later this week and bring a few things with me." The queen's offer made Avila blush, but she tried to control it. Although she hadn't thought about that aspect of her new life, she realized that it shouldn't have been a surprise; of course she'd need new clothes to go with her new title. She only hated the part that it forced her to rely on others.

With a slight bow again, she said, "Thank you. I appreciate the kindness, and will be looking forward to your visit."

The queen smiled again. "Please, I am sure it will be enjoyable. For now, let us get back before my son sends more people to fetch you."

With that, they both headed outside. Once they were with the guards, Avila could see there were several waiting for the queen. With a quick wave, the queen headed off in the opposite direction of where Avila needed to go.

Avila returned the wave and then headed back the direction she had come. Angelo was directly behind her. She paused in her walking and turned to look at him. "Thank you for that opportunity. I really appreciated getting to visit that wonderful place in silence."

He gave her a nod. "My lady, thank you for your kindness."

Avila was beginning to understand what it meant, not only to be in the castle, but also to have responsibilities. She didn't want to make things awkward, so she turned back with a smile and continued walking.

She made it back to the room with just a few minutes to spare. She really didn't have time to freshen up, but did anyway; she thought showing up at the table with dirt on her hands would be far more impolite than arriving a few minutes late.

Thankfully, Galdren understood her tardiness. Especially when she relayed what had kept her, though he did seem taken aback at the reminder that she needed a dress. At least he looked reassured, and perhaps a bit amused, that his mother already had plans to rectify the lack.

Avila wasn't thrilled about his suggestion of a whole new wardrobe as well, but his argument that she needed to dress the part of a member of the household made sense. She grudgingly agreed to the fitting, and the rest of the meal was spent in comfortable conversation.

Once the meal was finished, the two of them bade each other good night, and headed to their respective rooms. It was still too early for sleep, so Avila decided it would be a great time to vo-im her parents. They were both glad that she seemed to be settling in, and happy that she had met the queen and it had gone well.

Avila thought it was a little strange that they were so excited about that—not about the meeting, but that she got along with the queen. However, she was beginning to get tired, and she knew she still needed to vo-im Lissa as well. When she mentioned it, they seemed a little reluctant to cut the conversation short, but didn't argue. Although, Lila did make Avila promise to call back soon with more time to spend going over everything new.

As soon as she disconnected with her parents, she immediately called Lissa. She had no doubt her friend had plenty of questions, and couldn't put it off; not without Lissa going off on a reminder of what best friends meant the next time they spoke. The thought of that had her chuckling when the line connected and Lissa's face filled the screen.

Lissa must have caught the sound, as she immediately grinned as she said, "I knew it! You said you weren't sure about the move, but you're enjoying it, aren't you?"

Avila gave her friend an exasperated look, but didn't get to respond before Lissa continued, "So what's it like? Where did they move you? Are you still close to Prince Hottie? Is he still being extra nice to you? Do you have servants?"

Despite the nature of the deluge, Avila chuckled at the back-to-back questions.

That had been Lissa's nature since they met, and Avila was comforted by the familiarity, even if she wasn't sure about her answers. Still, there was no point in worrying Lissa when there was no real reason to worry. "Okay, one question at a time. First, yes, I am in the rooms next to Galdren's, though I wish you would quit calling him that. He is my friend." She paused and pursed her lips when Lissa rolled her eyes, but didn't call her out. Instead, she tried to answer the rest of the questions. "Yes, I do have servants, but it's all a little surreal. For now, I think it's going to take time to get used to."

Lissa gave her a dirty look, but Avila could tell it was teasing. Especially when her friend exclaimed, "I'm so jealous. I know the situation might not be what you planned, but you can't tell me you regret it. We both know that would be a lie."

For a moment, the reminder made her think of her relationship with Galdren. Would it have been better to have never met him? Perhaps, but she still had to admit that Lissa was right. She managed a soft smile as she responded, "No, I can't say I regret it. I may flounder sometimes, but I'm not sorry it happened, even if I wish the situation was not what it is."

Lissa must have noticed the melancholy note in her friend's voice, because she immediately changed the subject to the shenanigans going on at the university. After that, the conversation flowed into a detailed description of Avila's new rooms, but by that time, she was sufficiently cheered by Lissa's awe. The conversation helped her put things in perspective.

Even so, she was glad when she had to stifle a yawn and Lissa agreed to let her go so she could get to sleep. Avila was in a shockingly good mood when she finally made her way to bed.

22. NOT SO BAD

The next morning, Avila was up before her alarm, due to another nightmare. At least this one had not been particularly bloody. Despite the dream, she was glad she'd woken early. It gave her the chance to use the bath for the first time, and she needed to destress. She had thought about it the previous night, but it had been late when she finally got off the line with Lissa. Plus, her lady's maid, Meru, had come in right after, and she hadn't wanted to bother the girl. At least she had managed to get Meru to smile before she left. It was nice to know she was making some headway in not being a stranger to all the servants.

After she finished and dressed, she went out to the sitting room and sat in the bay window, looking out over the gardens. The sun had started coming up a short while earlier, but it still had not peeked up above the buildings surrounding the courtyard. As she was looking out and admiring the rosy glow on the slight cover of frost, she noticed that there were several people scattered about the plants. It took her a moment to realize they were tending to them. It even looked like one person might be feeding some of the animals. That explained how they could have enclosed gardens with small animals that didn't eat every plant in sight.

She sat enjoying the sunrise for a while, absorbed in the activities outside, and fascinated once again with how the frost slowly started to melt as the sun showed its face. She could not feel the chill of the air outside through the window; it was well insulated. It had her almost wishing she had decided to go for a short walk in her spare time to enjoy the morning crispness, but she knew she didn't have that much time to spare now. It gave her a small feeling of glee to know that, if she had wanted, she would have been allowed to, even if she couldn't go alone.

The quiet knock on her door brought her out of her reverie. She knew it was probably the professor, so she turned to the door as she called out and greeted him with a smile as he entered. For some reason, she was feeling very optimistic. Things were starting to fit into a pattern again, and it hadn't taken much time. Although she knew more changes were coming, the things she had experienced already gave her hope that she would be able to adjust better than she had thought. It didn't hurt that she found she was happy with most of the arrangements—at least, the ones that mattered to her.

The professor smiled at her, then quickly got to work setting things up for the day. Though there was some small talk between them, it faded as lessons started in earnest. The pattern their lives had been in for months now was so familiar it was easy to fall into, no matter the change in location.

There was a brief distraction for both breakfast and lunch, but Avila was pleased to note that Michael, who seemed to be the one assigned to wait on her suite during the day, did not get embarrassed at her thanks, and even had a small smile in return. Although she didn't make a big deal about it with the professor, she was secretly delighted.

After lunch, the day slipped smoothly back into the routine. As the days were wont to do when she was fully absorbed in her work, it was the end of their time together before she realized that much time had passed.

As the professor was packing up the last of his things, Avila looked out the window to see a bright blue sky. It only took her a moment to decide that she was not going to spend her afternoon indoors. By the time the professor finished, Avila had already grabbed her coat and was walking out the door with him, much to the surprise of all three males.

It was Angelo and David again, whom she smiled to as she walked out. She gave the professor a quick wave goodbye, then turned to Angelo. "Angelo, could we please head outside again today? It is quite beautiful."

"It would be my pleasure, ma'am." His accompanying bow was short, and since she already had her coat, he motioned for her to lead the way.

Once they were outside, it did not take Avila long to get lost in the pathways once again. She stopped near the hedge maze, and considered exploring it a bit, but decided that would have to wait. She had time, but not enough to potentially get lost for a few hours.

Instead, she started to head back toward the castle entrance and finally noticed the way the walls came up on all four sides of the gardens. She then turned to Angelo with curiosity. "Could you tell me what is surrounding this area besides the royal apartments?"

"Well, ma'am, we're facing the royal apartments now, as you know. To the left is the common access area of the castle. Although there are windows from there looking into this area, there is no direct access from there. To the right are the servants' quarters, the kitchens, and several other functional areas of the castle. There is also no direct access from that area to this one. The gardeners are let in through the area behind us. There is a set of doors back there for staff use and for the counselors and other nobility that have quarters in that part of the castle. However, there aren't many that live there since it was not designed for families."

His explanation was long, but it gave her a much better idea of how things were laid out. It made her shiver a little to think that there might be people watching from unseen windows. At least, since access was so limited, it was highly doubtful she would actually run into many people.

"Thank you." By that time, they were already back in the hallway. It had been an uneventful walk, but enjoyable, especially since it wouldn't be much longer before it got too cold to spend a lot of time outdoors. It was a good thing there was a library close at hand to keep her occupied.

She left Angelo at the door to her suite with a wave and her thanks. He bowed and closed the door behind her. Since it was still a short while until dinner, Avila thought about calling her mother before she had to get ready, but her plans were interrupted by a knock.

Angelo opened the door when she called out and bowed as he said, "Ma'am, there is a messenger here for you."

Avila was thrown since she had not been expecting anyone, but quickly regained her composure. "Please, show them in." The woman that entered was dressed in finer livery than she was used to seeing. She also had a small rose embroidered on the front of the shoulder of her jacket that Avila had never seen previously.

The woman bowed briefly before speaking. "Lady Durant, I have a message from Queen Lorne. She has asked that I wait for your response." With that, the messenger handed her a small envelope.

The envelope itself was of fine parchment and sealed with wax, something Avila had never seen before. When she broke the seal, she found the note was handwritten on the same paper. It was short and to the point. The queen wanted to know if she could make three in the afternoon the following day work, even though it was a little earlier than she would typically have been finished.

The queen had said she would try to come to visit that week, but Avila had not expected a written request, much less a messenger waiting for her reply. It was a little overwhelming, but she knew she couldn't keep the woman waiting for long.

"Would you prefer a written response?" Avila knew it was silly, but she was a little intimidated by the thought of having to respond to the request in writing. Even though she knew she didn't have to measure up to the queen, a part of her felt like it would be insulting to follow up her invitation with anything less than perfection as well. She also knew she wouldn't be able to come up with a perfect written response on the spot.

"I can take either a written response or a verbal one if you would prefer, ma'am." Avila tried to hide her relief at the woman's words.

"Thank you! Would you please tell Her Majesty that three o'clock tomorrow will work perfectly? I will make sure to be ready for her arrival."

The woman bowed again, then backed to the door. After she had left, Avila thought about how she would explain to Professor Gilbert. She was sure he would understand, especially if she put in extra effort to get done early.

With the distraction, it was close enough to dinnertime that she went ahead and cleaned up. Once she was ready, she walked into the adjoining room to find that Galdren had not yet arrived, but Etta was setting up the sideboard with the courses. Every meal she had eaten in the castle so far had been superb, even when she hadn't felt like eating, and this one looked like it wouldn't be any exception.

She didn't want to bother Etta, so she went to her seat while she waited for Galdren. Etta was very much like Olva in that small talk was not something she was big on.

It wasn't long before the door to Galdren's suite opened, and he entered the dining room. While the door was open, Avila caught a glimpse of a room almost identical to her own, but it was blocked from view quickly.

Avila stood as Galdren walked in. His smile at seeing her already waiting for him was contagious, and she gave him one in return. "Did you wait long?"

"No, I only sat down a moment ago."

Galdren walked behind her chair and placed his hand on it. When she realized what he was waiting for, she jumped to sit quickly. Even though she was used to his manners, she had become distracted by his nearness. Once she was seated, he pushed her seat in and took his own.

Etta began to plate the first course as soon as they were both comfortable. Avila waited until it was plated and Etta was back by the sideboard before speaking. "I know you said you were going to ask your mother something about a tailor when she came to visit, but she has asked to come tomorrow afternoon. I wasn't sure if you had the opportunity to speak with her yet."

Galdren looked up from his meal. "Yes, I spoke to her about it earlier today. What time is she expecting to be here?"

"She has asked to come at three. I know it is a little early, but I am sure I can juggle my workload with Professor Gilbert." At Avila's response, Galdren frowned slightly.

"Three? I will not be available until at least half after four—ah, well, I understand. I am sure you will have a wonderful visit." Avila was mystified by Galdren's answer and a little bit worried that it would just be her and the queen, but from their first brief meeting, she had hope that they would get along fine.

"I certainly hope so, although the prospect of picking out a wardrobe in her presence, I must admit, sounds a bit daunting. She seems to have a smart sense of style, and I am not sure I fit into that category." Avila forgot for a moment that although she was comfortable around Galdren, they were talking about his mother, as well as the queen. When she realized how it might sound to him, she looked at him a bit horrified, only to find that he was smiling at her.

"You have nothing to worry about. You'll be in great hands as far as that goes, but I would advise you to let her have her way; things will go much smoother for you. Take it from my own experience." He was almost grinning by then, so Avila wasn't sure if she should believe him or take it as teasing.

After that, they both settled into the meal with small talk and soon finished. Although it had only been a few days, Avila was already getting used to how their dinners were proceeding; familiar, but formal. She only hoped things wouldn't be too different once she began to attend dinners with the household.

She still had not had the opportunity to talk about that with Galdren, and this night was not any different. After dinner was over, he had to leave again.

Although Avila was in the palace with Galdren so close, it did not change the fact that he was a busy man. Sometimes, it felt like she was seeing him less now than she had previously, though she tried not to worry about it. Instead, she took some time to vo-im her mother, like she had promised.

As soon as the screen came to life, she smiled at the woman that had raised her. Lila was alone this time, but that was all right. Avila was just glad to be able to speak to her parents at all. "How was your day, Mom?"

"Fine. Not much out of the ordinary. It's you I'm worried about. How are you settling in? Are you eating like you should?"

Avila wanted to chuckle at her mother's worry, but she managed to keep it in. It wasn't as though the woman didn't have justification for the question. It had happened once or twice that Avila got too caught up in one project or another and forgot to eat. She managed a nod, though she couldn't keep from grinning. "Of course. Everything is fine so far. It's even getting easier to deal with everyone. Plus, I'll be getting a new wardrobe tomorrow. Queen Lorne is supposed to visit in the afternoon."

A look flashed through Lila's eyes that Avila was unsure how to interpret. It had almost seemed worried, but the following grin made her unsure. However, Lila started talking again, and she didn't get to ask. "So, I know you said last night that you got to meet the queen, but you didn't say much about what happened. What did she tell you?"

The question seemed oddly worded, but Avila tried her best to answer. "Not much really. We talked about the gardens and her hand in them, and then a little about the ball." Avila paused as she was reminded of another question she had. "By the way, will you and dad be attending this weekend? I didn't get to ask yesterday."

Avila knew she wasn't imagining it this time. Her mother definitely seemed nervous, and she looked away as she answered, "No, dear, Thomas and I have a company function we have to attend that night." She'd looked back by that point, but Avila could only see concern as she continued, "I'm really sorry. I know it would have meant a lot to you if we could be there, but I promise, you'll be fine. All that mess with the rumors should be cleared up now. They didn't release a public statement or anything, but when you moved, they put it into the public records that you are a ward of the royal family, even if they didn't say why."

Avila couldn't hold back a frown. "I guess that does clear things up, but somehow I doubt it will make all my problems go away."

Lila gave her a comforting look. "I know. I wish I could erase it all for you, but you are strong enough to get through it. Just remember that you have people that care about you, and you'll be fine."

Avila still wasn't convinced, but she also didn't want to dwell on it. Instead, she asked about the function her parents would be going to. After that, the conversation didn't last long. Avila promised she would call again when she had time, and Lila reassured her everything would work out once again before they hung up.

23. VISIT

Avila was awoken the next morning by her alarm, but she quickly turned over to stop it. She thought back again to how that must sound to Galdren on the other end and was thankful she had gotten to it quickly this time.

With the busy day she knew she had in front of her, she didn't want to dally long, and when she walked out to her sitting room, she found that she was early again. Seeing that, she was able to relax a little and thought about watching the sunrise, but instead decided to walk to her table and start setting things up for the day. She wanted to be ready to start as soon as the professor showed up.

Once she was done, it was still a little early, so she decided it couldn't hurt to go watch the sun rise the rest of the way while she waited. Although the sun was mostly up, it had barely cleared the buildings of the square. The frost was still glistening and thick everywhere.

She didn't get much of a chance to appreciate what looked like the start of another beautiful day, however, as a quick knock soon announced the professor's arrival.

When he came in, he looked slightly startled to see everything ready to go, but it only showed in his slightly raised eyebrow. Avila smiled at him. Having the ability to know what he was thinking without having to ask was something she appreciated, and knowing he could do the same for her felt comforting. It had been nice having someone she was close to nearby over the past few months; it made things a lot easier to handle.

Those thoughts hit her out of nowhere, and she had to turn from him for a moment. She hoped he wouldn't think anything was wrong. It appalled her that she was so emotional these days, and it always came out of nowhere.

She was back to rights shortly and met him at the table. "Professor, I would like to ask a favor this morning. I have a little bit of an ulterior motive for having everything ready when you got here."

He raised his eyebrow at her again, but she just gave him a wry smile and continued, "Her Majesty, Queen Lorne, has asked for an audience this afternoon. She would like to come to visit me, actually. The thing is, she said she would need to come a little early, like at around three. I accepted the invitation with the hope that I would be allowed to finish my work early today. I promise I won't skip anything; I would just like to make as much haste as possible."

She finished the last part in a hurry before the professor could interject. He didn't make any attempt to, however. He shook his head at her instead. "Of course. I would never think of inconveniencing the queen. I will make sure you have everything you need to be done before three. The rest will be up to you."

Avila grinned at him and sat down, ready to get started. The professor tried and failed to hide his laugh as he got right into it.

Avila made sure to concentrate on what she had in front of her and found that the day was passing quicker than she realized. Breakfast and lunch both came and went with her barely taking any time for them. With the extra effort, she was able to finish the day's lessons with time to spare.

Once she completed her last lesson of the day and the professor was getting ready to leave, he commented, "I know you can't keep up that pace every day, but if you can find the motivation to try at least a little, you will be graduating in no time. I shouldn't be, but I am surprised again by what you can accomplish when you put your mind to it."

Avila wasn't sure if that was a compliment or not. If she'd put in extra effort every day, she might have already been able to catch up, but with everything going on, she had done what she had to and no more. She knew it wasn't a terrible thing, but she felt a little bad at his reminder that she hadn't tried harder.

The professor frowned at the shadow that passed over her face. "That was not meant to be a reprimand. I know you are already working hard, and there is no need to push yourself harder. You just never fail to impress me when you do push yourself."

Avila blushed a little at his compliment that time. "Thank you, Professor. I know you were not trying to criticize. I just thought that I might have pushed myself a little harder, but I know I don't want to burn out either. Thank you though, I know I wouldn't have gotten even this far without you." As far as she was concerned, she didn't think she would ever be able to thank him enough.

Her words brought a smile to the professor's eyes, and a glint of pride before he quickly gathered his things. With a quick wave back to Avila, he was out of sight once the door closed.

Avila had finished before usual, but she didn't have much time before the queen would arrive. She looked around to make sure everything was still in order, then went to freshen up. Not that she needed to, but she wanted to make a better impression than she had the last time she met the queen. Once she was done, she went and sat stiffly in her sitting area near the fireplace while she waited. Time seemed to slow to a crawl.

Eventually, there was a knock on her door, followed by Angelo. He stepped in to announce the arrival of the queen. Instead of walking back out, however, he held the door open, and a man that was very apparently a guard entered the room. He was followed by the queen herself and then another woman wearing the same livery as the man.

Angelo closed the door behind the woman, then walked to stand behind the seat Avila had been sitting in. She gave him a funny look, but he didn't appear to notice. She didn't have time to ask either, so she let it drop.

With the queen standing in front of her again, she was reminded of how imposing the woman was without even trying. There was just something in her stance.

Avila quickly caught her thoughts before they could run wild and gave the queen a deep bow. "Your Majesty, welcome, and thank you for your visit today. You have given me a great honor." Avila remembered her last conversation and hoped that they could once again get to that point, but with the current setting, she felt it would be better to err on the side of caution and then follow the queen's example.

When Avila stood, it seemed to her that the queen's smile almost seemed strained, but if it had been, the moment was gone. She was the picture of grace. "Please, sit with me. I know I asked for this appointment earlier than I had anticipated. I hope it did not cause any issues for you?"

The queen was already making herself comfortable across from Avila, and the two that came with her took up spots behind and to each side of her. Once Avila could see she was comfortable, she followed suit and sat as requested.

"Your Majesty, it was no problem at all. I was able to finish everything early today with a little help from my tutor. Thank you for your concern, though."

That time, Avila was sure that she did see a small crease between the queen's brows before she spoke again. "Avila, please, I do believe I requested you to be a little less formal. There is no need to be so tense."

"Ah, yes, ma'am, you did. I will try to keep that in mind, thank you." Avila slightly lowered her head to the queen as a show of acquiescence and respect.

"Well, thank you for agreeing to see me so early. I appreciate you making the time. How are you settling into life here so far?" Avila could see the same smile on the queen's face that she had used in the hothouse. She could tell it was designed to try to put her at ease.

Once again, she reminded herself that she wasn't going to get anywhere if she stayed as stiff as she was. She took a deep breath, letting it out slowly and smiling back at the queen. "So far, I am happy to say that things are already settling into a pattern. I know there are still many things I will need to adjust to, but I am heartened by the way things have gone up to this point."

"Good, I am so glad to hear it. I had hoped it wouldn't be too intimidating for you." The queen's smile had relaxed into genuine joy at Avila's response. It didn't take much for Avila to get caught up in her exuberance. She was beginning to see that the queen had a charming personality.

"Thank you, ma'am. I have to tell you, the gardens have been a major help to me. It is nice having such a wonderful place to look to or visit to relax. Galdren told me that not only did you orchestrate them, but you get as much enjoyment from them as I do, if not more." It hadn't occurred to Avila that she had once again called Galdren by name until she noted the other people in the room shuffling uncomfortably. She berated herself and hoped it wouldn't get her in too much trouble.

Surprisingly though, the queen did not mention it at all. Her eyes were alight. Avila thought it might have to do with the turn in the conversation. "Ah, yes. Did he also tell you that I would be out tending it myself if I could?" The queen laughed. "Not that he would be incorrect. That might be one of the reasons I took an instant liking to you."

The queen's blunt statement had Avila blushing. "Well, um, thank you, ma'am. I understand how you might feel, but I certainly wasn't expecting that to be your territory. It was a pleasant surprise."

Avila worried her candor might be offensive, but when she looked up, she found the same light in the queen's eyes, and her smile was just as brilliant.

"It is so nice having someone that can appreciate everything that has gone into my little project. Have you had the opportunity to navigate the maze?"

"No, ma'am, I have not had the opportunity as of yet, but I do plan on looking into it as soon as I have a few spare hours."

"That's too bad, but I understand. I won't ruin it for you, but there is certainly a wonderful spot there for those with the patience to find it." Before the queen could continue, there was another knock, and David opened the door and announced the arrival of the tailor.

Avila, who had completely forgotten clothes for the ball were the main reason for the queen's visit, motioned for David to show them in and turned to see the queen standing again as well. "Good, I am glad they were able to get here. Where would you like them to set up?"

The queen's question stumped Avila for a moment. She had not thought about that. After another moment, she answered, "Ma'am, the table should have enough space to set everything up. Is there anything in particular they need that is not already here?"

The tailor had already come in, and at Avila's words looked to where she had pointed. "Lady Durant, this will be sufficient space to set up, but I am sure you will want to try some of these items on before we can tailor them for you."

At the man's words, Avila was thrown once more. She also hadn't considered having to try things on with other people around. She stared blankly back at the man for a moment.

"Of course, if we could have her lady's maid called, we can make short work of this. Avila, could you call for her?" At the queen's suggestion, Avila jumped into action. Since she didn't have a com unit to call anyone, she turned to Angelo, who was still in the room with her.

"Angelo, could you please call for Meru, or ask David to? The sooner, the better, please." He bowed at her request and stepped away but not out of the room. He made sure to keep her within sight. Again, this made Avila frown, but she didn't have time to ask.

He made the call and reported that she would be in shortly. With that settled, the tailor immediately captured Avila's attention and began to show drawn designs for the rest of the wardrobe to both the ladies. There were a great many dress suits, which Avila thought suited the queen perfectly. However, when she thought of wearing them herself, she became uncomfortable. She tended to wear pants all the time, and the thought of being asked to switch to dresses made her panic.

Before the tailor could get far with the designs, the queen spoke up. "These are all wonderful designs, but they don't seem to suit the Lady Durant. Can we skip the everyday dresses for now and move on to the other items you might have for everyday wear?"

Avila wasn't sure how the queen had figured that out already, but she was not going to complain. The tailor set aside the thick stack of drawings he had been going through and pulled out a different set instead.

Once he started going through them, Avila was more than pleased. There were still some suits, but they were pantsuits, cut sharp to accentuate a feminine figure while still being flexible. There were other pieces as well, things Avila was already used to wearing: sweaters, pants, and many other items that could be considered common, but the way they were designed made them seem less dreary.

Avila had not seen anything yet that she didn't like, although she wondered if her sense of fashion was a little off when she looked between the drawings and the queen. She couldn't see the queen wearing most of those items. She was far too elegant.

Before Avila could raise any objections, the queen had already stood. "I love this second set. I think the whole lot would do nicely. Do you have any cloth selections for us to look through?"

Her acceptance of the less-than-elegant set of designs made Avila pause. It wasn't that she didn't like them, but she did want to make sure to try and fit in. "Um, ma'am, I do agree that the second set of designs was stunning, but well . . . I am trying to find my place here, and I want to make sure I do what I can."

She wasn't sure if she got her point across well enough, but she didn't want to disagree with the queen, especially since she preferred that set as well. Apparently, the queen understood. "You will make a stunning impression no matter what you are wearing, my dear, but there is no sense in making you suffer to suit an ideal."

The queen's reassurances and smile were enough to put Avila at ease, although it was unexpected. Given what she knew of the woman so far, it should not have been.

The tailor had already retrieved the cloth samples and laid them out for Avila and the queen. The quality was fantastic on all of them, light and not stiff at all. The knits were incredibly soft. Everything was in natural shades as well. Someone must have forewarned the tailor of her preferences. There were muted reds, various shades of green, and many other earth tones with a few pale colors thrown in for contrast. It was a beautiful setup, and before long, fabrics for the entire lineup were decided.

Avila was surprised that it had been so easy, but honestly, there hadn't been much choice involved. The queen had been adamant about getting the whole set, so it was only a matter of which material for each piece.

Once that was done, the tailor bowed to the queen and reminded her about the matter of the dress as well. Avila had completely forgotten about that with everything else going on, but the queen did not seem disturbed in the least when she turned to her.

"Avila, I hope you don't mind, but I wasn't sure how much time we would have left and thought it might be easier if I narrowed down the selections before coming over. I had them send me the choices and picked two for them to bring."

"No ma'am, of course, that is fine. I am sure whatever you have picked out will be beautiful. You have wonderful taste." The queen only smiled at her response and motioned for the tailor to bring the dresses out.

For a moment, Avila forgot to breathe. Both dresses were simple as far as formal wear went. Neither had any lace, frills, extra embroidery, or anything else to detract from the elegant lines. That being said, they were both absolutely stunning.

Avila's gaze was first drawn to the green dress, of course. It looked to be just past knee length. The skirt flowed smoothly from the top, curved at the waist, and then fell into gentle folds. It had a V-shaped neckline and Avila wondered if it might be a little revealing, but her gaze was soon dragged onward. The material was such a dark green that it almost looked black, and it had full-length sleeves. She had a hard time pulling her gaze away from it.

When she finally looked at the second dress, she was thrilled again. That one was pale lavender, not a color she would have usually picked out, but beautiful nonetheless. The dress was sleeveless and gathered at the shoulders, with a U-shaped neckline and folds across the chest. It was full length and curved in at the waist, then fell in gentle folds all the way to the floor. The dress had a classic feel to it.

Looking back and forth between the two, Avila found she was having a hard time deciding. Suddenly she remembered she was not alone in the room and quickly turned back to the queen with a slight blush.

She found her smiling. She was obviously enjoying seeing Avila's pleasure, which had Avila smiling back. "Would you like to try them both on before you decide? Honestly, that is part of the reason I wanted to come early. I thought it would be nice if we could do this uninterrupted."

Avila glanced at both dresses again. The thought of trying them both on was exciting but a little intimidating. When she looked back to the queen, the woman was already motioning to Meru, who must have come in at some point during the presentation. "Did Avila say your name was Meru?"

"Yes, Your Majesty." Meru bowed and then kept her head down respectfully.

"Good, would you please take both of those dresses to the Lady Durant's dressing room and assist her in changing? Avila, once you have them on, if you don't mind, I would like to see them."

Avila almost felt like she was back in her old life shopping with Lila again, and the thought had her momentarily choked up. It made her wish once again that her parents would be able to attend the ball. However, she knew it was a futile desire, so she gathered herself so she could properly respond. "It would be my honor, ma'am. I won't be long."

With that, Avila followed Meru into her sleeping room. Avila opted for the green one first, and it did not take them long to get it on. She was surprised at how well it fit. It looked like there might be a need to bring it in some around the waist, but otherwise, it was perfect. She was a little embarrassed by the fact that the V-neck plunged as much as she thought it might. She had exposed cleavage, something she was not used to. It was still a beautiful dress, and she had promised to show it off, so she had Meru open the door to let them know she was coming out.

When she walked out, the queen beamed at her. "Absolutely stunning! I knew that dress would suit you. What do you think?"

Avila turned red at the compliment but tried her best to answer truthfully. "I agree, ma'am. The dress is stunning, but I am not sure I can wear it. Honestly, it makes me a little uncomfortable." Avila glanced down when she said this, and luckily didn't need to explain any further.

"I understand. While I think it looks gorgeous on you, it is your decision to make." Avila couldn't help but grin at the queen's kindness. Now that she had shown the dress off, she quickly made her way back to her room to change again. It wasn't until she was back in the room that she realized she had still been in her socks. It was embarrassing, but not worth changing. Besides, the next one would cover them anyway.

The lavender dress was just as easy to put on, and thankfully the bust line was not nearly as revealing. It was still lower than Avila was used to, but she could live with it. When she turned to look in the mirror before she left the room, she had to stop for a moment. The drastic contrast between the pale dress and her skin and hair was striking.

She shook her head to remind herself people were waiting and again had Meru open the door to let them know she was ready. When she stepped out, she thought she heard a couple of sharp breaths, but she only saw smiling faces when she looked around. Even Angelo was smiling at her.

She couldn't help but smile back. It seemed like the decision was made already. At least it hadn't been hard. "I guess that means this will be the dress." She was still smiling when she turned to the queen.

"It looks like it," the queen said with a smile. "Does it look like the fit is fine, or will there be any adjustments necessary?" She motioned Avila over.

This dress was a little loose in the waist just like the other one, but otherwise fit fine. It didn't take the tailor long to notate the correct measurements and mark where the fabric needed to be taken in. "Ma'am, if you will change back and let me take this, I can have these adjustments completed tonight and the dress back to you by morning."

At his words, she once again made her way back into her sleeping room and changed back into her regular clothes. Once she had the dress off, she couldn't help but smile at it again as Meru hung it up while she was dressing. Although she may never quite get used to life in the castle, she had to say, the entire afternoon with the queen had been nice. It gave her a feeling she really couldn't describe.

When she walked back into the room and handed the dress back to the tailor, he already had everything else ready to go. Before he left, however, he turned around. "Ma'am, I forgot to show it to you, but that dress has a shawl as well since it is sleeveless. It is only a light one, since fur was not an option, but I can go ahead and leave it with you if you would like."

At the man's word's, Avila's good mood dampened slightly. She had forgotten that fur was still very much a fashion accessory since she had not seen any evidence of it in the last several months. She guessed that was only due to who she'd been exposed to and silently thanked the goddess that it seemed the royal family was not part of the crowd that partook.

She came to her senses when she noticed everyone in the room was still looking in her direction, waiting on a reply. She managed a smile for the man anyway, since he had at least been trying. "Thank you, I'll go ahead and take it."

When he brought it out, she was delighted to see that it was in the same silken material as the dress, but with embroidered edges. The stitching was the same color as the material, and it had a single fastener in the front. It was definitely a classic dress. She only hoped she had made the right choice for the crowd she would be joining that weekend.

24. DANCING LESSONS

Once the tailor left, Avila handed the shawl to Meru. "Would you please hang this up for me? Once that is done, I won't need you again until tonight." Meru bowed and took the shawl.

Once Angelo showed her out, Avila turned to the queen. "Thank you so much for everything today. I can't even begin to show my appreciation."

"Well, you are quite welcome, but honestly, it is me who should be thanking you. This is just a small token of my appreciation, and I hope that we will be able to continue our conversations. Today, however, I have run out of time. I do believe I have had as much fun as you." The queen's smile was warm as she stood to leave.

Avila already felt like she could become friends with this woman if circumstances allowed it. Since the queen seemed to feel the same way, she hoped they would get the opportunity. "Well, I do hope so, because I was delighted. I am not sure when we will get the opportunity to meet again, but I hope it is soon." Avila's smile was just as warm as the queen's.

The queen took Avila's hand and gave it a quick squeeze before releasing it and turning for the door. "I will make sure it is not long at all. Please have a good evening."

"You as well, ma'am." Avila waved her out the door with her two guards and Angelo following behind them. He closed the door again once he was back outside with David after giving her a brief smile and a bow.

Avila took a moment to take a look around. It had been such a whirlwind of an afternoon that she had not realized how much time had passed. It was already dark outside. With a start, she looked to the nearest timeglass to note that it was already past her usual dinnertime.

She ran into her bathing room and freshened up as quickly as she could. Once she was done, she ran into the adjoining dining room. She wasn't surprised to see

Galdren there waiting, but she was shocked to note that Etta wasn't there.

"Oh, Galdren, I apologize! I let time get away from me. Why didn't you let me know what time it was, or join us?" She was a little embarrassed that she had kept him waiting.

He stood and smiled at her. "Please, don't worry about it. If I know my mother, she would have told me to leave anyway. I have a feeling she tried to arrange things so I would be busy as it was."

Avila had already figured out that had probably been the case, so to have it confirmed made her giggle. "Well, I still apologize for taking so long. I didn't expect that. So, what are we going to do about dinner since it is so late?"

"Well, now that you are here, I am going to call for Etta, and she will bring up something. I hope you don't mind simple fare tonight." He motioned for her to take her seat.

"You mean to say we are going to have a meal like we used to? Why, oh, why? Seriously, are you asking me if I would complain about that?" She was still in an excellent mood and couldn't resist teasing him a little. Usually, it was the other way around, and she was enjoying the opportunity.

He laughed at her jibe. "Have a seat. I'll have it brought right up."

She took her regular seat to the left of the head of the table and watched as he walked to a com unit she had never seen previously. It only took a moment for him to ask for their meal and rejoin her.

"From your mood, I am guessing that things went well this afternoon? I can ask that much at least, right?" She hadn't thought about keeping any details from him, but at his words, she considered if maybe she should at least keep her dress selection a surprise. Something about the idea appealed to her.

"Well, I can say we went through a lot of different designs, and with your mother's help, I am sure that my wardrobe will be more than sufficient. Did you give her any pointers about my preferences?" The thought struck her as she recalled the two very different sets of designs.

"I did let her know what style of clothes you preferred, but it was only general information. I take it you liked what was picked out?" He grinned at her.

"Yes, I did, thank you!"

By that time, their meal had arrived. Avila was pleased to confirm that it was indeed simpler fare. At least they would not have to sit through several courses—a good thing after her busy afternoon.

They ate in relative silence, just enjoying each other's company. The meal was a short affair, with everything cleared away soon after they were finished. Once they were done, Galdren stood and held a hand out to Avila.

She took it, and he helped her stand. It was the little gestures like that one that always made her smile internally. She knew he was only trying to be courteous, but it never failed to make her feel amazing.

Galdren opened the door to her suite but didn't enter. He stepped back and allowed her to go first. Once she was in her own rooms, he stood in the doorway watching her. "I am glad you enjoyed your afternoon. I am looking forward to seeing the fruits of your labors." He gave her another of the smiles she loved to see.

"I am looking forward to showing you. I hope they meet your expectations." She was only teasing him a little; she really did hope he liked them.

He smiled at her quip. "I am sure I will love them. For tonight, I hope you sleep well." He was still smiling as he turned to go.

Before he closed the door, Avila called out to him, "You too, Galdren."

Now that she was alone, she realized how tired she was. The afternoon had worn her out more than she expected. She went ahead and prepared for sleep without bothering to call anyone. It wasn't long at all before she drifted off.

The following day ran in much the same pattern as the previous days had. However, not long after the midday meal was cleared away, another knock came on Avila's door.

Curious who it might be, Avila called out. Lee entered the room. "Ma'am, the installers are here to put in the com units. Is now a good time?"

"Of course, show them in." Lee stepped aside and let a group of three people in, then followed them into the room and took up a position near Avila. Once inside, they all bowed briefly.

"Ma'am, we apologize for any intrusion, but we can take care of this quickly. We were instructed to install one of the units near your sitting area for your convenience. The other will go in your sleeping chambers near the bed. Will there be anything else before we get started?"

"No, thank you. Please go right ahead and let me know if you need anything." After the exchange, Avila watched them bring in several tools and pieces of equipment.

There was some noise, but she could tell they were doing all they could to make sure she was disturbed as little as possible.

Even with the slight noise in the background, Avila was able to get back to work and soon stopped paying much attention to the workers. In a surprisingly short amount of time, the man that had addressed her when they started was patiently waiting near her table for her to finish her task.

Once she was done and turned to him, he gave her a quick bow. "Ma'am, we have completed the installations. Would you like to take a moment for me to show you how to work them?"

Avila glanced at Professor Gilbert, who gave her a quick nod. With his approval, she stood. "Yes, please, I would appreciate that." Together, they walked to the unit installed by the sitting area.

"This can function in two different ways. If you touch this button on the left, it will pull up a directory of every available person or department. You can then scroll through them on the screen and just touch the one you would like. It will automatically connect. If you know exactly who you are trying to connect to, you can touch the button on the right and simply state the name. It will connect in the same way. The unit in your sleeping chambers functions the same, with the exception that it also has a direct connection open at all times to the adjoining rooms. Do you have any questions, ma'am?"

His explanation was thorough, and Avila felt that she could figure it out without any trouble with a little experimentation. "Thank you, I believe I understand the gist of it. I appreciate you explaining it to me."

With that, he gave her another bow and walked to the rest of the group. They finished cleaning up the last of their things and quietly left. Avila barely noticed, as she was already back to her studies. She was making every effort to catch up after the previous day's discussions with the professor.

When Professor Gilbert started gathering his things, Avila gave the timeglass a startled look. Before he could finish, they were both surprised by another knock at the door. She wondered who it would be this time, since she was sure there wasn't anyone else she had been expecting.

She was delighted when it was Galdren who entered. He smiled at both of them before stepping up to the table. "I hope I am not interrupting. I tried to make sure it would be time for you to be finished for the day."

"If that was your goal, then you are right on time. I was just getting ready to leave." The professor had gathered the last of his things and was getting ready to walk out the door. "Was there something you needed to speak with me about before I go?"

"No, thank you, Frederick. I appreciate it, but I just wanted to make sure I wasn't interrupting Avila's studies."

"In that case, Your Highness, please have a good evening. Avila, I will see you next week." He was gone as soon as he finished speaking.

"So, to what do I owe the pleasure of this visit?" Avila asked, as she'd just realized it was the first time since her first day that she had seen him before mealtime. The fact that they had not spent much time together since she moved hit her a little hard. She wondered if it would always be like that.

If he noticed her melancholy, he didn't make a note of it. Instead, he put a hand on her arm and guided her to the sitting area. Pointing to a seat, he took the one directly across from it.

"I needed to talk to you about tomorrow, and I had not had time before now. I hoped you would be free this afternoon, as there is a lot we need to go over."

Avila sat at his direction. She had started to look forward to the ball after the queen's visit the day before, but at the idea of having to remember a lot of rules, she felt her uneasiness start to return. "I imagined there would be some things I should know, seeing as how I'm new to all of this. So, where do we start?"

"Honestly, Avila, your etiquette is perfectly fine. I worried about it when we first came here, but you managed to adjust to the meals with no issues. Besides, this is a ball, not a banquet. There are just a few things we need to go over to make sure you are prepared."

Avila was a little taken aback at his words, but she wasn't going to complain. It was nice to hear her manners were acceptable. "So, if it isn't my table manners, what do we need to go over?"

"Well, the first thing I need to let you know is that I will not be by your side for most of the night. I will obviously be keeping an eye on you, but because of my position, I will be with my parents for the majority of the evening. The ball is about you anyway, so I am sure you will be more than busy. Because I cannot escort you myself, I will make arrangements for you to have a double guard to the ball."

Avila hadn't realized it, but she had been counting on Galdren's presence as moral support. The thought of being alone with a group of strangers for the majority of the evening was daunting. "Galdren, I understand what you are saying, but I—I am not sure I can handle it alone." The admission was painful for Avila, but she was already fighting the panic just thinking about it.

"Avila, you are amazing. I know you will be fine, and I promise I will be watching. If it looks like things are getting out of hand, I will get you out of there. Can you agree to that?"

Avila knew Galdren would not do anything to put her in danger, so that made her feel a little better. Once she calmed down a little, she nodded. "I will make my best effort. I promise that much." She followed up with a smile.

"Great." He looked relieved. "As for the rest, it's mostly formalities. The rest of the guests, my parents, and I will already be in attendance by the time you are due to arrive. At half past eight, you will be escorted by your guards and announced. When you are announced, you should pause at the entrance for a moment. After that, you are free to mingle until the ball starts.

"You will be given opportunities to meet many people, and I have also asked that Councilor Raban serve as your escort during that time. He will wait for you by the entrance and introduce himself to you then. I apologize for not being able to arrange a meeting earlier, but he knows almost everyone and will be a great asset for you."

Avila was trying to take it all in. It was comforting to know that she would have an escort for introductions, at least. She just wished it was someone she knew. She briefly wondered if she would know anyone there at all.

"I understand so far. None of that seems too difficult, just a little intimidating." She smiled again to let him know she was still all right.

"Good, well, the rest will all be up to you. Do you know how to dance, by the way? I never thought to ask."

Avila had to laugh at him for his thoughtlessness. "And what if I said no? Would that change anything about tomorrow?" Although she was teasing him about it, she was a little worried. She knew the basics of dance since Lila had insisted she learn for some reason, but that had been years ago. It wasn't a skill she felt she had needed and so had not bothered to keep up with.

At Avila's teasing, Galdren had the grace to look a little abashed. "Well, obviously not, but I could always try to give you a few pointers, at least."

"Well, if it eases your mind, I did have lessons many years ago. I haven't danced in a long time, but I am sure I can pick it up fast enough." Avila didn't want Galdren to worry about it.

"Hmm, if it has been years, it might be good that I brought it up. Let me get some music, and we can see how rusty you are." With that, Galdren walked to the adjoining room. He was only gone for a few minutes and brought back a small device that he set on the table.

He then motioned for her to join him before he turned back to the portable music player. With a touch, music filled the room, and he held his hand out to her.

For the first time in days, she had to focus on not blushing as she took his hand. His other hand went to her waist while her hand went to his shoulder. It was already familiar. They waited a moment to get in rhythm with the beat of the music, and then he began to move.

Avila stumbled at first, as she was focused on his touch and not paying attention to the music, but Galdren was good at leading. It didn't take long before she was moving along with him.

They danced without any words, moving together effortlessly. After the first song ended and the next started, she smoothly transitioned into that one as well. When that one ended, however, Galdren stopped while the music continued.

They both stood there together for a moment without moving. Finally, Avila broke the silence. "I guess I am not as rusty as I feared. That's good, at least. I shouldn't make a fool of myself that way, anyway."

She wasn't sure why the mood in the room had become so tense, but it was palpable. Not that she didn't understand her own feelings, but she was trying not to let that get in the way. Her attempt to lighten the atmosphere seemed to work, as Galdren smiled at her and moved to stop the music. "I doubt you would have made a fool of yourself anyway, but it is nice to know we don't need to make excuses as to why you can't dance. I am sure you will have many requests, just make sure to save at least one for me."

His smile made her heart flip as she realized what he was asking, but she reprimanded herself. Of course. She was the guest of honor; it would be rude if someone from the royal family didn't make the request. It only made sense for it to be Galdren, since they were friends.

As he put the device in his pocket, he turned back to her. "Also, one other thing. I have made arrangements for someone to come and assist you with your preparations. They will be here by one in the afternoon, so please make sure you are here. I know that is early, but from what I understand, it could take some time."

His announcement caused Avila to give him a confused look. She was usually ready in a matter of minutes, not hours. What could they be planning that would take them half the day? That also raised another question for Avila.

"You say that like I won't be seeing you again until the ball." She posed it as a statement, but the question was evident.

"I apologize, but I will be unavailable tomorrow at all. Dinner will be served in the adjoining room as per usual, but I will not be able to attend. I am sure you will not be alone, though."

She knew he would be busy with arrangements, and the goddess only knew what else, but it was still disappointing. She had wanted to show her dress off to Galdren before everyone else got to see it. With a small shrug, she smiled and said, "I understand; it wasn't anything important anyway."

He furrowed his brow, but didn't push her. "Please try to sleep well tonight. I am sure tomorrow will be a busy day for you, and you will need it. I look forward to seeing you tomorrow evening."

With those parting words, Galdren walked toward his chambers. "Galdren, I hope you sleep well too." Avila watched his departing back until he closed the door.

Although she knew he had been right, she was still too wound up to go straight to sleep. To wind down and to distract herself, she reached for a book before bed. Her thoughts were already too jangled to call anyone, but reading was a good way to try and relax.

She sat down on the couch with her current novel, and after reminding herself several times that she should not be thinking of Galdren, was able to get absorbed in the story.

It was a little over an hour later that her stomach reminded her that she had been too distracted to call for a meal, and a bit chagrined that Galdren had not thought to do so either. He was probably distracted with plans, but that didn't help her hunger. Still, it was already late, and she doubted eating would do more than cause even more nightmares than usual, so she decided to wait. As she headed toward bed, she had to firmly keep thoughts of the following day from her mind. It took some effort, but once she lay down, she walked through some breathing exercises and finally relaxed into sleep.

25. PREPARATIONS

The next morning, Avila was up early. Since she didn't have any plans until after noon, she wasn't sure what she would spend her morning on. No matter what it was, she decided she would pamper herself a little to make sure she wasn't too wound up before the ball.

She got up and went to the bathing room; if there was ever a time for a long bath, then today was that day. After the tub was filled with steaming water and she added a scented oil that she'd found, she slipped in and could instantly feel herself relaxing. It wasn't until her fingers started to wrinkle that she finally decided it was time to get out and face the day.

After drying off and getting dressed, she still had several hours before her one o'clock appointment. She thought about taking a walk around outside, but saw a slight drizzle when she looked. Normally that wouldn't be a problem, but after her bath, it was less appealing.

Instead, she called for breakfast. Thankfully, the meal was quick in coming, and once she finished, she decided it might be an appropriate time to look into the library. With that thought, she walked out the door. It surprised her to see Lee and Jacob arriving while two others, a man and a woman she did not know, turned to her as she opened the door.

"Good morning, ma'am. Is there something we can assist with? My name is April, and this is Brian, by the way. I think this is the first time we have met." They both bowed at the woman's introduction. Before Avila could answer, Lee and Jacob had arrived.

"Good morning, ma'am. We apologize for inconveniencing you with the changing of the shift, but if you would wait one moment, one of us will take you wherever you would like to go." They all bowed at Jacob's statement.

"Please, take care of what you need to. I only wanted to go to the library, so it is no problem." Avila waved away their concern and stepped back so they could continue with their shift change.

April and Lee exchanged a few words, status updates, and the fact that nothing had been out of the ordinary. Once they finished, April and Brian both bowed with a chorus of "ma'am" before turning away to leave.

Lee took up his position by the door, and Jacob walked over. "You said you wanted to go to the library, ma'am?" he asked.

"Oh, yes, thank you." Avila felt it was a little ridiculous to need an escort to cross the hallway, but she wasn't going to voice that opinion. The last thing she wanted was for Galdren to hear about it.

Jacob extended his hand to indicate he would follow her. She took the few steps to the large double doors but paused before opening them. They were carved wooden doors, something you didn't often see anymore, and they were beautiful. She shook herself out of her review and opened them.

She was surprised to find that for such large, heavy doors, they opened easily. Once they were open, Avila stepped inside. The first thing she noticed was the hush. It was so quiet she could feel the silence pressing against her ears. With the complete lack of sound, the noise of the doors closing made her jump.

Once she really looked around, though, the room made her gape in awe. The middle of the room extended up to a vaulted ceiling, and a balcony with book-shelves lining every wall ran all around the edges of the room. The far wall from the door had several large windows that went from the ceiling to the floor, flooding the entire room with a muted light. Avila could only imagine how bright it might be on a sunny day.

On the ground floor, there were rows of neatly lined shelves. Along the walls, under the balconies, there were more bookshelves interrupted every so often by what looked like reading nooks. Some had tables with chairs, while others only had comfortable looking seats in a loose circle. The whole room was obviously designed for reading.

Avila jumped again when she heard an unfamiliar voice. "May I help you?" The voice belonged to a woman who looked to be quite a bit older than Avila. Her hair was completely grey, and her eyes were framed in a face that showed more than a few wrinkles. At the moment, those eyes were glaring at Avila.

"Pardon me; I wanted to see what was available to read. I hope that won't be a problem." Avila wasn't sure if it was just the way the woman usually looked or not, but her expression hadn't changed.

"How did you get into this library? It is off-limits to anyone that isn't part of the royal family." Avila was sure she wasn't imagining it now. The woman was definitely not happy to see her.

She flushed a little at the woman's thinly veiled hostility. She hadn't had to deal with anything like that in a long time, and it took her by surprise. She heard Jacob move behind her but held out her hand to stop him from saying anything.

"His Highness, Prince Galdren, explained to me that since I am staying directly across the hall, everything in this wing would be accessible to me. I would not want to inconvenience you, so if you will excuse me, I will just look around. Please go back to what you were doing." Avila saw the woman's eyes grow round at the mention of her staying in that wing; she must have realized who Avila was. Avila wasn't in the mood to be accommodating, though. She turned away from the woman before she could say anything else and walked to the first bookshelf.

Avila picked up and replaced several books without seeing anything. After a few minutes, she sighed and tried to let it go. So far, she had met with very few people that were anything other than respectful. She wasn't going to let someone like that ruin today of all days.

She finally started seeing the titles closest to her. From the looks of it, they were all strategy books. With another sigh, she stepped back from the bookshelf at looked at the other bookshelves close by. She found there were content labels at the end of each shelf and soon found the fiction section.

It didn't take long for her to get lost in title after title. She wasn't planning on reading anything at the moment, but she was looking for things to note for future reference. After some time, she had a mental list of at least a dozen titles she wanted to read at some point.

When she turned to leave, she found the grumpy librarian was nearby. Her expression had not improved much, but it was markedly more respectful when she spoke to Avila. "Did you find anything you would like to check out, ma'am?"

The woman's words surprised Avila. She hadn't expected to be able to check anything out and was thrilled with the prospect, even if it meant dealing with this woman. "Actually, yes, I did. I wasn't certain I would be able to check them out, so I only noted them for future visits, but if I could take at least one, for now, that would be wonderful."

Avila noted the surprise in the woman's face. She took a deep breath and reminded herself it was best to kill them with kindness. She couldn't control the way any given person treated her, but she could control her own reactions, and this wasn't worth getting stressed over.

"If you would bring your selection to the desk there, I can assist you." The woman pointed to a desk near the door that Avila had not noticed when she entered. Once Avila turned back to the bookshelves, the woman went to wait near the exit.

Avila went back to the fiction section and deliberated for a few minutes on which one she wanted to take. After looking at two of the selections again, she picked the action story and headed to the desk.

"I would like to take this one, please." Avila handed the book over.

"Of course, please sign here, and I will mark down which title you have taken. You can keep it as long as you would like and bring it back once you are finished." Avila signed the ledger where indicated and took the book back.

"Thank you for your help today. I hope to come back often." Avila made a point of giving the woman a pleasant smile as she left.

Once they were back in the hallway, Jacob opened her door for her and bowed as she entered. Avila thanked him before he closed the door. She was slowly getting used to how most people treated her here, but it sometimes made her stop and wonder why her life had taken the direction it had.

When Avila entered the room, she checked the time. It was already much later than she thought. She wasn't going to have much of an opportunity to read before whoever was coming arrived.

With a sigh, she thought it would be good to ask for some lunch while she had time. As she was getting ready to go back to the door, she remembered her com units had been installed the day before. There was no time like the present to try it out. She diverted to the com unit and hit the button on the left. Since she wasn't sure exactly who she needed to ask for, she thought it might be better to start with the directory.

Once she had it pulled up, she was almost flummoxed by how many choices there were, but it didn't take long to locate one called *"Kitchens."* She thought that might be the correct one and decided to try it. Once she touched the name, a woman's voice came on the line. "Hello, kitchens. How may I help you?"

The woman sounded like she was a little rushed, and Avila was suddenly nervous, but she had already started, so she pressed on. "Um, this is the Lady Durant. I wasn't sure if this was the correct connection, but I wanted to ask about having lunch brought to my room?"

"Of course, Lady Durant. We can have something sent right over. Is there anything in particular you would like?" Avila was a little thrown by the question. Usually, the meals were preplanned. She had always liked them, but having a choice was different.

"Well, I hadn't thought about it, really. Whatever you would normally bring will be fine. Thank you!" Avila started to relax. Ordering had been easier than she had feared, but she supposed that was the reason for the com unit in the first place.

"You're welcome. Someone will be there shortly with your meal. Was there anything else you need?"

"No, thank you." Avila watched the screen go blank. That had been relatively painless, she supposed. She opened the book she'd just checked out and sat down to wait.

She had barely gotten started when there was a knock at the door. That was even quicker than she had anticipated. She called out, and Lee escorted a young woman Avila had never seen before into the room.

She came in and set up the meal and, with a bow, turned to leave. Avila didn't want to pounce on her like she had Michael on his first day, but she made sure to thank the girl before she left the room.

She noted the meal was a steaming vegetable soup with a thick slice of bread to accompany it—the perfect meal for such a dreary day. She went ahead and started eating while it was still hot. Once she was finished, she made herself comfortable on the settee with her new book. She got lost in the pages quickly but was interrupted again before she got very far. She sighed at the intrusion but put the book down again.

After she called out, Lee led in a whole group of people carrying an array of different implements Avila had never seen. She assumed they were the people she was told to expect to prepare her for the evening.

Before Lee left her alone with the group, she asked if he would have someone come and collect the remains of the meal. She had forgotten she needed to call them back to pick it up. He did open the door, but only passed the message along to Jacob and then walked back to take up a position near her. She frowned at him, then realized they were probably told to not leave her alone with anyone other than Galdren or the professor. It bothered her, but she had more than enough to worry about already and decided to not ask.

Once Jacob was in position, the whole group bowed as one. A smart-looking woman stepped forward. "My lady, my name is Savanah. We are here to help you prepare for this evening. We have a lot to get through, so if you could point us to a place, we can set up and get started."

Avila indicated the area next to her worktable, where there was plenty of open space. The others immediately started setting up the equipment they'd brought with them while Savanah turned back to Avila.

"Ma'am, we would like to start with a haircut first. Is there any particular style you would prefer?" Avila took an involuntary step back at that. She had not been expecting a haircut. She could use one, but it was still unexpected.

"Um, well, I wasn't expecting anything like that, so I hadn't thought about it. Honestly, I think I would only need a trim." She liked her current style well enough. There wasn't much work to it.

"We can do that as well. If you would have a seat here, we can get started." Avila hesitantly stepped up to the seat she indicated. After she sat down, Savanah immediately started combing through her hair.

While Savanah was working on her hair, two of the others stepped up as well. One of them had a small collapsible table. "Ma'am, while you are getting your hair cut, we will start working on your nails if that is all right with you."

Avila was beginning to wonder what she had gotten herself into but just nodded. She remembered Savanah afterward and apologized for moving. After she gave her consent, the two moved in. The one with the table took her right hand and started soaking it in some sort of solution. The other one took hold of her left leg. Once the woman had Avila's sock and shoe off, she started soaking her foot in a different solution, this one warmer. It actually felt nice.

Avila had never been one to pamper herself, but decided to relax and enjoy it while she had the chance. She closed her eyes and listened to the snipping of her hair being cut. She wasn't sure what the two taking care of her hands and feet were doing, but she felt them massaging and buffing. Once they finished one side, they swapped places and finished the other side as well.

Savanah completed her trim before they finished with her hands and feet, so she held out a small mirror for Avila to look into while they finished. They finally let her go, and Avila felt almost as relaxed as she had after her bath.

Savanah asked her if she would like to shower quickly and clean up before they proceeded. Avila thought that might be a good idea. No matter how good Savanah was, it always felt better to shower after a haircut.

Avila only took a few minutes for a simple rinse off since she had just bathed that morning. While she did that, they managed to clear up everything.

Avila had not bothered to dry her hair, so the first thing Savanah did once she was seated again was start drying. While she was working on that, the other two, Amelia and Kate, went back to her hands and feet.

This time, they started by shaping her nails and then applying color. When Avila had the opportunity to look down, she noticed that it was a gorgeous lavender close to the color of her dress. It didn't take them long to finish, and they admonished her to keep still for a short time to let the color set.

By that time, Savanah had already started styling Avila's hair. She hadn't bothered to ask what the style would be, but the woman had begun by pulling most of it back. There were tendrils left in the front that framed Avila's face that Savanah slightly curled and then let lay. Avila couldn't tell what she was doing with the rest that had been pulled back, but she could feel regular tugs and pins being placed.

26. BALL

ome time later, Savanah stepped back and announced she was finished. Avila went to go look and couldn't believe the transformation. She usually pulled her hair back or braided it. Now, it was pulled into a complex set of loops pinned across the top of her head, all coming together at the crown to continue in waves past her shoulders. Avila didn't think she would be able to reproduce the effect herself.

"Do you like it, ma'am?" Savanah looked a bit anxious as she asked.

"Yes, I love it! I never would have thought of this myself, thank you!" Avila made sure Savanah understood how grateful she was for the work.

"Good, I'm glad. We just have your makeup to finish, and then you can eat before changing." Avila was a little overwhelmed by all of the steps. She was beginning to understand why they said it would take all afternoon. It was already nearly dinnertime, and they still had to finish her makeup. Her hair alone had taken most of the afternoon to complete.

Avila once again sat down for Savanah to get to work. While Savanah worked on Avila's makeup, Kate and Amelia cleaned everything else up. The makeup didn't take as long as her hair, thankfully. Avila was pleased to note that the woman hadn't used much since she wasn't used to wearing any to begin with.

Savanah handed Avila the hand mirror again to see the difference. She couldn't believe what a significant change a little bit of color could make. It was understated but beautiful. She felt like she was looking at an entirely different person in the mirror.

Avila couldn't thank the three women enough before they left. Once they were gone, she remembered she was supposed to dine alone that evening and decided to check the adjoining room for Etta. She was pleased to find the capable woman already waiting for her when she arrived. The meal was a simple affair again, so it did not take long to finish. By then, her nerves had caught up to her once again. She thanked Etta for the meal and asked her to send Meru in to assist.

When Meru arrived, Avila was surprised to see several things in her hands in addition to the adjusted dress. "What is all that?"

"Ma'am, I was asked to bring these to you. These shoes were designed to go with the dress you picked out, and there are several pieces of jewelry here. I was asked to have you choose the ones you would like to use for the night."

"Who asked you to bring these to me?"

"I was stopped on my way here by a courier from the queen. She asked if I could deliver these. She also asked me to pass on the message apologizing for the oversight." Avila couldn't believe it. Things had already gone beyond her expectations, but this was excessive. Since it was sent via courier, though, she couldn't decline it without the possibility of causing a misunderstanding or offense.

With a quiet sigh, she turned to her room to get changed. Meru followed her in, and with a little assistance, she was soon standing there in nothing but her underthings. She reverently stepped into the dress, and Meru helped her adjust it so it would lay just right. Once done, she checked her reflection once more to make sure her hair and makeup were still intact.

She couldn't believe how she looked. Everything still looked perfect, but to her, she didn't look at all like herself. She turned to Meru to finish the last touches. The girl held out several selections arranged on a velvet tray for Avila to choose from. The set that caught Avila's eye first was a necklace and earring set that was silver-based and set with a variety of colored diamonds. The setting was made to look like twisting vines with small bright flowers scattered throughout. Avila was thoroughly entranced.

She didn't look twice at any of the others and had Meru help her get the necklace and earrings on. "So, what do you think?"

"Ma'am, it isn't really my place, but I believe you are absolutely beautiful."

She had gotten so used to Meru that she hadn't thought asking would be inappropriate; she had only wanted another person's opinion. She felt a little bad for putting her on the spot and reminded herself to keep her position in mind, especially this evening. "Thank you, Meru. I appreciate the compliment. I apologize if I made you uncomfortable."

"No ma'am, if you don't mind me saying so, I appreciate knowing where I stand with you." Meru blushed a little at her straightforward statement, but she was smiling. Avila was happy to see that her efforts weren't a waste.

"Good, thank you too! Now, I think it is time for me to be headed out. Is there anything I am missing other than the shoes?"

Meru helped Avila strap the low heels on and then quickly turned back to the armoire. "Don't forget your wrap, ma'am."

Avila took it gratefully and walked with Meru to the door. When she opened it, both David and Angelo turned to her. She was pleased to note the appreciative smiles from both men before they bowed. She never really thought of herself as pretty, at least not by Aril's conventional standards, but it was a nice feeling to be noticed.

"Ma'am, are you ready to leave?" Angelo asked as he stepped forward.

"Yes, I believe it is close to the time I am expected to be there."

"If you would please give me one moment, I would be happy to escort you." With that, Angelo stepped away and pulled out a com unit. The conversation was brief, and from what Avila could hear, he was letting someone know they were on their way.

He stepped back after the call and indicated the double doors. "Ma'am, if you would stay by my side until we are joined by Adam outside this wing."

Avila nodded and headed toward the doors with him. When they reached the double doors, the two guards pulled open a smaller set of inset doors Avila hadn't noticed before. Once they passed through, there were three more guards on the other side.

Two of them simply nodded at Angelo once they got an unobstructed look at his face. The other stepped up to Avila and bowed. "Ma'am, my name is Adam. I have been asked to assist in your detail tonight. It is my honor."

Avila was a little surprised at his formality but tried to take it in stride. "Thank you, I appreciate your help." Avila hoped she was living up to the expectations everyone seemed to have of her.

Once Adam joined them, the procession changed a little. Angelo led the way since Avila had no idea where she was going, while Adam followed her. They walked down several different hallways that progressively got more crowded.

It didn't take them long to reach their destination. Avila was once again greeted with a large set of double doors. This set was already open, and she could see a huge crowd of people milling about inside the room.

Angelo stopped just before the doors and stepped aside to present Avila to the nearest doorman. "The Lady Durant." With that, he stepped behind her.

The doorman motioned for her to step forward. Once she was inside the room, she stopped on the top step like she had been instructed and waited for the doorman to announce her. She had to repress a flinch as his voice boomed out above the din. "May I present the Lady Avila Durant."

The noise in the room suddenly went down several notches. She could almost feel every set of eyes in the room turn in her direction, and her nerves suddenly had her locked up. She knew there was something she should be doing right then, but she couldn't think of what. The best she could do was smile, and she knew it had to look forced.

She was rescued by a voice to her right. She turned to the sound of her name and found an older gentleman standing there, smiling at her. It took a moment, but she finally remembered that she was supposed to be meeting a councilor. "You are Councilor . . . Raban, correct?"

He gave a small bow at her question. "You are correct, Lady Durant. I will be your escort for the first part of the evening. Would you like to join me?" He offered his arm. She took a deep breath to try and calm her nerves and placed her hand on his forearm. Once she had accepted, they descended the steps into the crowd.

The next hour passed by in a blur for Avila. Many people approached her to introduce themselves, and Councilor Raban was always right there to give her information on who was whom. When they were not being approached, the councilor was sure to point out people he thought might be vital for her to know. She only hoped she could retain a fraction of the information she was being presented with. The good news was that she didn't have time to be nervous once she started making rounds.

Once the first hour was up, an announcement was made for everyone to move to the ballroom, as the ball would be starting shortly. Avila wondered if what was coming would be any easier than the last hour.

She started making her way to the ballroom with the councilor, stopping along the way for a few brief introductions. Before they made it into the hall, a young man that Avila had not yet seen stopped them.

"Lady Durant, my apologies for my tardy introduction, but I wanted to be sure to make your acquaintance." The man gave her a small polite bow.

"Of course, there is no need for an apology."

"Thank you for your graciousness. I am Lord Nathanial de Legris. I know you are headed to the ballroom; it would please me if you would allow me to escort you. I have wanted to get an opportunity to speak with you for years."

Avila wasn't sure what to make of this request, so she turned to her current escort for some guidance. He gave her a small nod and patted her hand before letting it go. "Lady Durant, it has been my great pleasure to escort you this evening. I hope you enjoy the ball."

With that, he continued on into the ballroom, leaving her with the stranger. She supposed if there had been any danger, he would not have left her alone, but it still made her uncomfortable. There was no point in being rude, though, so she took the offered arm and stepped toward the ballroom.

"So, Lord de Legris, you said you wanted to speak to me for years? Did you follow my work previously?" Avila could only assume that was what he meant.

"Please, call me Nathan, if you don't mind, that is. As for your work, well, my father is the Duke of Armand, which I am sure you recognize from your previous work, being that our family is responsible for the Southern Peloun Reserve."

Avila was a little overwhelmed already. He was obviously excited; his speech had gotten less formal and faster the closer they got to the ballroom, but she understood what he was trying to say.

"I worked with people from all three of the major reserves, but it never occurred to me the royal family was watching over it directly. I mean, I knew the king's brother was responsible for an adjoining estate, that is where most of my queries were directed through, but I guess I never thought about it in those terms. So that means you were there when all my questions were reviewed?"

"Of course! I had always hoped you might be able to visit the Armand estate and the Peloun Reserve, but you just disappeared after the bill was passed."

Avila wasn't sure how to react. She had been hearing similar things for the past hour and still didn't have a good response. She never thought she had made any kind of impression, especially on people she had never met, and was a little bemused at Nathan's apparent excitement.

"Well, I didn't really disappear. I just spent time focusing on other things. I didn't expect anyone to be following the bill, really. However, I would like to visit all the reserves someday, so your offer is appreciated." She meant it, too.

All three of the reserves across the planet were said to be beautiful in their own unique way. Each covered a different landscape. From what she remembered, Peloun was in a drier climate but still had an abundant array of wildlife that had adapted to the harsh environment over time.

"It would be my honor to receive you. I know my father and brother would be just as thrilled to have you grace our estate."

Avila was definitely feeling embarrassed now. She wasn't sure how to take the young man's enthusiasm. They had reached the ballroom, though, and it looked as if the dancing would begin soon.

"My lady, would you do me the honor of dancing with me tonight?" Nathan bowed to her when he made the request. Avila hesitated only a moment, but she didn't get to answer.

"I believe the first dance is reserved for me." Galdren's voice completely took Avila by surprise. That was the first time she had seen him all evening, although she had not had time to look for him.

When he reached out his hand, he gave Nathan a nod. "Maybe you can get the next one."

Avila took Galdren's hand without thinking. She couldn't seem to take her eyes off him. He was wearing a formal black suit with a white shirt and a deep purple sash that crossed from his right shoulder to his left hip. His slim coronet only caught her eye when the light glinted off it. Its golden color blended in well with his sandy hair.

The music started once they reached the middle of the room, and for a few brief moments, it was just the two of them sweeping across the empty floor. As far as Avila was concerned, they were the only two people there.

For Avila, the music ended much too quickly. She didn't even notice that neither of them spoke while on the ballroom floor until she was being asked to dance by another person. She thought she caught Galdren smiling ruefully as he walked away, but she didn't have much time to wonder. There were actually several gentlemen waiting for her response; Nathan was only one of them.

She hadn't known him long, but he had already made an impression on her. Since his was the first face she recognized, she gave him a bright smile and held out her hand.

"Sorry, gentlemen, I suppose you will all have to wait until the next round." Nathan bowed over her hand as the music started up again. Avila was delighted to find he was almost as good a lead as Galdren. It must be part of the family training.

Nathan was not silent, though. Throughout the dance, he regaled her with tales of trips into the savannah with his brother and father, and how drastic the difference was when he moved north to the capital.

Before she realized it, the dance was already over, but Avila was having a wonderful time. She knew it was largely due to Nathan and his ability to make her forget how nervous she was. She would need to make sure to thank him if she ever had the chance.

She ended up dancing with many more people and with Nathan several more times. She never danced with Galdren again. She wasn't sure if he danced at all, but she did look for him. The few times she saw him, he was always sitting with his parents. She felt a little guilty that she was having fun while he was attending to his duties, but she reminded herself that this night was about introducing her, so she supposed it was all right to mingle.

After the last dance was announced, Avila found that she was far more tired than expected. She also wasn't sure where to go or what to do. She couldn't completely hide her relief when Nathan found her and offered to escort her back.

"I am sure I will have a guard waiting for me, but I would love to have your company until we reach them." Avila smiled at him freely. She felt like she could easily be friends with the energetic young man.

He held out his arm, and she linked hers through it. She was happy to find she was leaving in much higher spirits than when she arrived. The way things had gone tonight, she felt she might actually be able to fit in, something she had not wanted to admit how worried she was about.

When they got to the double doors, she was not surprised to see Angelo and Adam standing there waiting for her with a contingent of other guards. They stood at attention when she arrived.

Since the two guards would be taking her the rest of the way, she turned to Nathan and gave him a slight bow. "Thank you for making this a wonderful night. I enjoyed talking to you, and I hope to have the opportunity again."

He didn't even try to contain his grin as he responded, "My lady, the pleasure was all mine, and it would continue to be my pleasure if I were able to share your company at some future date."

Avila couldn't help but smile back at him. He had the kind of smile that was infectious. "In that case, I hope it will be soon. Please have a good evening." She waved at him as she turned to follow Angelo back the way they had come.

By the time she reached her rooms, the euphoria of the night had started to wear off. Her feet were beginning to ache from all the dancing, and she could feel the exhaustion pulling at her.

Meru was already waiting in her rooms for her when she arrived. Between the two of them, she was quickly divested of all the hairpins and other accessories. She gave the necklace and earrings a silent, rueful goodbye before they went back into their velvet case.

She knew she probably needed a long soak, but she was afraid she might fall asleep in the tub, so she opted for a quick cleanup in the shower instead. Once she was finished, she fell into bed completely exhausted and was asleep before she realized she had even crawled under the covers.

27. MAZE

It was already bright outside when Avila woke up, and the drizzle of the previous day was completely gone. Grumbling to herself for sleeping in, she rolled out of bed.

Luckily, it was still only Sunday, and she had the whole day to recuperate. It was a good thing balls didn't happen more often. She hadn't overindulged in anything, but every part of her was aching. Her body was not used to that level of activity. She felt a little ashamed at having gotten so out of shape.

Those thoughts and the sunny day propelled her into deciding the day would be an enjoyable one to spend outside. She didn't take long to dress and was out of her room quickly. Lee and Jacob were the two waiting. They turned with a bow, and Jacob stepped forward to volunteer to take her wherever she needed to go.

They started toward the garden entrance together, but Avila had an idea and turned to Jacob before they made it. "Jacob, do you think it would be a problem to ask the kitchens for a bagged meal? I was thinking about tackling the maze today, but I might want to stop for lunch at some point if I do. Today looks like a lovely day for a picnic anyway."

"Of course, ma'am. That will be no problem at all. Is there anything in particular you would like me to ask for?"

"Oh, well, not really, but make sure they pack enough for you too. If you are going to have to stay with me, I wouldn't want to inconvenience you."

"Thank you for your concern, ma'am. I will put in a request, and someone can meet us near the maze if that is acceptable to you?"

"Yes, thank you." At her consent, Jacob took out his com unit. He quickly described what they needed and instructed the person where to send someone to meet them. It didn't take him long at all, and they were on the way.

Avila was excited to get to see the maze, especially after speaking with the queen.

She wondered what could be in the center. However, they didn't make a straight line for their destination, as she wanted to take her time and enjoy the sunny day. It was always nice after the rain, even if it was cold. The air just seemed fresher to her. She didn't take too long, though, since someone was supposed to be meeting her. When she noticed a person walking from the other side of the square, she headed in the direction of the maze to meet them.

Before she got to the meeting spot, she was surprised to find the person she had seen was not the kitchen staff, but Nathan. It took her a moment to reel in her shock and greet him properly. "Lord de Legris, good morning! Pardon me if I seem a little shocked, but I have to say, you are the last person I expected to see this morning."

"Ah, you wound me. Are we back to lord and lady? I had hoped you might have enjoyed my company enough to be comfortable calling me by my name. Either way, it is a great pleasure to see you this morning as well, *Lady* Durant." His slight jab was utterly nullified by his sparkling smile.

"My apologies Nathan, I didn't mean anything by it, really. I was just surprised to see you. This is the first time I have seen you in the gardens, or really anyone for that matter."

"No need to apologize. I am not surprised you haven't seen anyone. These gardens are pretty secluded, even as far as residents go, but I enjoy a walk on the weekends when I have time. I moved back to the castle just over a week ago, so I haven't been out here in a while."

"Ah, that makes sense. It seems this is becoming a bit of a getaway location for me. In fact, I was just about to tackle the hedge maze. Have you been through it before?"

Avila didn't think it could have been possible, but Nathan's smile grew even larger. "Yes, I have, but it has been years. From what I understand, Queen Lorne has been busy making improvements everywhere, the maze included. I would love to see what she has done with it."

"In that case, would you like to join me? Only if you aren't busy with something else, of course. I wouldn't want to impose on your day." Avila started to feel like she had been too bold, but she found it was easy to be open with Nathan.

"Are you sure it wouldn't be an imposition for you? You looked like you were walking to meet someone when you were surprised by my presence."

His reminder made Avila start and look around. A young woman she had never met before was patiently waiting several feet away with a package.

"Oh, excuse me, Nathan, let me take care of this." He watched her with amusement as she walked to the girl. As she approached, the girl bowed.

"Lady Durant, the meals you requested. You should have everything you need for a picnic, but please let us know if anything is unsatisfactory." She handed the package to Avila with another bow, showing her the handles and how to carry it easily across her shoulders while leaving her hands free.

After the girl left, Avila turned back to Nathan. "I apologize for that, but that is who I was meeting. I thought I would make a day of it and asked for a picnic. The offer still stands if you are interested."

"In that case, it would be my pleasure. Would you like to take the lead?" Nathan gestured toward the maze and stepped aside for Avila to go first. If he noticed Jacob at all, he didn't mention it, and Avila noted he did not have a security detail of his own.

Avila only paused for a moment at the wrought iron gates before stepping through into the green passage. It wasn't long before they had gone far enough for the walls around to cut what little wind had been blowing down to nothing.

The walkways were not narrow, but they were tall. It didn't take long for Avila to start feeling completely isolated from the rest of the world. It wasn't a bad feeling. Instead, it was calming. It reminded her a little of her walks in the woods, when she would go to let nature calm her frazzled nerves.

The maze didn't have the wild feel to it, but the quiet was appreciated. It wasn't that there wasn't any conversation. In fact, Nathan was a wonderful conversationalist. The more she got to know him, the more she liked him. He had a way about him that was excited but not loud; it was like he sensed the calmness from the environment and kept his tone low.

Avila didn't count the turns like she should have; she was thoroughly enjoying the walk and not paying attention. After more than an hour, she started to wonder if they were going in circles.

Nathan must have picked up on her nervousness, because he placed his hand on her arm. "I am sure we are getting close to the center. If I remember correctly, this maze is pretty large and complex. I am sure it won't be long." He gave her another smile to make her feel better.

Avila appreciated his effort, and knowing she wasn't alone made her feel better. Not to mention that Jacob had a com unit, so there was no way they could really get lost. Trying to keep that in mind, she decided to relax and enjoy the walk again.

However, she did start paying closer attention to where they were going and made sure they didn't take the same route twice.

Thankfully, Nathan had been right. After just a few more turns, they saw an opening ahead of them. Avila was excited to see what waited at the center. When they got to the gap in the hedges, she was not disappointed.

A large crescent-shaped pond went from the opening to halfway across the clearing, and a wide footbridge arched from the gap in the hedges across the water to a covered deck that extended over the water for several yards on each side of the path.

The path continued up a slight rise to a gazebo that had arches built into each of the seven sides. The side facing the trail was open, but the others had a half wall and a type of evergreen vine Avila had never seen covering each of the arches. It gave the gazebo the same feel as the hedge maze: quiet and calm.

An open field surrounded the gazebo. It looked well tended, and Avila could envision it being filled with colorful blooms in springtime. Still, it seemed right that this area was left closer to its natural state and didn't have winter flowers.

Avila did notice a low ring of evergreen hedges around the field. There were no blooms, but there were many bright red berries. The bright color among the dark greens and greys of winter was beautiful. Avila knew she would have to visit during spring as well. This was the kind of place that would be beautiful all year.

When they got to the gazebo, Avila looked around. It was a spacious area with covered benches under every arch but the entrance. It was a lovely place to eat lunch. Plus, her sore muscles could use a break.

At the thought of lunch, Avila realized she was starving. She hadn't thought about breakfast, and it had taken them longer to get to the center than she had anticipated. She sat on one of the benches and pulled the pack around to see what they had.

She was pleased to see the pack had several small bottles filled with various colored liquids. Avila opened one to find it had juice. She grinned as she continued to pull other items out of the pack. There were several wrapped sandwiches—enough to feed their unexpected guest, even. There was also an insulated jar that held a fragrant soup that was still warm when Avila opened it.

She was more than pleased with the variety. She had to insist that Jacob join them, and he finally relented. He didn't sit with them, but he did consent to eat what he was offered.

Avila was in excellent spirits. Nathan was so easy to talk to, and he had so many insights into animal rights and ecology that it was truly interesting to speak with him.

They had finished their meal some time ago, and it was already late afternoon by the time Avila decided they better head back just in case it took them as long to get out. Fortunately, they both seemed to have a better idea of the way going back than they did coming in. Or at least, they were paying more attention, because they were out in a relatively short amount of time.

Avila was laughing with Nathan about something he had said as they exited the maze when she was brought up short by the sight of Galdren waiting a few feet away from the maze's entrance with Randy and Baxter. She realized a little guiltily that Galdren had not been in the front of her mind all day long. It was the first time in a long time. Following hard on the heels of that thought, she chided herself for thinking it mattered.

She did worry that she had strayed somewhere she should not have, though. She hadn't thought it would be a problem since Jacob was with her all day, but she couldn't shake the feeling. It probably had something to do with the stormy look on Galdren's face.

By the time they reached him, he was wearing a smile, but Avila could tell it was forced. If Nathan noticed, however, he didn't say anything about it as he greeted his cousin, "Ah, good afternoon, Your Highness. I didn't really get the chance to talk to you last night, so I'm glad to see you today!"

"Nathan, I'm glad to see you are doing well. When did you get back to the capital?"

"Just over a week ago. I was thrilled when I found out I made it just in time for Lady Durant's ascension. That was the best coincidence I've had in years!" Avila noticed Galdren's jaw clench, but his voice betrayed nothing.

"Given your family's assistance in her endeavors in the past, I am sure even your father will be disappointed to have missed the occasion."

"I would like to say he might rethink his policy of self-isolation if I told him, but I would probably be lying. It's unfortunate, as she is as charming and beautiful as she is intelligent." Avila had been staying out of the conversation, but at Nathan's remarks, she turned to him with a red face.

"Wait, wait, let's not, please." She had a hard time getting a coherent response out, but Nathan understood well enough. He chuckled a little at her and gave her a pat on the shoulder.

"Don't let it get to you." She dropped her gaze and let it slide. Nathan turned back to Galdren. "So, was there something you needed from me?"

"No, actually, I had been looking for the Lady Durant."

"Well, in that case, I will bid you both farewell. First, allow me to say I had a wonderful time today, my lady. I hope we have the chance for many opportunities like that in the future."

Avila was no longer sure of how she should react. She could feel the weight of Galdren's stare even though she wasn't looking at him. She only deliberated for a moment before she decided that it didn't matter what Galdren thought. He had already made it clear what his boundaries were with her, and she didn't see why it would be a problem for her to cultivate new friendships. Especially since that was the purported reason for her recent move.

Once she made up her mind, she gave Nathan a small bow back. "As did I, Lord de Legris. I look forward to our next meeting." She gave him a sincere smile as he walked away.

When she turned back to Galdren, he just motioned for her to follow him. She tried not to pay attention to his abrupt attitude since he was obviously trying to be polite. Still, it grated on her nerves. She didn't know what his problem was, but he didn't need to take it out on her.

Once they were back in her room, she walked ahead of him to the sitting area. After she was seated, she finally looked at him. "So, you said you were looking for me?" She knew her attitude was brusque, but Galdren's actions toward her had brought back images of the previous weekend. She just barely managed to hold in a shudder at the memory.

She noticed the shock on his face at her curtness, but he quickly had it under control again. His eyes returned to their stormy look, but it was a tempered storm, a fact Avila was grateful for. At least this time, he didn't look blinded by his anger.

"Yes, I wanted to speak with you about the upcoming changes in our daily schedules. I do believe I mentioned that we will be joining the rest of the household for dinners starting tomorrow?"

His words caused Avila to cringe a little. She had conveniently forgotten about that. She wasn't sure if she was ready, but it did help that she already knew the queen and Galdren. The fact that she usually got along well with both of them eased the knot of nerves in her stomach a little. It was just a matter of not making a fool of herself. "Yes, I had almost forgotten. Are there any particular rules or other things I should know, beyond common sense etiquette?"

"Your table manners are impeccable, so that won't be an issue. Mainly, you should remember that you don't sit until both the king and queen are seated, don't eat before either of them, and don't try to start a conversation with either until they have started talking to you." Galdren's gaze had finally calmed now that they were talking. Avila's worry about what had caused his mood was still in the back of her mind, but she pushed it aside for the moment. She had more important things to worry about.

"Well, I'm glad to hear I won't embarrass myself, and you, just by my ignorance. Is that it, or is there more I should be prepared for?" She honestly wasn't too worried about her manners. Her biggest concern was making sure she didn't act too familiar with Galdren. In the privacy of her rooms, it wasn't a big deal, but she didn't want to add fuel to any scandal by calling him by name. Not to mention it would probably be frowned on in general.

"The only other thing you will need to know is that while dining with the family is not a formal occasion, it isn't casual either. You will need to put some effort into presenting a certain kind of front. I know this will probably be the hardest part for you, but you'll get used to it quick enough."

Avila knew he hadn't meant anything personal by it, but it still stung. She tried to convince her heart he was talking about not acting familiarly with him, but it refused to believe anything except the fact that he thought she wasn't good enough without "putting in effort." "I will make sure to present myself well and will keep the company in mind during all conversations. You don't need to worry that I will embarrass you."

That was the second time in the last several minutes that her tone with him was harsh. She watched his jaw clench and wondered for a moment if he was going to call her out for it. She wasn't sure what she would say if he did. Thankfully, it wasn't an issue as he continued like nothing was wrong, "I have no doubt that you will be splendid. You already have the majority of the people that will be there enchanted with you, and your brilliant mind will make up for the rest. I wasn't trying to scare you; it was just supposed to be a reminder."

Avila blushed; she knew he was exaggerating, but it did help to know that she had already formally met most of the royal family. As she thought that, she had to contain a giggle. If anyone had told her a year ago that she would be friends with most of the royal family, she would have asked if they had lost their mind. She couldn't help but wonder who else would be there besides Galdren and his parents. "I appreciate your reassurance. Who is usually at dinner?"

"It is normally just the family." He paused and looked unsure about whether to continue. "That includes any extended family that might be in residence. Also, there could be visiting dignitaries, but that is a rare occurrence. With Aril being the farthest out of the planets in the Alliance, we usually only get visitors if there is business to be done."

Avila wasn't looking forward to possibly facing royalty from another planet. She would hardly call her interactions with the royalty from this planet normal. However, she was delighted to find that Nathan would probably be there as well. The thought had her smiling again. "Well, I can't say that I am thrilled with the idea of trying to interact with foreign dignitaries, but I think I can handle the rest."

Galdren gave her a sincere smile finally. "I'm sure you will be fine. I will be there as well, so don't worry too much." He stood at that point. "I still have a few things to do this afternoon, so I will see you tonight. As for tomorrow, I will make sure to come get you. It isn't far, but we will need to pass through the commons, and I don't want you to go alone."

Avila gave him a nod and a bright smile. "I will see you later, then." She was in a much better mood than she had been when he first found her. It helped that she could look forward to her introduction to the "family" meals instead of dreading them like she had been.

Once Galdren left, Avila wondered if she should go back out and resume her walk, but when she looked outside, she saw the sky had become slightly overcast. That combined with her still-sore muscles helped her decide that the rest of the afternoon would be better spent reading. When she curled up in one of the chairs, it didn't take her long to get lost in the pages.

28. FAMILY DINNER

Monday morning found Avila still slightly sore from her weekend, but it had toned down enough that she could relish the feel. She decided that she would have to ask Galdren to help her find some way to exercise more thoroughly. She couldn't keep going like she had been. She hated the idea of not being able to take a regular walk in the woods if she got the chance just because she was so out of shape.

Despite moving a little slower, she was up and around before the professor came in. She was in a bright mood. The thought of dinner the coming night was now something she was looking forward to. Her bubbly attitude carried her through the rest of the day. Professor Gilbert even commented on her continued drive, as she was through his curriculum more than an hour before her scheduled time.

When the professor left, Avila found that she still had several hours before dinner. She was on her way out the door for an afternoon walk, but stopped at the thought that she didn't know exactly when dinner would be for sure. Galdren had left that detail out. If it was at the regular hour, she could be back with time to spare, but not knowing had her turning around to pick up her book instead.

She paused before curling up with it. She decided that getting changed first might be a good idea too, in case she didn't have time later. It didn't take her long to find something she felt would be appropriate. Once she was satisfied that she wouldn't embarrass herself or Galdren, she moved to get back into her book.

She paused when she picked it up and changed her mind again. She hadn't talked to her parents or Lissa since before the ball, and she was sure they would love to hear how it went. As expected, both her parents were apologetic again for not being able to go, but she reassured them that she had thoroughly enjoyed herself, so it was no problem.

Lissa wasn't as willing to let it go. She had to hear every detail about the dress and the dance. She was even more excited when Avila told her about Nathan. It made Avila laugh when she was forced to detail nearly line for line all of her interactions with the young man before Lissa was willing to say goodbye.

By the time she got offline, she barely had time to start reading when she heard her door open. She looked up to see Galdren and gave him a big smile as she stood. Her mood was still as bright as it had been all day. "Galdren! I'm glad I decided to stay in after all. Do we have to leave right away?"

Galdren couldn't help but smile at her exuberance. He had been afraid she would be nervous, so he was glad to see he wouldn't have to coax her into a better mood before they went to dinner. "We have a little time, but not much. Was there something you needed?"

"Not at all, well, other than freshening up. I just wasn't sure about the time. You never told me when I would need to be ready." She didn't give him time to respond before moving toward her bedroom. "I'll be right back."

He couldn't help but shake his head at her bemusedly. He had no idea why she was in a good mood, but was thankful for it. It would make her first meal with everyone go smoother. True to her word, she was back in moments with a bright smile. "I'm ready when you are."

"We have a few minutes still before we have to leave. Is there anything you would like to go over before we head out?" He was trying to make sure she was as prepared as she could be.

She deliberated for a moment before shaking her head. "The only question I have is if there will be any visiting dignitaries. If not, then I should be fine."

It was Galdren's turn to smile. "None that I am aware of." He didn't lose his smile, but he still gave her an evaluating look. "I'm not sure why you are so much more confident about it tonight than you were when we last spoke, but I am glad to see it."

Avila's smile lessened some as she answered, "I thought about it and realized two things. First, I will know most of the people there, if what you explained holds true. Secondly, I know you would not willingly put me into a position that would harm me or cause me embarrassment. As long as you are guiding me, I know I can't fail." Avila snapped her mouth shut as soon as the words were out.

Galdren was stunned at her words; he understood precisely what kind of boon she had just offered him. He had not exactly given her many reasons to trust him, and it took him a few moments to formulate a response. "I am glad to hear you think that. I will do everything in my power to make sure you have every reason to continue to believe so."

A bit of color came to her cheeks at his words. She turned from him to try and hide it, changing the topic while she did so. "Will I need to bring my coat?"

He couldn't help but chuckle at her obvious embarrassment. She never liked it when her softer emotions showed openly. He found it amusing, as she never had a problem with openly showing her anger. He didn't push her, though, and allowed the change of topic with no comment. "No, we are only going down the hall. We can go ahead if you are ready."

By then, she was back under control and had turned to him with another of her brilliant smiles. "All ready."

He offered her his arm. This was new for her, but she knew he was only being polite. She knew her face warmed some when she tucked her hand into the crook of his arm but couldn't help but smile anyway.

He had been correct in that it wasn't far. He led her back through the double doors at the end of the hallway before turning down the hall to the left. She realized this was the hall that ran the length of the garden. She was pleased to note that although it was considered part of the commons, it was still not a high-traffic area. She had not seen anyone other than the five of them, as Randy, Baxter, and Angelo had followed them as soon as they left her rooms.

When they entered the dining hall, she almost paused in the door when several sets of eyes turned their way. Galdren didn't allow her to. His hand was firmly over hers on his arm, and he pulled her forward. She couldn't help but wonder if they were late, as both the king and queen were already there. Her unease faded when she caught Nathan's eyes. He gave her a big smile, and she couldn't help but return it.

When they reached the table, Galdren left her at the seat next to Nathan while he moved to sit across from her, next to his mother. Once he released her arm, she turned to the king and queen with a respectful bow. She didn't move until the queen spoke up. "Avila, I am so glad you could join us! Please take a seat."

She sat at the queen's insistence and gave her a smile at her warm welcome. "Thank you, Your Majesty. I am thankful for the opportunity."

Her words caused the queen to frown slightly, but Avila's worry wasn't allowed to blossom, as the queen quickly let her know why she was displeased. "How many times must I tell you there is no need for that? Ma'am will be sufficient, no matter the company."

Avila was a little embarrassed by the slight rebuke, but was more than glad to hear she had blanket permission to not address the queen by title. "My apologies, ma'am. I had thought to err on the side of caution, but I will keep your words in mind."

At her straightforward answer, the queen gave her a big smile. Her gaze was drawn to Nathan when he chuckled and said, "The same goes for me. I would hope we are past the point of needing such formality."

She gave him a smile. "Thank you!" She turned her gaze to Galdren at that point. He was smiling at her as well, but for some reason, it looked forced. She couldn't help but wonder what was bothering him. She couldn't allow his mood to worry her too much, though. She had to focus on getting through the meal. The first one would be the hardest. Once she had an idea of what was expected, she would be much more comfortable.

The only person that had yet to say anything was the king. Avila remembered Galdren's advice to not speak unless spoken to and tried to avoid catching his eye until or unless he addressed her first. Her unease was halted when he finally spoke up. "Lady Durant, we are pleased circumstances have allowed you to join us. I am sure I speak for all of us when I say we are grateful for everything you have done and look forward to aiding you in your future accomplishments."

Avila could feel her face burning up to the tips of her ears, though she knew she couldn't reprimand the king for saying anything. The fact that it was coming from him in the first place made it almost surreal. She also knew she couldn't remain silent. She gave him a respectful nod before responding, "Your words bring me honor. I only hope that I can live up to such high praise and expectations."

She was amazed when he gave her a small smile in response. "I have no doubt you will more than excel in anything you put your mind to." He then turned to glance over the rest of the table. "Let dinner begin."

When the first course arrived, Avila was a little worried to note that it would be a larger meal than she was used to. She only hoped it wouldn't be considered rude if she couldn't finish. There was no way she would be able to. At least she knew which fork to start with. Her worries about the meal were interrupted by Nathan. "I must say, I had not been joining these dinners since I came back. Normally they go off into political tangents I would rather not follow, but when I found that you would be joining us, I couldn't resist."

Avila was certain that the blush was not going to leave her face by that point. "I'm glad you find my company pleasing. I will admit that having you here does make it easier." She looked away from him to try to hide the blush that still dusted her cheeks, so she only caught a glimpse of the way his eyes flashed brighter for a moment before she was looking across the table.

She noticed Galdren was frowning until he caught her eye. The expression was erased immediately and replaced by a forced smile. It made Avila wonder if she had said or done something wrong. Had she already embarrassed him and not even realized it yet? She thought back over the last few minutes and couldn't think of anything. If she had, she would just have to ask him later, as no one else seemed worried and now wasn't the time.

It looked like Galdren was about to say something, but he paused when his mother lightly touched his arm. The woman gave him a reprimanding look that made Avila's eyes widen, but she didn't have long to wonder what it was about before the queen looked at her and asked, "Avila, how did you enjoy the ball?"

That question started a trend for the rest of the evening. Avila soon found herself part of multiple conversations, some of which included Galdren. He finally seemed to relax and enjoy the company and meal. By the time the last course was finished and the king stood, Avila felt a warmth fill her that she hadn't felt since her life was changed. She didn't feel like she was a prisoner. Instead, she felt human again, with worth due to her own personality and not because of who she knew. It was a nice feeling, and one Avila was glad to note would probably continue. The irony of the fact that it was due to the royal family did not escape her.

When the king and queen turned to leave, Avila made sure to give them a deep bow along with her smile. A part of her had a hard time believing the meal went so well, but she wasn't going to voice that feeling. Instead, she turned back to Nathan and Galdren. They both seemed to be waiting, although Galdren didn't look pleased about it. She ignored the tightening of his jaw and turned to Nathan with a smile. "Thank you for once again providing such engaging conversation. I can almost see the way the savannah looks from your descriptions."

His smile only widened at her remark. "You should never take my word for it. I promise that it would be much more wonderful for you to see it in person. My invitation still stands. If you are interested, I will be going back on business eventually. You would be welcome to join me."

Avila couldn't help but feel a spark of excitement at the offer. She hadn't taken him seriously the first time he mentioned it, but after speaking with him extensively, she understood the offer was real and open. However, that didn't mean she could say yes on her own. All of her actions would depend on Galdren's approval, so she glanced over at him. She almost flinched at the sight of the storm in his eyes. As she realized how he must feel about the request, she found it was much harder to keep her smile up when she turned back to Nathan. "I will keep the offer in mind. Maybe someday."

All the joy she had felt during dinner was fading fast. When she noticed Nathan's brow furrow slightly, she turned back to Galdren. She could tell Nathan had picked up on her mood change and didn't want to discuss the cause. "Galdren, I wanted to thank you. This was an amazing opportunity, and I am glad I will get the chance to do it more often. For now, though, I find that I am quite worn out. Could we go back to the rooms?"

"Of course." Galdren gave Nathan a polite nod before continuing, "I will extend my appreciation for the invitation as well. I am certain your father would love the opportunity to meet Lady Durant. We can discuss the idea further at some point. For now, we must go." He didn't wait for Avila to take his arm that time. Instead, he reached for her hand and tucked it into his arm before turning and leading her away. She looked back over her shoulder one last time and gave Nathan a wave as they walked away.

The next several days passed in peace. During one dinner, Queen Lorne mentioned that she was expecting a shipment of new plants from off-planet and asked if Avila would like to be there when they were added to the hothouse. Avila had enthusiastically accepted the invitation, and that was precisely where Galdren found her on Thursday afternoon, talking excitedly about the new shipment with the queen.

The two had their heads together and were looking at all the information that had come with the exotic flowers when he walked up. He couldn't help but chuckle at the sight. "If I were to guess, I would say you have found a new species. What did you find this time?" He leaned down and gave his mother a quick peck on the cheek to take any harshness from his words.

If she noticed he was teasing her, she didn't show it. Instead, she held up the report they had been pouring over. "Look at this. I have never seen this variety of colors in one plant. They are called sun lilies because of the way they emit light. Have you ever heard of a plant that can produce light on its own? Isn't it amazing?"

As amused as he was at his mother's enthusiasm, he couldn't help but agree. It was a plant unlike anything he had seen before. "They do seem unique. Do you already have a place for them?"

"Yes, I had to set aside a separate section for them. There is the possibility they could harm some of the other plants, or even be harmed by some of the more aggressive growers. Their light is supposed to not only attract bugs, but—" She stopped speaking when a group of men carrying several open crates stopped in front of them, catching her attention. "Oh, they're here!" The smile she shot both Avila and Galdren before she turned back to the men was brilliant. "Please follow me. I will show you where they should go."

Avila moved to follow the queen when Galdren put a hand on her arm before calling out to his mother's retreating form, "Mother, I need to speak to Avila for a moment. I will send her in as soon as we are finished."

The queen turned back to him with a slight frown. "Don't keep her long. These flowers are from Talamh and I told her she could be here for this."

"Yes, ma'am. I will have her back to you shortly." He gave her a respectful nod before pulling Avila a little farther away from the bustle surrounding the hothouse. "I do apologize for interrupting, but I had something important to ask you."

Avila gave one wistful look back but was smiling when she turned to him. "That's all right. I would most likely have been in the way while they are transplanting anyway. So, what did you need to speak to me about?"

Galdren couldn't help the smile that came up at her question. He was excited to see how she would respond. "I have been working on something this week, and I finally have everything completed so I can be free this weekend. The only thing remaining is you. Would you like to go to Nerada this weekend? We can visit one of the other nearby Talamh communities as well."

Avila looked stunned. "This weekend? It isn't too short of a notice?"

His smile softened at her questions. "That is why I have been working on getting everything finished and set up. I didn't want to say anything if I couldn't get it done on time. If you would like to go, I will have everything ready."

She flashed him a radiant smile. "Of course I would love to go! Thank you so much!" She looked like she might hug him, then seemed to think better of it.

Galdren returned her grin before responding, "Good. I will get you all the details by tonight. For now, why don't you rejoin my mother before she comes looking for you? I'm quite sure it would be unpleasant for me, at least, if it comes to that."

She shook her head at his teasing. "She is the second sweetest woman I have ever met. If it came to that, it would only be something you deserved."

"The second sweetest?"

"Well, I may be a bit biased, but I think Lila is the sweetest. She did raise me, after all."

He chuckled at her response. "I will allow that you are indeed biased, but it is understandable."

She started to reach out to smack his arm lightly but caught herself at the last moment. Instead, she took a step back and grinned up at him. "I'll see you later. Be prepared to hear all about these wonderful new specimens! I was even told I might be able to keep one in my room if we can manage the right setup." She didn't wait for a response before she turned and headed back toward the hothouse. He could only shake his head with a chuckle at her retreating form.

29. NERADA

Saturday morning found Avila up and ready early. Galdren had told her they would be leaving just after dawn to try and get to their destination before it was too late. They would be taking the royal family's private telepad to Nerada, but from there, they would need to use hovercars.

She also double-checked her bag. While winter was in full swing in Arinel, in Nerada, it would be summer. Nerada was in the middle of the southern continent, so she would need to be prepared for the immediate difference when they arrived.

She couldn't help but check the mirror one last time as well. It wasn't that she was trying to primp, but she still didn't feel entirely comfortable in the clothes she was wearing. When Queen Lorne had found out they were going to the spaceport, she had ordered a few sleeveless summer dresses sent over. When Avila had tried to object, the queen was quick to point out that the dresses would be much cooler than pants. Avila had never been to the southern hemisphere and had no idea how hot it could get in summer. She finally relented and agreed to wear them, but she couldn't quite get the feeling that she wasn't fully dressed out of her mind.

Her thoughts were interrupted when Galdren entered. "I see you're ready to go." She gave him a smile that answered his. "You told me we were leaving early."

Galdren had been about to respond when he suddenly stopped, and his eyes flicked down to her legs. They widened for a moment, but he shook his head and looked back up. Avila couldn't help but wonder if she really looked that strange, but wasn't about to ask. Thankfully, Galdren had already started speaking. "We will be expected at the telepad shortly. Do you have everything packed?"

She pointed to the bag next to the door with a smile. He picked it up and held out his arm. "Let's go then." She turned to grab her coat before she took his arm, but he stopped her before she put it on. "You won't need that."

She gave him a confused look but didn't contradict him. She was sure he knew what he was doing. "All right. Lead the way then."

She was surprised to see Angelo waiting with Lee and Jacob but didn't get the chance to ask about it before Galdren handed her bag to Lee and turned to Randy. "Is everything ready?"

"Yes, sir. Your things are already there waiting for us." Galdren gave him a nod before taking Avila's hand and putting it on his arm.

When they started off, both Lee and Angelo followed. This fact confused her for a moment, and then she realized Galdren had picked the two of them to accompany them as her own personal guards. She couldn't help her smile at his thoughtfulness.

When they arrived, Avila wasn't sure what to think of the unremarkable building. It was tiny and paled in comparison to the public facility in Arinel. That one was a large, bustling part of the central travel hub in the city. Not everyone could travel via teleport, partially due to a lack of destination locations, but the cost was a daunting factor as well. Even so, it was a growing part of intraplanetary travel.

When they entered, she was surprised that all the room contained was a large, raised platform with a pedestal off to the side. She had expected something a little different. There was only one person waiting for them, and he bowed when they entered. "Your Highness. Everything is programmed for your trip. Your things are already waiting for you on the platform. I will be happy to transport you as soon as you give me the signal."

Galdren gave him a nod before turning to gesture for the rest of the group to get on the platform. Several bags were waiting on the platform already, and Galdren turned back to the telepad operator once everyone was up. "You may begin."

Avila didn't get a chance to think of anything else before she felt a tingling wash across her skin. It was sudden and unexpected, but the surprised cry didn't even make it out of her lips before the room around her suddenly changed. She realized she was grasping tightly to Galdren's arm when he chuckled at her. "I apologize. I should have warned you about how it would feel. I forgot that you have never traveled that way before."

She only gave him a shaky nod. She was afraid if she tried to speak, she might get sick. After she stepped off the platform, she took a better look around. There weren't windows, but there was a skylight in the ceiling far above them. The room was much larger than the one they had just left, and a woman was standing a short distance away, bowing to Galdren.

Avila hadn't noticed that the rest of the group already had their things and was waiting by the exit while she looked around. When she realized they were waiting on her, she gave Galdren a sheepish smile. "I apologize for being so distracted."

He shook his head at her. "Don't apologize. You shouldn't forget that this trip is for you. Although I know you wanted to come to try to see into your past, that doesn't mean I expect you to not look around. The spaceport is a wonderful place to visit, and I expect you will enjoy it."

She gave him one of her particularly bright smiles before following him out. Once they were outside, Avila couldn't help but stop. The heat was instant and suffocating. She had known it would be summer here, but knowing it and experiencing it were two different things. She was instantly glad that the queen had convinced her to wear a dress.

She was pulled from her thoughts when Galdren took her hand and once more put it on his arm. "I don't want to get separated. We have transports waiting for us, but they are on the other side of the facility."

She nodded her understanding. She couldn't help but wonder if he realized that his proximity to her in such a way might give strangers the wrong impression. Especially since they were headed into a busy port. Any worries she had about it were quickly forgotten when they stepped out of the private telepad's enclosure.

Avila felt like she was trying to look in several different directions at the same time. The sight of the massive spaceships in the distance was awe-inspiring, and the crowd was just as interesting. Although the exit from the private telepad led them into a hall that allowed them to circumvent the public portions of the spaceport, the large windows provided a clear view down into the crowd of people coming and going. When Avila caught sight of a flash of blue, she slowed to get a better look. She stopped completely when she saw a group of people whose iridescent skin flashed shades of blue and green when they moved.

She remembered learning the basics of the Allied planets, but there had not been a lot of emphasis on anything other than the fact that all known races were humanoid. Still, only a couple of planets had races similar to those who lived on Aril. Avila was awed at the variety that life created under different circumstances. She was also relieved to note that she wasn't as odd as she had been made to feel her whole life.

She realized Galdren had stopped when she did, as her hand was still on his arm. She gave him a sheepish grin as she started walking again. "I apologize for that. There is just so much to see. Are you sure two days is enough time?"

There was a teasing note in her voice, but Galdren seemed to realize she was only partially joking. He pulled her to a halt as he gestured around them. "Avila, do not feel rushed. We have nowhere to be. If you see something that you want to check out, let me know. That is why we are here. If we can not see it all in two days, then we will see more the next time we come. This is only the beginning."

Avila felt herself relax under his earnest gaze, even though she felt a familiar warmth warring for attention. She could tell that he meant every word of that, and it reassured her to know that no matter the circumstances, he was still her friend. He still cared.

Still, it wouldn't do either of them any good for her to start acting like a fool in public. Instead, she managed a nod. "Thank you. I'm sure there will be lots to see." Galdren gave her a smile that made her need to look away. He was already too close. When she thought about that in conjunction with the windows, she wondered again at what he was thinking, but it didn't take her long to notice that the glass was one-way. That was a relief.

They continued walking, and eventually stopped at a waiting extended hovercar. Even though the vehicle had come from a reliable source, it still took the four guards nearly an hour to go over it thoroughly to ensure the occupants' safety.

While they worked, Galdren took Avila to the side and pointed out some of the things they might see while in Blathane, the community they were scheduled to visit. It was a strange feeling for her. Some of the things he mentioned went straight over her head, but others felt oddly familiar. Even some of the customs or items she didn't recognize by name initially, she felt drawn to when he showed her pictures. It was both frightening and exhilarating to know that at least a small part of her past was in reach, even if she couldn't remember it directly.

By the time the hovercar was deemed safe, Avila was so excited that she could barely sit still. It would take them another hour and a half to get out of the city and to their destination. She could hardly wait. To try and keep herself occupied, she stared out the window.

When Avila heard Galdren chuckle, she looked back with a frown. He immediately shook his head as he said, "Please don't stop on my account. I just realized how refreshing it is to see you enjoy the sights. I have been here often enough that I sometimes forget to notice all the wonders. It's pleasant being reminded of them again." Avila wasn't sure how she felt about that sentiment, but there was too much to see to let it worry her for long.

When they arrived in Blathane, the first thing they did was head to the hotel where they would be staying. It was a small enough community that there were few choices. When they walked in, Avila was taken aback to see people standing at attention in castle livery. There were more than just a few, too. She looked over to Galdren to ask what that was about, but he preempted her.

"They arrived yesterday to secure the location. They will remain until after we leave."

Avila was once again reminded of how different this life was than anything she had ever known. It was nearly stifling. Thankfully, the feeling did not last long. Randy dealt with the arrangements, and they were all up to the suite of rooms in short order. She was thrilled when they walked in to deposit their things. The room was tiny compared to her suite back at the palace, but it was cozy.

The sitting room had a desk and several chairs. She was pleased to see there were two sleeping rooms, which were both connected to the bath. That also had everything she had gotten used to recently, though again, on a smaller scale. She had to repress a chuckle at how her perceptions had changed. Less than a year ago, she would have thought the rooms were the most opulent thing she had ever laid eyes on. A little part of her mind wondered how she would feel if she were forced to go back to her old life and home, and realized she would be disappointed. It was funny how things changed when she wasn't paying attention.

The group hardly did more than drop their stuff off. Galdren asked Avila if she wanted to freshen up, but she was too excited to see what was out there. She didn't bother to do more than splash some water on her face to help cool her off before they were off again. Galdren had barely been able to slow her down enough to remind her to be mindful of the heat. Her only response was to grin before she dashed down the stairs. The rest of the group was hard-pressed to follow in a dignified manner. At least she remembered that people were watching when they made it to the foyer and slowed as well.

Instead of taking the vehicle again, the group opted to walk. The streets were crowded, but not as much as they would have been in Arinel. Plus, most people moved out of the way before anyone had to say something. Avila cringed internally at the fact that there was no way she would be able to experience the city to its fullest—not when there were four hulking guards with weapons nearby and even more following at a distance. She was shocked that the streets hadn't cleared out completely at their arrival.

At least Galdren was doing his best to keep her preoccupied. He kept pointing things out as they walked, and it wasn't long until she forgot the limitations of the trip. As she looked around, the confirmation that she was not alone in the universe was both thrilling and overwhelming. When she caught snippets of speech, the accents and even the occasional foreign word made her smile brighten. The accents were much like the one she had when she first arrived on Aril. Hers was all but gone now, but hearing it from others was like music to her ears. It was just confirmation that the people around her really were from the same planet—from Talamh.

After the group of six had been wandering for well over two hours, they made their way to a section of the town where there were many businesses. Avila wasn't interested in shopping, but it was fascinating to see the different specialty shops. Some of the things, especially the food items, she had never seen before, though others did tug at her forgotten memories.

While they were looking over a line of wrapped baked goods, the shop owner came out to greet them but froze when he caught sight of Avila. The man's eyes widened, and he stood there with his mouth open. That lasted for several seconds before too many things happened all at once.

The shop owner fell to his knees and reached out to Avila. Immediately, Galdren pulled her back and pushed her toward Angelo, who was next to her with his gun up as soon as she was secured. Both Randy and Baxter did the same for Galdren. They all froze like that when the man finally started to speak.

He had ignored the rest of the group's actions; his eyes never left Avila. He was still holding his hands out, but he did not try to grab her. Instead, it looked as though he were entreating her. His voice was broken as he said, "Your Majesty, you are alive! Our hope, our light, it has survived. We thought you dead with the king."

Avila was stunned by the whole ordeal. Everything had happened so quickly that she wasn't sure how to react. At a loss, she gestured for the man to get to his feet. "Please, get up." He was older, and seeing him down on his knees made her cringe. She tried not to think about his words.

The man started crying when she spoke to him. The guards, clearly figuring the man didn't seem to want to attack, relaxed their stances but stayed alert. Baxter and Lee moved to help the man back into his shop, but before they could, a young woman came rushing out of the store and helped the man to his feet.

The girl bowed to the gathered people and gave Galdren a scared look. "Please forgive us, Your Highness. My grandfather meant no harm, I promise." Her eyes shot to Avila when the man continued to talk about the light returning. They widened for a fraction of a second before she lowered them and said, "I am sure there has been some misunderstanding. The past has been hard for him to let go of. Please do not take offense."

Galdren finally stepped forward and waved off the girl's concern with a smile. "No harm has been done. Though, it might be best to have him rest for a moment. Too much excitement could be detrimental."

The girl gave him another quick bow before she looked around at the rest of the group. It was clear that she understood his meaning well enough. They didn't want to cause a scene, and to prevent more drastic measures being taken, it would be best to get the man off the street. The girl's eyes lingered with curiosity on Avila for a few seconds longer than the rest, but she tore her gaze away and bowed one last time. She then pulled on her grandfather's arm. "Come in and let me make you some *ciuin buaidh.*"

The old man resisted for a moment, but he finally noticed the five tense men as well. Fear passed through his eyes before they settled into resignation. He looked back at Avila once more before he turned to his granddaughter. They could barely hear him as he answered, "Yes, I think that might be good."

Once the two were back in the shop, Galdren turned to Avila with concern in his eyes. "Are you all right?"

She nodded. She was more confused than upset. Plus, there was something roiling inside her that she couldn't quite place. That man had been addressing her when he said "Your Majesty," not Galdren. She hadn't missed the way the girl looked at her either. What had that been about?

She was pulled from her tumultuous thoughts by Galdren's hand on her arm. His look was even more concerned than it had been. She managed to push back the unsettling feeling and give him a tight smile. "I'm fine. A little confused, but not harmed."

He did not look convinced. "Do we need to return to the hotel?"

Avila shook off the last of her discomfort and took a step back. She avoided looking around again when she answered. "Not at all. It would be a pointless trip if I don't get to see anything. Though, I will ask that we head to another street, please." Galdren's jaw was tight, but he didn't argue. Instead, he nodded to the others, and they all fell into formation again, this time with Randy and Angelo out front.

The next thirty minutes were still so tense that Avila hardly saw anything around her. Instead of looking at the shops and the novel differences, she found herself watching the people. She wasn't sure what she was looking for, but she wondered at each glance her way. Were they looking at her because she was with the crown prince, or was it something else? It wasn't until they stopped for lunch that she finally shook off her worries. No matter what that had been about, she wasn't going to get answers by fretting.

The rest of the day was uneventful. Avila was nearly overwhelmed by the amount of culture that surrounded her. So much of it was familiar, even though she couldn't remember it.

Galdren had arranged for them to have a special dinner, so they made their way back to the hotel to clean up. Avila had started to flag a little and was uncertain about making it through the dinner. However, her excitement and energy returned in spades when they arrived at the restaurant and the host bowed to them before he greeted them in Canain, the native language of Talamh. She was even more pleased to find that she understood him and was able to answer in kind.

The host's smile was bright when he stood and looked at Avila, and a moment later, he gestured for everyone to follow. "Your Highness, please follow me. We have a room reserved for you."

The meal was just as unique as the rest of the day had been, and Avila was surprised to find that the more she saw, the more it all came back to her. Not any specific memories, unfortunately, but the things that would have been seen every day on Talamh. It almost felt like the return of dear friends after a long absence.

As the meal wore on, Avila was thrilled to interact with the servers and host. Even the owner of the restaurant came over. She did feel a little awkward when they had realized she could speak Canain fluently and switched to accommodate her, since that left Galdren and the others out. However, when she looked at him with a questioning glance, he shook his head with a smile and made a small gesture for her to continue. She was grateful for the chance, and took full advantage of it. She did try to make sure to translate for him often so he would not be entirely left out of the conversation.

It was late when they finally made it back to the hotel, and even though Avila was dead on her feet, she still could not shake off her smile. When the restaurant owner had joined them, he was more than happy to tell her things he could remember of Talamh when she explained her lack of memories. She was sure part of it had been the fact that she was with Galdren, but she had a feeling that even if she had not been, the man would have been happy to share.

She had noted the man's melancholy, but he did not let it color his retelling. It saddened her to know that her home planet was occupied, which was why they were all on Aril. Still, the few people that had mentioned it to her had not lost hope that they would see their home again someday. It was enough to buoy Avila's spirits. She wasn't sure why, but she thought that maybe, it was because she hoped to see it one day too. Even if she couldn't remember, she had a feeling it would be worth the wait.

Her last thoughts before she fell to sleep were of all the future possibilities. She had no doubt it would not be the last time she visited Blathane, and she was still smiling when she finally drifted off.

30. WHAT IF?

The next day was as eventful as the previous one had been. The hotelier provided them with what he said was a traditional breakfast before he recommended that they check out the open-air market. Avila was thrilled with all of it. She didn't even think to argue when Galdren insisted that she pick something out to take back with her.

She hadn't wanted to get anything large, but she finally found a thin bracelet of finely woven silver. The design looped around, then back in on itself. The stall owner had explained that it represented the knot of eternity. There was no beginning, and no end. It was supposed to represent the cycle of life, death, and rebirth that was common to the belief structure on Talamh. Despite not remembering the concept, it still resonated within her, and she wore it for the rest of the day.

All in all, it was an exceptional trip. By the time they headed back to Nerada and then Aril, Avila was both tired and satisfied. It was late when they got back to their rooms that night, but her excellent mood carried into her sleep, and her nightmares couldn't touch her.

The next few weeks seemed to fly by. Professor Gilbert seemed thrilled to see Avila in such high spirits, and even more so when she shared the tales of her adventure. The only thing she didn't mention was her run-in with the strange shopkeeper. She didn't tell anyone about that. It wasn't that it bothered her, per se, but she still had no idea what to think of it. That meant she tried not to.

She hadn't even mentioned it to her parents, though if anyone knew anything, it might have been them. Still, it wasn't worth bringing up. It wasn't like she had much time to talk to them anyway. She vo-imed them at least once every few days, along with Lissa, but none of them had been able to visit since she moved, and the conversations were usually short by necessity. She did vow to make arrangements to see them soon when she had the chance to speak to Galdren about it.

Nathan had been just as thrilled to hear her tales as the professor had been. The two of them spent nearly every afternoon in the gardens after her lessons were done for the day. The only time they didn't was when the rain or duties prevented it.

Avila noted that Galdren didn't seem to be fond of his cousin, but he was never rude. Though, the interactions between the two men were usually only at dinner time. That she didn't see the prince often anymore still bothered her, but any time she thought about it, she reminded herself that it was not her business anyway.

If she wasn't with Nathan or the professor, she was in the hothouse with Queen Lorne. The two of them were still trying to ensure that the new arrivals were going to survive the trip. Thankfully, they had only lost a couple of plants so far. They had even moved one to Avila's room as promised. So far it was doing well, though she had to be mindful that it not get too much sun.

It was during one of those meetings near the end of her second week back from Nerada that the queen turned to her with a soft smile. "I had almost forgotten, but there will be a party this weekend. One of our cousins has just come of age, and we will be celebrating here. It would be wonderful if you agreed to attend."

Avila tried not to grimace. She had enjoyed herself during the last ball, but she couldn't bring herself to look forward to them. Still, the look the queen was giving her was hard to turn down. "I would be happy to if you think I would not be out of place."

Queen Lorne came dangerously close to rolling her eyes as she waved off Avila's concern. "You are part of this household. It would only be strange if you never attended such functions."

Avila still wasn't sure she agreed with that sentiment, but she wasn't going to argue. "All right, then. Will it be as formal as the last one?"

After that, the two of them got drawn into a discussion about what Avila would wear. She wasn't thrilled that the queen insisted on bringing more dresses for her to look at, but somehow, she still ended up looking at several the next afternoon.

This time, she was told she could keep all the dresses and accessories she liked for future use, but the one she picked out for the party was scarlet. The color was showy enough that she almost declined it, but once she tried it on, she found it complemented her complexion well. It was floor length with a high neckline, and the sleeves were fitted and went to her wrists. A sheer sewn-in cape-like attachment fell from her shoulders to the floor and covered most of her arms, but the fabric flowed well enough that it did not hinder her movement.

The fitted bodice had tiny embroidered vines in a similar color to the dress that circled the waist before crisscrossing over the chest and around the neck. Even though Avila loved it, she did wonder if it was too flashy. The queen assured her it was not.

Once that was decided, Queen Lorne waited until the tailor and his crew were gone before she gestured to one of her guards, and the woman brought over a case. Avila eyed it as the woman handed it to her, then hesitated as she looked over at the queen. The other woman only smiled and put her hand over Avila's on top of the box. "I was told you didn't even bother looking at any other pieces. Consider them a gift. They should go well with almost anything."

Avila's eyes widened when she realized what the queen must be talking about. She opened the case to see the vine necklace and matching earrings. When she looked up again to object, the other woman only shook her head. "Don't bother. I'm sure you have already been told how stubborn I can be. Let me have this."

That response had Avila floundering. After a few seconds, she slowly closed the box and gave the queen a nod. "Thank you." That was all she could produce; she was too touched by the gesture. It seemed to be enough for the queen, as they soon got caught up in another conversation about a possible new addition the queen was thinking of adding to her hothouse collection. It was another exotic, but if she did decide to have them shipped in, it would be the following year.

The next day found Savanah and her crew back in Avila's rooms. It didn't take quite as long as it had last time, but Avila was learning the woman was a perfectionist. She refused to declare the preparations finished until she was fully satisfied with the look. At least they were done with more than enough time for her to eat something before Meru arrived to help with the dress.

Once again, Galdren was not able to escort her personally. It was something that she was getting used to, even if it did bother her, especially when she thought about how close they had seemed during the trip to Blathane—but perhaps it had all been in her imagination. They were still close friends, even if they didn't speak as often. She forced those thoughts from her mind as Angelo led her out of the family wing. They weren't going to do anything to help her mood.

Her forced smile became a real one when she walked out of the family wing to see Nathan waiting with Adam. His eyes lit up when he saw her, and he dropped into a low bow. "It is as though I have been graced by the goddess herself."

When he stood, he took her hand and grinned at her. Avila felt her cheeks heat slightly at his compliment, but she shook her head. "There is no need for flattery."

He gave her a wink as he brushed a kiss across her knuckles. "Who said it was flattery?"

Avila pulled her hand back and tried to give him a scowl, though the effect was ruined by the pink tips of her ears. "Why are you here?"

He rolled his eyes at her obstinance before he took her hand again and tucked it into his arm. "I was told you did not have an escort. I would hope that I am sufficient."

"Oh." As close as the two of them were becoming, she had not thought of him wanting to escort her anywhere. She knew it meant little as far as affection went, but she was pleased that he held her in high enough regard to wish to do so. She finally managed a grin to match his. "Well, if that is the case, then lead on, Lord de Legris." He rolled his eyes again at her use of his title as they headed toward the ballroom.

When they paused in the doorway, Avila felt a little uncomfortable when they were announced. She hadn't thought about how it might look that they arrived together, but from the looks she caught, she felt some people were reading more into it than there was. At least it wasn't long until Nathan had her forgetting about the rest. The group in attendance was different from the one last time, but there were still many people she recognized.

When it was time for the ball to start, Avila allowed Nathan to guide her into the ballroom, but she felt her heart lurch when they stayed back and watched as Galdren led a stunning young woman onto the floor. She couldn't ignore the whispers of how good the two looked together and wondered if perhaps the girl was one of the few that would be in the running for Galdren's bride. He would eventually have to marry.

That thought left a burning sensation in her stomach. Thankfully, Nathan was quick to grab her attention as he pulled her onto the dance floor. His smile was strained, and she knew he had realized something was wrong, but he didn't mention it. Instead, he told her a little about the girl that was the honoree of the proceedings, and currently dancing with Galdren.

She wasn't exactly relieved when Nathan told her the girl was their cousin in little more than name. The relation was so distant that the only reason they still called them cousin was because the girl's family was loud in proclaiming their relation to the royal family. He also told her that the girl was supposed to be the epitome of what a young royal should be. She could tell he hadn't meant it as a compliment, but that didn't make her feel any better. She had to push back visions of what might happen to her when Galdren did finally find someone.

Nathan led Avila through several more dances, and she was even asked by a few of the men they had talked to earlier. Still, she could not banish the picture of Galdren dancing with the beautiful tall blonde. Finally, she had to beg off the next dance and headed to the refreshment table. Nathan offered to go in her stead, but she smiled and told him to go mingle. He clearly didn't like it, but he seemed to understand she needed a few moments away from everyone and nodded to her before walking to where the queen and king were standing with Galdren.

Avila was grateful that he had not insisted more. She was also thankful that he was there to help her keep her mind off things she shouldn't be thinking of, but that didn't keep her from feeling overwhelmed.

When she got to the refreshment area, she didn't even bother looking at the selection; she just grabbed the closest drink. However, she nearly spat it back out again when the saccharin flavor crossed her tongue. It was more like syrup than fruit juice. She managed to swallow it to keep from making a fool of herself, but she also put the half-empty cup back on the tray of discards.

When she turned around to face the dance floor once again, she was pulled up short by the sight of the blonde she had seen dancing with Galdren. It took her several seconds to remember the girl's name, but she finally bowed. "It's a pleasure to meet you, Lady Dunoire. I hope your birthday celebrations are to your liking."

The girl eyed her for a moment before she accepted a drink from the attendant. With the cup in hand, she stepped until she stood next to Avila. She looked out at the crowd and smiled before she lowered her voice and said, "Why are you here?"

Avila was taken aback. She wasn't sure what had motivated the question, but she still tried to be polite. "I beg your pardon that we have not had the chance to meet yet, but I'm sure the queen invited me so that I could remedy that fact."

The girl finally turned to face her. She was still smiling, but it never reached her eyes, and her voice was cold. "That is not what I meant. Surely you thought about how it might disgrace me to have you here? You may be a budding scientist of some renown, and even be touted as a ward of the royal family, but that doesn't negate what else you are."

Avila felt her blood run cold. There were always those who did not accept her presence in the capital, but none had been so forthright about it in years. She faked a smile to match Lady Dunoire's as she answered, "What else? And what else do you believe me to be that would be so disgraceful?"

The girl covered a huff with her cup. Her smile was back in place when she lowered it, but Avila did not miss the tension in her jaw. "Look around you. Do you see any others like you?" The girl paused long enough to catch Avila's eye before she continued, "Your kind are not welcome in the capital for a reason. Even if that were not the case, I have no desire for the prince's harlot to be paraded about during a celebration meant for me."

Avila's smile froze. This was precisely what she had been afraid of. Some people were going to believe whatever they wished, no matter the evidence. She was still trying to work through a reply when the girl lifted her nose a little and added, "It's even more disgraceful that you flaunt your connection to Lord de Legris. As though it were not enough to bed the royal heir." She then turned to Avila with a sneer. "You should leave."

Finally, Avila managed to find her tongue. She gave the girl a cold smile of her own, and her eyes flashed as she said, "Do not worry, my lady, I will ensure that we never speak again. Since harlotism is obviously a communicable disease, I need to make sure I don't catch it." She then bowed her head slightly. "If you'll excuse me." She turned back to the refreshment area and walked to the far end.

From the corner of her eye, Avila could see the Lady Dunoire stare after her for a few moments with an expression that was just shy of murder. It took the girl several seconds to bring it back under control. She huffed once more and practically threw the cup in her hand before storming off.

Nathan was wearing a bright smile when he got to where Galdren was standing. He bowed to them all before he turned to his aunt. "You are lovely as ever, ma'am."

Lorne chuckled at his pandering, then waved him closer. "Come, tell me how the night goes."

Nathan's smile faltered for a split second, but he managed to cover it as he joined them on the dais, and it was as brilliant as ever when he gestured across the room. "The Lady Dunoire is exceptionally lucky to have you at the head of her arrangements. This will be a night she won't soon forget, I'm sure."

The queen's expression fell slightly as she raised a brow at him. "While I am sure you are correct, that was not what I meant. How has the newest member of our household been this night?"

Nathan's smile faded a little as he looked across the room. It did not take him long to locate Avila. He was surprised to see the ball's honoree approaching her, but he didn't comment on it. Instead, he turned back to the queen. "She fits in exceptionally well, at least when she is not thinking about trying to." He shook his head and gave her a lopsided smile. "She seems to be the only one to not realize how brilliant she is."

The queen returned his smile with one of her own. "I am sure that will change in time. Thank you for offering to escort her. I'm sure she appreciates having a familiar face nearby."

He gave her a nod as his eyes sought out the woman they were speaking of once again. They narrowed as he watched the two women talking. Something seemed off, but his attention was drawn by Galdren. "Nathan, would you speak with me a moment?"

Nathan looked over at his cousin with curiosity. It was unusual for him to bring up anything of import during one of these things, but he still nodded. "Of course. Do we need to leave?"

Galdren seemed to be fighting a frown as he shook his head. "Not at all. This is something I have discussed with the queen already."

Nathan gave him another curious look and wondered again why it couldn't wait. When he looked over at the thrones, the queen waved them off. "It is nothing to worry about."

Galdren's expression didn't seem to agree, but he still stepped to the side. He got right to the point as soon as Nathan joined him. "I understand that your offer for Lady Durant to visit the Peloun Reserve was sincere. I am sure she only declined because I have previously expressed my wish for her not to go anywhere unattended, and I cannot spare the time to go with you."

It took all Nathan had not to frown at the reminder. He was one of the few people who was privy to the full reason Avila was part of the castle household, and he didn't care for it. Still, there was little he could do about it.

He was not given a chance to voice any of his thoughts before Galdren continued, "I have sworn to protect her, and if she goes, I will not be able to." He then paused and gave Nathan an intense look. "However, I know she wishes to visit the reserve. If I were to allow it, would you give me your word that you would do the same in my place?"

Nathan was struck dumb for several seconds. The offer was the last thing he had expected. Still, he already had an answer. "I give my word that she will be safe with me."

Galdren's jaw clenched. Avila might not understand what was going on, but Nathan had no doubts as to what motivated the prince's expression. That didn't make him back down. He stood there and waited for Galdren to find the words. "When I ask for her safety to be ensured, I mean against all threats. Physical and emotional."

Nathan raised a brow at that. He had to swallow a barbed retort about Galdren's actions where the woman was concerned. Now wasn't the time. Instead, he managed a nod. "I would think to do no less."

Galdren's fists clenched along with his jaw that time, but after a few seconds, he gave his cousin a nod. "Then I will agree to allow her to go with you when you go back to your father's estate. Since you will only be gone for a few weeks, it is acceptable for her to return with you. We can discuss the details tomorrow since you will not be leaving until the end of next week."

Nathan was stunned. That was the last thing he had expected. Still, he wasn't about to decline. He gave his cousin a bright smile that he also turned to the king and queen before bowing. "Well, if that is the case, I believe I have happy news to share. If you will excuse me, please."

Galdren watched him leave with stormy eyes. No one except maybe his father heard his mother's words. "This is the right thing. You are giving her the space she needs to learn and grow in more ways than one. Take solace in that."

He knew she was right, of course. He had already decided that if he were to fulfill his duties toward Avila, then he could not keep her isolated. That did not make it hurt less to watch the jaunt in Nathan's steps as he walked back to where Avila was waiting.

31. HAPPY NEWS

Nathan was shocked when Lady Dunoire walked by with barely a pause. He thought he heard her mumble out a greeting, but she was off before he could respond. Her swift departure had him worried as he looked around to find Avila.

When he finally saw her, she was at the far end of the refreshment area and had just downed a drink. She put a hand on her chest and grimaced, then reached for another. His eyes widened, and he rushed forward. He made it just in time to pluck the drink from her hands and gave her a cheery smile when she glowered at him. "I think perhaps you should be looking for a different refreshment. These are not usually the downing variety."

Avila sighed and shrugged. "I figured that out after the first one." She tried to smile back. "I apologize for leaving you alone so long."

Nathan's smile fell and his eyes narrowed as he looked at the tension in her jaw and the tightness in her eyes before he set the cup down and put her hand on his arm. His voice was low as he led her away. "What happened?"

She nearly grimaced at his question, then shook her head. "Nothing worth talking about."

He pulled them both to a stop before they reached the dance floor. "Why don't you let me be the judge of that?"

Her eyes were hard when she looked up at him. "I apologize, but no. I handled it already."

Nathan suddenly had a horrible feeling that he knew what had gone on between the two women, but this was not the place to keep prying. Instead, he took a deep breath and tried to smile again. "Fine. Then why don't we have a change in subject?"

She eyed him warily, and he had to remind himself of where they were to keep from winking at her. "I have some excellent news. Would you like to hear?"

Her expression did not change at all when she responded, "I have a feeling you're going to tell me anyway."

The deadpan look she was giving was too much. He chuckled as he patted her hand. "Of course, but I promise you'll be glad I did."

When her only response was to try and pull her hand away, he finally relented and stopped teasing her. "I spoke to my cousin just before I came to find you. Much to my surprise, he told me he was willing to give you permission to visit the Peloun Reserve when I go back next week."

His words instantly had her expression changing. She grasped his arm tightly and lowered her voice. "It is not funny to joke like that."

Nathan's grin toned down into a soft smile. "No jokes. I promise. He said it would be all right for you to stay until I have to return."

She swallowed a few times before she looked over to the dais. Galdren was not looking in their direction, but the queen was. The woman gave Avila a bright smile before she turned again to her husband. Avila then looked back at Nathan. It looked like she might hug him.

Her voice held more than a little excitement as she asked, "So, we are going with you next week? And we'll be gone for, what? Three weeks? What kind of clothes will I need? Will we have time to visit the savannah?" All signs of her previous bad mood were gone.

Nathan's chuckle turned into a laugh. "Woah, hold on—one at a time. First, Galdren has said he will not be able to go with us, so it will just be the two of us. And your guards, of course. As for the rest, we can go over the details tomorrow." He paused and made sure he had her attention since she looked like she had walked into a wall. There was a mix of emotions in her eyes that he tried to mitigate as he said, "Avila, I have to warn you that I will be there for business. Part of what I do is work as the liaison between the duke and the palace. However, I will make sure we have time to let you see as much of the reserve as you can handle."

Eventually, she managed to shake off her stupor. "I apologize. I'm just shocked." She then managed to grin at him. "But I am still looking forward to it! This is the chance of a lifetime, even if you will be busy most of the time."

Nathan was glad to see a real smile from her instead of the fake one she had been trying to pass off earlier. He returned it as he pulled her toward the dance floor once again. After that, neither of them noticed the passing of time as they got lost in conversation about what was to come. Though, the night did end earlier than anticipated. Just the one drink was enough to make Avila loopy after a short while. Nathan had to fight his laughter the whole way back to the family wing. He was almost loath to see her go, but he knew it had given him plenty of ammunition for their next conversation.

The following day, Avila could hardly sit still. She was still trying to deal with her conflicting emotions about what was to come. On the one hand, she was going to go to Peloun. It was more than she expected after her trip to Araleen went so poorly. She was positively giddy with thoughts about what she might see.

On the other, she was going without Galdren. That was the crux of her confusion. She tried to be elated at the thought that he was willing to trust her to go somewhere without him, but she could not entirely erase the doubt that he might have an ulterior motive. Especially after her conversation with the beautiful Lady Dunoire. The timing was too close for her to not at least consider that there could be a connection. Was he sending her away at the girl's suggestion?

Even if she didn't think about that, which was difficult, she still had to consider why he had been willing to let her go after he had been so adamant that her safety was only guaranteed with him. It wasn't until she thought about it that she realized she had subconsciously been allowing his words when she first moved to give her hope that there was more going on than there actually was. It was a hard pill to swallow, but she forced herself to admit it.

When it got to the point that pacing around her room was not enough, she decided to go for a walk. Unfortunately, it started raining not long after she entered the gardens. Instead of heading back to her room, she raced to the hothouse. At least she would be able to walk around in there and not feel as cooped up.

She was thrilled when she entered to find Queen Lorne already there. The woman gave her a bright smile as she gestured for her to come over. "I understand that you will be leaving for a few weeks?"

Avila hadn't doubted Nathan, but hearing it confirmed by the queen shot electricity through her veins. Despite her worries, she practically bounced on the balls of her feet and had to swallow a squeal of excitement. "I haven't spoken to Galdren about it yet, but Nathan told me last night. I can't wait to go!"

Queen Lorne's eyes dimmed for a moment, but her voice didn't show it. "I'm glad to know you are so excited about it. I must confess, that is the one reserve I have never been to, so I envy you."

Avila stopped in shock. She had expected the queen to have visited all of them. Still, she shook it off. "Well, I can promise to bring back plenty of sketches for you."

The queen wasn't given a chance to respond, as they were interrupted by Galdren. "I thought I might find you here."

Avila turned to him with a grin, but it faded slightly when she caught his eyes. His expression was genial, but there was something missing. Some warmth that she usually saw that wasn't there. However, she wasn't given the opportunity to reply, as he immediately added, "I hate to pull you away from the hothouse, but I need to speak with you. I will be busy this afternoon."

The queen patted Avila's arm with a smile. "Don't worry, these will still be waiting."

Neither the queen nor Galdren showed anything other than a smile, but Avila couldn't shake off the feeling that there was more going on. Still, she doubted they would tell her if she asked. Instead, she motioned toward the door. "We can speak here if you wish. If not, I hope you brought an umbrella. I hadn't thought to bring mine."

He chuckled at her quip and turned toward the door. "I thought that might have been the case, so I brought an extra. Besides, I believe Lee should have one as well."

Avila stopped and tapped her chin. "Huh, I hadn't thought of that."

Galdren nearly rolled his eyes, though he didn't say anything as he motioned for her to follow.

When they got back to her rooms, Avila immediately went to stand in front of the fireplace. Galdren took a seat nearby before he spoke. "Nathan already told you that I agreed to allow him to escort you to the Peloun Reserve, correct?"

Avila turned and tried to keep her grin to a manageable level. "Yes!" She then paused as it occurred to her that his mood might be an indicator that he was actually upset because he couldn't go as well instead of the conjectures she had previously been considering. She gave him a grin as she added, "You know, it would have been nice if you could come too, but like I told your mother, I can bring back lots of sketches."

Galdren didn't respond right away. She watched as his expression became guarded, which didn't help her mindset, but he finally said, "While I appreciate the offer, and I am sure my mother will love your sketches, there is no need for you to worry on my behalf. I have been there before. Plus, you should focus on making the most of your trip."

Avila gave him a curious look. He hadn't denied he was upset about not going, even though he had already been. It made her all the more curious and worried as to why he was troubled. "Are you sure?"

Galdren sighed and looked over with a wry smile. "You never give up, do you?"

She only raised a brow in response. He chuckled at the sight of it before he shrugged. "I am sure. However, since I will not be able to personally ensure your safety, I will admit to being uncomfortable after what happened previously."

Avila's smile instantly dimmed. She tried not to think about the last reserve visit, and his reminder was like a slap to the face. Still, she knew he hadn't meant it that way, so she tried to keep her discomfort to herself. "Well, that's one thing I'm sure you don't need to worry about. I'm going with my guards, right? Plus, I doubt Nathan would allow anything to happen that might mar his good name."

Despite the somber turn in the conversation, Galdren managed a real smile as he said, "I am sure you are correct. From what I understand, my uncle has wanted to meet you as well, so I doubt you will have much time to yourself anyway."

She gave him a doubtful look. "If you say so." Her fingers were finally warm by that time, so she turned to take a seat before she gave him another curious look. "I doubt that was all you wanted to speak to me about, or you would not have pulled me back here. What else is there?"

He shook his head and smiled. "I felt it would be prudent to discuss the details and possible situations. I have a meeting scheduled later to go over the finer points with Nathan as well."

Avila had to fight not to roll her eyes. She had a feeling she was about to be given many more rules to follow. She only managed to stop herself at the memory of the recent reminder of why he was so protective. Even if she still wasn't sure what motivated him to send her, she didn't doubt that they were at least friends. When her only response was to look at him expectantly, he continued.

Over the next hour, he laid out who would be going, when she would be leaving, the routes they would be taking, and lastly, what she was to do in case of emergencies. She would have liked to say it was more than she needed, but it was all she expected. Still, she didn't complain. Instead, she thanked him for the trouble he was going through to let her go and waved him out before she headed back out to the hothouse. At least it had quit raining.

The next morning, Avila hit her first snag. She had forgotten about her studies in her excitement to go to the Peloun Reserve. Now, she had to figure out what to say to Professor Gilbert. She hoped he wouldn't be too upset. Even with everything that both Nathan and Galdren had already gone through, she would reschedule the trip if necessary. Not that she wanted to.

She was up and pacing when the professor finally came in. His brow rose when she turned to him with an earnest look. He set his things down and approached her. "From that look, I would say you have a favor to ask."

Avila chuckled awkwardly and gave him a half-shrug. "I suppose that is close enough to the truth."

When he gave her an expectant look, she took a deep breath and decided to get it over with. "I was invited to spend the next three weeks at the Peloun Reserve and said yes before I thought about what it would mean for my studies. It wasn't until this morning that it even crossed my mind, so we can rearrange things if we need to. Unless you want to go too? I'm sure that can be arranged."

The professor chuckled. "I don't think that would be as easy to arrange as you are inferring. Besides, would it not be better for you to focus on other things while you are there? I'm sure there will be plenty to keep you busy."

Avila froze before she jumped forward and grabbed his arm with a grin. "Does this mean you are all right with me going?"

He patted her hand before he extricated himself and went to pull out his papers. "While I am not fond of the delay, this is the type of opportunity that I told you would come your way. So few people are invited that it would be ridiculous for me to stand in the way of this trip."

Once he had everything out, he turned to her with a somber face. "That being said, do expect me to send work with you. It would be counterproductive if you were to lose focus entirely."

Avila was still grinning as she took her seat. "Of course. No matter what, I will dedicate at least a few hours a day to make sure any work you send gets done."

Avila watched as he put his hand over his face to conceal his obvious laughter. She tried not to grin when he finally looked up and started pulling out the things for her lessons. That was the last it was mentioned, and they quickly got to work. They did have a lot to fit in before she left, after all.

The rest of the week was a flurry of activity for Avila. The queen seemed nearly as excited as she was and helped Avila make sure she would have appropriate clothing: more summer dresses, and even shorts. The last was an unexpected addition, but Queen Lorne assured her that it would be acceptable where she was going. It was hot there by Arinel standards, all year round. To wear more in the summer would be intolerable. Since she would be in the field often, the shorts would be indispensable.

Avila was mortified when she finally saw all her luggage together. She had never traveled far before the trip to Nerada, and that had only been one night, but she still had the feeling the two suitcases and small trunk were more than what she really needed. It wasn't as though she couldn't wear the same thing more than once. Although, she had to admit she didn't see the queen often wear the same suit. She had the fleeting thought the night before she left that perhaps next time, she would ask to pack a little lighter.

32. ARRIVAL

That Saturday morning found Avila back at the transport facility with many more people than the last time. Galdren had come to see her off. Both Randy and Baxter were with him, like always. Plus, she had three of her guards—Angelo, Jacob, and April. Nathan was also there with a small contingent of his own.

It was the first time Avila had seen him with a guard, so she gave him a questioning look when they all walked in. He was confused until she glanced over his shoulder. He then laughed as he motioned for them to put everything on the platform where Avila's luggage was already stacked.

Nathan's voice still held laughter when he approached. "I see you weren't expecting me to have guards as well. Do I not seem royal enough to warrant them?"

Avila frowned at his prodding. He laughed and patted her shoulder. "Don't worry. They only come when I am outside the palace complex. Unlike you, I don't need to be watched around the clock."

Her frown grew, though she made sure to show the humor behind it. It came out in her voice as well when she finally responded, "Well, I suppose that just means you aren't as important after all."

Nathan laughed again but wasn't able to respond before Galdren joined them. Despite his blank face, or possibly because of it, Avila felt that something was bothering him. If it was, he didn't get to say anything before Nathan held up a hand. "Yes, I already know. Keep her safe, and never let danger come near her. I have already given my word that will be the case."

Galdren frowned but nodded. "I do appreciate your promise."

He then turned to Avila. He smiled, but it seemed forced. She wasn't going to call him on it. Some things were better left unsaid. At least his voice didn't show any irritation. "Please ensure that you never go anywhere alone."

She raised a brow at the statement and tried not to laugh at his constant reminders. "I know. I promise. Besides, we both know I will never be anywhere without at least one of my guards, and I trust them all."

Galdren took in a deep breath as he nodded. "Of course." He then stepped back so they could all get onto the telepad. Once they were in place, he nodded to both of them before the operator activated the machine.

This time, Avila was better prepared for the gut-clenching feeling and managed not to stumble upon their arrival. She was still grimacing as the rest of the team took their luggage.

Nathan laughed at the sight of her but held up both hands when she glared at him. He winked as he said, "I know, not a word."

Despite her discomfort, Avila grinned at his efforts. It was hard to stay upset with Nathan for long. Thankfully her disorientation was gone quickly, and the group was on the way.

The trip was going to be a long one, as the reserve was near the continent's southern tip. There was a rocky mountain range at the far southern edge of the reserve that curved north between Peloun and the rest of the continent. It kept most of the ocean air from reaching far inland, served as an excellent natural barrier, and helped provide a thriving environment for a wide variety of all forms of life in one location. That made for a wonderful setting for a preserve, but it also meant that it would take them the better part of two days to get there via hovercar, as Nerada was still the closest port with a telepad. There were not many cities between the spaceport and the mountains either. After the peaks, there was nothing outside of the duke's outposts.

They ended up stopping late that night at a remote walled location. Avila eyed the whole thing with distrust until Nathan explained that they were already technically on his father's lands. This was an outpost situated for just this purpose—to be a guarded stopping point on the way to Peloun or to Nerada. He also assured her the next day's travel would only be half as long.

As awe-inspiring as the trip had been so far, she couldn't say that she wasn't glad the next day would be shorter. Being in a hovercar all day was not her idea of fun, no matter how beautiful the view was.

Thankfully, the next day was just as short as Nathan promised it to be, a fact that had Avila grinning as the hovercars finally came to a stop in front of an imposing building. When she stepped out into the arid air, it nearly took her breath away, but her instant discomfort was soon forgotten as her eyes focused on the structure in front of them.

It was nearly half as large as the castle in Arinel, though the architecture was completely different. Where the castle had tall, imposing stone walls and thick doors with carved arches and weighty knobs, this place was full of open domes and fountains. The front doors were certainly as imposing as any others she had seen, though they seemed to be made from a lighter material, and images were carved into the wood.

She was no less impressed when they walked into a bright hall lined with large open windows that let in the sunshine. She was thrilled when she saw another fountain in the center of the room lined with a plethora of feathery leaves that seemed to dance in the mists raised by the falling water.

She was trying her best not to look like an uncultured bumpkin as she followed behind Nathan. However, she knew it was a lost cause when she saw the many plants that also lined the windows. Thankfully, she was drawn back to the moment when she heard a voice call her name.

She looked around with a bright smile to see an older version of the man standing next to her. He was smiling. She noted it didn't quite reach his eyes, though his voice was full and warm when he spoke. "It is an honor to host you here at Peloun, Lady Durant."

It suddenly struck her who he was. The Duke of Armand was second in power only to the king. Thankfully, her smile only faltered a little as she curtsied in return. "The honor is mine, Your Grace. I cannot express how thrilled I am with this opportunity."

Nathan tried to stifle a chuckle next to her, but she barely had time to give him a confused look before his father spoke once more. "I am sure that my son has already expressed a dislike toward formality. Please, call me sir if you must, but there is no need for titles. I hope over the next few weeks that we have plenty of opportunities to work together."

Avila smiled brightly. Despite her instinct toward a more formal approach, she could already tell that it would not be difficult for her to relax around the man. He had an air about him that was similar to Nathan's. She nodded as she responded,

"Of course. I am unsure what work there is needed, but after everything this estate has done to help me, I would be more than willing to lend a hand in any way possible."

The older man chuckled slightly, then gestured toward a woman standing off to the side. She approached and bowed to Avila as the duke continued, "This is Evette. She can show you the rooms you will have while you are here and help you settle in. For now, I must beg your forgiveness, as I still have much to do. I hope to see you again at dinner."

She gave him another bow as she answered, "Of course, I look forward to it."

With that, the duke walked away and disappeared into one of the long halls. Avila's attention turned to Nathan when he finally spoke once more. "I'll leave you in Evette's capable hands, but if you feel up to it, I might have time to give you a tour of this place once you freshen up. Unless you would rather rest, of course."

Avila had to remind herself not to grab her friend by the arm as she grinned back at him. "I would love to see more of this place. It's gorgeous. Just give me an hour. I think that should be enough time."

Nathan chuckled at her enthusiasm but still shook his head. "Well, I do still have a report to give as well, so it might be closer to a couple of hours before I can get away. Still, that should give us plenty of time to look around before dinner."

Avila's smile dimmed, but she nodded as he waved and walked off. Once he was gone, she turned to the woman that had been patiently waiting. "Thank you for your help while I'm here."

The woman gave her a shallow bow as she responded, "It is my pleasure, Lady Durant. If you would, please follow me."

Avila followed the woman down one of the other halls. She almost felt like she was part of a procession as all her guards, two other gentlemen carrying her things, and one of the house guards all fell into step behind or beside them. At least it was something she was getting used to, so it didn't bother her as much as it would have a month ago.

When they finally got to the set of rooms assigned to Avila while she visited, Evette opened the door and let Angelo sweep the room. When he gave the all-clear, the rest followed. It did not take the maid long to direct the rest of the group as to where everything should be put and show Avila the facilities at her disposal.

Avila was impressed with the rooms. They were not as large nor as opulent as the ones she used in Arinel, but there was a comfort to them that instantly put her at ease. It likely had to do with the abundance of plant life in the space. It was almost like being outside.

Once her things were put into place and Evette was sure Avila was settled, the maid left while Jacob and April took up spots outside her door. She wasn't thrilled that they would be working overlapping shifts—not because there would always be two people with her, but because they would be working longer shifts to implement the coverage. She had already said something to them about the long hours, and each had reassured her that it was fine.

After everyone left the rooms, Avila did a little exploring and was pleased to find a large tub that nearly rivaled hers back home. She sighed at the thought of a bath to work out the kinks from the long drive but resigned herself to waiting for that. Instead, she took a quick shower and changed into one of the nicer sundresses. If they were only to be walking the halls of the castle before dinner, there was no point in having to come back and change again.

Since she still had a little time to wait before Nathan came to get her, she decided to go ahead and pull out the work that the professor had sent with her. There was no point in putting it off, especially when she could already tell there would be more than enough to keep her busy.

She was concentrating on reading to the point that she nearly jumped when there was a knock at the door. She stood as soon as April ducked her head in. "Lord de Legris is here." Avila smiled at the woman before she closed the book and pushed it aside. The rest would have to wait.

As soon as she stepped outside, Nathan greeted her with a grin. "I hope everything is to your liking. And that you didn't get too bored while waiting."

Avila was too excited not to share his grin. "The rooms are lovely. You know how I feel about plants. As for being bored, didn't I tell you that the professor sent work for me to complete while I was here?"

Nathan's eyes widened slightly before he chuckled. "I didn't realize you were serious. He really expects you to work while you are here on vacation?"

Avila huffed at her friend, though she wasn't actually upset. "Of course I was serious. This is technically not a vacation. It is an opportunity for me to expand my horizons and become better acquainted with all that is involved with taking care of a reserve, as that is my chosen line of work once I'm finished with my studies."

Nathan held up both hands in surrender, but he let the subject drop as he took one of her hands and tucked it into the crook of his arm. When they started walking,

April fell into step behind them while Jacob stayed by the door. Nathan ignored them like always and began pointing out the different aspects of the architecture as well as the various plants, most of which Avila had heard of but never seen in person.

It wasn't long until the two of them were lost in conversation. Avila hadn't realized that the sandstone palace was one of the oldest on Aril. Even more ancient than the one in the capital. She had long known that Aril hadn't always been ruled by a single king, but she had forgotten that the current royal family had once come from these southern reaches. It wasn't until the planet joined the Trading Alliance that the need for a single king was realized and Arinel was co-opted as the capital.

Avila had just commented on how amazing the structure looked for something that was more than a thousand years old, and Nathan was happily explaining the extensive work that went into keeping it that way, when they were interrupted by a young man Avila had never seen before.

He bowed to both of them before he spoke. "Lord de Legris, Lady Durant, I have been asked to remind you that dinner will be served in fifteen minutes."

Nathan thanked the young man and assured him they would be there shortly. He then turned to Avila. "Do you need to freshen up, or can we head straight to dinner?"

Avila furrowed her brow slightly as she answered, "Do you feel I need to change?"

Nathan rolled his eyes as he took her hand once more. "That isn't what I meant at all. However, I am aware that most women always find something they feel they need to do before dinner."

She had no idea how to respond to that nonsense, so she ignored it in favor of asking about the arrangements. "So, will dinner be a formal affair, like in Arinel?"

Nathan paused and pulled her to a halt. He seemed to be thinking about something before he answered. "In the basic sense, yes. However, things here are a little more relaxed in general. My brother is out today and tomorrow, but when he returns, they might become—well, perhaps silent is the best word."

As soon as he saw her troubled expression, he shook his head. "Don't worry, it has nothing to do with you. Let's just say that my brother and I have not seen eye to eye for quite some time."

Avila wanted to find out what caused her friend to have such a twisted expression, but they had reached the dining room by that time. She tabled the question for the moment.

As soon as they walked in, the duke turned from where he had been standing next to one of the windows. His smile was just as charming as any of Nathan's, even if there still seemed to be something missing. "Ah, Lady Durant, I am pleased you feel up to joining us for dinner."

Nathan had already guided her to the seat prepared for her, but she didn't sit right away. Instead, she returned the duke's smile as she responded, "I can only imagine the number of things I could learn from you. I do believe I am just as happy to have this opportunity."

The duke gestured toward her chair as he answered, "Please, sit. Although there may be much for us to share, there is no need to rush. Let us enjoy the meal."

Once she sat, Nathan pushed her chair in before he went around to take the one across from her. Since it was only the three of them at the table, it was not long until they all got caught up in conversation, though most of it was carried by the two younger people. The bulk of the talk revolved around the trip and some of the plans already laid out for the next few weeks. Avila was thrilled to learn that they already had quite a bit set up.

The dinner as a whole was a relatively intimate affair for something that would usually have been considered a formal dinner. But Nathan had said they were more laid back. It wasn't surprising since the household seemed to be rather small in comparison to the one in Arinel, though that did not mean it was lacking in any way.

The food was unfamiliar but still tasty. Nathan explained that the main dish was a mix of some local fruits and vegetables, along with a springy loaf made from bean curd cut into chunks and fried to add a mix of textures. Avila was thrilled to find she loved the combination, but she did have questions. "Did you say there was fruit in this as well?"

Nathan chuckled as he picked up one of the items on his plate with his fork. "Yes, these are a type of fibrous fruit that grow in the wetter parts of this area." He rolled his eyes when she gave him a skeptical look. "Not all fruit has to be sweet."

Avila laughed at the look and let it pass. She wasn't inclined to complain, as it was tasty. However, as soon as her laughter rang out, the duke spoke, which was noteworthy since he had barely said anything throughout the meal. "It is good to hear such lovely laughter grace these halls again. I had almost forgotten what it sounded like."

Avila felt her smile fade a bit as she noted the wistful look in the man's eyes. He wasn't looking at her, so much as looking through her. She had to repress a shiver as she looked over and saw that Nathan was wearing a frown. However, when their eyes caught, his smile instantly returned as he tried to smooth things over. "I will agree that it is a lovely sound. I hope this will be far from the last time we get to hear it."

That was too much. Avila looked down at her plate to hide her blush. Thankfully, neither of the men commented on it, and the meal soon continued as though it never happened. Not long afterward, the duke stood. The other two were instantly on their feet, though the older gentleman only gave them a smile. "It has been a pleasure, though it is getting late, and I must turn in. I look forward to hearing your perceptions of this place as you visit."

Avila bowed her head in respect as she answered, "I will make sure I note everything. I would also like to thank you again for this opportunity."

He waved off her thanks with a tired smile as he turned to his son. "I have already spoken with Talor. The vehicles will be ready in the morning. Do not worry overmuch about the reports, I am sure you can handle them when you return."

For a moment, Nathan looked a little uncomfortable, but it was gone by the time he answered, "Thank you. I will ensure nothing is left out, though that does mean things will be a little later each night." The duke gave him a curt nod and Avila another smile before he turned to leave.

33. NATURE IN ACTION

The next morning Avila was up before the chime rang out on her timeglass. She considered trying to go back to sleep, but her excitement had already started to bubble up. At least it was only a half hour early.

She decided against taking a long bath, but she did shower and change. It did not take her long before she was ready for the day. Since there was still time before breakfast, she took a look around the room to see if any of the bookshelves she had seen contained more than props. Much to her surprise and delight, there were several about the surrounding area. Though, when she thought about it, she shouldn't have been so shocked. The only people likely to be staying in these rooms were either family or visiting dignitaries. Having information about the land would surely be welcome by any of those.

It was not long before she became engrossed in a book about the relationship between the most common local flora and how the fauna interacted with it. Finding symbiotic relationships in nature was common, but it seemed in this region, it was far more necessary than she had initially thought.

In the plains within the mountain range, the rainy season was short and left the rest of the year dry. Bulbous plants that looked like stones grew there. They had adapted over time to not only hold water but also to withstand burrowing creatures. The symbiotic part came when it was time for the plant to reproduce.

Instead of releasing pollen to fertilize or grow seeds, that part of the process was internal. The tiny seeds were then left to float in pools of water the plant created near its base to draw in the local fauna. The seed casings were made of the same hardened shell the plant used to prevent intrusion, but by the time they passed through the digestive tract of whatever animal might have sipped them up, they were softened enough for the growing plant to break free.

She had just gotten to the part where it described the survival rate depending on the animal when she was startled by a knock at her door. She set the book to the side with a sigh as she called out for them to enter. Angelo poked his head in with a nod. "Ma'am, the lady's maid is here to assist you in preparing for the day."

Avila stood and gave him a confused look that then slid to the woman waiting patiently behind him. She gestured down to her body as she answered, "As you can see, I am already ready. You can send my thanks to whoever sent you, but there is no need for help. At least until it's time to leave."

The woman gave her a slight bow as she answered, "Of course, my lady. I have also been instructed to bring you to the dining hall once we are finished. If you are prepared, I can lead you there now."

Avila grinned at the woman, thankful that she wasn't insisting, then looked around and grabbed the small pack that contained specimen bags and her sketch pad. "All right, lead the way, please."

The woman gave her another bow before she started down the hall. Angelo fell into step behind them. Both Nathan and his father were already in the dining room when she walked in.

They both stood with smiles as soon as they saw her. Nathan eyed the bag before he raised a brow and commented, "I should have known you would have been ready."

Avila chuckled as she set the bag next to the chair Nathan had pulled out for her. She waited until the other two were seated again before she answered, "Well, I did wake up before the alarm, but I couldn't go back to sleep. Instead, I found a fascinating book in the room and kept myself occupied."

Nathan shared a confused look with his father. When the man's only response was to shrug, they both turned back to her, and Nathan asked what they were both wondering, "I vaguely remember that bookshelves were in each of the guest suites, but I don't recall there being anything particularly fascinating in them. What were you reading?"

Avila nearly rolled her eyes at him, but stopped when she saw the duke was watching as well. No matter how laid back they were, it would do to remember the man was second only to the king. She still gave Nathan a long-suffering look when she answered, "I suppose my idea of fascinating and yours are simply two different things. I was reading about these amazing plants that are supposed to be common in this region. They look like stones. What were they . . ."

Nathan chuckled. "Leave it to you to get excited about plants. It's no wonder you get along so well with—"

Avila looked up with confusion when he suddenly cut off. Her confusion only grew when she noticed the duke's eyes narrow slightly, though he didn't say anything. Instead, Nathan started speaking again almost immediately. "They are called nakala stones. I am sure we will come across many while you are here if you would like to examine one. Though I would recommend that you don't try to drink the water. It doesn't harm the animals of the plains, but for us, there are some . . . interesting side effects. The seeds are coated in more than the hardened shell for protection."

That sent Avila's mind off on another tangent. He hadn't made the side effects sound fatal, but it would surely be detrimental if it was enough to issue a warning. Not that she had any plans to find out for herself, but the idea that differing physiology between species would create such drastically different effects from the same stimulus was an exciting topic. Did it have more to do with how the animals had adapted, or was it another defense mechanism of the plant?

She was pulled out of her whirling thoughts when she heard Nathan laugh. He was grinning when she looked up. "I can already see the gears turning in your head. Instead of trying to figure it out now, why don't you wait until you can see one for yourself? The faster we finish here, the quicker we can be on our way."

Avila immediately picked up her fork, which brought a laugh from the duke as well. After that, the conversation was minimal. Soon, the table was cleared and the duke stood to bid them a good day.

Avila noted that Nathan was frowning slightly as he watched his father leave, but when he turned back to her, he did so with a smirk. "Since you brought your bag, I suppose that means we can go straight from here?"

Avila answered his smirk with one of her own as she grabbed the bag and put the strap over her shoulder. "Lead the way." Nathan chuckled at her enthusiasm but didn't comment further.

Despite the delay while security checked the transport, it was not long before they were on their way. The talk in the hovercar was minimal while Avila scanned the land they were traveling through.

She had already been told that, given the circumstances, they would not be able to go more than a couple of hours out until the weekend. Not that she was bothered by that; they had barely been out a half hour, and she had already seen several things she wanted to ask questions about or look up later.

She was shocked when Nathan called them to a halt before they were even out an hour. When she shot him a questioning glance, his only response was to grin and wink at her. He then opened the door and gestured for her to follow.

Avila was sure he had a reason, but she still gave him a skeptical look. Mostly to get back at him for the wink. He then led her to a group of stones a short distance away. Several small, lizard-like animals scurried away into holes she hadn't noticed until they got closer. She almost followed them, but Nathan gently grabbed her arm to pull her closer to the stones. His voice was barely above a whisper as he pointed to the odd grouping. "You were asking questions about these earlier, so I thought you might want to see them in person."

She was confused, but only for a moment. It didn't take her long to realize the rocks weren't actually rocks. Her eyes lit up as she rushed forward to examine them. Even standing next to them, she could not tell that they were not stone. The brown surface matched the earth around them, and they were covered with a fine layer of grit. When she turned to Nathan, her voice was just as low. "Would it be all right if I touched them?"

She could tell he was trying not to laugh at her. When she frowned at him, he finally relented. "They aren't hothouse babies. Life out here is rough. You would be far from the only thing to have touched them. Just don't touch the water."

She gave him a nod before she reached a tentative hand out. She only let her fingertips touch it at first, but when there was no reaction, she allowed them to slide until her palm rested on the warm surface.

If she had not known better, Avila would have still thought them stone. The surface was rough and absorbed the sun's light the same way boulders would. She frowned as she began to wonder how they processed nutrients. Perhaps that would be something she could study later.

For now, she lifted her hand and gently rapped her knuckles against the side. Even though she half expected it, the hollow sound still took her by surprise. As soon as the sound faded, she pulled out her sketch pad from the bag she had thankfully grabbed when exiting the hovercar. She skirted the bundle of strange plants slowly to ensure that if any wildlife was about, they would have ample opportunity to leave.

It didn't take her long to find what she was looking for. At the base of the next nakala stone over was a small indent partially covered by a wild weed. She gently pushed the smaller plant's leaves to the side to better see the small pool of water.

The water was murky, though she doubted the animals in the area cared. What she found impressive was how it almost looked like the pool had been created by an underground reservoir that had made its way to the surface to partially erode the "stone."

It did not take her long to sketch the setup. It was only as she was standing that she wondered what part the other plant played in things. It was apparent the small, leafy weed was taking advantage of the water source, but it didn't seem to be ill-affected. Perhaps it, too, had a part to play in the symbiosis of the region. She doubted this was a random occurrence with the way everything in the dry plains had to fight to survive.

When Avila stood once she was satisfied with her sketch, she nearly fell over. Nathan had been right behind her and was watching with interest. He was, thankfully, able to steady her. Though he did smirk at the scowl she shot him. Instead of commenting on the near miss, he pointed to the sketch pad. "I have heard you mention that you like to sketch the things you observe, but I didn't realize you had talent. You could sell those with a little work."

She scoffed as she headed back to the vehicle. "I doubt that, but even if it were true, I won't be parting with any of them. Unless there is something I need to study that must be done in a lab, I would rather use my drawings."

By that point, they had reached the hovercar. Instead of arguing, Nathan reached into a little compartment and handed her a capped bottle. She took it but gave him a curious look. He didn't allow her the chance to ask. "I am positive you are not used to the heat or sun. Even though you haven't complained yet, I don't want to take the chance of you getting dehydrated."

Avila looked chagrined, as she had been wiping the sweat from her brow as he spoke. Still, she gave him a smile and took a long drink of water before she answered, "I was too excited to notice; I'm glad you thought of it. By the time we head back, I have a feeling I will be even more appreciative."

He laughed at her quip, but it wasn't long afterward that their conversation once again drifted into a lull. When they finally arrived at the stopping point for the day, Avila was thrilled to find that they were not far from a "village" of rodent-looking creatures. Nathan explained that the group of creatures was called a village because they had a pack-type mentality with a structured hierarchy despite being in the rodent family.

She desperately wanted to get a closer look, but she knew it would spook them. She was even less inclined to do so when he explained that the tiny creatures would become quite aggressive if they felt their homes were under attack. He had even seen them drive off one of the big cats. A feat she had a hard time imagining, but he assured her it was true. With that being the case, she satisfied herself with watching them through a spyglass.

By the time they were ready to head back, Avila had a small stack of sketches. It had only been one day, and already she had more information than she knew what to do with.

They managed to make it back in time for a late lunch, though it was rushed. Nathan did still have duties to attend to while he was there. As soon as the meal was over, he turned to Avila with an apologetic smile. "I hate to eat and run, but the reports won't file themselves."

Avila waved off his concern with a grin. She pointed to her bag as she answered. "Don't worry, I already have more than enough to research. With everything we saw today, I am beginning to think it would take a lifetime to understand the variety of life in this region. I am surprised you have managed to learn so much."

He gave her a mock-glare as he said, "If I didn't know any better, I would say you doubt my intelligence."

She chuckled at his quip as she shook her head. "Not at all. However, I do know that you have always had other duties as well. Even the second-born son of a duke would not be exempt. It's impressive that you were able to learn so much about this land and still keep up."

Nathan glanced away at her earnest compliment. A moment later, he turned back to her with a grin. "You shouldn't throw those types of statements around so casually. Other men might get the wrong idea."

Avila was thoroughly confused by his statement but didn't get to ask, as he immediately added, "Unfortunately, I do have to get going. Evette can lead you back to the rooms, and if you need anything, please reach out to her. Otherwise, she will be back to get you for the evening meal."

Avila made a shooing motion as she answered. "Don't worry about me. Between the tasks Professor Gilbert sent with me and all the things I would like to look up now, I doubt I will have a spare minute. Just make sure you don't work yourself to death, either. I know this can't be easy for you, so thank you."

Nathan's smirk was back in place as he waved off her concern. "Until later." Once he was gone, Avila followed Evette toward her room.

That night, dinner was much the same as it had been the night before. The only significant difference was the fact that the duke insisted that she call him by name.

She was fighting a blush when she tried for a rebuttal one last time. "Your Grace, I understand that this household is less strict about certain things, but surely it would not be proper for me to call you by name."

The man chuckled as he shook his head. Despite the turn the conversation had taken, he was only amused. "I am no king."

"Perhaps not, but you are second only to the man that is."

For a moment, the duke's eyes seemed to harden, but the expression was gone so fast, Avila wasn't sure what she had seen. His smile was back in place as he answered, "Perhaps, but in this household, we do not live by formalities. We are still close enough to the wilds that we cherish the bonds we make, even if they are to be fleeting. Now, please agree. I will not insist that you call me Zach. Zachariah is enough."

Avila knew her face had to be as red as the tart fruits served with dessert, and there was no hiding it. When she caught the sound of Nathan trying to smother his laughter, she finally relented with a sigh. "I will agree . . . Zachariah."

The duke smiled at her as he spoke. "See, not so difficult, was it?"

She decided that it would be better to not answer that, as she still felt uncomfortable, so she changed the subject to the fascinating things they had found that day.

The rest of the week went in much the same pattern. Despite only having half a day to explore, Avila still found so many things she had never seen before. It was the experience of a lifetime, and she knew she was barely scratching the surface.

The following weekend was the first time they were allowed to travel farther. The section of the mountain range that blocked off the southern ocean was still too far to reach in a day, and given the safety concerns, it was a trip that would have to be postponed until better arrangements could be made. That didn't keep them from getting close enough to see them in the distance.

Even though the range was barely more than a hazy span across the distant horizon, Avila could tell that the land, flora, and fauna were affected by the natural barrier. The closer they got to the mountains, the fewer nakala stones she saw. They also got caught in a brief thunderstorm right before they decided it was time to head back.

Avila was thrilled at the way the dry plains seemed to become a vibrant show-case of colors for the tiniest bit after the storm. Nathan explained that the rain was unusual but not unheard of outside of the rainy season due to the way the mountains would occasionally trap low pressure fronts. Unfortunately, they had to leave the riot of color behind as they headed back for the day. Not that she didn't find the rest of the plains beautiful as well, but it was a muted and dignified type of beauty. There was a grace in the savagery of the near-barren land that was sometimes hard to look away from.

It was late when they returned that night, and the duke had already retired. As much as Avila enjoyed his company, she wasn't too upset that the meal with Nathan was a hurried affair. She was already looking forward to bed, especially since she knew the next day would likely be just as long, and she still had homework she had barely touched. That thought haunted her as she went to sleep. She knew she would need to take more time for her studies over the remaining two weeks, or her work would never get done.

34. HAUNTED BY THE PAST

The next week and a half flew by. Some days Avila felt as if there simply weren't enough hours in the day. At least she finished all her assignments and would be able to enjoy the last few days exploring Peloun without distractions. She was also thankful that she had thought to bring extra sketch pads, as she had filled the first one before the end of the fifth day.

As for the adventures, she had already resigned herself to the fact that she would likely never get to see everything she wanted to. There was just too much to see and not nearly enough time, but at least she had good company.

She had noticed a subtle shift in Nathan the longer they stayed. Despite his laid-back attitude, the longer they spent in the plains, the more she could see how this wild land had shaped him. He had been forthright from the moment she met him, but here, that became daring. As vibrant as his personality was, each day, it became brighter. She wasn't sure which of them enjoyed the outings more.

She doubted he had noticed the shift, since it wasn't anything drastic, but she still kept it to herself. They were only a few days from heading back, and already she felt a pang at the idea of leaving. She could only imagine that it was worse for Nathan. At least he seemed adaptable.

Those thoughts led to more about Arinel and the ones that lived there. Specifically, a tall, blonde, green-eyed one that she had been trying to keep off her mind the whole trip. Even though she was busy, she thought of him often enough. It was hard for her not to wonder what Galdren would think of the things she had seen. Whenever the thoughts did come up, she reminded herself that he had said he had already been, so it wouldn't be new to him. It was a small consolation as she buried her thoughts of him again and again.

Nathan had said they would be headed to a new area that day, and it didn't take long to see that he hadn't been exaggerating. As they neared the planned stopping point, they started into something that could almost be considered a forest. It definitely could be when compared to the flatlands that made up the majority of Peloun. The flatlands weren't completely barren, as the grasses grew in abundance, but rarely had she seen anything else other than the nakala stones and the small plants that usually surrounded them. Avila was in awe.

The trees weren't dense, but they were far from anything she was familiar with. Though barely taller than the hovercar, they were broad. They also didn't grow close to each other, but part of that was likely due to the way the roots spread more than a dozen yards around each tree. The leaves were also interesting. They almost seemed sunburnt, but Nathan assured her they were always like that.

Despite her interest in the strange trees, when Nathan pointed out why they had visited this area, her attention was completely diverted. There were large nests placed in the nooks and crannies in most of the trees' broad branches. However, they were not occupied by anything avian. Instead, there were families of primates jumping through the limbs and sometimes from tree to tree, which didn't look like an easy feat. Due to how far apart the trees were, the branches of the closest ones were still several feet apart.

Much to her surprise, Nathan asked if she would like to get a closer look at them. It wasn't an opportunity she was willing to pass up. He grinned as he took her to the edge of a cluster of trees and then had her sit. Once they were both down, he took out several small fruits from his bag and rolled them toward the trees. Once they were out, he gave her a mock-stern look as he whispered, "Make sure you stay still and silent. You can sketch them later."

She answered with a nod before they settled in to watch the hooting animals. Their patience was rewarded soon after, when several lanky primates dropped to the ground and tentatively headed for the fruit. Avila couldn't help but grin when they finally darted in to pick them up, and instead of running back, stopped to stare at the two humans.

There were three of them, and they were bolder than most wild animals she had ever seen. Two of them were content to munch on the fruit while staring, but the third hopped over until it was only a couple of feet away—almost close enough that they could have touched it if they tried.

She had to fight not to giggle when the thing turned its head this way and that as though it were trying to solve a riddle. She gasped when it started making cooing noises at them. Despite the warning to be still, Avila couldn't help but look over at Nathan. He returned her curiosity with a shrug before he mouthed the words "just watch."

She frowned at him for a moment but finally turned back to do as he suggested. The animal was still watching them intently, and it got to the point that she was beginning to wonder if it would eventually come up to them.

Before that could happen, the animal jumped back with a screech that was immediately picked up by the rest of the primates in the area. The cacophony was so loud that Avila had to cover her ears. However, she wasn't given a chance to ask about it, as Nathan was already on his feet and dragging her up.

He pulled her behind him with enough force that she nearly lost her balance. She was going to reprimand him, but he was already yelling at the nearby guards, "Grab the tranquilizers and be ready!"

Thankfully, they were not far from cover. Nathan shoved her into the vehicle unceremoniously and quickly followed after. She turned to glare at him, but any words she thought to speak were drowned by the stark terror in his eyes. By that point, the two guards had followed them in and slammed the door shut behind them.

It was then that a scream pierced the tense silence. Avila's attention was jerked to the grove. She saw a blur pass near the transport and tried to follow where it went. When she heard another growl, she finally saw what had caused the commotion.

Near the roots of one of the trees, she saw a giant animal hunched over. It wasn't until it jerked its head up that she realized what it was. The giant cat was a third of the hovercar's size and nearly the same color as the grasses, with thin stripes of darker brown scattered across its fur. She couldn't see the eyes, but she knew they would be yellow. She was staring at one of the apex predators in all of Aril—a vari.

It was only when she noticed the smear of red across the cat's maw that she understood what had happened. She had to slam a hand over her mouth to hold down the bile that threatened to come up. It wasn't that she didn't know predation was a part of life, but it still sickened her to watch it.

Thankfully, Nathan had them quickly on the way. The vari barely noted their departure, as it was still busy with its meal. It wasn't until they were out of sight that Avila finally relaxed with a sigh.

Nathan was immediately by her side. "Are you all right? I know that had to be terrifying."

She managed a smile as she answered, "Well, I will admit that I never expected to get that close to a vari, but I'm fine." She paused when she noticed the fear had still not left her friend's eyes. Her smile fled, and her brows furrowed as she reached out to him. "Are you?"

Nathan looked away as he answered, "Of course, I was only worried. There is no telling what my cousin would do to me if something happened to you."

Avila was taken aback by his sudden mention of Galdren. Not that the prince had never come up during her stay, but he almost made it sound like there was more going on than there was. To keep from snapping at him while adrenaline was likely high for both of them, she mumbled a nondescript response and allowed the conversation to drop. After that, the ride back was nearly silent.

When they finally made it to the castle, Avila was surprised by the level of activity when they walked in. She turned to ask what might be going on and saw Nathan frowning. When he caught her looking, he sighed and gave her a forced smile before he answered her unspoken question, "It looks as though my brother made it back earlier than expected after his delay."

Avila could tell something was bothering Nathan but didn't get the chance to ask what it was, as he continued, "I apologize, but I must leave you to have lunch alone. If Benedict is here, then I am sure Father will have things to go over before I return to the capital in a few days." He took a step away. "Please get some rest before dinner. I know today was a rather—exciting day."

He didn't give her a chance to respond before he bowed and turned to leave. She watched his back with a frown for a few moments before Evette came to lead her to her rooms. Since she was alone, she decided she could take lunch there.

Despite having several things to research, Avila had difficulty concentrating for the rest of the afternoon. She somehow managed to finish the last of her assignments and even started trying to sketch the things she had seen that day from memory. Not that it was going well. Too often, she was distracted by thoughts of the last look Nathan had sent her before he walked off.

He had told her that he didn't get along well with his brother, but it seemed more than that. She thought part of the problem might have stemmed from the encounter earlier in the day; he hadn't seemed himself afterward.

She sighed and erased a stray mark once again before setting her pencil down. Her concentration was shot, and it didn't help that she was trying to recall every detail without any kind of reference.

As she stood to stretch out a knot in her lower back, Evette arrived to take her to dinner. She looked at the timeglass in surprise and gave the maid a furtive request to wait while she freshened up. She still hadn't changed from her shorts, but she was able to clean up and change in less than ten minutes, though she felt even worse about her tardiness when she was led into a quiet dining room.

As the three men stood, she turned to the duke with a bow. "I apologize for keeping you waiting. I was working and lost track of time."

The man gave her a smile. "It was not too long. Please join us."

Avila walked to the seat she had been using and whispered thanks to Nathan for holding out her chair. Once she was seated, the third man caught her attention. "It is a pleasure to meet you, Lady Durant. I am Benedict de Legris. My father speaks highly of you, which doesn't happen often."

She lowered her head with respect at his greeting. "Thank you, Lord de Legris. I cannot speak to other's opinions of me, but I can say that both your father and brother have shown me nothing but thoughtfulness. I can only hope I have returned it in kind."

The other man's eyes narrowed slightly, but his smile didn't dim. "I have been told my father convinced you to call him by name. If that is the case, I believe it would be quite awkward for me to be the only one you call by title, don't you?"

Benedict's smile had widened as he spoke, and for the first time, Avila could see the similarities between the brothers. Though, it was easy to tell Nathan was the youngest. She managed to return the smile as she answered, "Of course, as long as you are fine with calling me Avila."

He gave her a curt nod. "It would be my pleasure."

The meal was served by that point, so the conversation fell away as they all ate. It wasn't until the second course was on the table that Avila noticed Nathan had hardly touched his food. He hadn't said anything yet, either. She had just resolved to ask him what the matter was when her attention was pulled away by Zachariah.

"So, tell me what wonders you uncovered today. I must admit that it is revitalizing to hear of the marvels of my lands through the eyes of a newcomer."

Avila gave her friend one last worried look that he ignored before she turned to the duke with a smile. "I'm glad to hear my visit isn't entirely pointless." She took any possible offense out of her statement when she ended with a grin.

Thankfully, the duke understood, and he chuckled as he answered, "Given your history, I doubt anyone could think it pointless. Still, that does not answer my question.

What adventures did you have today?"

Now that the danger was far away, Avila was thrilled about the glimpse she'd been given of one of the most challenging species to spot. Not only did the vari have a low population, but they were wary and were hardly ever seen outside of the rare motion capture images. It was one of the things that made them a deadly predator, but it also made the scene from earlier in the day one to get excited over. Barring the gruesome part, at least.

She could hardly contain herself when she answered, "We went to see a nesting area for the kohnahv. Which was wonderful, as one of them came right up to us. I wish we had been given more of an opportunity to stay, but I suppose I must be a cat magnet, because a vari attacked them while we were there. As horrific as that was to see, it was still an incredible opportunity. I can only think of a few people that have ever laid eyes on the beast in person."

Benedict had not spoken a word since his introduction, so Avila nearly jumped out of her seat when the man slammed his hand on the table and practically yelled, "Again? Was one murder not enough?"

She looked over to see Benedict standing and glaring daggers at Nathan. Her friend had gotten to his feet as well, but his jaw was clenched. She could also see pain in his eyes. Thankfully, he wasn't given a chance to respond, as the duke had stood as well.

His voice was not loud, but it cut through the tension immediately. "Ben, that is enough. I have already given my opinion about this matter. Do not push me. Especially here, as we have a guest."

The elder of the brothers looked at his father with unmasked rage, but he managed to growl through clenched teeth, "Then I will excuse myself." He didn't wait for a response before storming out.

Several moments after he left, the patriarch of the household turned to Avila with tired eyes. Any joviality that he had while speaking earlier was long gone. Still, he managed to give her a smile as he said, "Please forgive my son. Rest assured, this has nothing to do with you."

She had to swallow once before she could respond. "Thank you for the reassurance, but is everything all right?"

She looked over when Nathan slumped back into his seat with a sigh. He ran his hand over his face before he shook his head and answered for his father, "This is nothing new, Avila. Please do not let it bother you."

No matter what either of the men said, she could not help but be concerned. She had never seen Nathan so despondent. Before she could press the matter, Zachariah added, "He has the right of it. I know it may not be easy, but please do not let this bother you." He then gave her a polite bow before he stepped away from the table. "I do apologize for my abrupt departure, but I believe it would be best if I handle this now. Please enjoy the rest of meal, and I will see you both in the morning."

It was nearly a minute after he left before Nathan sat forward with another sigh, and by that point, Avila could not keep her questions to herself. "Do you want to talk about it? I'm afraid I'm done with dinner either way."

Nathan managed a half-smile, but it quickly fell. He didn't answer right away. Instead, he seemed to be lost in thought. She had begun to believe that he had no intention of answering when he finally said, "Would you like to go for a walk?"

His request was so unexpected that Avila didn't know how to respond at first. She finally gave him a curious look. "A walk? At night?"

He chuckled weakly at her response before he stood and held a hand out to her. "I promise it will be nowhere dangerous."

She wasn't sure if it was his reassurance or the haunted look in his eyes, but she took his hand and allowed him to pull her to her feet. He didn't speak right away. Instead, he tucked her hand into the crook of his arm and led her through several halls and up a few flights of stairs.

As curious as she was about where they were going, she could not bring herself to break the silence. At least, not until he led her through a small door and they walked out onto part of the roof. She gasped as she took in the view around them. The savannah was spread out below, and the tall grass, silver in the moonlight, stretched as far as the eye could see.

Nathan took her to the low balcony that surrounded the rooftop. Still, it was several minutes before he spoke. "It's beautiful here, isn't it?"

Avila was still in awe when she turned to him. "This whole place is phenomenal, but this—this is magical."

He chuckled, but it barely lasted a moment before he leaned on the low wall. There was another pause before he started speaking again. "I know you are aware that my mother has been gone for years, but I have never told you how or why."

It only took a second for Avila to put two and two together to realize why he was bringing this up now. She put a gentle hand on his arm. "You know, you don't have to tell me if it is difficult. I only wanted to help."

Nathan shot another half-smile in her direction before he looked back out over the plains. "I know. Which is why I am telling you this now."

Instead of saying anything more, Avila settled on the wall next to him and waited. It took him some time to put his thoughts together and start the tale. "When I break it down, there isn't much to the story, but it had such a massive impact on our lives."

He paused and took a deep breath before he continued, "My mother would often take Ben and me out into the savannah. She considered it part of our education, since it is our family's responsibility to take care of this reserve. That trip—it was no different than any of the others. Or so we thought."

"It wasn't the kohnahv nest we visited that day, but it was just as interesting. There are so many things to see out there." Nathan's face took on a pinched quality, and Avila placed a hand on his arm.

He couldn't muster a smile for her when he glanced in her direction, so he turned away. "I went farther than I was supposed to. Not that I did so on purpose, but I was following a trail that led away from the trees. It wasn't until I started hearing shouts that I realized how far I had gotten."

"I ran as fast as I could. I was only eight, but even then, I could hear the terror in my mother's voice. She was frantically looking for me. When she saw me, she picked me up and started running with me. I had no idea what had happened, but I didn't argue. I—"

He cut off with another grimace but stepped away when Avila tried to comfort him. His back was to her and the moonlit savannah when he kept going. "We were almost back to the transport. We were so close to safety, but—it wasn't close enough."

"A vari had attacked the herd we were watching, but it must have caught sight of us. The guards tried to tranquilize it before it could reach us, but it didn't work fast enough. We were knocked down when it jumped on us, but my mother managed to roll away. Thankfully, the sedative was starting to take effect, so the vari had slowed, but it was still deadly. The guards had come to help us both to the transport, but the man helping my mother could not keep the cat from attacking again. They were both mauled before the vari finally succumbed to the tranquilizer."

"They tried to—we headed back immediately, but there was no—by the time we got back, she was already gone." By the time he finished, his voice was choked with years of unshed tears.

When he tried to turn from Avila again, she simply walked around until she could embrace him. He finally pulled her into a crushing hug as she said, "It wasn't your fault. No matter what your brother says, and I doubt he really believes it was either. It isn't the best way, but people cope differently. I wondered why both you and your father would occasionally become melancholy."

They stood together like that for several minutes. When he finally let her go, he turned to wipe at the dampness on his cheeks. Before he could try to say anything else, Avila spoke again. "I understand why you were so scared earlier, but you did the right thing. We couldn't have predicted that vari would be there, but you kept your wits and got us both to safety before I even realized what was going on. I can't say that this won't always hurt, but you can't keep blaming yourself."

Instead of saying anything else, he pulled her into another embrace. They stood like that for several more minutes before he sighed and pulled back. By that time, he was able to give her a real smile, even if it was still small and edged with sadness, and his voice was no longer choked when he spoke. "Thank you. I have known for a long time that everything you said is true, but it helps to hear it from someone else."

She smiled up at him and wrapped her arm around his as they headed to the door. "Anytime."

Nathan was in a better mood than he had been since that morning. Not that he hurt any less, but sometimes sharing a burden made it easier to carry. He wished Avila good night, then headed to see if he could find his father.

35. DÉJÀ VU

Avila held tightly to the hand of the man next to her. Her other one clutched the collar of the coat she wore. She no longer had the bandages wrapped around her head, but that was even more reason to keep the hood from falling back to reveal her face. Not that there were many people out to see it.

It was late into the night, which made the chill that much more biting, but she hardly noticed it over the rush of blood pounding in her ears. Mikael had finally found a transport that could get them off-planet, but if they were caught before they arrived at the warehouse, all would be lost. Despite the darkness, it was even more of a possibility than during the day, as there were no crowds to hide in.

She still could not remember everything, but things were slowly returning—enough for her to know her place in this disaster and her duty. Especially after having spent months among her people. The level of despondency was palpable and entirely unacceptable. Had the Trogand even tried to help the victims caught in the middle, she might have second-guessed herself. She was only one person, and barely more than a child. Yet, the terrors they continued to perpetrate against the populace was enough to keep her livid.

Avila was pulled from her thoughts when Mikael suddenly jerked them both into a narrow alley. Her already speeding heart rate picked up a notch as she tried to listen for footsteps that might be following them. She almost let her shoulders slump in relief when she realized it was only because he was taking a shortcut to the back door of their destination.

Once he opened the door with a keycard he had been given, they slipped inside and paused. According to their contact, the ship was already loaded and was waiting for the best conditions for takeoff. When silence was the only thing to greet them, they soundlessly made their way through the narrow walkways between thousands of stacked crates, all looming high overhead.

Avila felt her hope blossom when she finally saw the ship through the tiny spaces in some of the stacks. She could also hear the quiet murmur of the voices of the men that waited. Despite how tired she was, her pace picked up as they neared their destination.

When they were a few feet away from the last crate, the waiting men turned to them, and silence fell. Then, suddenly, a familiar voice rang out. "I am glad to see that not all of the people on Talamh are ignorant fools. Let it not be said that there is no power in money."

Standing at the front of the new group was a tall, bald man with a goatee and thin mustache. At first she couldn't place the voice, but she finally realized where she knew him from when he spoke again. "Ah, Princess, I will admit that you have done well so far. Or, I suppose, the people hiding you are the ones to admire. Though I will say, you should be more careful who you trust. Unfortunately, it will be the last lesson you will have the chance to learn."

Avila ignored Mikael's hand on her arm as she tried to step forward. She didn't make it far, but that didn't stop her from glaring at the man when she answered, "You! You are the one who killed them all. In the ship—Larissa—"

When her voice cut off, the man only smirked. "Yes, the nanny. I had hoped she would be more cooperative with a gun at her head. I suppose it doesn't matter, as I have you now." He then gestured to the men behind him. "Kill them all, but make sure the girl is recognizable."

As soon as the man uttered those words, chaos erupted from all sides. The Trogand forces started firing, but the men with the ship were not idle. Several of them rushed forward to help cover Avila and Mikael. Though, instead of taking her and running, Mikael pushed her toward one of the other men and yelled, "Run!"

She wasn't given a chance to object before the other man picked her up and did as he was instructed. She could barely make out Mikael as he somehow managed to get behind one of the crates.

Almost as soon as he did, the world seemed to stand still as an explosion engulfed the other side of the warehouse, including most of the Trogand men. Including Mikael. Avila screamed his name, but it was cut short as the blast knocked them all from their feet. She felt shrapnel hit her in several places as they went down, but she hardly noticed. Her mind was already in overload as the picture of her last protector being swallowed by flames kept repeating in her head.

Time seemed to slow as she fell with the man holding her, but the world darkened when they finally hit the ground. She felt her head bounce on the concrete, but even that pain was lost to the blackness overtaking her mind, and she barely heard the words of several men as they lifted her. Hot tears and the heat of the flames were the last things she knew before darkness swallowed her whole.

Avila jerked awake with her chest heaving and her throat raw. She ignored the sticky feeling of the sweat drying on her skin as she looked around with wide eyes. It was several seconds before she recognized the room. As soon as she did, she slumped back into tears.

She wasn't given long to dwell on the fiery images from her dream before the door burst open and Nathan came running in. He was followed quickly by Angelo and April. She wanted nothing more than to curl under the sheet and ignore them, but she knew that wasn't an option. Instead, she sighed and preempted the question she could see in Nathan's eyes. "It was a nightmare. I apologize if I woke you."

Nathan was still looking at her with wide eyes as he sat on the edge of the bed. "Are you all right? It sounded like someone had attacked you."

Avila managed to give him a half-hearted nod as she pulled her knees up and hugged them. When several moments had passed, and he realized she wasn't going to say any more, he placed a hand on her arm to get her attention. When she looked up, he said, "Will you be able to go back to sleep? Do you need to talk about it?"

She almost turned him down without a thought, but as he looked at her with nothing but concern, she recalled their last conversation and gave him a wry smile. "Maybe talking will help."

Before he could ask more, she turned to Angelo and April. "Would it be all right if you two waited outside?"

Angelo frowned slightly as he answered, "Ma'am, we are here to ensure your safety."

She smiled back at him. "I know. But this is Nathan."

Her guard still looked torn, but he finally gave her a nod and a salute before he and April walked out and closed the door behind them. Once they were gone, she turned back to Nathan with a sigh, though she somehow managed a smile at how ridiculous the whole thing was. It was as though the universe was trying to add as many bad things into one day as possible. Her voice was low when she finally spoke. "I get them all the time. They started after my accident in Arinel. Most of my nightmares are bloody, horrifying things, but I usually handle them better. It isn't often that they are this vivid."

Nathan's tone held a bit of censure, along with concern, when he answered, "You have never mentioned this before. Why?"

She scoffed at the question, but it didn't hold any bitterness. Instead, she hugged her knees tighter and rested her chin on them. "Do you blame me? I would rather not think about them if I don't have to."

Instead of getting upset at her dismissal, he tugged on her arm gently until she unfolded her legs and joined him on the side of the bed. He put one arm around her shoulder while he answered, "No, I don't blame you. I can't say that I haven't done something similar, but that also means I know that it might help if you talked about them."

Avila let out a weak chuckle, but she didn't move away from him. Instead, she rested her head on his shoulder as she tried to explain. "Honestly, they aren't usually clear. Most of the time, all I can remember is the sense of fear and pain. Though ones like—like tonight. Those are terrifying. It was nothing but death, blood, and—this one had flames. They consumed everything."

Nathan's arm tightened around her shoulder, but he didn't speak right away. When he did, his voice was hesitant. "I know you can't remember your past, but do you think they have anything to do with that? You did say you believe you came from a planet that recently went through a civil war, didn't you?"

Avila stood in a rush and paced a few feet away. She covered her mouth with her hand as though the act could hold back the tumultuous thoughts his question provoked. It was an idea she had considered herself, but she didn't want to believe it. There were so many horrid things in those dreams. If they were true, she wasn't sure how she would handle it.

It was nearly a minute before she turned back to face Nathan with a frown. She hadn't even considered the fact that she had only been wearing her sleep shorts and a tank top until she caught his gaze, and he looked away. She felt a slight blush creep up at the impropriety of the situation, but she was still too frazzled to care more than that. She ignored the embarrassment as she answered, "If they are memories, I'm not sure I ever want to find out."

Nathan stood and moved to wrap her in a hug. Despite the situation, she appreciated the gesture. It helped to calm her, knowing that she had someone she could talk to. After several moments, he pushed back far enough that he could look down with a grin. "You know, no matter what happens, I will be there to talk to if you need it."

She gave him an answering smirk as her words from earlier were paraphrased and given back. Though, it quickly fell when she noticed there was something else in his eyes. Something she had not seen before. Not from him. She was given little opportunity to try and figure out what it was before he leaned down and gently pressed his lips to hers.

Avila froze in shock. It was the last thing she had expected from Nathan. However, he didn't stop at her unresponsiveness. Instead, he pulled her closer and moved one hand up to cup her cheek. As strange as it was, it was not unpleasant.

He was gentle and coaxing, and it was not long until she leaned into him and allowed him to deepen the kiss. For a few moments, she allowed herself to just feel, not think.

Somehow, she wasn't shocked that Nathan was incredibly talented. His lips were soft on hers, yet he was still insistent. His other hand moved to pull her flush against him while the one that had cupped her cheek slid back until his fingers tangled in her hair. Not enough to hurt, but it allowed him to keep her in place while he took advantage of the way she molded to him.

Avila wrapped her arms around him and felt warmth flow into her at the feel of his muscles under the shirt he wore. Even though she had never considered this as a possibility, she could never have denied that he was an attractive man.

Despite all that, something was off. After her initial shock, she had wanted to feel something. To have that spark happen. Nathan was her best friend, and she had no reason to deny herself. She knew beyond a shadow of a doubt that he would be good to her. Still, his lips were not the ones she saw in her mind, and that thought sent ice down her spine. Plus, there was a sudden sense of wrongness. This was too familiar, and yet jarringly different.

When his lips moved to dot the corner of her mouth and then her jawline with more soft kisses, she finally found the breath to speak. "Nathan—Nathan, please—"

That was all she had to say before Nathan stilled. Even if she hadn't finished the sentence, there was no mistaking the tone. He pulled back far enough to look into her eyes and was not surprised to find confusion and pain there, though he doubted either were directly because of what had just happened.

For a split second, he thought about leaning in once more. She hadn't pushed him away. He would even go so far as to say she had enjoyed the kiss. Something told him that if he persisted, she would not deny him. But he also knew it would possibly break something between them. Something that he had come to treasure.

He didn't let her go, but he did sigh as he rested his forehead against hers. He managed a half-smile at the fact that she hadn't tried to pull away yet, though it was several moments before he calmed enough that he could speak coherently. He stood a little straighter and looked down with a sad smile. "My cousin is a lucky man."

Avila pulled away and gave him a shocked look that quickly turned to a frown, though her anger was belied by the way her face turned red. He didn't need to see more to know what she was about to say. "I don't know what you mean. I only stopped you because this was unexpected, and I don't want to start something when we have both gone through something emotional today. I value your friendship and don't want it to sour."

Nathan closed his eyes for a moment and clenched his jaw. A moment later, when he opened them again, he gave her a wry smile. "Maybe you're right. Perhaps it would be best if I leave you to go back to sleep. I would only ask that we put this behind us."

Avila nodded stiffly. Nathan hesitated for a moment. He had so many things that he wanted to say. So many ways that he could press his suit. He knew that it wasn't entirely unfounded. Under different circumstances, he had no doubt that they would work. Still, he could not bring himself to say more. Instead, he turned to the door without a word.

He stopped with his back to her when she called out, "Nathan? Thank you for checking on me." He paused with his hand on the handle for a moment before he shot her a strained smile. He didn't say anything else before he walked out and the door clicked closed behind him.

The next morning, Avila was relieved and pleased when she entered the dining room to see Nathan chatting in the corner with his father. When both men turned her way, she was greeted with smiles. If both of them seemed a little strained, she chose not to comment. They still needed to get through the next few days, and no good would come of her saying something.

Instead, she joined them at the table. Once they were all seated, she noticed that Benedict was missing. She thought about asking but decided against it. Again, there was no point in dredging up painful topics. Instead, the three of them engaged in light conversation over the meal.

Unfortunately, that tiny bit of awkwardness carried over through the rest of the day. Not that she and Nathan did not speak, but their conversations were short and rarely delved into anything other than the things they were observing. By the end of the day, Avila found herself hoping the last day would go by quickly. That, or a miracle would happen, and things would just go back to the way they were before. Though, she wasn't going to hold her breath for that one.

The following morning, she was shocked to find all three of the de Legris men standing in the hall. Their conversation was hushed, so she didn't hear any of it, plus they stopped as soon as they saw her. She almost felt awkward when she approached, but even Benedict greeted her calmly, "Lady Durant, I must apologize that we had so little time to speak while you were here. Perhaps there will come a time that you can visit again. If so, I would very much like the opportunity to make up for what was missed."

Avila furrowed her brow, since it almost sounded like he was saying goodbye. Still, she managed to keep it out of her voice. "Of course. It would be my pleasure. If I ever get the chance, that is."

He smirked at her last quip, but at that moment, the duke cut in. "I would like to extend an open invitation, Avila. You are welcome to visit any time you wish."

Avila was a bit stunned by that. She had been sure this would be a one-time visit, as the household did have to work around her presence. Still, she wasn't going to say no. Getting other people to say yes might be a different story, but for the moment, she could dream. "I don't know how often it would be, but I would love to return."

Despite their smiles, the feeling that they were saying goodbye became even stronger. Especially when she looked over to Nathan and saw that his smile was strained, though his voice was even as he said, "I apologize for the last-minute notice, but something came up last night, and it was decided it would be best if we start the return trip today. I know we had more planned, but . . ."

When he hesitated and looked as though he was struggling to find the right words, Avila took pity and cut in. "There is no need to apologize. I realize things happen. Though I'm afraid I will need a little time to gather my things. When did you wish to leave?"

Nathan was caught between looking chagrined and relieved, but he was quick to answer, "I thought that would be the case, so we are not scheduled to leave for an hour and a half. That should give us time for breakfast. Afterward, Evette can assist you in gathering everything. Would that be enough time?"

Avila nodded. "Of course, but I believe if we are to stay on schedule, we should get going."

At her reminder, Zachariah gave her a slight bow and said, "Lady Durant, I do apologize once again, but Ben and I have something else to attend to. This will be where we part."

Avila was slightly disappointed that they had to leave a day early, but to know she was already going to have to say goodbye to her charming host was more of a shock. She managed to hide it as she returned the bow. "Please do not apologize. I only hope that it will not be long until I can see you again."

The older man chuckled. "As do I." With that, both Zachariah and Benedict gave their last farewells before they turned to head to the offices.

As soon as they were gone, Nathan gestured to the dining room. "Breakfast should be ready."

The meal passed quickly and mostly quietly before they both headed to gather their things. Although Avila did not have much, Evette's help was still a blessing, especially since what little she did have had become scattered across the sitting room.

Thankfully, with the help, they were on the road a little before the planned time. Avila almost felt like she was leaving home again as she watched the plains fade as they traveled farther away. She hadn't been lying when she said she wanted to return. This place was far from the woods she had retreated to when she was younger, but still the first that had touched her so deeply since then.

36. FRIENDLY DISTANCE

It was late Saturday when they finally arrived on the telepad in Arinel. Avila was bone-tired and ready for bed. Part of it was the long drive, but not all. There was still a tenseness between her and Nathan that neither was prepared to confront. Although she knew it would need to happen sooner or later, in a vehicle when other people were watching was not the right place or time. If they couldn't clear the air, their friendship would suffer, and she didn't want that to happen. She didn't believe he would like that either.

However, all thoughts of her tiredness and the problems with Nathan disappeared as soon as her eyes landed on the person waiting for them when they arrived. Galdren was standing near the platform with Randy and Baxter.

Despite knowing better, Avila could not hold in the grin that emerged as soon as she saw him. It was only then that she realized how much she had missed him. She had thought they were growing apart after she moved into the castle. However, after this trip, she'd realized how much time they still spent together, even if it hadn't been the same between them since the move.

She didn't even care that he was not smiling. As soon as the field around the platform disappeared, she jumped down and went directly to him. "Galdren, it is so good to see you! I wish you could have been there. I know you said you have already gone, but there were so many extraordinary things to see, I don't think I even touched on half of them."

She was so giddy that she barely registered when his shoulders relaxed and a smile finally graced his face. "I am glad you enjoyed the trip. If anyone could catalog that place in one lifetime, it would be you. However, I will ask that you regale me with your adventures tomorrow. It is late tonight."

Avila was still too happy to let his words bother her, especially as she heard a familiar note of teasing in them. However, that came crashing down when Nathan joined them. Her friend was smiling, but it never quite reached his eyes as he said, "I hate to pop in and leave, but I will agree that it has been a long day. Plus, I have duties in the morning."

He then turned to Avila. "It was my honor to escort you. I hope that my family may once again host you at some point in the future. Until then, thank you for accompanying me."

Avila floundered for a moment, but she finally managed to find something to say before he walked away. "It is me that should be thanking you. I hope you rest well tonight. I also hope to see you soon. Don't let your work keep you too busy."

He managed a ghost of the smile he usually reserved for her, but she had the horrid feeling that it would be some time before she saw him again. Still, as much as she wanted to grab him and make him promise not to avoid her, she couldn't bring herself to. Not here. She didn't even realize her gaze had turned to a frown as her friend walked away.

When Galdren called out to her, she came back to the moment. She could see the curiosity in his eyes, along with the worry, but she was glad that he didn't ask. Instead, he stepped back so the others could grab her things, and they could leave.

The next two weeks passed by in a jarring mix of familiarity and foreignness for Avila. Several mornings she woke with the thought that she would get to see something unusual, only to be reminded that she was back in Arinel. A fact that was more than affirmed each time she stepped outside. Winter had not yet let go, though they were on the tail end of it finally.

To balance that was the fact that each day since she had been back, Galdren had managed to find time to visit for at least a short while before they had to go to dinner. It was a pleasant change from before she left, and it helped to offset the fact that she hadn't seen Nathan once outside of dinner each night, and their interactions there were still strained, at best.

Most days ended with her feeling a whirling mix of frustration and hopelessness. She was tired of things changing so drastically every time she turned around. She'd already had to endure more changes in the last nine months than any person should be forced to. Was it too much to ask to just be able to hold on to a friendship that meant so much to her?

The only thing that kept her from snapping at the least opportune moment was the fact that Professor Gilbert had been thrilled with everything she brought back—especially when she confirmed she had completed all the assignments he sent with her. They spent several days going over the sketches she had made while there.

The only thing she hadn't mentioned to anyone was the vari attack. After hearing about Nathan's past and how he had reacted when it happened, she didn't want to cause him more problems. Even though it had turned out fine, she didn't want Galdren to get upset over nothing. Unfortunately, that meant she also kept it from the professor, Lissa, and her parents.

When Saturday came around, late snow unexpectedly hit the capital, and despite the cold, she was thrilled to go and explore in it. It was a rare enough occurrence, and it was nice to have something unusual happen.

Once she got ready, Jacob escorted her out into the gardens' white landscape. Avila considered starting a snowball fight—she hadn't been able to have them often, as this much snow was rare in Arinel. Still, when she turned to grab a handful of white powder, she decided against it. She doubted Jacob would find it as humorous as she would. Plus, as much as she appreciated the people assigned to guard her, she couldn't exactly call them friends, and a snowball fight with an acquaintance wasn't the same thing.

Instead, she walked around to see how the winter flowers were doing. Unfortunately, they were almost all buried. It then started to snow softly again. It was one thing to play in the snow and an altogether different one to be out when it was snowing. Still, she wasn't interested in being cooped up in her room, so she opted to head to the hothouse.

She was not surprised to see a familiar guard near the door, and she grinned as he nodded when she entered. She didn't bother wandering around and instead went directly to the back, where she knew the queen would be. As soon as Lorne saw her, she stood with a smile. "Avila, I'm glad you came out here today. I had hoped to talk to you."

That made Avila give the other woman a curious look, but she didn't have to wait long to find out what was going on. Lorne gestured for Avila to join her as she continued, "I found out something amazing last night, and I thought you should know. We will have a guest soon, and I do believe you are the reason he will be visiting."

Avila wasn't sure what to think about that announcement. Surely it had to be someone important if it was someone the queen would consider a guest and not a simple visitor. If that was the case, she didn't know if she would be up to dealing with it, not after the last couple of weeks. Still, the queen only had a smile at the news, so perhaps it wasn't as bad as she was thinking. Though it wouldn't have been the first time the older woman thought she could handle more than she felt she could.

Lorne chuckled and pulled Avila down to sit next to her on one of the benches. "You don't have to look so frightened at the idea. I have a feeling you will appreciate what is coming."

When Avila only lifted a brow, the queen laughed. However, she got herself under control quickly and finally broke the suspense. "Zachariah, the Duke of Armand, has decided to end his isolation and will be coming to stay for an undetermined amount of time. He should be here sometime between now and next weekend."

Avila couldn't respond for several seconds. She had already figured that his wife's death had to have been the catalyst for his isolation, as they happened at the same time, but that didn't explain why he had decided to break it now, after so many years.

Her voice held both her curiosity and confusion when she finally said, "I must admit that after my visit, I understood why he stayed there. It is surprising he has decided to come visit, and I don't know what I might have to do with it."

The queen didn't answer right away. Instead, she shook her head and asked, "Did Nathan tell you what happened?"

Avila was temporarily thrown by the change in subject, but when she realized what the question was about, she looked away to keep the older woman from seeing her grimace as she answered, "Not until right before we returned, but yes. He told me about his mother."

A melancholy note lingered in the queen's voice as she said, "Zach never blamed anyone but himself for my sister's death. When he apologized to me, he said he should have been there. I tried to tell him no one could have prevented it, but I think he may still think that way sometimes."

Avila was so shocked that it again took several seconds before she could form a coherent response. "Did you say sister?"

The queen's brow drew down in confusion for a moment before it cleared and was replaced by a sad smile. "Yes. I suppose it isn't common knowledge outside of the castle. However, when our marriages happened within a year of each other, it was quite the gossip. Not that we had planned for it to work out that way."

That knowledge made Avila even more curious about why Zachariah had chosen to end his isolation. Still, she wasn't given long to think about it, as the queen stood and walked to the plants she had been looking at earlier.

When Avila joined her, Queen Lorne finally spoke again. "Given the momentous occasion, we will be throwing a ball in his honor. I doubt he will be thrilled about it, but we will keep the guest list small. Still, I do believe he would appreciate your presence."

Avila swallowed a sigh. As much as she disliked the events, she wouldn't miss this one. "Of course. I am glad that he has decided to come." After that, the conversation steered toward the plants.

Avila was slightly disappointed that Zachariah didn't arrive until late Friday night. She had hoped to speak to him before the ball. Instead, she was forced to endure another several hours of primping for an activity she would have forgone if it had been for any other reason. At least she knew she would have good company that evening.

The dress she chose that night was emerald green and had a high neckline with a fitted bodice that laced up the back instead of the typically hidden zipper. It was beautiful, but she was more than grateful to have Meru there to put it on. She doubted she could have laced it herself.

As Meru was helping her with the last of the preparations, she found she was conflicted. She hadn't thought about it before that moment, but she wondered if Benedict would be there too. If so, would the two brothers be able to keep it civil? Or would Nathan go at all? That last caused a pang. She was hopeful that he would be waiting, but something told her it was a hollow hope. She tried to push those thoughts aside as she headed out.

Angelo bowed as she exited, and she fell into step behind him when he stood. When they reached the common hall, Avila paused to look around. When the guards were the only ones there, it took all she had not to grimace. Still, she didn't want to cause a scene, so she was already moving again before either of her guards could ask what the problem was.

She was still moving on autopilot when she was announced, but that changed as soon as she stepped down off the entrance platform. A familiar voice caught her attention, and she turned to see the guest of honor headed her direction.

His smile was cordial when he took her hand and bowed over it, though she did see a familiar melancholy in his eyes when he stood. At least his voice showed no signs of it when he said, "Lady Durant, I am pleased to see you could attend. A familiar face and lovely smile are sure ways to help me adjust back into this life."

He paused and looked around for a moment before his brow furrowed. "I expected Nathan to be with you, was he delayed?"

Avila had to clench her jaw shut to keep from snapping, as it wasn't the duke's fault. It was several seconds before she could respond. "I apologize, but I haven't seen him in a few days. He has been busy, but I have no doubt he will be here."

The duke's eyes traced her face for a moment. She had no doubt he had already figured out that something had happened, but he didn't ask. Instead, he held out his arm. "Well, then I suppose my son will simply have to deal with missing this opportunity. Would you agree to walk with me instead?"

Despite her mood, Avila couldn't stop a grin from forming at the way his cheek dimpled slightly when his smile widened. It seemed Nathan had gotten that trait fairly. Her only response was to put her hand on his arm before he turned and began to mingle.

As grateful as Avila was for the smaller crowd, she was amused to find out that Zachariah was even more so. She might not have realized it if he hadn't said something when yet another group of distant relatives walked away after giving their well-wishes and greetings.

"I had hoped things had changed, but I suppose that was too much to ask."

When she gave him a curious look, he continued with a wry smile, "Don't mind this old man. It is simply that I have been gone far too long. I suppose one does get used to quiet with solitude."

Avila felt torn about how she should respond. On the one hand, she understood exactly how he felt, but she was also glad to have another friend close enough to visit. He must have realized her dilemma, as he chuckled and patted her hand. "Don't worry. I do not regret this choice. I am certain we will have many opportunities to share ideas in the coming days. However, I believe I have held your attention far too long. I see some of your friends are waiting for me to release you."

Avila had no idea who he might be talking about, as she hadn't heard Nathan announced, and she knew Galdren would not approach her during one of these events. Before she could ask what he meant, he had released her and gave her a slight bow before he turned and disappeared into the crowd.

She stared at the spot he had disappeared from in confusion until she felt a presence behind her. When she turned to see who it was, she had to bite her tongue to keep from groaning, though she couldn't keep the frown from her face when she spoke. "Lady Dunoire." That was all she could muster, as she didn't want to lie and say it was pleasant to see the other woman.

Her irritation was multiplied by the fact that the obnoxious female was not alone this time. Several other young women were standing with her. She could immediately tell that none of them were happy with her presence, even if they were smiling.

She wasn't given a chance to figure out her escape before the young blonde spoke. "I see that you are once again enjoying yourself."

There was a snide emphasis on the word "enjoying" that put Avila's nerves on edge, but she refused to rise to the bait. "Yes, I am. It is a wonderful opportunity to see a friend."

There were several giggles at her statement, but the Lady Dunoire only sneered. "A friend? I suppose that makes sense. Although, I must say that you seem to *make friends* at an alarming rate. Do you believe they don't speak to each other?"

Avila nearly rolled her eyes at how juvenile they all were when she heard several more snickers, and one of the other girls added, "Perhaps that is the wrong question, Becky. Do you think they don't know she is *friends* with them all? I'm sure none of them could be close to her, considering how often she flits around."

Before Avila could try to get around the group of girls, a different one spoke up. "Now, now, let's not be rude. After all, haven't we all been taught to be kind to the less fortunate? I'm sure she is doing all she can to rise above her heritage. I mean, Daddy has often told me the straits those poor refugees are in. Who can blame her for taking advantage of friends that can help make her life better? No matter the cost."

That was the last straw. No matter how tight a rein Avila had on her temper, that was just too far. It wasn't their opinions about her relationships, as the people that mattered knew the truth. However, she couldn't stand the way they were talking about her people. They had no idea what leaving their home for a chance at survival had to be like. They had no right to speak of the people of Talamh as though they could possibly judge a situation they could never understand.

She somehow managed to keep from yelling at the twits, but her voice was colder than ice when she said, "You speak of me flitting around as though you have no idea what it is to be a butterfly. I'm sure there are more than enough men here to hold your interest. There must be several that are only looking for a beautiful, shallow, vapid arm accessory. I apologize, but I must leave. My brain has met its quota of drivel for the day."

As Avila stormed past the small group of girls, one of them reached out to grab her arm tightly. All she did was look at the girl, but her rage must have shown in the tightness of her jaw and the flashing in her eyes because she was released just as quickly. Lady Dunoire called out to stop her, but she ignored it. For the first time, she was thankful that several eyes were turned their direction. She was so livid that she didn't care that many of them wore frowns. At least that also meant that the idiots didn't try to follow her.

Despite her experience the last time, Avila headed for the refreshment bar. She had never been one to drink, but anything to keep her from trying to strangle the lovely Lady Dunoire and her asinine friends would be welcome. At least she didn't down the first one she picked up.

She had barely finished her drink when she was surprised by a familiar voice to her side. She looked up to see the guest of honor standing there with a bemused expression. "I did not believe you to be the type to drown your problems."

Avila's eyes narrowed, though he did not seem to be reprimanding her for her choice. No, the longer she stayed silent, the more curious he appeared. She did sigh when he raised a brow at her silence. She finally shook her head as she said, "It isn't that I am trying to drown my troubles. Think of it as my way of saving lives. I doubt many people would appreciate a bloody ballroom floor."

She frowned as soon as the words were out. She wasn't sure why she had told him that, as she hadn't mentioned anything to anyone the last time. However, he immediately started chuckling. Instead of answering her questioning glance, he took her by the arm once again. "The dance is about to start, and as the guest of honor, I will lead the first one. I would be honored if you would share it with me. You are the one that opened my eyes to what I have been missing, after all."

Avila was staring at him in shock but didn't resist when he pulled her toward the far room. Especially when he shot her a mischievous grin as he said, "Besides, I am sure this is a far more productive way to show the Lady Dunoire that you don't care a whit about her opinion."

Avila felt like her eyes were about to pop out of her head at the look he gave her. The man was far more perceptive than she had given him credit for. That, or he knew what the girl was like. She didn't get to ask which it was, as a late announcement was made, and they both turned to see Nathan walk in.

Zachariah pulled Avila to a stop while they waited for his son to join them. It wasn't long, as most of the crowd had already gone to the next room. Nathan flashed them both a smile, but she wasn't warmed by it. Something was missing.

Still, his voice didn't sound any different than usual when he greeted them. "I am glad that I made it before the end of the night. I was afraid I would not be able to get away."

Zachariah nodded as he said, "The important thing is that you are here."

Nathan looked between them before he looked around to note that there were not many people left. He looked chagrined when he said, "It seems as though I am holding up the proceedings. There is no need to keep everyone waiting; I will catch up with you later."

Zachariah turned to Avila with a raised brow, and it took her a moment to realize he was verifying that she still agreed to the first dance. She was flustered by the whole situation, but she still managed to say, "I agree. We should go before they send someone to find you." Something odd passed through Nathan's eyes as she turned, but she didn't have time to ask.

There was quite a bit of murmuring when she and Zachariah walked onto the dance floor, but she tuned it all out as soon as the music started. Thankfully, dance lessons seemed to have been part of the royal upbringing, and she was thrilled to find that her partner was even smoother than his son and nephew—which was saying a lot. At least his smile was not strained, nor was he silent, and he easily managed to keep her mind off all the things bothering her.

They shared one more dance before he gave her a bow and left her in the hands of a gentleman that had been waiting. Avila accepted graciously but soon regretted that decision. After the second time she tripped over his feet, she began to wonder if he was doing it on purpose. He apologized both times, but there was a glint behind his smile that had her on edge. As soon as the dance was done, she declined the next one and made her way to the sidelines.

She nearly grimaced when she watched the young man join the group of girls from earlier. They all sneered at her, and it was easy to tell the damage had already been done. When she looked around, more than a handful of people were giving her looks ranging from discreet frowns to outright sneers.

If she hadn't also caught the queen's questioning look and the fact that Zachariah was there on the dais as well, she would have likely walked out. There was no reason to subject herself to the crowd's rude behavior. It didn't help that Nathan was nowhere to be found. A friend to talk to would have been excellent at that moment.

She decided that she was finished with dancing. She wouldn't leave until she had a chance to say good night to Zachariah, as that would be rude, but she wasn't going to stay in the ballroom either. Coming back into the ballroom later, when she was sure he was no longer with the king and queen, was always an option. She barely managed to conceal her frown as she made her way through the crowd and back into the other room. At least they had snacks and drinks. It was better company than the people surrounding her.

37. CONFESSION

Galdren was in a better mood than he had been in for some time. He refused to admit the cause of it, not even to his mother—not that she didn't probably know. However, even he could admit it was likely to be short-lived. The situation hadn't changed, after all. Though Nathan had avoided him and Avila both for the last few weeks, he doubted it would stay that way, if for no other reason than Avila was likely to get fed up and take action.

At least he could enjoy the reprieve and pretend that his heart had not led him down a disastrous path. He had taken on the responsibility to take care of Avila, which meant that no matter how much he might want something more, friendship was all he could share with her. Anything more would validate every whisper that said he kept her for gratification alone. He refused to allow that.

He tried to keep those thoughts in mind as he made his way through the ballroom. Although, not all of his cheer was due to things he couldn't focus on. He was also pleased that his uncle had finally decided to end his isolation, especially since he knew his parents had been trying to convince the man to visit for years.

Galdren could not hold back his grin when he saw his uncle lead Avila onto the dance floor. She had definitely made an impression, that was for sure. He was glad that her trip had been so successful on more than one front. If only he could figure out what had happened between her and Nathan. She refused to talk about it, but he could tell it bothered her. Despite enjoying more time in her company, he still felt prickles of guilt that it had come at the expense of something she cherished.

He refused to focus on that for the night. Instead, when his uncle finally joined them, he was the first to extend a hand. Zachariah shook it with a soft smile, but his first words were aimed at the king and queen. "I believe I should thank you both for this. Although, I must admit I am slightly rusty. At least there is excellent company to be had."

The queen returned the smile as she answered, "I cannot express how pleased we are to see you here. I am sure it will not take long for you to acclimate. Things are not always this hectic."

A look passed between the two of them that nearly erased Zachariah's smile. However, when he turned toward the crowd, it came back. His voice was light when he spoke to Galdren again. "To be honest, I am shocked. I left the Lady Durant to another gentleman thinking that either you or Nathan would be more than pleased to swoop in and keep her company, and yet here you are, and Nathan is nowhere to be seen. I almost feel guilty. Despite this party being in my honor, she is the one that should be thanked."

For a moment, Galdren was at a loss for words. He had no idea how to respond to that without saying something that would be best left unsaid. Thankfully, he didn't need to, as his mother said in his stead, "Come now, it hasn't been so long that you do not know how things can be misconstrued. Though, I am shocked that Nathan is not with her. They have been practically inseparable since they first met."

Galdren could have gone without the last part of her statement, but she wasn't wrong. It did make his brow furrow momentarily while he looked around for both Nathan and Avila. He felt a slight twinge of worry when he could see neither of them in the crowd.

He concentrated on looking for the two of them to the point that he missed the rest of the conversation. He didn't realize it until his uncle stepped away with a parting remark about rejoining his party. Even after the man was gone, he could not find Avila, though he finally saw Nathan. His cousin and uncle were speaking to each other on the far side of the room. He was forced to let go of his worry when his mother called him over and tried to remind himself that Avila would not have left without saying good night to the duke, so she had to be around somewhere.

It was nearly an hour later before Galdren saw Avila again. She had just returned from the refreshment area. More than once, he had thought about sending Randy to go find her, but he curbed the urge. It wouldn't help anything if he took such action for no reason. He already knew things were less than ideal and saw no reason to cause unnecessary problems.

Unfortunately, it did not take him long to figure out that something was wrong before she had made it far. He frowned at the look he could see her giving a group of girls, and his worry only increased when he saw that one of them was Lady Dunoire. Between one breath and the next, things seemed to have escalated. He could not hear what was said from where he was standing, but he noticed that Avila had raised her voice. Many of the guests had stopped what they were doing and were already whispering to each other at the unfolding scene.

Galdren decided that the crowd's perceived image of what their relationship was could be damned. He immediately turned to Randy and whispered, "Get her out of here. I'll meet you outside."

Randy saluted before he started weaving through the crowd. When Galdren looked back once more, he was grateful to see that his uncle was already by her side, and even more so when it seemed that the man was frowning at the group of girls and not Avila.

He did not wait to see more. He gave his parents a quick bow before he turned to leave out the side door with Baxter in tow. He was gratified that his mother's response was a worried look, and his father only gave him a nod as he passed.

A few minutes later, Randy came around the corner with several people behind him. Galdren had expected Avila and her guard, but he was surprised to see his uncle as well.

Avila looked like she was ready to do bodily harm to someone, and his uncle's expression wasn't much better. He didn't get a chance to ask before the older man said, "I am glad that I was close enough to hear that conversation. Despite what rumors may come of this, Lady Durant was more than justified. Given what I heard, had they been speaking to me, there would have been far more drastic repercussions. I do hope that going forward it is made known she is not to be harassed as she was tonight, regardless of what gossip may float around."

Galdren was shocked at how angry his uncle sounded. He had always been known for his calm, tempered demeanor. Unfortunately, that made his worry all the stronger. He managed to give the duke a polite bow as he responded, "Of course, I will do whatever is necessary to prevent further problems."

Zachariah ran his hand down his face before he sighed. "I will leave her in your care. It would be best if I return to handle the rest of this fiasco."

Avila had been standing to the side and silently fuming. However, when Zachariah said he was returning, she turned to him. "I apologize. This was supposed to be for you, and I have ruined it. I hope that I can make it up to you."

The duke shook his head as he answered, "This is not your fault. Please do not blame yourself. Though, I do suggest that you perhaps find a better way to deal with things like this going forward. I know how difficult things can get if you do not watch your every move."

Avila's face flushed, and she lowered her eyes to the ground as she responded, "I will heed your advice."

Both men gave her another concerned glance before the older of the two sighed and turned back to the ballroom. Once he was gone, Galdren gave the guards a look that had them dropping back a short distance while he tucked her hand into the crook of his arm and started leading her down one of the side halls.

Although they were both silent at first, it did not take him long to notice that she was less than sober. She still had not looked at him, but her expression kept alternating between furious and mortified. He also noted that she stumbled a couple of times. Had she not been holding his arm, she might have fallen the second time. He knew she was not the type to typically drink more than a glass of wine at a time, which made this behavior worrisome.

He decided it would be best to walk back to the family wing via the less-used hallways. When they were nearly to the family wing and were relatively assured of their privacy, he finally asked, "Avila, can you tell me what happened? You can't expect me to believe it was nothing."

He was shocked when she finally looked up at him, and rage was burning in her eyes. It showed in her voice too. "I know we cannot control what people think, but if that sad excuse for a petty cow thinks she can get away with calling me a whore to my face and disrespecting every person from Talamh and not deal with the repercussions, she has another thing coming. Goddess, she is such a brainless twit. I know it stems from unfounded jealousy, but I am so done with their insipid stupidity."

Galdren was taken aback by how furious she was. He had never seen her so angry. Though, if that was indeed what had happened, then he didn't blame her. Before he could respond, Randy said from just behind them, "Sir, perhaps it would be best to continue your discussion inside."

He looked back at his most trusted guard and nodded. The man was correct. It wouldn't do to have someone come by and hear any of this. He could tell that Avila was not done, but she snapped her jaw shut and looked away when their eyes met. He repressed a sigh as he led her to her room. He had a feeling the night was not going to end as pleasantly as it had started.

Once the door was closed behind them, Avila dropped his arm and started to storm toward her bedroom. He called out before she could reach it, "Please, wait. I understand that you are angry, but I cannot help if you don't explain."

Her eyes flashed when she spun around to face him. "Help? Like you have each time before? You already know what the problem is. I am nothing more than a second-class citizen, no matter what you say. The fact that you own me only makes it that much worse."

Galdren was aware enough to know she wasn't angry at him, but it still felt as though she had slapped him. He took a step closer, but she held up a hand to stop him. "Don't. I know it isn't you. It isn't your family either, but tonight was worse than it ever was when I was younger. You have no idea what it is like to have to deal with people who think you are less than they are just because you look different."

He ignored her glare and pulled her into a hug. She stiffened at first but relaxed against him when he said, "You are correct. I can't relate, but that doesn't mean I won't help."

She closed her eyes as she rested her forehead against his chest. Her voice was broken when she finally spoke again. "Galdren, I learned how to handle it years ago, but I could have used a friend tonight. Someone that was able to stand by me and not run when things got a little uncomfortable."

Galdren had to close his eyes against the pain her words caused. He hadn't been there for her through any of the events she had been to at the castle. He knew there had been valid reasons for it, but hearing her now, he wished he could go back and change that. It didn't seem as though his public distance had served any purpose but to make things harder for her.

He wasn't given a chance to say that before she pulled away. She was no longer yelling, but he could now see more of her hurt behind the anger. She took a few steps away before she spoke again. "I don't know what either of you are thinking, honestly. You are both supposed to be my friends, and yet you've both done the same thing. How can you think it is acceptable to kiss me and then ignore me? I know I was the one that stopped him, but it was because I wanted to save our friendship. How am I supposed to take this?"

Galdren couldn't have moved at that point if he needed to. She had to be talking about Nathan. That was the only thing that made sense. Nathan had kissed her. That was why they weren't speaking. He knew he had no right to the burning rage building within him, but all he could picture was his cousin kissing Avila, and it made him sick. He barely even registered that she had said she stopped him.

Before he could get himself together enough to think of a response, she continued, "And don't even get me started on you. I know we said we would put this behind us, but do you have any idea how much it hurt that you kissed me and then acted as though I had done something wrong? Goddess only knows that I was already falling in love with you then. Having you reject me so thoroughly after that—I can't even begin to describe it. I have had about enough of all of this."

Galdren's brain suddenly felt as though it had short-circuited. Surely he had misheard. He was so busy trying to gather his wits that he didn't even hear as she continued to rant.

It was several moments before he could focus on her again. She was pacing, but he cut her off mid-sentence by grabbing her by her upper arms. She frowned and looked like she was about to start ranting again, so he said the first thing that came to mind. "Say that again."

Her frown deepened. At least she didn't try to pull away as she said, "Which part? Where I said that you are thoughtless or—"

He cut her off with a shake of his head. "No. Before that."

She gave him a confused look, but he could tell the instant she realized what he meant, as her eyes went wide and she tried to pull away. He refused to release her, but her voice was nearly frantic when she said, "No. Oh goddess, please forget I said anything. I know you have already made yourself clear, and I don't want to lose your friendship too."

Despite the desperate look she was giving him, he refused to move. He couldn't. It took several heartbeats before his voice would work. "Please. I need you to say it. I want to make sure I didn't dream it."

His words caused her eyes to widen for a moment, but not for long. She shook her head, but when his steady gaze did not waver, he felt her slump in defeat. Her voice was barely more than a whisper when she said, "I love you, Galdren. I have cared about you for some time, but I didn't realize how much until we moved here."

Galdren felt as though he had run into a wall. His breath caught, and his brain refused to work. He felt simultaneously light-headed and weak-kneed. It wasn't until Avila tried to pull away once more that he came to his senses. One of his hands went to cup her cheek and turn her head up so he could look into her eyes. He saw pain and confusion, but when he smiled, he also saw hope.

He was so giddy he almost laughed. Instead, his thumb brushed across her cheekbone softly as he said, "I don't know where to begin. Though, I need to ask if you are sure. The idea of it—I can barely express how happy it makes me, but I do not want you to feel obligated. I care too much to think to force you."

Avila's eyes widened, and one of her hands went to grasp his wrist. He allowed her to pull his hand off her face, but he still gently switched her grip so that their fingers were intertwined. He wasn't sure she noticed, as her eyes were focused on his. Her voice was so soft that he barely heard her when she said, "You care about me? In what way? You are acting as though you are not upset, but surely it can't be that. You—you made it clear you didn't want me."

In a sudden burst of clarity, Galdren understood how foolish he had been—they both had been. His chest constricted at the thought that he might be too late, especially with everything else she had said, but he had to try. He had gone far too long already without considering that her feelings for him could be the same.

He closed his eyes and gently pulled her into an embrace. "No, Avila, I meant what I said. I know you said that I own you, but I have never believed that. My only desire has always been to help you. That night, I felt like I was only feeding into the belief that you belonged to me. You were so scared when I found you. I thought I had crossed a line. Not because I did not want to, but I never want you to feel compelled."

He could feel her heart rate speed up, and it was several seconds before she pushed back and looked up with wide eyes. "Compelled? Galdren, I thought you knew me well enough to realize if I didn't want something, I would say so."

He searched her eyes for a moment. When all he saw was consternation and hope, he finally smiled. "You are correct. I should have known better." He then cupped her cheek once again before he leaned down and softly pressed his lips to hers.

He only let it linger a moment, but he felt the soft sigh of her breath as he pulled away. He looked down to see her eyes were still half-lidded. It caused a spike of desire to shoot through him, but he curbed it as he said, "Avila, I should have said this long ago. I love you. Please forgive me."

In response, she wrapped her arms around his neck and pushed herself up until their lips met once more. His resolve to take things one step at a time was tested when her kiss became insistent. He was barely conscious of the way he pulled her flush against him as he lost himself to the feel of her.

Neither of them were thinking past the moment, so it came as a shock when someone knocked on the door. They reluctantly pulled away from each other, but it was still several seconds before Galdren felt he could speak clearly. "Yes?"

The door opened to reveal Meru standing behind Angelo. "Ma'am, your lady's maid is here to help you."

Galdren only needed one look at Avila to know that she didn't know how to respond. It was even worse that her cheeks were bright red. That made him smile, but he tried not to focus on why as he answered for her, "Could you please give us a moment? I will be right out."

Angelo saluted before he closed the door. He had to take a deep breath when he turned back to face her, and his touch was feather-light when he ran his thumb over her bottom lip. The action caused her to gasp, which he managed to not let distract him. "Perhaps it is a good thing that we were interrupted. I would rather continue this discussion when you are in full control of your faculties."

Galdren had to swallow a groan when her response was a slight pout. It took all he had to not do more than brush his lips across hers once more before he stepped away. "Have no fear; I have every intention of continuing this conversation in the morning."

Avila huffed once, but she couldn't conceal her smile as she nodded. "I will hold you to that."

Galdren somehow managed to step away. He paused once he was at the door and looked back with a soft smile. "I hope you sleep well."

"You too."

He realized that if he didn't force his feet to move, he would likely not be able to. With that thought, he reluctantly turned to walk out. As soon as he was out the door, the girl, Meru, made her way in to help Avila prepare for bed. That was another thought he had to force out of his mind. He could already tell things were about to become much more complicated, but he could not find the will to regret it.

38. FIRST STEPS

The next morning, Avila woke to the sun shining through the tall windows. That would have typically been a sight she relished, but her head hurt too much. She rolled over with a groan as she tried to remember why she might be in such pain. It did not take long for the events of the previous night to come back—all of them.

She let out another groan as she buried her face in the pillow. She wasn't sure if she was ecstatic or mortified. Her behavior before she left the ball had been less than stellar after her second confrontation with Lady Dunoire, but what happened when she and Galdren got to her room more than made up for it. Part of her wondered if that had even happened. Galdren had said he loved her. Her giggle at that thought was muffled.

She also remembered that Galdren had said they would continue the conversation this morning. Her stomach knotted at the thought, but it still motivated her to get up and into the shower. By the time she was finished and dressed, she was sufficiently sobered, and thankfully the hot water had helped with the splitting headache. Although her mind was still a mess, at least all of the "what ifs" that kept popping into her head made sure she wasn't a giggling idiot when she walked out of her bedroom. That was a good thing, too, as Galdren was sitting in front of the fireplace.

He stood as soon as she walked out. They both stood there silently for several seconds before he gestured toward the small table in front of him as he said, "I did have a few things that needed to be attended to this morning, but I have asked my parents to handle them. I thought it might be best if we had some time to talk. Breakfast should still be warm if you would like some."

Despite, or perhaps because of, his statement, Avila felt even more awkward than she had. Still, she silently moved to sit next to him. Just as he said, the porridge was still warm. She took her time preparing it to her tastes. Neither of them spoke until she put the half-finished bowl back on the tray.

As soon as Galdren saw it, he handed her a warm cup of tea with a smirk. "I had hoped you wouldn't be suffering this morning, but I give my word that this will help both your head and your stomach."

Avila felt her cheeks heat, but she took the cup gratefully. She started feeling her stomach settle after a few sips, and hoped it would help her head too. She didn't put the cup down, but she did turn to Galdren. Though she couldn't hold his gaze, she decided that she needed to say something, or it would only get more awkward. "I should apologize for last night. I know I had more to drink than was wise, which didn't help the situation."

There was a slight pause before he answered, "Which part are you apologizing for? If it is about the events before we left the ball, I will say that it was not your fault, no matter how people may twist the truth. As for the rest, I had hoped an apology would not be your response now that you are sober."

She could feel her ears burning by that point, and she nearly stumbled over her words as she responded, "No! That isn't it at all. I mean, yes, I was talking about the scene before we left. The rest—"

She cut herself off and looked into his eyes, only to see that he seemed nearly as uncomfortable as she felt. She was suddenly plagued by doubts, but she realized that this needed to be resolved no matter what happened. "I will also apologize for the way everything came out, so suddenly like that, but I won't recant what I said. I meant it."

His eyes did not leave hers as she spoke. Even though she felt she was about to combust from the embarrassment, she didn't look away either. Despite knowing that Galdren was not the type to lie, she was still afraid that he would change his mind. He was the crown prince, after all.

Those types of thoughts plagued her until he gently removed the tea from her hands. He then pulled her to him and wrapped her in an embrace. He held her there silently, and she wasn't sure what to think of it until he finally pulled back and cupped her face in his hands. His eyes were shining as he looked down into hers.

"I am not sure where to begin. I suppose I should start with an apology as well. I spent so long thinking only of doing what is best for you that I never considered you might have other ideas."

Avila pulled his hands down and shook her head, but she still managed a smile to keep her words from coming out as harsh as they might have otherwise. "How many times do we have to go through this? Ask me instead of deciding for me."

Galdren sighed as he rested his forehead against hers. "You are correct."

They sat together like that for several moments before another thought occurred to Avila, and she sat back. "Galdren, what does this mean? I can't begin to express how happy I am at the thought that you care, but that doesn't change the fact that you are the crown prince. You are the heir to the throne, and I am basically nobody—no, worse than that. I'm foreign. I can't believe that seeing me would be beneficial for you or accepted by the populace."

There was no hesitation in Galdren when he frowned and answered, "You have never been a nobody. As for the rest, I have no obligation to anyone other than my parents, and neither would have a problem with this. They have told me before that they would rather I follow my heart than be trapped in a loveless relationship. There is no need for you to worry about that."

Despite his adamant reassurances, Avila was still unconvinced. On top of that, she had more questions. Ones that she had never considered before, as the situation they were in had seemed impossible just the day prior. It took several seconds to put her thoughts together coherently. "What—what does this mean? For us, I mean. No matter what you say about our positions, I don't think it would be a good idea to just make a public announcement. Nor do I believe that we can keep it hidden unless we never leave this room. That could cause problems as well."

When a furrow formed between his brows, she quickly continued, as there was one more question more important than the others, "Even if those weren't issues, don't we need to discuss what this is? I mean—" She cut off and had to look away with a blush. "I do love you. I have for some time, and I don't doubt what you say, but that doesn't—"

Avila's jaw snapped shut on the last of her question when Galdren turned her to face him. His eyes held mirth, but his voice was soft when he said, "You are overthinking this. Most of those issues will resolve themselves in time, as we come to them. The questions about us, well, there is no need to define it. Not yet. We barely came to the realization that we care for one another. It isn't as though we are talking about marriage. Just relax."

Avila choked on the air she was breathing when he mentioned marriage. At least it was not in the context of wanting to discuss it. She probably would have locked herself in her room had that been the case.

It again took several seconds before she was able to gather herself and respond, "Okay. I suppose you are correct. We don't have to tackle everything now."

Despite her words, Avila was still tense. This was all new to her, after all. She wouldn't have known what to expect if it had been a man that didn't have all the responsibilities Galdren did. The fact that he did have so many made it much more difficult to face.

She was pulled out of her worry, literally, when Galdren tugged on her arm. She had no idea what he planned, but her face flamed when the next thing she knew, she was in his lap. That managed to effectively stop her frantic thoughts, and she knew he could tell it. His smirk was too self-satisfied.

He put an arm around her waist and pulled her closer. "I cannot say where this will lead, but this feels right. It has every time I've held you. I only wish I had thought to say something sooner. For now, we can enjoy this. Everything else can come later."

He didn't give her a chance to respond. Instead, his lips covered hers in the softest of kisses. No matter her worries, it was not long until she relaxed and wrapped her arms around his neck. This did feel right.

However pleasant kissing him was, she knew they couldn't stay like that forever. Eventually, she pulled back and grinned up at him. "Besides confirming that I love you, what did you have planned for the day?"

Avila felt a warmth fill her from the inside out when she noticed the effect her words had on Galdren. His smile was the brightest she had seen in some time. He moved so she was sitting next to him instead of on his lap, but he still hadn't removed his hand from her waist when he finally answered, "While staying here is enticing, I don't know that it would be wise. I had planned on asking if there was anything you wanted to do. I am yours for the day."

Avila's heart tripped at his statement, but she managed a smirk to cover it as she answered, "Just for the day?"

Galdren laughed at her prodding. He then brought her hand up to brush his lips across her knuckles before he said, "Pardon the lack of clarification. I meant you have my presence for the day. All else is yours as long as you desire."

His statement sent that warmth curling tighter, but she did her best to ignore the impulses it caused. Instead, she pointed to her half-empty cup. "Let me finish that, and then maybe we can go for a walk. It looks like a perfect day for it."

Galdren glanced out the window before he turned back with a wry smile. "At least the snow will be gone, even if it isn't warm." He paused and brushed a strand of hair off her face. "While you try to finish breakfast, I will make arrangements so that we may visit the city park. It would hardly take a day to walk the gardens."

Avila's eyes widened, and she grabbed his hand with a grin. "That sounds amazing!"

Galdren chuckled at her exuberance, but still pulled away, and his eyes flashed when he answered, "We can not leave until you get ready, so I suggest hurrying."

She rolled her eyes at his teasing but still turned to the tray. She eyed the porridge ruefully, as she doubted she could finish it now. At least they would likely take something with them, so it would not be long until her next meal. She then grinned at Galdren before jumping up. If they were to go anywhere outside, she needed to change.

It was late morning when they finally arrived at the park. The sun was bright and had already thawed the last of the frost through the bare limbs. That didn't mean it wasn't still cold, but Avila barely felt it as they started down the silent path. Although, that was likely due to her arm through Galdren's

The small group continued on wordlessly, with the three guards following at a short distance. Avila was loath to break the calming quiet, and the rest followed suit. It wasn't until they came to a clearing with several benches that she finally turned to Galdren with a smile. "Thank you. I really miss walking in the woods, and this is close enough. Though, I will admit that I rarely did it in winter."

She looked around for a moment before she squeezed his arm and looked back. "Isn't it beautiful? I love autumn, but I should have paid more attention to winter. There is something calming about the sight of the world getting ready for rebirth."

Galdren pulled her closer to his side as he smiled down at her. "It is indeed lovely, though not nearly as lovely as you."

Avila's grip tightened on his arm again, and several seconds passed before she burst into laughter. It grew louder when she caught sight of his consternation, but she somehow managed to calm enough to say, "I appreciate the compliment, really I do, but don't you think that's a bit trite?"

The look he gave her had her biting her lip to keep back further laughter. She didn't want to offend him. At least it looked as though he understood she was only teasing when he smirked down at her. "Perhaps, but I must admit that my attempts at poetry are less than satisfactory, and my singing voice could scare the birds. Unfortunately, that leaves me with trite commentary."

Avila rolled her eyes as she pulled on his arm, and they started walking again.

She was still smiling as she said, "I don't need poetry or serenades. As long as we can keep doing the things we have since we met, I will be happy."

He pulled her to a halt and cupped her chin. When their eyes met, his voice dipped into a whisper. "Anything you ever want, if it is in my power to give to you, it is yours. If all you want is my time, you have it with every bit of hope I have that it will make you happy."

Avila was suddenly caught between wanting to cry and blushing. She settled for pulling far enough away so that she could turn her head. Her voice was as low as his had been when she answered, "That's more than I could ask for." She didn't give him a chance to respond before she pulled him farther down the path. He followed with a smile and let silence reign once again. For the moment, it was enough.

It was not long before dinner when Galdren and Avila finally returned. Despite her initial hesitance, she had not let go of his hand since they left that morning. Even after they arrived back at the palace, Galdren made sure Avila knew he would not hide their relationship. Each time he said something, it made her fear lessen. She doubted their relationship would be accepted without comment, but at least she knew the person that mattered most wouldn't be affected.

Avila hardly wanted to part so they could clean up for the family meal, and Galdren was just as reluctant. Unfortunately, they both knew they could not forego dinner. Especially as there was something she had to do once there. At least it did not take long to clean up and change.

When she stepped out of her room, she was unsurprised to see Galdren waiting, though it still made her smile. He hooked her arm through his as they headed out. When he caught sight of her blush, he leaned a little closer and whispered, "You know, we go to dinner like this nearly every evening. It isn't new."

Her lips thinned as she looked up at him, but the effect was ruined by the mirth shining in her eyes. When he winked at her, she lost it. At least she was able to keep her laughter quiet. She was still smiling when they walked into the dining room. When she saw that everyone except the royal couple was already in the room, her smile waned as she realized this was the opportunity she'd wanted.

Avila let go of Galdren's arm and approached Zachariah and Nathan. She gave them both a polite bow before turning to the elder of the two. "Sir, I would like to apologize again for my behavior last night. I would also like to thank you for your assistance."

The duke smiled as he shook his head. "Think nothing of it. Despite how it may have seemed, the result was less troublesome than you might think. I am glad to see you back to yourself. You look to be in good spirits, if your smile when you came in was anything to go by."

Despite willing it not to happen, Avila felt her cheeks heat. Not that the man had mentioned anything untoward, but the thought of why she had been smiling had her fighting a grin again. When his gaze turned curious, she looked away. Thankfully, the king and queen had just entered, and everyone moved to take their seats. She was grateful for the forced change of subject. She paused when she caught sight of a shadow that passed over Nathan's eyes, but he turned to take his seat before she could figure out how to approach him.

The rest of the dinner proceeded much like they always did. Zachariah confirmed that Benedict had stayed behind to take care of the estate while he was gone. Avila was also grateful that her misdeeds from the night before were only brought up in passing. They moved on as soon as they assured her things had been handled. Part of her wanted to know the outcome, but in the end, she was happier to let the subject drop and move on.

Her only problem for the rest of the evening was that she felt her face was going to break from smiling so much every time she caught Galdren looking at her. It wasn't helped by the way his eyes seemed to glint with unsaid words each time, and his smile was fit to match hers.

By the time dinner was over and everyone had given their goodnights, Avila was glad for the reprieve. She felt like she was going to burst and was conflicted as to why. Part of it was that she wanted the world to know about her happiness, but the rest was because she knew that wasn't a great idea. Not yet. She settled for giving the others smiles before she once again took Galdren's arm.

Nathan was the last to leave, and the look he gave her as they walked out was the only thing to dim her happiness. It hadn't been angry, only resigned. He turned before she could say anything, which caused a new pang to pass through her. She resolved that soon, she would track him down, and they would have it out. No matter what had happened, he was still her friend. She refused to give that up without a fight.

Despite her worries about Nathan, her focus was once again on Galdren by the time they were back to the rooms—especially as he followed her in. She gave him a curious look when he shut the door, but he ignored it in favor of pulling her into an embrace. She rested her head on his chest as he said, "Well, that was certainly an interesting endeavor."

Avila chuckled as she pulled back enough to look up at him. "See, this is why I wanted to have a plan."

Galdren looked away at her statement, but she could still see the corners of his lips turn up into a smile. When he didn't say anything right away, she leaned back into him and continued, "Don't worry that I feel slighted. I understand this is a precarious position for both of us. We'll figure it out."

He sighed before leaning back and tilting her chin up so he could see her eyes as he answered, "It isn't that I am worried about their reactions. I only want to make sure that whatever comes out will not harm you."

She squeezed his sides lightly before she stepped back. She kept her smile so he would know she wasn't upset. "I know. I already said not to worry. You are the one that told me we will take it a day at a time, so that's what I plan to do." She looked away with a blush. "Besides, none of the people in that room are stupid. I doubt that any of them missed that something has changed. It wouldn't surprise me if they already have it figured out by the time we say anything."

The last of Galdren's worry left his eyes as he chuckled at her remark. He then pulled her closer once more and cupped her cheek. "You are correct. I'm not sure why I didn't think of that myself."

By that point, something had changed in his expression, and Avila felt a familiar warmth course through her. He didn't say anything, but her heart clenched in anticipation when she saw his eyes flick down to her mouth. She didn't wait for him to move before she lifted onto her toes and ended up meeting him halfway.

Her hands skimmed from his side to his chest, and she grabbed his shirt to steady herself as his kiss turned less than chaste. Instead of stopping him, she slid her hands up to his shoulders. No matter how many times he kissed her, it still took her breath away.

The warmth she had grown to enjoy was starting to turn into an insistent, unfamiliar heat as one of his hands tangled in her hair and the other pulled her even closer. His kiss strayed to the corner of her lips, and then her jaw. When she felt the scrape of his teeth lightly against her earlobe, she made a sound that was foreign to her. She had no idea what to make of the feeling coursing through her, but was too lost in her desire to be closer to him to try and focus past what he was doing.

She was on the brink of begging, though she wasn't sure what for. The words were on the tip of her tongue when Galdren pulled back. She had to blink a few times before she could focus on his face. The look in his eyes sent a spike of desire running through her, but she forced herself to listen to him instead of pressing against him again.

His voice was more than a little strained as he said, "Avila, I believe it might be best if I leave now."

Avila felt her longing instantly cool. He must have seen it in her eyes, as he pulled her closer. "Do not think it is because I do not want this. On the contrary, I'm afraid if I do not go now, I may step beyond a point that we are ready for."

Avila knew she was innocent in many ways, but it didn't take much for her to figure out what he meant. She was glad her face was buried in his chest as she responded, "I understand." That was all she could muster for the moment. Thankfully, he didn't try to move her.

After several moments he finally pushed back with another sigh, but he was smiling when he looked down at her again. "Don't worry, I plan to be back in the morning." He then kissed her forehead and stepped away. She could see the strain in his eyes as he added, "Good night."

Despite her earlier worries, Avila had no doubt that the tension she could see was for the same reason she felt dissatisfied. That thought sent shock waves through her. She was wanted. It was a heady feeling and had her grinning back at him. "I hope your dreams are good ones."

"As do I. At least, I doubt that they could possibly be bad." Then his smirk had that warmth flooding back in, but he didn't give her a chance to respond. Instead, he opened the door and gave her one last wink before closing it behind him.

Avila didn't move for several seconds. When she finally did, she couldn't stop smiling. Somehow, she doubted that her dreams would be bad that night, either.

39. UNEXPECTED NEWS

When Monday morning came, both Avila and Galdren were more than a little disappointed to have to attend to their respective tasks. At least they both knew the time apart would only be temporary. Avila was particularly pleased when Galdren returned an hour before they had to go to dinner. Not that it was any more time than they had been spending together before things changed, but she found new enjoyment in his company now that she no longer felt the need to police her thoughts.

Over the next several weeks, things between the two of them gradually grew more comfortable. Even meals became less tense. Not that they had mentioned anything to anyone else yet. Avila had even kept it from her parents and Lissa. That last was the hardest, as her friend was insatiably curious, but Avila knew the time wasn't right yet. She would tell them before it came out publicly, but for now, she was content to simply share time with Galdren. Besides, he had agreed with Avila's initial assessment. There was no way his parents didn't know, but their confirmation of that fact could wait along with everyone else.

Many aspects of their relationship were growing each day, but one, in particular, was more difficult for them both to cope with. Avila was not shy by nature, but she was inexperienced in any kind of intimate relationship. She had never had time to explore the concept before. Now, there were many days that it showed. She did not push Galdren away, but she often felt overwhelmed. Thankfully, he seemed to always have that in mind, though some days were more challenging than others.

This day was the last in a long line of days that had found the two of them sitting on her couch after dinner. It started with a conversation as they unwound before bed, but it was not long before Avila found herself being pulled closer to Galdren. She had been teasing him and laughing at the look he was giving her, but it cut off as his arms circled her waist and was replaced by a breathless noise when she saw the look in his eyes as he spoke.

"Have I mentioned that I adore the way you don't seem to care about my position? Not when it is just the two of us." He paused and placed a soft kiss along her jaw. She leaned her head to the side without thought as he followed it with another on her neck. She shivered as his breath ghosted over her ear when he continued, "I cannot begin to explain how difficult it is for me to keep my hands to myself most days."

Avila had a snarky remark on the tip of her tongue, but it was lost when his lips covered hers, and then her arms went around his neck as he pulled her into his lap. She quickly forgot what they had even been talking about.

In an effort to get as close to him as possible, Avila shifted so that she was straddling his legs. The groan that came from him as she pressed forward made a shaft of fire race through her. She reveled in the sound as she cupped his face and held him in place for a kiss like he so often did to her. The feeling of power and need was a potent combination.

Despite her position, or rather because of it, Avila nearly groaned in pleasure as well when Galdren pulled her flush against him. His lips found her pulse point before they drifted down to her collarbone. That, combined with the feel of him pressed against her, was enough to cause sensory overload. She leaned her head back as he pulled her shirt down a few inches and placed a hot kiss at the top of her cleavage.

In the next instant, Galdren had switched their positions. It took her addled mind a moment to understand how they had gone from her in his lap to her on her back with him hovering over her. However, she saw no need to think about it further as he pressed closer and claimed her lips once more.

Her arms had already gone around his shoulders, and her nails were tracing random patterns across his shoulder blades through the fabric of his shirt. She had no thoughts beyond what she was feeling—at least until she felt one of his hands under her shirt on her waist. It was such a foreign sensation that she immediately stilled.

As her mind started to clear, she realized this was farther than things had ever gone between them. She wasn't displeased with that fact, but her stillness must have clued Galdren in to the fact that all was not well. He pulled back and braced himself on one arm so he could look down into her eyes. It was several seconds before either of them could breathe evenly. However, as soon as he was steady, Galdren pushed a stray strand of her hair back and gave her a wry smile as he said, "Perhaps it would be best if I left for tonight."

Avila felt a sudden urge to stop him. She grabbed his shoulders as she said, "Don't go. I give my word that I was not upset. It was only unexpected."

Instead of moving to kiss her again, Galdren sat back and pulled her up with him. He held her close to his side but shook his head as he responded, "I don't doubt you, but this is something that should not be rushed. Please forgive me for being so forward."

Avila could tell that he had already made up his mind, and this was a lost cause, but that didn't stop her from trying anyway. "I do not think you were forward."

Before she could say more, he cut her off with a swift kiss. He smirked down at her frown when he pulled back. "I know, but this is important. I want it to be special for you when it finally happens."

Avila felt her cheeks flush at his reminder, but she still wasn't done. However, before she could speak again, he placed a soft finger over her lips. "Avila, we have a lifetime for this. Take your time, and have no fear that I will not wait."

His words painted images in her mind of things she was both thrilled about and terrified of. Still, she could tell there was no budging him. When he dropped his hand, he gave her one more swift kiss and squeezed her fingers before he stood. "Sleep well."

"You too." That was all she could manage to get out before he turned and went back to his own rooms. Once he was gone, Avila flopped back onto her couch with a groan. She knew he wasn't wrong, but that didn't stop the frustration. She groaned again as she pushed herself to her feet. A long shower before bed was what she needed. She hoped by then that the worst of it would pass.

Nearly a week later, a distraction appeared. Avila and Professor Gilbert were finishing up for the day when a familiar guard followed Angelo into the room. They both bowed to Avila when her protector said, "Ma'am, the queen is here to see you. Are you available?"

Avila shared a shocked look with her teacher, but his only response was to start clearing his things. The queen wasn't someone you turned away. Instead of saying more, she nodded to Angelo. "Of course. Surprise or not, I always enjoy her visits. Please don't keep her waiting."

Angelo saluted before he opened the door again, and the queen entered along with her other guard. As soon as she was in the room, Professor Gilbert bowed. "Ma'am, it is always an honor to see you, but I have finished here for the day. Unless you need my presence, I will excuse myself."

Lorne smiled as she answered, "Frederick, please do not worry. I apologize if I have interrupted, but something urgent has come up that I need to discuss with your student."

Professor Gilbert put the last of his papers away before he lowered his head once again. "Of course, ma'am. It is no inconvenience. The day was nearly over." He picked up his things and gave Avila a nod before bowing once more. "I will leave the two of you to your visit. Good day."

Avila watched him go with mixed feelings. Usually, she enjoyed the queen's visits, but with the recent changes in her life, she was slightly apprehensive. Had the woman finally come to confront her about her relationship with Galdren? There was little else she could think of that might be considered urgent. At least the older woman was still smiling. She chose to take that as a good sign.

Once the professor was out the door, Lorne gestured to the sitting area. "I apologize again, but I wanted to speak with you before my son had a chance to find you."

That statement did not soothe Avila's fears, but she still joined the other woman when she sat. She couldn't find her voice, so instead, she waited for the queen to continue. The older woman's eyes turned somber when she spoke. "Avila, I understand why you might be apprehensive about why I am here. However, I have come to ask you this myself because I believe it is what is best."

Had it been any other person talking, Avila would have been on her feet as soon as those words left their mouth, if for no other reason than her anxiety would not let her sit still. She somehow managed to fight the urge to fidget as she said, "What could I possibly be apprehensive about?"

She cursed the waver in her voice, but thankfully it didn't seem as though the queen noticed. The woman chuckled before she answered, "My apologies, I am getting ahead of myself. We are hosting an ambassador from Talamh, and I felt it would be important for you to attend the welcoming ball."

Those few words were all it took for Avila to forget her worry about her relationship. She couldn't decide what part was more shocking—that the queen wanted her to attend another ball after the last fiasco, or that it would be for a person from her home planet. Or perhaps not. The more she thought about it, the more she realized the ambassador was likely to be someone from the new government. She wasn't sure why, but the thought left her feeling nauseous.

It was several seconds before she could school her thoughts enough to come up with a coherent answer. "Please do not think that I am ungrateful, but I must ask why you believe my attendance would be important? From what I have learned, anyone coming from there now would be one of the many reasons my people are refugees. Why I am a refugee. That doesn't even consider my last mishap."

Lorne surprised Avila when she sat forward and took her hand in a comforting grip. Her eyes held only concern when she answered, "I know it may not be comfortable, but that is precisely why you should be there. No matter what has happened, is that not still your world? Do you not want to know the hands that guide it now? Your memory may be gone, but surely you wish to know the fate of any of your people that remained."

Avila paused at the earnestness coming from the queen. She still wanted to say no. There were so many reasons for her to avoid the scene altogether, but she could not. The older woman had a point. The thought of seeing anyone from the new Talamh government made her nausea stronger, but she could not deny that she needed to know.

Her dreams came to mind and reminded her why she did not wish for that knowledge, but she couldn't force the idea out of her head. She finally nodded. "I do not want to go. Even though all I have is fragmented dreams as reminders of what might have been, the thought of facing that makes me sick. But I will. You are correct that I need to. If for no other reason than to learn to move on. Perhaps this is what I need to finally be rid of my nightmares."

When she agreed, Lorne gave her a soft smile and patted her hands before she sat back. "I knew you would see the good in it."

Avila still wasn't sure she agreed, but she let it drop as the queen had already changed the subject. The next half hour was spent going over the woman's plans for the gardens now that spring was just around the corner.

When Lorne finally stood to leave, Avila was still unsure of her choice, but she kept it to herself as the woman walked toward the door, a decision she was grateful for when the queen turned back with one last smile. "I am glad you chose to go. I look forward to seeing you there."

Avila had a response on the tip of her tongue, but it was cut off when Lorne turned to her guards. "Please give me a moment." The two of them bowed before they stepped out.

When Angelo gave Avila a questioning look, she nodded. "Please." She wasn't sure what the queen wanted to discuss that needed so much privacy, but she trusted her.

Once they were all gone, Lorne took her hand again, and her smile brightened. "I won't keep you long, but I also wanted to tell you one more thing. I am happy that you and my son seem to have worked through your issues. Whatever comes of this, know that I will not object. His happiness is all I want."

Avila was stunned into silence. With everything else, she had forgotten her earlier fears about the queen's opinion about her and Galdren. Her response was the last thing Avila had expected. She was still too stunned to say anything when Lorne patted her hand before she let go. The queen gave her one last beaming smile before she walked out. It was several minutes before Avila was able to move.

Galdren was frowning as he made his way toward his father's office. The news about their upcoming guest had just passed his desk, and he wanted to talk to his father about keeping Avila away. He wasn't worried about the incident at the last ball, but he also did not want her to have to dredge up painful memories. The idea that her nightmares were twisted fragments of her past had already occurred to him, and he did not want them to become worse.

He had just raised his hand to knock on the door but stopped when he heard his mother's voice. He was loath to leave, but didn't want to interrupt. She seldom visited his father when he was in his office, so it was surely important. The internal debate on whether to leave or wait came crashing to a halt when he heard something that caught his attention.

While he knew eavesdropping was impolite, he had realized they were speaking about Avila. His feet became glued to the floor upon hearing his father's next words. "Do you believe this is a wise decision? Things could go horribly wrong."

His mother's dismissal was quick. "Of course. No matter what happens, she will need to face this. Besides, she has no memory of what happened. So many years have passed that it is unlikely they will come back."

"And if they do?"

The king's voice had a hard note to it that was rare. It had Galdren's nerves on edge. His mother's response did not help. "Then you have already made your decision on what should happen. I have faith that she will make the best choice."

After that, their voices dropped low enough that Galdren could no longer hear them. Not that it mattered. What he had heard was enough to make him worry.

He was also fighting a mix of curiosity and disappointment. It was evident that his parents knew more about Avila than they had shared with him. The thought that they felt they couldn't tell him made him wonder what about her could possibly warrant that level of secrecy.

Unfortunately, he knew it was something he would have to discover another day. He could not interrupt, especially not after having heard that. Instead, he turned to go back the way he had come, his mind now full of possibilities and more than a little worry. One thing he had garnered was the fact that somehow, his mother had already convinced Avila to attend the coming ball. He only hoped the ominous words he'd overheard turned out to be nothing.

40. AMBASSADOR

Saturday evening, Avila was once again standing in her room as Meru helped her finish dressing. Savanah and her crew had already left. Despite the pretty azure dress, Avila was still distracted. She was thinking back to Galdren's objections later the same night that the queen had visited.

He had been adamant that she should not go to the ball. He didn't want her to be hurt. Part of her had agreed. She still wasn't sure she could face whoever was coming and not either break down or lose her temper. Just thinking about the people from Talamh that she had already met made her angry on their behalf. She understood why the king had chosen to host the ambassador, but that didn't make her happier about the situation. Unfortunately, despite her reserve and Galdren's objections, she knew this was something that had to be done, if for no other reason than to get closure.

Once Meru clasped the vine necklace around her neck, Avila glanced once more at her reflection. When she verified nothing seemed amiss, she thanked the girl and followed her out. She stopped in shock as soon as she was out the door. "Galdren, what are you doing here?"

He held out a hand as he smirked. "You sound as though you do not want me to escort you."

Avila nearly stumbled over her words. "That's not it at all! It's just—" She cut off as he took her hand and tucked it into the crook of his arm.

He waited until they were near the outer hallway before he spoke again. "I am aware that you may be hesitant, but I had planned on escorting you no matter the reason. I am tired of caring about what others say. Besides, I am still not convinced this is a good idea. I would rather be nearby tonight."

Avila felt her cheeks heat at his declaration, and though most of it was from the warmth his words caused, some was from thoughts of the probable fallout from his actions. Still, if he refused to let it bother him, then she could follow suit. It wasn't as though she didn't have plenty of other things to worry about that night. Plus, his mother's words were still ringing through her memory, and she felt much better about their prospects.

When the two of them walked into the ballroom and were announced together, the silence that fell was eerie. It was broken only a moment later, and the murmur of the crowd was louder than Avila had ever heard. She felt her nervousness pick up, but Galdren placed his hand over hers as they descended the steps. That comforting gesture helped to calm her. It was made better when she looked toward the dais to see the queen smiling at them. Avila's brow furrowed when she noticed the king was not there, but she did not let it hold her attention. There were too many other things to worry about.

As soon as they stepped off the platform, they were surrounded by a throng of people. Avila was grateful for Galdren's presence, as he deftly led them through it. Unfortunately, they had to stop often to listen to people wishing the prince well or for other small talk. She had no doubt that some had many other things to say, but they kept it to themselves. Not even the typical horrid whispers could be heard.

Instead, she noticed that most of the crowd surrounding them consisted of councilors and their families. Given that, it was no shock that much of the talk revolved around the ambassador and their hope to gain a powerful ally. Avila was curious as to why they hadn't met whoever the person was yet, as the ball was supposed to be in their honor. Though, when she remembered that the king wasn't at his throne either, it made her wonder if other talks were going on behind the scenes. Not that it had anything to do with her.

She brushed those thoughts aside as one of the councilors' wives turned to ask about her necklace. Avila was a little uncomfortable telling anyone that it had been a gift from the queen, so she kept that part to herself, but she was more than willing to admit it was her favorite piece. By that point, there was a lull in the men's conversation that Galdren took advantage of. He excused them both before he turned and led her toward the refreshment tables.

He stopped a short distance away and dropped her hand so he could face her. His voice was low enough not to carry when he spoke. "How are you?"

Avila could not hold back her smile. "I'm fine. With you here, there will not be any trouble. Don't worry. Besides, even if you step away, they can all see you will be back. No one is going to cause any issues tonight."

He didn't look entirely convinced, but he finally nodded. "Would you like something to drink?" He paused, and a sparkle lit in his eyes as he smirked. "Though, I will not fill any requests for something alcoholic."

Avila had to clamp her lips shut on the laughter his words evoked. As embarrassed as she had been over that night, she knew he was teasing. Still, now wasn't the time or place to say what was on her mind. Instead, she gave him a nod. "Yes, please. All I ask is that it not be something too sweet. I don't care for syrup."

He chuckled when she wrinkled her nose and ignored the look she gave him as he stepped away. "I will not be far, but it may be a few minutes. They do look rather busy."

Avila waved him off. "I will stay right here, don't worry." He only hesitated for another moment before he turned to get them both refreshments.

Once he was gone, Avila could tell that several people considered approaching her, but most of them looked to see that Galdren was not far away and turned to mingle again. She could not hold in her smile. It was nice to attend one of these functions and not be harassed.

Then she heard a familiar voice on her other side. "I cannot believe you dared to show your face here again after what you did. Especially not on the arm of the crown prince. Have you no shame?"

Avila didn't bother holding back her sigh as she turned to face the Lady Dunoire. At least this time, she only had two other girls with her, and they were both looking around nervously. Avila smiled coldly at them all as she answered, "I do believe you have that backward. It isn't me that was caught disrespecting my peers and causing problems. You are obviously the one that needs to learn a bit of humility. Though, it does seem like you don't learn from your mistakes. More's the pity."

The girl looked like she was about to have an apoplectic fit. Still, before anything else could be said, a foreign male voice spoke up behind Avila. As different as it was, it was also familiar, and it had her frozen in place. The rest of the room seemed to disappear as he spoke. "Princess Avila Treunmhor."

Time slowed as she forced her feet to move and turned to face the man that had spoken. What she saw had her breath locked in her lungs. The man was older than she remembered, but there was no mistaking who he was. His bald head and cold eyes were just as terrifying as the last time she had seen them.

The sight of this man from her nightmares caused a cascade of locked memories to rush through Avila's head. She wanted nothing more than to drop where she stood and scream as they threatened to tear her apart from the inside out, yet she somehow managed to lock her knees. Her voice was colder than ice when she finally spoke. "You."

Avila was shocked when, instead of attacking her, the man bowed respectfully. "Your Highness, it is a . . . pleasure to see you alive and well. We had long thought you dead."

Despite her terror, Avila took a step forward. Her rage allowed her to bury the fear. Before she could say anything, she was pulled back into the present by a condescending female voice beside her. "I believe you have the wrong person, sir—there is no one worthy of that title here."

Avila looked over at the young blonde and didn't bother to hold back her disdain. "Be silent."

Before she could turn back to face the more critical threat, Lady Dunoire huffed and practically yelled, "You have no right to speak to me with that tone! You are far too full of yourself. You think yourself my peer, yet you are a nobody."

Avila's eyes flashed, and her voice became hard as she glanced over at the younger woman. She didn't care that others had gathered as she said, "I said be silent. You are correct that I am not your peer, yet it is you that speaks above your station. Your incessant prattling is of no consequence here. You have no idea of the wider Alliance and how insignificant your part in it is. If you have nothing better to go on about than your petty jealousy, then find another nobody to speak to. I have no time for it."

She ignored the girl's sputtering as she turned back to the man. He was smirking at the scene, though he also ignored the younger woman. His eyes were entirely focused on Avila. "Your Highness, don't you think it would be prudent to be kinder to these people, who are protecting you?"

Despite the stream of varied emotions she was still fighting, Avila felt a rush of dread. She understood implicitly the threat he had not spoken. Her fists clenched by her side as she answered, "No one here is protecting me. To them, I am no more than another refugee."

The man smirked at her answer, but the look in his eyes caused a chill to go down her spine. He glanced over her shoulder before he answered. "Oh? Are you sure they feel the same way?"

Avila didn't want to rise to his bait, but she could hear a ruckus behind her. She was shocked to not only see Galdren making his way through the crowd, but both Zachariah and Nathan as well. Despite the crush of people, once everyone realized who was coming through, the crowd parted, and it was only a moment before all three men were by her side.

Galdren sent a glare to Lady Dunoire that had the younger woman backing into the press of people, but his gaze was instantly back to the stranger as he said, "What is going on here?"

The stranger gave Galdren a bow and a polite smile when he stood to answer. "Your Highness, it is a pleasure to meet you. I must beg your forgiveness for my tardy introduction, but I had a few last-minute things to attend to."

Galdren glared at the man before he glanced at Avila. She knew he had to see how upset she was, but she couldn't find the words to reassure him. Thankfully, she didn't need to. His voice was clipped when he turned back to the stranger. "That does not tell me what has happened here."

The man never lost his smile as he gestured toward Avila. "Pardon, I was merely letting the princess know how worried we have all been for her. No one had seen her in so many years that we feared the worst."

Avila vaguely heard several gasps and Nathan's frantic whisper, but she was too focused on the man in front of her to care. "How dare you? How can you stand there and say that with a straight face when my family's blood stains your hands?"

The man's eyes flashed, but his voice was still cordial. "My apologies, Your Highness, but I'm afraid I had nothing to do with their deaths."

Avila was shaking so badly that she was afraid she would fall. Or punch his nose. His perpetual smile had her seething. "Perhaps not. But we both know you did kill every other person I ever loved. Your solicitous attitude is as false as your premise for being here. I am no longer that child who hid in terror from you."

The man's smile slipped, but he managed to keep from losing it. However, they were interrupted when the king arrived. He stepped in between them, but faced the man. "I must beg your pardon, Ambassador. I will have this sorted out shortly, but please stay and enjoy the rest of the party. My wife will be here to help in any way she can."

The stranger gave him a nod, but the king had already turned to the rest of the group. "If you would join me in my office, please. I believe we have things to discuss."

Avila had no doubts that they did. She was still too rattled to fully grasp how tenuous her position was, but she knew that this was not good. She gave the king a nod and finally turned to the others. She saw the queen standing a short distance away. The woman gave her a worried look, but Avila didn't know how to respond.

She wasn't even sure what to say to Galdren. The look on his face was shocked and maybe a little hurt. Zachariah and Nathan were not much better.

Instead of trying to figure out what to say to any of them, she turned and followed the king out. She was surprised when the three men followed, but she couldn't focus on it. The ambassador was still giving her that cold smile as she left.

The walk to the king's closest office was silent, but that changed as soon as the small group was behind closed doors. Galdren turned to his father immediately. "What happened back there? You know what is going on already, yet you have told me nothing."

The king looked at his son blankly for a moment before he finally responded. "I will not object to your presence here if you will keep silent. I asked Princess Avila here to speak with her about what happens next, and I will not tolerate interruptions."

Galdren took a shocked step back. Before he could respond, his uncle stepped forward and pinned the king with a stern look. "I am aware that this may be a matter of state. I will even concede that we should not be directly involved, but no matter what the outcome is, you cannot expect us to stand idly by. Especially not after what I heard out there."

Before Zachariah was even done speaking, Nathan had stepped up to Avila's side. He looked over at her with confusion, and his voice was low as he asked, "So, it's true then? You really are the missing princess?"

Avila had to look away. She had wanted to mend things with Nathan, but she couldn't face him now. Not that she didn't think he deserved an answer. They all did. However, she could barely keep her frantic thoughts in place long enough to think straight. She merely nodded before she looked over at the king. "Your Majesty, I imagine you asked me here to give me an ultimatum. I understand that Aril has always been neutral, and I do not expect you to change that on my behalf."

Galdren gently grabbed her arm and turned her to him, but she couldn't meet his eyes either. When she wouldn't look at him, he turned back to his father, though he didn't let her go. "You cannot be sending her away. No matter who she was, she is a citizen of Aril now. She has a place here."

For a moment, the king's eyes reflected his heavy heart, but he hid it again as he answered, "You are both correct. Now that Her Royal Highness, Princess Avila Treunmhor, has regained her memories, there is a choice to be made."

He paused long enough to ensure that Avila was looking at him before he continued, "My son is correct in that you do have a place here on Aril. I knew who you were when you arrived and your guardians gained citizenship. Your life here, as it is, can continue if you so choose—all aspects of it, including the Life Debt. To accept that, you must officially denounce any intention of trying to reclaim your throne. You will forever be a citizen of Aril, and will no longer be allowed to pursue any activities against the Trogand, as Aril has always been, and always will be, neutral—as you said yourself."

Galdren made a frustrated noise but did not speak when the king sent him a quelling look. The older man then looked back at Avila. "However, you also have the choice of pursuing your past. It is up to you, but you need to be aware that Aril will be closed to you if you choose to leave. We cannot afford to become embroiled in foreign affairs. Though, I will grant the verification of your identity. That is all I can offer."

Avila's voice was barely above a whisper when she answered, "Your Majesty, that is a choice that I am unprepared to make right now. Could I humbly ask for some time?"

He nodded once. "I will allow for one week. After that, you must choose."

She gave him a polite bow. "Thank you. May I be excused for the evening?"

The king's eyes once again showed deep tiredness as he said, "You may. I will expect your answer soon."

She somehow managed a curtsy before she turned to walk out. When she did, she was confronted by the sight of the three men, who had not left. Zachariah looked somber, but both Nathan and Galdren were livid. She shook her head before either of them could speak. "Not tonight, please. I can't."

Both men grimaced, but they didn't speak. Galdren stepped forward and gently took her arm to lead her out and back to her room. Nathan moved to follow as well, but Zachariah grabbed him before he could. Avila barely heard the older man as they walked out. "Not tonight, son. Give her time. For now, stay with me. I have a few more questions." Whatever his questions might have been were cut off by the closing door. Silence was the only sound as Galdren and Avila made their way back to their rooms.

41. LET ME FORGET

When they arrived, Galdren followed Avila into her room, but she stopped just inside the door. Her face felt numb when she turned to him. Too much had happened, and she still had not been able to process it all. Despite the fact that she had managed not to break down, she was barely hanging on. She couldn't look up into his eyes as she said, "Galdren, could I please—I need time. I can't talk about this right now."

Instead of answering, he pulled her into a tight embrace. She couldn't relax; if she did, she was afraid she would never stop crying. Despite how stiffly she was standing, Galdren simply held her like that for a while. "I will not ask you to talk to me tonight. I still want you to know that I don't care who you were. All that matters is who you are. Regaining your memories does not change what we have shared. I still love you."

Avila knew he meant well, but his words cut through her like a knife. She pushed back with more force than she intended to, but she couldn't apologize. She couldn't speak at all. Her tears had already started to fall, and she needed space. When he reached out to her, she shook her head and stepped back. She managed to choke out, "I'm sorry," but that was all she could muster before she turned and ran to her room. She doubted he would follow, but she locked the door anyway.

As soon as the lock clicked, she dropped to her knees and let the tears fall. The pain of all her memories hurt so profoundly that her sobs felt like they were ripping her apart. She hugged herself and laid her head against the door while misery claimed her.

Avila had no idea how long she sat there like that, but her sobs had finally subsided, and she was left feeling hollow. She still hadn't moved, even though she vaguely felt her legs going numb. She didn't plan on moving either until a knock startled her, and she nearly fell over backward when it sounded again, this time accompanied by a familiar female voice.

"Ma'am, it's me, Meru. I'm here to help you change for the night."

Avila considered sending her away. She had no desire to face anyone. However, when she shifted and her legs tangled in the skirt of her dress badly enough to trip her when she tried to stand, she reconsidered. She was far from all right, but nothing was going to be solved by ignoring everything outside her door. Especially when she couldn't even stand.

She let out a sigh as she reached up and flipped the lock open. Meru gasped when she came in and saw her on the floor. Avila wasn't sure if she was relieved to see how distressed the girl was on her behalf or ready to tell her to leave anyway. She swallowed that last urge and shook her head as she tried to head off the questions. "Please, Meru, don't worry about me. I just think my leg went numb from sitting awkwardly. I'll be all right. The skirts didn't help."

Despite her attempt to put the girl at ease, Meru's lips were still pursed as she helped Avila to the side of the bed. Once she was seated, the girl immediately started to work the pins out of her hair. The dress could come after her legs were back to normal. Silence reigned for several minutes. It wasn't until the last pin was removed that Meru finally spoke. "Ma'am, please forgive me if this is forward, but if you need anything, I would be willing to help."

Avila had thought she had no more tears to cry, but she found she was mistaken. Meru's words were a reminder that she still had a life. A good one. One she could be proud of, no matter what else happened. One that included people that cared for her.

When Meru saw her tears, she immediately tried to comfort her. "Oh! I didn't mean to upset you. Please don't cry."

Avila hugged the girl, but thankfully, Meru must have realized that whatever was wrong was something horrible, as she didn't try to move. Avila eventually realized how awkward it had to be for her, so she stepped away. She wiped at the tears as she tried to explain, "I apologize. This is not your fault, so please do not worry."

Despite her reassurances, Meru did not look convinced. "Ma'am?"

Avila took a deep breath to try and regain a semblance of calm before she shook her head. She even managed a smile, though it felt fragile. "Everything will be fine."

Meru hesitated for a few seconds, but she finally nodded. "Yes, ma'am. Allow me to help you remove that dress, and then I can run a bath for you. Will you need anything else?"

Avila wasn't able to answer verbally, so she shook her head. Meru was still obviously worried, so Avila tried her best to hold it together until she was gone. She ended up staying in the tub until the water started to cool. She was once again hollow as she finally climbed into bed. That didn't mean her head wasn't full. Too many questions, too many memories, and too much heartache were all she had.

She ended up lying there for at least an hour, and sleep seemed impossible to find. It wasn't helped by the fact that she was terrified to close her eyes. She knew when exhaustion won, there would be nothing but more nightmares to tear her apart.

She turned over in frustration and looked at the timeglass. It was already after midnight. Then her eyes settled on the old com unit. It hadn't been turned on since the full ones had been installed, but the small gadget had never been removed. The sight of it was a stark reminder of Galdren and all that he had done for her. Especially those little gestures that had meant so much.

Avila was sick to death of crying, but she could not stop. Instead, she sat up and grabbed the unit from her bedside table. She sat and looked at it for a few seconds and let memories of the last year fill her. So much had changed, but they weren't bad changes. Not once she let her fear go. She wiped away her tears as she thought about her last sight of Galdren. He hadn't deserved to be pushed away. Out of everyone, he was the one person that she could turn to, no matter what.

As those thoughts consumed her, she was gripped by the urge to see his face. To apologize and see if he would be willing to help. Even if it was just to keep the fear at bay. She was already at the door to the room between theirs before she considered that he might not appreciate her going to him in the middle of the night. It only took her a moment to decide that she at least needed to see his face.

Despite her nearly desperate need to see him, she still hesitated. Would he want to see her now? It was late, and she had been the one to push him away. Finally, she sighed and knocked. There was only one way to find out.

Even though she had reached out, she was suddenly unsure of her actions. Perhaps he wouldn't be able to hear. His rooms were likely set up similarly to hers, and if so, he would probably be sleeping in his bed. He would never know she was there.

She had turned and was facing the door to her own rooms when the door behind her opened. She spun to see Galdren standing there in his sleep pants with a confused look. "Avila? What is—"

He cut off as soon as their eyes met. She barely heard him curse under his breath as he immediately pulled her into a crushing embrace. Avila grasped him just as tightly.

Several seconds passed before he let go enough to pick her up and carry her back to his sitting room. She barely noticed his room was nearly a mirror image of her own before he sat down with her. His eyes were concerned as he brushed at the fresh tears that had started to fall, even though she willed them not to.

"Avila, what can I do? I can only imagine how confused you must be, but you don't have to do any of this alone."

She couldn't hold his gaze. No matter her decision to come to him, she was still fighting so many things. She had no idea how to answer. She hadn't exactly been thinking clearly when she decided to knock on his door. Instead, she laid her head on his chest and soaked in his warmth. He allowed the silence and obliged her need to be held.

It was several minutes before Avila finally sat back and looked up. She could see a hint of hurt in his eyes and wished there was something she could do to stop it. After swallowing once, she said, "Galdren, I don't want to think about any of it. Not right now. I can't—"

Her voice became so thick that she couldn't continue. Galdren cupped her cheek and tilted her head to face him. "You don't have to handle it all at once. Take your time. I'll be right here."

Instead of leaning into him again, Avila wrapped her arms around his neck. She pushed away all thoughts of pain, choices, and tomorrows. Instead, she pressed her lips to his. He didn't respond at first, then pushed her back with a worried look and cupped her cheek. "Avila?"

She shook her head to keep him from saying anything else. Deep down, she knew this was a bad idea, but she needed something to reaffirm that life still went on. She needed to focus on something other than death and destruction. "Please, don't push me away. Not tonight."

His other hand came up to frame her face, and his eyes only grew more concerned. "This is not a decision you should make while you are grieving."

She reached up and pulled his hands down. Her grip was tight as she swallowed to make her words come out. "Maybe not, but I don't want to remember. Please. Help me forget."

Galdren looked torn for a moment, and it was several seconds before he did anything. Instead of answering, he stood with her in his arms. Avila immediately wrapped her arms around his neck, though she was still apprehensive. At least, until he headed toward his bedroom. The action sent a new wave of conflicting emotions through her. Uncertainty and anticipation were the most prevalent. However, it was a moot point when he laid her down and then sat beside her.

She wasn't sure what to think, but it wasn't long before he clearly set out his intentions. "Avila, I won't leave you alone tonight. You can sleep here with me, but I don't—it isn't the best choice to take advantage of your emotional vulnerability."

Avila felt warm and cold at the same time. She loved that he cared enough to think about what was best, even now. However, his words reminded her of another situation. Instead of objecting, she pulled on his hand until he relented and laid down next to her. She then leaned up on one arm so she could look at him clearly before she answered, "I know. I understand what you are saying, and I love that you care. But not tonight. I need you. I need this. Please."

Galdren sighed as he pulled her closer again. His lips were soft on hers, and she melted into him. Unfortunately, he didn't let it go on for long. His voice was husky as he tucked her under his chin once again and held her. "Rest easy tonight. I will be here as long as you need me to."

Avila ignored her tears as she realized there would be no changing his mind. At least he held her tightly enough that she felt she wouldn't fall apart. She let it comfort her as she finally closed her eyes. Despite her inner turmoil, it was not long until the warmth of his embrace helped her relax enough to eventually drift into sleep.

Avila felt like she had barely slept at all when she jerked upright and clamped her jaws together on a scream. She looked around frantically to try and figure out where she was—and looked down and noticed an arm was still slung across her hips. Her attention was then jerked toward Galdren as he mumbled in his sleep and tightened his grip on her.

The sight of him instantly worked to calm her, though her heart rate was still erratic. She had just woken from another nightmare. There were no vivid details, but more a sense of being trapped and in life-threatening danger. The fear still felt like it coated her skin as she tried to calm down. She pressed one fist to her lips to try and stifle any sounds. She had already worried Galdren enough.

Several minutes later, she had finally gotten herself under control. She started to lie back down, but when she tried to move Galdren's arm, he made an indistinct noise before his hand slid up to her waist and pulled. Suddenly, her heart was in her throat for a whole different reason.

Logically, she knew he was still sleeping and had no idea what he was doing, but that didn't keep a familiar warmth from trickling into her limbs. She thought back to his words earlier and felt embarrassment fill her. Still, when she lay next to him again, she knew she wanted him for an entirely different reason now. It was hard not to with the way his sandy hair fell across his eyes, and how his lips were tilted in an almost-smile.

She quit resisting the pull of his hand and slid down next to him once again. When she did, his arm tightened around her. She had to swallow once and wondered if she would be able to get back to sleep at all. It was dark enough that she knew dawn was still at least a couple of hours away. Despite her thoughts of earlier, she pushed up enough so that she could gently press her lips to his.

She only let it linger a moment, but she still felt him shift against her. The feel of him caused her breath to hitch, but she ignored it as she brushed her knuckles across his cheek and softly called his name. She held her breath as she waited for a response. After a second, she was rewarded with the sight of his beautiful eyes.

She smiled up into them as he blinked a few times to clear the sleep from his thoughts. It was a few moments before his brow drew down in confusion and he asked with a voice still husky from sleep, "Avila? Is everything all right?"

She didn't answer. At least not verbally. Instead, she ran one hand up his chest until she cupped the side of his neck. She pulled herself closer at the same time and kissed him like she was starved for the taste of him. He was still groggy enough that he didn't try to stop her. Instead, a groan escaped as he pulled her closer to him.

A moment later, he shifted them slightly, so he was leaning over her. She welcomed his kisses as they drifted down the side of her neck. It wasn't until he came to the collar of her nightgown that he finally came to his senses.

He was still lying partially on top of her, but he pushed himself up and looked down with growing concern. "Avila—"

Before he could say more, her eyes opened, and she placed a finger across his lips. She didn't want him to try and stop again. Not now. Her skin already felt like it was on fire, and the sensation of his body pressed against her had her wanting more. It wasn't the first time, and she didn't want the feeling to end.

She could hear the breathlessness in her own voice, but she ignored it. "Don't say anything." She then wrapped her arms around his chest and pulled him down once more.

He only resisted for a moment. She immediately drew him into a kiss. He was still holding back, but that changed when she slid one hand across his back, to his waist, and then across his stomach. She reveled at the way each muscle tensed under her touch. Even more so when she heard him try to stifle a groan.

As much as Avila knew she wanted this, wanted him, she had no idea where to go from that point. Learning about this behavior in biology was nothing like experiencing it. So far, she had let her instincts guide her, but she hesitated at the edge of his waistband. She felt a trickle of apprehension for the first time since she started. Would she know what to do?

She was pulled from her thoughts when Galdren sighed above her. He shifted so that he was lying next to her and cupped her cheek. She could tell he was not unaffected by his breathing, but his voice was still calm when he said, "I did not ask you to stay for this. I won't lie and say I do not want you, but please don't force yourself for me. I love you without it."

Avila suddenly felt equal parts embarrassed and frustrated. She knew he was only trying to do what he thought best, but she was done putting it off. She felt herself blushing, but she still reached out and took his hand and placed it over her heart. When he tensed, she held his hand there. "Galdren, I know you do. But haven't I asked you before to consult me before you decide what is best for me? I—I want this. I want you." She had to pause and look away before she could continue. "Any hesitation I have is only because I need a little guidance."

Neither of them moved for several seconds. Finally, Galdren pulled his hand from her grip and turned her to face him. He searched her eyes for several seconds, and she saw his widen slightly before he whispered, "You mean that?"

Her only response was to nod. Thankfully, that was all he needed. When he leaned in again, his kiss was more insistent than it had ever been. Avila was more than happy to match his enthusiasm. However, when she tried to wrap her arms around him again, he sat back enough to capture them both and gently pinned them to the bed next to her head. Her breath caught when she looked up and saw how intently he was looking down at her. She was so distracted by the fire in his eyes that she nearly missed that he had started speaking.

"If this is what you want, then let me guide you. I don't want to hurt you."

Avila hadn't forgotten everything she had learned, but she had also not thought about it in conjunction with herself. Her apprehension was returning, but they had come too far. She didn't want to stop. She finally nodded, and his eyes flashed before he leaned in for a quick kiss.

His breath was hot on her ear when he whispered, "I promise to make you forget the pain."

She shivered as he immediately moved to place a series of hot kisses down her neck and collarbone. He let go of her, but she didn't move to grab him again. Not that she could have. He had already started to undo the laces on the front of her gown, and he placed a kiss for each inch of flesh that was exposed.

While he made her breathless with kisses that continued down the middle of her chest, one hand had moved to her thighs. He gently bunched the cloth up until her legs were exposed, and she gasped at the feel of his fingers as they brushed against the inside of her thigh.

Instead of moving on right away, he gently moved her legs, so he could kneel directly over her. One hand slid up to her hip while he leaned closer to kiss her again. Avila could feel herself start to shake, but even she wasn't sure if it was nervous anticipation or pleasure. The two feelings were so intertwined that she could no longer differentiate. That didn't mean she wanted Galdren to stop.

By the time he started to pull the gown up and over her head, she was too enthralled with what he was doing to be embarrassed when he looked down at her. That feeling wasn't helped when she saw his eyes. They looked reverent before he lowered his head to start running kisses down her chest again. This time, he paused to cover one dusky nipple. She tried to stifle the moan the sensation caused.

When Galdren noticed, he leaned up to whisper once again. "Don't hide anything from me. Let me hear you."

Avila couldn't have held in her moan again if she had wanted to when his thumb ran under the edge of her panties at the same moment he spoke. Galdren smirked down at her when he repeated the motion. She barely heard him speak again. "Just like that. Don't hold back."

There was no way she could have responded. When his lips went back to her chest, one hand had dipped below her panties. The first touch was tentative, as though he was waiting to see if she would push him away. She was too far gone to even consider it, no matter how foreign the sensation was. She could think of nothing but Galdren.

When he was confident that she was not anxious, he paused long enough to slip the last barrier down her legs while also sliding out of his pants. Avila watched with wide eyes as he leaned over her once again. He held himself away from her and kissed her gently, as though he was trying to reassure her. She was nervous, but the heat of his body radiating toward her was calming, and any fear she had of what was to come was washed away in the flood of desire she felt. Her arms went around his neck, and she pulled herself up until she felt his hot skin against hers.

Neither of them could hold back a moan at the contact. The fact that Galdren seemed to be losing himself as well made Avila feel sexy and wanted. It all fed into her desire for him. He didn't stop kissing her as his hand slid down her stomach. When she felt him touch her most intimate area, her gasp was low. She grabbed his arms to steady herself. She felt something tightening, a feeling building that she didn't understand. It was almost overwhelming, but Galdren did not stop, even after her fingernails started making half-moon marks.

When the tension finally broke, Avila wanted to scream, but her breath was caught for several seconds before an unintelligible sound escaped. She felt like the world had suddenly sent her spinning, and the only thing that kept her from falling was her grip on her lover. She couldn't feel anything but his hands on her.

It took several moments before she was able to breathe normally. She opened her eyes to see Galdren hovering over her. Despite the cloud of euphoria she was in, the stark desire in him was enough to send a fresh wave of want through her.

He leaned in and kissed her once more before he whispered against her lips, "I love you. Trust me."

Instead of answering verbally, she wrapped her arms around his shoulders. When he lowered himself to rest against her, the feel of him was nearly more than she could handle, but she didn't try to move. Instead, she relaxed and kissed him again.

He shifted above her as his kiss deepened. One of his hands brushed against the side of her breast, which had her arching into his touch. When she did, he eased forward. The sudden sense of fullness had Avila stilling, and the pain that followed ripped through the last of the euphoria she had been feeling. Still, she did not pull away.

As the worst of the pain passed, Avila looked up to see Galdren tensed. She could tell he was waiting to see if she was all right and let out a long breath before she shakily reached up and cupped his face. Her kiss was gentle, but it was enough of a reassurance for him to start moving again.

Avila buried her face against his chest to hide her expression. The pain was harsh at first, but she knew it would pass. She was surprised when he leaned back and pulled one of her legs up slightly. The action made her self-conscious, but not for long. The new position gave him enough room for one of his hands to go back to the sensitive spot right above where he was moving slowly in her.

It was not long that the sensation sent shock waves through her again, and the pain was forgotten. When he leaned into her once more, she wrapped her arms around his shoulders, and her legs went around his hips without conscious thought. All she could think was to get as close to him as possible while they started moving in sync.

The sound of his ragged breathing next to her ear only added to the pleasure that was coursing through her, and the same pressure from before started to build. Although she had a better idea of what to expect, that did not keep her from crying out as the sensation broke over her again.

Her grip on Galdren tightened as the world disappeared around her. All she could feel was him. All she could hear was his cries as he started trembling, and his voice soon joined hers as their pleasure twisted together. Avila had no idea how long it went on, but she relished in the feel of Galdren as he practically collapsed above her. She held him tightly as they both tried to catch their breath.

Several moments passed before he rolled to the side and took her with him. She nestled into his chest as her perception of the rest of the world finally started to return. Neither of them moved after that for some time.

Avila had almost started to doze when Galdren finally spoke. She could hear his voice reverberate under her ear. "Are you well?"

Avila could not hold back a chuckle. She pushed herself far enough up to look down with a grin. "Is that even the right question? Perhaps it would be better to ask if I have rejoined this planet. I'm certain I must have left it at one point."

His smile joined hers as he brushed a damp strand of her hair behind an ear. The look of affection he gave her nearly took her breath away. "Good. I am glad."

Her smile softened as she pushed herself far enough forward to brush her lips across his. "Galdren, I love you. Now and forever."

He pulled her closer and deepened the kiss. When he finally pulled back, she could see a shadow of the desire they had just shared, but his voice was soft. "As much as I would like to make love to you until dawn, I think we both need sleep."

Avila sighed as she shifted so that she was lying against his side instead of on top of him. As much as she didn't want to admit it, she was tired. All of her limbs were heavy, and her eyelids felt weighted. She covered a yawn as she laid her head on his chest. "I think I will have to concede." She felt his chuckle and his arm as it wrapped around her, but those were the last things she noticed as she slipped into a satisfied and dreamless sleep.

42. SHATTERED DREAMS

Galdren did not want to move. He could see the sun shining brightly through his eyelids and he knew it had to be far past when he usually would have been up, but he was far too comfortable. When he was conscious enough to realize it was because Avila was still pressed to his side, a smile spread across his face.

His arms tightened around her as memories of earlier that morning came back in a rush. He had to admit that if it wasn't for the feel of her skin against his, he might have thought it a dream. However, he could feel her heart beating steadily by his side and her breath as it washed over his shoulder. Unfortunately, each of those sensations only worked to remind him of what had transpired. When he could feel his desire stirring once more, he gently disengaged from her and sat up.

She hardly moved when he pulled the cover back up. As he watched her, he realized she must have been exhausted. Their activities notwithstanding, she had likely not slept before she came to him. Not that he had slept much more.

He had been livid when he saw Lady Dunoire speaking to her, but his anger at the younger woman paled when he heard the exchange between Avila and the ambassador. Somehow, he hadn't been shocked to find out that she was the last surviving member of the House of Treunmhor. He had seen several clues, but had ignored them all until he couldn't anymore.

He still wished that she had never gotten her memories back. When she had pushed him away the night before, it hurt, but not because of the action itself. He wanted to help, and he had no idea how.

She was so desperate when she finally came to him that he had been frightened for her. He still had no idea what she was thinking. Not to mention the ultimatum. The thought that she might be forced to leave and never come back made his blood run cold. He didn't want to think about never seeing her again. He refused to.

He felt guilt creep in as he watched her even breathing. He had not wanted to take advantage of her distress, no matter what she had said, but when he woke to feel her against him, conscious thought was hard to find. When he finally did come to his senses, they were both already entangled. At least he had no doubts that she had enjoyed herself. He made sure she did. Plus, despite his niggling worry, he doubted she was going to regret the decision.

With a sigh, he finally looked at the timeglass, only to see that it was nearly midmorning. He was shocked that his valet had not been in to wake him. He then frowned at the thought that the man might have come and gone again when he saw he was not alone in bed. He did not like the idea of anyone else seeing her in this state, but he was also worried that it could cause more problems that she absolutely did not need on top of everything else. Still, what was done was done. With another sigh, he stood to get cleaned and dressed.

Less than half an hour later, he was standing next to his bed once more. He had things to do, but he was still hesitant to leave her, and he did not want to wake her. He knew she needed sleep. Especially since it seemed like she had slept without nightmares for the first time in a long time.

Still, he could not put off the conversations he needed to have with both his parents. Instead, he penned her a quick note before picking up her clothes, folding them, and placing them on the table next to the bed. He then put the letter on top of them before he bent and gently kissed her forehead. He was both pleased and worried when she didn't stir even after he covered her once more. At least she was resting well.

He only hesitated for a few seconds before he turned to leave. He knew where his mother would be at this hour, and he had several things to speak to her about. He doubted he could change his father's mind by himself, but that didn't mean he wouldn't try. His face hardened as he walked out and closed the door softly behind himself.

Avila rolled over with a yawn and a stretch. She felt surprisingly refreshed, though she was unexpectedly sore. She yawned once more before opening her eyes with a smile. She couldn't remember any nightmares, and that meant it was an excellent morning.

Her thoughts came crashing to a halt when her eyes landed on the unfamiliar bedcurtains. She sat up and looked around before she looked down. A blush burst onto her cheeks as memories of the previous night came back. She looked around again and felt disappointment fill her that Galdren was already gone. Though, she knew she shouldn't be surprised. He was a busy man.

In her second inspection, her eyes landed on the note and pile of clothes next to the bed. Her blush deepened, but she ignored it as she read the note. It wasn't much, but it did explain that he hadn't wanted to wake her and that he would see her later. It ended with an *"I love you"* that made her smile.

She felt odd putting her nightclothes back on, but she certainly wasn't about to walk to her room with nothing on, even if it was through places that no one else should be in. Once she was dressed, she immediately headed back to her own quarters.

When she entered her room, she blushed at the sight of her made bed. That meant at least one person knew she had not slept in her own bed the previous night. She brushed the thought aside. It didn't matter for more than one reason. She trusted the people that worked in these quarters. Plus, she did not regret her decision.

Unfortunately, thoughts about the court and their opinions brought everything else back. Things that she had been trying not to focus on. She sat on the side of her bed for several minutes as she fought to control her tears. Her reprieve was over, and now came the time for decisions. At least her time with Galdren had allowed her to achieve an objective enough distance that she was no longer overwhelmed. She still had an ache in her heart that refused to budge, but she could think clearly.

Despite knowing that Galdren would not like it, she realized she had questions that needed to be answered, and there was only one man that could answer them. With that thought, she rose to take a quick shower and get dressed.

It was a relatively short amount of time later that she opened the door to her quarters to see Lee and Jacob standing there. She squared her shoulders and prepared herself for the need to convince these two to go along with what she needed. Despite her worry, her voice was strong when she spoke. "I know it is out of this wing, but I need one of you to please escort me to King Rougir. If he is busy, I will wait for him, but it is imperative I speak with him."

Both men bowed before Jacob stepped back. "Are you ready to leave now, ma'am?"

Avila stared. Despite not wanting to question her luck, she could not keep from asking, "Why did you agree so easily? I know you have been told not to take me out of this wing without Galdren or his approval."

They both looked slightly uncomfortable, but Lee answered. "Yes, ma'am, that is true. However, we received orders this morning to take you directly to the king if you asked to see him."

"Oh." That was the best she could think of. Still, she didn't have time to stand around. Several things the king had mentioned the night before needed clarification. Not the least of which was the mention of her guardians. She still wasn't sure what her choice should be, but she needed to know all she could. She gave Jacob a nod, and he fell into step beside her so they could leave.

The closer they got to the king's office, the more nervous Avila became. She was able to hide it, but thoughts that he would be unwilling to tell her anything kept invading. He had said his only concession would be to verify her identity. Until or unless she chose to take up the mantle of her family's responsibility, she was just another citizen under his rule. Would he even agree to speak with her if it wasn't to hear her decision?

She certainly wasn't planning on deciding yet. As guilty as it made her, she was still unsure of the path she should take. Yes, her people deserved better. They deserved their homes. However, she was just one person. If they had not managed to change the fate of their planet in over a decade, what could she possibly do? If she was honest with herself, the thought of trying to retake her throne terrified her. Even so, the guilt that kept pricking her was enough for her to realize she was unwilling to let her heritage go without question.

She was pulled from her thoughts when a gratingly familiar voice called out to her. "Princess, what a pleasure to see you this morning. After your abrupt departure last night, I was afraid we would not have the chance to speak again."

Avila stopped in her tracks as the ambassador approached. His smile made her gut twist, and she had to resist the urge to smack it off his face. When he drew even with them, she noted that Jacob had shifted so he was partially standing between them without obstructing their conversation. It helped to calm her, and she managed to not lash out at the monster in front of her.

Her voice was still cold when she answered, "It is unfortunate. That I have to see you again, that is."

His smile took on a condescending tilt, but he didn't rise to her insult. Instead, he gave her a bow. "Things happened so quickly last night that I am afraid we have yet to be properly introduced. I am Shior Bana'ak, Ambassador for the Trogand Federation."

Avila knew he had said that last part to goad her, and it worked. She bristled at the thought of the people that dared to claim they were a valid world government when they still stood precariously at the top of a mountain of bodies. She didn't yell, but her voice was scathing as she said, "Do not posture on my behalf. I know what you really are and what those you serve stand for. It is not for the people you claim to rule. It is only for your greed. Talamh has long been the hub of galactic commerce, in and out of the Trading Alliance. Don't think your motives are misunderstood. Had you any sense of duty, we would not be here."

Instead of getting upset, the man's smirk widened. "Ah, Princess, surely you are in no position to preach to me about the ills of my employers. The blood on my hands stains yours as well, does it not?"

Avila's back stiffened when she understood his meaning. It took all she had to not let her rage and despair cause tears to well up. After several seconds, she hissed, "Do not think to lay the blame for their sacrifices at my feet. I wept for them. I still grieve their loss, but I did not force them. You are the one that called for their deaths when you could not have mine."

He merely shrugged at her. "I see that you will believe what you wish. However, I would like to remind you that years have passed. Times change, as do people. Perhaps you should consider which battles are worth fighting. Especially as you are here and not there."

He took a step closer but stopped when Jacob shifted his gun to be more visible. The man smirked at the alert guard but then ignored him in favor of Avila. "Do remember that you are alone without these people to hide you from the vast galaxies." His smirk twisted to match the coldness in his eyes as he continued, "It would also serve you well to remember that Aril is the most isolated and smallest of the allied planets. What is worth protecting, Princess? These people took you in, did they not? Would you have violent eyes turn to them for harboring a fugitive?"

Avila's blood ran cold at his implied threat. She knew that if she were to abdicate, they would have no reason to come to Aril. However, if she became a thorn in their side, they could well take up arms against this planet and claim it was for standing against them. The Alliance might not get involved if they felt the attack on Aril was justified. Even if they did not and chose to help, the Alliance might not know until it was too late. There was a reason Aril stayed out of conflicts.

When she saw his smirk widen, Avila's rage burned through her fear. She squared her shoulders and responded, "Your threats will no longer send me running. I am not a child that will hide in the dark. I will face you and whatever else is coming. You will not find me cowering ever again."

The ambassador took a step back and looked her over from head to toe. She recoiled under his evident evaluation, even more so when his eyes came back to hers, and he smirked again. "You are correct about one thing. You are no longer a child. You have grown into a beautiful woman, nearly identical to your mother. It is a shame she made poor choices as well. She didn't need to die, but the past cannot be changed." He gave her another mocking bow before taking another step back. "Perhaps you can learn from her mistakes. The universe is full of possibilities, after all."

He did not wait to hear any more before he turned and made his way down another hall. When Avila took a furious step after him, Jacob stepped into her path. His eyes were hard, but his voice was apologetic. "Please forgive me, ma'am, but I cannot allow you to go after him."

Avila's fists clenched by her side, but she counted to ten in her head before she let out a deep breath and answered, "Thank you. I know it would not have been wise."

The hard edge to Jacob's eyes eased as he nodded and stepped back again. "Please follow me. We are nearly to the king's office."

She gave him an absent nod as she fell into step behind him. Her mind was already racing, going over every part of that conversation. It infuriated her that not only did he not deny his crimes, but he did not seem remorseful either. But that was only part of her trouble. Before she spoke with him, she had not known what her choice should be. If she was honest, she had been considering giving it all up to stay with the people she knew and loved.

However, was that the wisest course of action? The man had made it clear there would be repercussions for Aril if she stepped outside their sphere of protection. However, she was intimately familiar with the Trogand's tactics. She knew they would send an assassin for her even if she stayed. She was a loose end, and if nothing else, the Trogand were thorough.

She nearly stumbled at the thought of walking away from everything she had come to love about this planet—and it wasn't just her love for Galdren, though thinking about that had tears filling her eyes. Aril was as much home to her as Talamh had been. She had to blink several times to banish them. She could not afford to let her heart make this decision. Too many lives were at stake.

She had to pause for a moment and close her eyes against the wrenching pain. She already knew what she had to do. Not just to protect Aril, but for her people that had spent the last decade trying to rebuild wherever they could find a place to survive. In the end, it was no choice at all. She only hoped that her banishment from Aril would only be until she regained her throne.

The thought that it could take years was daunting and did not help the pain flowing through her. She could not ask Galdren to wait for her, but that didn't mean she could not hold out hope that he would.

By that point, they had finally reached a set of double doors. The guard outside gave her a respectful nod, and Jacob stepped to the side to join him. Avila closed her eyes once more to gather her wayward thoughts. No matter how long it took, no matter the hardships she would have to endure, she would hold on to hope. Hope that she would find a way to succeed, a means to free her people, and a path to allow them to find happiness. She would also hold on to the hope that someday, she would find happiness of her own and that her sacrifice would not be in vain.

For now, she could not think about the fact that she was once again losing everyone she ever loved. Instead, she would focus on her goal of finding a way to see them again. At least this time, it was a possibility. When she opened her eyes, she squared her shoulders and knocked firmly on the door. No matter the pain now, her future waited, and she refused to ever run again.

www.ingramcontent.com/pod-product-compliance
Lightning Source LLC
Chambersburg PA
CBHW020247200626
46816CB00001BA/172